A STRANGE MANUSCRIPT FOUND IN A COPPER CYLINDER

broadview editions
series editor: L.W. Conolly

A STRANGE MANUSCRIPT FOUND IN A COPPER CYLINDER

James De Mille

edited by Daniel Burgoyne

broadview editions

Library and Archives Canada Cataloguing in Publication

De Mille, James, 1833-1880

A strange manuscript found in a copper cylinder / James De Mille ; edited by Daniel Burgoyne.

(Broadview editions)
Originally publ.: New York : Harper & Brothers, 1888.
Includes bibliographical references.
ISBN 978-1-55111-959-5

I. Burgoyne, Daniel, 1966- II. Title. III. Series: Broadview editions

PS8457.E45S75 2011 C813'.4 C2011-904536-2

Broadview Editions
The Broadview Editions series represents the ever-changing canon of literature in English by bringing together texts long regarded as classics with valuable lesser-known works.

Advisory editor for this volume: Michel Pharand.

Broadview Press is an independent, international publishing house, incorporated in 1985.

We welcome comments and suggestions regarding any aspect of our publications—please feel free to contact us at the addresses below or at broadview@broadviewpress.com.

North America
PO Box 1243, Peterborough, Ontario, Canada K9J 7H5
2215 Kenmore Ave., Buffalo, New York, USA 14207
Tel: (705) 743-8990; Fax: (705) 743-8353
email: customerservice@broadviewpress.com

UK, Europe, Central Asia, Middle East, Africa, India, and Southeast Asia
Eurospan Group, 3 Henrietta St., London WC2E 8LU, United Kingdom
Tel: 44 (0) 1767 604972; Fax: 44 (0) 1767 601640
email: eurospan@turpin-distribution.com

Australia and New Zealand
NewSouth Books
c/o TL Distribution, 15-23 Helles Ave., Moorebank, NSW, Australia 2170
Tel: (02) 8778 9999; Fax: (02) 8778 9944
email: orders@tldistribution.com.au

www.broadviewpress.com

Broadview Press acknowledges the financial support of the Government of Canada through the Canada Book Fund for our publishing activities.

The interior of this book is printed on paper containing 100% recycled paper.

RECYCLED
Paper made from recycled material
FSC® C103567

PRINTED IN CANADA

Contents

Acknowledgements

I am grateful to the Department of English, the Faculty of Arts & Humanities, and my colleagues at Vancouver Island University. Richard Lane, who directed the Literary Theory Research Group with me, has been very supportive. Steve Lane provided guidance and supported my funding attempts. Marni Stanley helped me understand Orientalism. Craig Tapping read the proposal. Matthew Beedham helped with linguistics queries. Thank you to Ross MacKay for his willingness to read a draft. For their generosity and openness to dialogue, I want to especially thank Doug Stetar, Cynthea Masson, Katharina Rout, Anna Atkinson, Frances Sprout, Debbie Torkko, Terri Doughty, Dale Wik, Ian Whitehouse, Sally Carpentier, Clay Armstrong, Rick Conroy, Gregory Ball, and Dawn Thompson. Ros Davies, Sheila Davidson, and Faye Landels provided support on a daily basis. The librarians at VIU's library have been incredibly helpful—special thanks to Jean Blackburn and Mary Wood.

This publication was supported by funds received from the Vancouver Island University Research Fund and the VIU Work Op program. I want to acknowledge the help of my research assistants: Ashleigh Moody; Lori Arscott, who helped digitize the 1888 *Harper's Weekly* serial; Jan Beecher, who read the 1888 *Harper's* serial aloud (punctuation included) and helped me collect nearly everything ever written on De Mille; and Alison Pitcher, for her attention to detail. Thanks also to Bel Levasseur and to Riqui Ward. Jesslyn Gosling touched up and otherwise helped improve the images in this edition.

I want to thank Rick Gooding, my companion in so many other projects, for giving me his copy of *A Strange Manuscript* and affirming my interest in literature and science. Thanks to Janet Giltrow for her insistence on intelligence and rigour. Special thanks to Hazard Adams, Leroy Searle, Raimonda Modiano, Robert Abrams, Robert Corbett, David Baulch, Dean Leroy, Michael Smithson, and Alan Vardy. I am grateful to Jodi Salter for introducing me to the copper cylinder. Thanks to Trisha Boeur, Robyn Corson, and Shawna Lane for helping me understand De Mille's sources. Lloyd Keane helped me at the CEECT archive in Ottawa.

I want to thank Don Le Pan for his enthusiasm and generosity. I am grateful for all of the support and patience on the part of the editorial team at Broadview Press, especially Marjorie Mather, Leonard Conolly, Michel Pharand, and Tara Trueman.

Finally, I can't express my gratitude for the support and encouragement of my family, especially my wife Christina King, my children Jessica, Jacob, and Alex, and my parents Al and Nancy.

Introduction

On Saturday 7 January 1888, the front page of the year's first *Harper's Weekly; A Journal of Civilization*[1] featured a full-page illustration by Gilbert Gaul[2] with four men on a sailing boat, one holding a cylinder while another prepares to strike it with an axe. In the bottom right corner of the page begins Chapter 1 of *A Strange Manuscript Found in a Copper Cylinder.* Written by an unidentified author,[3] the novel was published in the next nineteen numbers, concluding on 12 May, each instalment accompanied by another illustration by Gaul.[4] That Canadian James De Mille's[5] finest novel should be published anonymously and posthumously is wrought with irony and complication, some of which took nearly a century to decipher.

Some of it was figured out almost immediately. On 21 May 1888, a review in the *New York Times* identified the author as "the late Prof. De Mille" (see Appendix F1). Professor of rhetoric and history at Dalhousie College in Halifax, Nova Scotia, James De

---

1 A New York political magazine published by Harper Brothers from 1857 to 1916.

2 American illustrator for *Harper's Weekly* and *Century* magazines, Gilbert Gaul (1855-1919) is best known for his paintings of army life and western subjects.

3 In a letter to Annie De Mille, James's wife, Harper Brothers explained that the anonymity of the novel was necessary to protect the book from being reprinted "on the ground that Professor de Mille [*sic*] having been a British subject, he might have been considered as not entitled to the protection of copyright in the United States" (qtd. in Monk 231).

4 The novel appeared simultaneously in the English *Penny Illustrated Paper* and also, beginning 24 March, in the Australian edition of *Illustrated London News.* The first book edition was published by Harper Brothers later in 1888, and other editions, by Chatto & Windus in London, Robinson in Montreal, and Macmillan in Toronto, were published between 1888 and 1910.

5 James was born with the surname De Mill but he adopted the spelling De Mille when he went to Brown University and used it for all of his literary publications. (However, it is spelled De Mill on professional documents at Dalhousie University.) I have followed Patricia Monk in consistently using De Mille when referring to James. Note that his surname is sometimes misspelled DeMille (without the space).

Mille was born on 23 August 1833[1] in Saint John, in the British colony of New Brunswick. The third child of Nathan and Elizabeth De Mill, James grew up in Saint John and then Wolfville, Nova Scotia, where he attended the boarding school Horton Academy and then Acadia College. After a year-long tour of Europe (1850-51) with his older brother Elisha Budd, James enrolled at Brown University in Providence, Rhode Island. He graduated with an MA from Brown in 1854, after which he returned to Saint John where he eventually established the Colonial Book Store in 1857. In 1858, he married his longtime fiancée Elizabeth Ann Pryor (Annie). Annie and James had three children: William Budd (1859), Louise (1865), and Ethel Maud (1872). James worked as a professor and chair of classics at Acadia College, in Wolfville, Nova Scotia from 1860 to 1865, before moving to Halifax and beginning the work at Dalhousie College that he would continue until his death on 28 January 1880.

He was the author of about thirty novels published between 1860 and 1877. His corpus includes religious historical novels such as *Helena's Household*, satirical romances such as *A Comedy of Terrors* and *The Dodge Club*, novels of sensation including *Cord and Creese* and *The Cryptogram*, and two series of books for boys: The B.O.W.C. (The Brethren of the White Cross) Series for juveniles and the Young Dodge Club series. Many of these novels were published by Harper Brothers, as serials and then books. In addition, De Mille wrote a large number of short stories, poems, and miscellaneous prose works. His most important scholarly book is *Elements of Rhetoric* (1878).[2]

One recurring concern in the reviews and in later criticism is the relationship between *A Strange Manuscript* and other works of fiction published in the preceding decades. The *New York Times* reviewer stresses that the posthumous publication (in 1888; De Mille had died in 1880) means that De Mille's novel wasn't derivative of the recent novels by Henry Rider Haggard, *King Solomon's Mines* (1885) and *She: A History of Adventure* (serialized in *The Graphic* in 1886-87). Other reviewers compared it to Samuel Butler's 1872 *Erewhon* (Appendix E5). A reviewer for *The Athenaeum*

1 The year of his birth has been disputed (given as 1833, 1834, 1836, and 1837) because there are no surviving birth or baptismal records, but the year 1833, given by the De Mill family historian Muriel Raymond, corresponds with other details of his life (Monk 32).

2 For more detailed information, see the Brief Chronology or see Monk, Chapters 6-8, and especially her lists of De Mille's published works in the Selected Bibliography.

(15 December 1888) wonders "at the strange law which has led the human intellect in the year 1888 to light upon the same ideas of topsy-turvydom which occurred to Mr. Butler in 1872" (see Appendix F4). As late as the 1970s, critics argued that De Mille owed a debt to Butler as well as to Edward Bulwer Lytton, whose lost-race narrative *The Coming Race* was published in 1871 (see Appendix E3).[1] The manuscript of *A Strange Manuscript* was found among De Mille's papers after his death, but when did he write it?

De Mille seems to have written *A Strange Manuscript* between 1866 and 1868.[2] In a letter dated 6 March 1880, De Mille's brother Alfred Henry De Mill recollects reading it "some years ago":

> The "Copper Cylinder" Mss is one of the first stories ever written by James & he was never able to make a satisfactory *denouement* to the plot in it, & consequently I do not think he ever offered it for sale. I read it over some years ago & told him that the concluding chapter could be so written with advantage, & [though] he certainly agreed with me, I do not know whether he has ever touched it since or not. (qtd. in MacLeod 103-04)

De Mille was writing stories when he was at Brown University in the early 1850s, but Alfred seems to refer to his first published novels, thus the 1860s. Malcolm Parks argues that the "known facts of De Mille's life in the decade support a date of composition no later than 1867 or 1868" ("Strange to Strangers Only" 63), while De Mille's biographer Patricia Monk concludes that "1866 [is] the earliest possible date for the composition of *Strange Manuscript*" (229). My own experience of working with different sources consulted by De Mille leads me to agree with them. Monk, who revisits the evidence provided by Kilian and Parks, says that a compositional date of the mid-1860s "must be considered definitive" (229).

If *A Strange Manuscript* was written between 1866 and 1868, its composition precedes *The Coming Race* and *Erewhon*, and it is strikingly original. But what then accounts for the remarkable similarities between these novels? In order to answer this question, we need to look more closely at *A Strange Manuscript*.

---

1 For example, in "De Mille and the Utopian Vision," George Woodcock assumes that De Mille wrote *A Strange Manuscript* in 1879.

2 Douglas MacLeod (in his unpublished MA thesis, 1968), Crawford Kilian (in 1972), and Malcolm Parks (in 1976) demonstrated that De Mille wrote the majority of the novel in the late 1860s.

Stories: Frame Narrative and Manuscript

There are two stories in *A Strange Manuscript*. The first is the frame narrative that takes place over two days, 15 and 16 February 1850, during a "winter's cruise" on board the yacht *Falcon* en route to the Mediterranean Sea from the Azores, the Canaries, and the Madeira Islands. The yacht is owned by Lord Featherstone, who is "weary of the monotony of high life [and] fond of seeking relief from the *ennui* of prosperity amid the excitements of the sea" (p. 99). He is accompanied by Noel Oxenden, "late of Trinity College, Cambridge," the restless Otto Melick, "a *littérateur* from London," and Dr. Congreve (a friend and medical attendant), the oldest of the group, a middle-aged man with gray hair, who knows an enormous amount about recent exploration and paleontological discoveries. Off the Canary Islands, in sight of Mount Tenerife, they find a barnacle-encrusted copper cylinder floating in the ocean. The cylinder contains two packages wrapped in coarse felt. In the smaller package there is a short letter from one Adam More, an Englishman who claims "to have been carried by a series of incredible events to a land from which escape is as impossible as from the grave" (pp. 53-54). He appeals to the finder of the cylinder to deliver the other package, a manuscript containing an account of his adventures, to his father in England.

This is the second story, and Melick proceeds to read it aloud to the others. The reading of the manuscript is interrupted several times. Melick stops reading at dinner when they take a break and discuss More's account. The Doctor continues reading until bedtime. In the morning Oxenden reads until dinner. And Featherstone reads the last part of the manuscript, stopping with a yawn, at bedtime—at which point the novel ends.

More is a mate of the ship *Trevelyan* (Bennet, master) which unloaded a cargo of convicts at Hobart Town on Van Diemen's Land in early December 1843. On the return voyage, the *Trevelyan* is caught in a slow drift near the Antarctic Circle (66° 33′ 44″ south) where they encounter a high promontory they name Trevelyan Peak. More and Agnew, the second mate, go ashore on the Captain's gig to hunt seals and they are separated from the *Trevelyan* by bad weather, drifting in the small boat for several days with the ocean current until they come into sight of volcanoes on what More believes is the Antarctic continent.

Agnew is killed by cannibals they encounter on the coast of Antarctica, and More is left alone, drifting in his boat, until the current enters a cavern, a subterranean river that takes More into utter darkness. More eventually finds himself on an inland tropical sea at the centre of the Antarctic continent, where he is welcomed by a remarkably hospitable people called the Kosekin.

Most of the desires and aspirations of the Kosekin are opposite those of the norm to which More is accustomed, and he spends a great portion of his story explaining these differences. Early on, the Kosekin are excessively generous, serving More and giving him multiple gifts. When they go into battle against the huge monsters that populate the South Pole the Kosekin are fearless unto death. More slowly comes to recognize that the Kosekin do not aspire to wealth, indeed they value poverty and wish for deprivation. For them the highest good is death, but to be in the continual suffering of hunger and squalor is sufficient if one doesn't receive the blessing of death. The discussion and recognition of these opposites produce a series of ironies and inversions that generate what Melick calls the satire of More's story. For instance, it is ironic that the extreme generosity of the Kosekin is their way of advancing, by becoming poorer, in Kosekin society. Inversion, the reversal of a normal order or relation, characterizes the Kosekin. For example, the Kosekin women are the active suitors in romance. But inversion is also dynamic or perhaps dialectical insofar as there are continual reversals in perspective and understanding that occur as More's story proceeds.

More is introduced to Almah, a woman unlike the others, who reminds More of "those oriental beauties whose portraits [are] seen in annuals and illustrated books" (p. 112). Unlike the Kosekin, Almah loves the light. She was born in another South Pole civilization and doesn't share their world-view or love of darkness. She calls him Atam-or, which in Kosekin means man of light. As they fall in love, Almah teaches More the Kosekin language and eventually leads him to understand some of the disturbing truths of Kosekin society.

The frame narrative on board the yacht *Falcon* may well be the most remarkable aspect of *A Strange Manuscript*. The complexity created by Featherstone, Melick, Oxenden, and the Doctor reading aloud and discussing the manuscript multiplies and compounds the inversions that occur as More comes to understand the Kosekin civilization. This complexity is probably what accounts for much of the late twentieth-century interest in the novel, and so it is worth looking at closely.

The use of a frame narrative in which a set of characters tell and discuss other stories is an ancient practice that lies close to the heart of the origin of the novel as a genre. An obvious comparison to More's castaway adventure, the fantastic voyages of Sinbad the Sailor were usually included in *The Thousand and One Nights* or *Arabian Nights Entertainments*,[1] with its frame narrative in which Scheherazade tells endless stories. The direct mention of Sinbad in Chapter 7 is followed by references to a plethora of other story cycles of middle-eastern origin or derivation, including *Hitopadesa*, a collection of ancient Sanskrit fables attributed to Narayana, *Rig Veda*, an ancient collection of more than 1,000 Vedic Sanskrit hymns, and *Lalla Rookh*, an oriental Romance written in 1817 by the Irish poet Thomas Moore (1759-1852). In this sense, the deliberate use of a frame narrative suggests that De Mille is interested in storytelling itself, with the nature of story, and especially how a story is framed and interpreted.

The basic fact that a frame narrative tells the story—in this case, the characters take turns reading the manuscript—emphasizes that stories are performances. Or, perhaps, more to the point, reading is performance. Each of the four frame readers interprets and analyzes the manuscript. The Doctor and Oxenden are highly educated, and they actively interpret More's experience as literally true. The Doctor contributes a wealth of current geological and paleontological information that dramatically transforms how a reader (at least a nineteenth-century reader) understands the plausibility of the fauna and flora More encounters. But the Doctor advances the hypothesis that the Kosekin have always lived in Antarctica, while Oxenden develops the theory that they are evolutionary descendents of the troglodytes of East Africa (Appendix D2). Together, the Doctor and Oxenden function like a self-explicating text: in effect, they indirectly disclose the source material that De Mille is using while writing More's narrative. For example, if De Mille consulted Richard Owen's *Geology and the Inhabitants of the Ancient World* (see Appendix B1) when he composed More's description of one of the monstrous creatures he encounters, the Doctor observes that it "may have been the *Cheirotherium*," and goes on to note, "On account of the hand-shaped marks made by its paws, Owen thinks that it was akin to the frogs" (p. 174). Melick is the most dynamic of the four. His contempt and scepticism for the manuscript almost seem like De Mille's literary conscience. He doesn't believe that More wrote the manuscript; instead, he sees the manuscript as a poor attempt at a sensational novel. At one

1 First translated into English in 1706, the common English title through the nineteenth century is *Arabian Nights*. See *The Arabian Nights Entertainments* (London: Routledge, Warne, & Routledge, 1863).

point, Melick observes, "His plan is not bad, but he fails utterly in his execution. The style is detestable" (p. 247). And he goes on to suggest that the writer should take Defoe or Swift as his model. Melick's claims that the manuscript is a "transparent hoax" (p. 100) perpetuated by a "gross plagiarist" (p. 247) are startling. In contrast, Lord Featherstone plays a largely docile role. He thinks the manuscript is a "deuced queer sort of thing" and he "hardly know[s] what to think about it" (p. 99). His role is summarized in the novel's closing lines, when he lays the manuscript down and yawns, with the excuse that he's tired and hungry for supper.

William New summarizes these tendencies of the novel by saying that "the author's focus shifts from the narrative itself to the processes of constructing narrative, and the equally problematic processes of interpretation" (101). Such attention to how the narrative is constructed can induce belief when these processes involve the history of Antarctic exploration (citing Ross's expedition, for example) or when they show how the flora and fauna are derived from geology. But they also draw attention to how More's report is constructed—how his experience and description of the Kosekin, for example, are mediated by antecedent texts. In this way, by revealing the mechanics of literary production, De Mille arguably destabilizes the way that Eurocentric discourses construct the imagined other. That is, he shows how experience of the world is shaped by representations of it. If another culture is represented as inferior or inhuman, this culture may be perceived as savage or primitive when it is encountered.

Lost Worlds: Satirical or Scientific Romance?

A Strange Manuscript can be located in several literary traditions including satire, fantastic voyages, lost-world and lost-race narratives, utopia, and scientific romance. It also exemplifies Antarctic fiction and, more specifically, the Antarctic utopia (Leane, "Romancing"). Justin Edwards treats *A Strange Manuscript* as an example of early Canadian Gothic. Readers of the novel have often traced a lineage of influence that includes Edgar Allan Poe's *The Narrative of Arthur Gordon Pym* and Samuel Taylor Coleridge's "The Rime of the Ancient Mariner." Melick's various suggestions that More should have taken Swift or Defoe as models and that whoever wrote the manuscript is "a gross plagiarist" provoke a reader to engage in comparative analysis. As I noted earlier, such comparison dominated the early reviews and has also preoccupied critics of the novel. What type of writing is *A Strange Manuscript?*

The most obvious suggestion, provided by Melick, is Satirical Romance—De Mille's own term for many of his other novels, especially those he wrote in the late 1860s.[1] If satire disturbs and changes how we see the world and ourselves, *A Strange Manuscript* makes a valiant attempt. Comparable to Jonathan Swift's Gulliver (see Appendix E6), More's slow recognition of Kosekin society, insistent comparison of it to his own world view, and general lack of self-insight make him a reliable vehicle for satire. One might say that More performs British ideology: as the man of light, the male protagonist and colonialist, he brings enlightenment to a society that wants nothing of it. Certainly, as R.E. Watters notes, De Mille was fundamentally satirical in orientation: "De Mille's critical and satirical temperament manifested itself at least as early as his college days" (x). And yet, oddly, there is reluctance among early reviewers of the novel to credit De Mille's use of satire (McGaw 53). The 3 June 1888 review in *The Brooklyn Daily Eagle* identifies a "vein of speculative philosophy" that "runs through it ... presenting a sharp contrast to all our conceptions of life," but it also asserts that *A Strange Manuscript* is "scarcely satirical" (Appendix F2). The 15 December 1888 review in *The Athenaeum* is harsher, characterizing De Mille as "lacking" in "wit and satire": "a string of impossible adventures does not make a work of imagination" (Appendix F4). A critic like J.O. Bailey, for example, writing in 1947, cannot accept that the book is satirical: "Yet no satiric purpose is clear in the book" (65). This is quite at odds with John Colombo, who in 1995 argues that "De Mille's dystopian novel offers a consistent set of moral reactions and an ethical critique of social values" (34). Perhaps the early reluctance to recognize the satire can be explained by Gwendolyn Guth, who argues, "it is central to De Mille's satiric design that although satire is evidently at work in the novel, the reader cannot dogmatically pin down the target of the attack" (40). Or perhaps, as Guth suggests, it is a variant on a Menippean satire or "anatomy"—"a satire of ideas, fixed intellectual patterns, systems of reasoning" (42-43).[2]

---

1 De Mille calls "Ashdod Webster and His Starring Tour" a Satirical Romance in a letter to *Blackwood's Magazine* dated 23 July 1879.

2 Named after the Greek cynic Menippus, Menippean satire attacks attitudes or behaviours rather than individuals. In *Anatomy of Criticism*, Northrop Frye calls this type of satire "anatomy." In *Problems of Dostoevsky's Poetics*, Mikhail Bakhtin identifies Menippean satire with the carnivalesque: describing the unsettling effects of fantastic adventures that mix styles and voices.

Closely connected to satire is the sense that the novel is utopian. In his important 1969 introduction to the McClelland and Stewart edition, Watters suggests that *A Strange Manuscript* belongs to the "genre of utopian fiction," defining utopia in a manner synonymous with utopian satire: the use of an imaginary country to critique an existing society (viii). Perhaps because De Mille's target is ambiguous, some critics have argued for a focused critique, while others see him attacking everything. Kenneth Hughes sees it as a "positive Utopia which satirizes an aristocratic class that serves no useful function" (123), while Glenn Willmott sees the "dystopian Kosekin society" as a reflection of the slave morality of modern culture (147), and Karyn Huenemann suggests that it critiques "the very foundations of Victorian culture: religion, ethics, morality, gender relations, and [...] the imperialist project" (194).

The profound questioning implied by Huenemann begins to explain why so much attention has been paid to the novel in the last four decades. Linda Lamont-Stewart, who has traced what she claims is a history of misreading the novel on the part of various critics, suggests that critical appreciation of the novel since the 1970s is due to a "postmodernist impulse to celebrate the self-reflexive, parodic, elusively ironic qualities of his work" ("Rescued" 34). Others agree with this suggestion: "a reactionary but radical Victorian text which is bizarrely postmodernist in technique and conception" (Keefer 130). Much of this commentary focuses on the frame narrative. For instance, Flavio Multineddu suggests that the different ways that the four readers try to make sense of More's story model how readers and critics interpret literature in general: "the interpretative problems that are posed by *A Strange Manuscript* [are] 'paradigmatic' of textual exegesis" (78). Richard Cavell's suggestion, in his analysis of De Mille's 1869 novel *The Dodge Club*, that De Mille enacts a "paradoxical questioning of originality, such that the novel becomes its own formal critique" (209), can easily be applied to *A Strange Manuscript*. David Ketterer claims that the "technique of reversing oppositional and hierarchical relationships would today be described as deconstructionist": "an aporia, an irreconcilable contradiction opens up that subverts all attempts at [determining] meaning" (9). The same sentiment is expressed by others: "There seems to be an infinite number of ways in which More's manuscript mocks its repeating series of readers, makes chaos of chronology and the secure location of readers and authors outside texts" (Beddoes 10).

In Chapter 26, Featherstone asks why the manuscript shouldn't be considered Scientific Romance. Scientific Romance, as a term, was being used in Britain from the 1840s onward to describe the intersection between popularized science and speculative fiction. For example, in the 24 March 1866 issue of his weekly journal *All the Year Round*, Charles Dickens characterizes Henri de Parville's "Un Habitant de la Planète Mars" as a "scientific romance."[1] Featherstone's question doesn't mean much to the Doctor or Oxenden because they are firm believers in its authenticity, but Melick dismisses the suggestion on the grounds that "there is precious little science in it" (p. 245). It is true that the manuscript proper lacks the obvious signs of science, speculative or otherwise. As Melick notes, it could be grouped with fantastic voyages such as Sinbad or *Robinson Crusoe* or fantastical satirical voyages such as *Gulliver's Travels*. And yet, the Doctor and Oxenden show that More's story can be assessed in scientific terms; they analyze the manuscript in terms of current geography, paleontology, evolution, botany, and so on. Of course, once the frame narrative is factored into the equation, the science is undeniable. In this sense, *A Strange Manuscript* can be located in the developing genre of Scientific Romance with obvious precursors such as Jules Verne's A *Journey into the Interior of the Earth* (Appendix E4) and contemporaries such as Edward Bulwer Lytton's *The Coming Race* (Appendix E3). My hope is that the following sections on Antarctica and nineteenth-century science will help show why Scientific Romance is an appropriate way to think of the novel. Leo Henkin's study of Darwinism and the English novel emphasizes the way that the introduction of paleontology and the idea of evolution transforms the fantastic into an analogy for how organisms respond to environment. He sees De Mille marking the threshold where satirical romance transitions into evolutionary romance, whose setting "represents the discovery of freakish instances of aberrant evolution, of quasi-human and semi-human beings" (183). In this sense, we might see to what extent De Mille anticipates a novel such as H.G. Wells's *The Time Machine* (1895).

Earlier, I wondered what accounts for the remarkable similarities between *A Strange Manuscript* and other novels that it has often been compared with. These include *She* and *King Solomon's*

1 French journalist Henri de Parville (1838-1909) published "Un Habitant de la Planète Mars" (An Inhabitant of the Planet Mars) in 1864 as a hoax in the French newspaper *Le Pays*. It was published as a novel the following year in Paris by Pierre-Jules Hetzel, Jules Verne's publisher. The story details the analysis by a scientific commission of a meteorite discovered in Colorado that contains the calcified body of a Martian.

Mines published in the 1880s, also those novels published in the early 1870s such as Butler's *Erewhon* and Bulwer Lytton's *The Coming Race.* One commonality is that all of these novels involve the discovery of lost races—in Africa, beneath the United States, in New Zealand, and in Antarctica. Thomas Clareson argues that "lost race" novels, dating from the 1870s to 1930s, reflect three intersecting areas of late nineteenth-century interest: 1. ongoing exploration, especially of Africa and polar regions; 2. geological discoveries and theories; and 3. archaeological discoveries and theories about ancient civilizations. These three areas can be seen vividly in the range of intertexts that are explicitly identified in the frame narrative of *A Strange Manuscript.* These intertexts radiate out in a circle that seems almost inexhaustible, but they have several precise effects. They root the adventure in eighteenth- and nineteenth-century exploration narratives, especially Antarctic exploration but also a significantly broader set of exploration narratives and scientific work derived from them. These include observations of indigenous populations, and botanical and paleontological work. In effect, the intertexts lead again and again to the intersection of scientific inquiry and European global expansion (imperialism and colonization). At one level, these intersections should be fairly obvious. The circumnavigation and mapping of the globe are scientific achievements, but they are also of inestimable economic and political significance. Botanical research gathered on exploratory expeditions such as those of James Cook led directly to the classification of plants and animals used for imperialist and economic purposes. Charles Darwin's observations while on the second voyage of the *Beagle* (1831-36) are usually recognized in scientific terms, but More's reference to Darwin's observations of the natives of Tierra del Fuego locates the science in terms of a racial hierarchy that has profound implications for European imperialism. In this regard, we might keep in view that More's ship *Trevelyan* was chartered by the British government to carry convicts to the penal colony on Van Diemen's Land (Tasmania).

One significant difference between *A Strange Manuscript* and other lost race novels is the instability produced by the frame narrative. In Chapter 26, Featherstone asks Melick if he still thinks that the manuscript is a sensational novel. The question stems from the earlier argument over the authenticity of the manuscript, in which Doctor Congreve and Oxenden provide reasons for their faith in it and Melick mocks it with "contemptuous scepticism," having ridiculed its literary merits and suggested that it is a "transparent hoax" (p. 100). These comments blatantly interfere with a reader's suspension of disbelief. Rather than Haggard, Butler, or Bulwer Lytton, they remind us of Poe. Both *The Narrative of Arthur Gordon Pym* and Poe's 1841 tale "A Descent into the Maelstrom" alluded to by More provoke readers to disbelieve: to recognize that they are reading a story, a construction rather than a fact.

Antarctic Exploration: Territory and Imagination

Copper cylinders had two principal uses by naval expeditions in the nineteenth century. If holes were drilled in them and a thermometer was placed inside, they could be lowered into the water and used to take the water temperature. If they were sealed, papers recording location and daily events could be placed inside them and they were dropped overboard; if the cylinders were later found, information could be inferred about ocean currents. The second use is recorded by John Ross and William Parry during their respective voyages in search of a Northwest passage in 1819 and 1826. In this sense, the title of De Mille's *A Strange Manuscript Found in a Copper Cylinder* immediately invokes a history of naval exploration even as it recollects Poe's 1833 Antarctic tale "MS Found in a Bottle," a story that ends when the ship plunges into a huge whirlpool at the South Pole and the manuscript is thrown into the ocean as the ship enters the whirlpool.

The lost world that De Mille projects—discovered by More, but already inhabited by the Kosekin—is one that reflects a range of European ideas and practices. Namely, this lost world confirms the long-standing European practice of defining Antarctica "by its assumed inversion of northern geography and its inaccessibility" as "oppositional and inverted" (Leane, "Antarctica" 27). Antarctica is bound into the history of European mapping and imagining of the world since at least the Ancient Greeks. In *Meteorology* (350 BCE), Aristotle projected a region called the antarctic at the southern pole that corresponded with the northern pole. This imagined region was reiterated by other ancient geographers and consolidated by Ptolemy, who drew imaginary maps of the world that projected a continental land mass labelled *Terra Incognita* enclosing the Sea of India: southern Africa extends east and enjoins Asia on the far side of India. Maps of this continent feature prominently among the maps of early global exploration in the sixteenth and seventeenth centuries: for example, European geographers such as Johannes Schöner and Abraham Ortelius included *Terra Australis Incognita* on their maps and globes (Hakluyt's 1599 map is an exception). It wasn't until James Cook's second voyage that this imaginary continent disappeared. Cook's chart (see Appendix A1, Figure 1) shows the paths of different voyages, but the South Pole is left blank. In this regard, it is worth noting Ralph Pordzik's study of the postcolonial utopia: he makes the interesting observation that in speculative postcolonial writing "the map of the world is often redrawn in order to provide the necessary space for the inscription into history of imagined societies" (20).

It is remarkable, if one follows the exploration literature, to see the delays and the gaps in exploration. (See the Antarctica Timeline in Appendix A.) It wasn't until 1773 that Captain James Cook's ship becomes the first to cross the Antarctic Circle (see Appendix A1). And along with sealing and whaling industries, the flurry of attempts that followed Cook resulted in a growing picture of a land mass beneath or behind the walls of ice. But this land mass remained a mystery, the blank inside of the quasi-circles drawn on the map by different routes.

A testament to De Mille's speculative strategy can be seen in the parallel timelines of the novel and the history of exploration. De Mille is exploiting exploration information that is current to the 1860s when he's writing. This is a strategy used by Poe in his only novel, *The Narrative of Arthur Gordon Pym* (1838). Poe goes into considerable detail about the explorations of Cook, James Weddell (1822), Benjamin Morrell (1823), John Briscoe (1831), and others. De Mille also notes Cook, but he emphasizes Charles Wilkes's US expedition (1839-40) and James Ross's British naval expedition (1841), both of which took place after Poe's novel was published, and which represented the most current knowledge when De Mille was writing. (See Appendices A2 and A3 for excerpts from Wilkes and Ross.) The delay of about twenty years in publishing the novel makes no difference. The next significant expedition following Ross didn't happen until 1892, when Captain Carl Larsen of the *Jason* landed on Seymour Island. While there was increasing activity on the Antarctic mainland in the first decade of the twentieth century, it wasn't until 1911 that Roald Amundsen's team finally reached the South Pole. De Mille, using More's fairly vague first-hand account and the Doctor's remarkably technical recollection of different expeditions, sketches the contemporary state of knowledge about the southern continent, and then he creates a lost world in the blank centre of the map.

More's story begins in the familiar setting of icy waters, icebergs, volcanoes, and barren coast line, but the land on the other side of the mountains is almost tropical, a balmy sea at the South Pole. Given twentieth-century knowledge of extreme subzero temperatures and an ice-covered continent, this warm sea is puzzling to say the least. In order to understand it, we need to look more directly at the Antarctic fiction that influenced De Mille and also at the rationale for the warmth provided by both More and the Doctor.

More and Agnew repeatedly allude to the theory of John Cleves Symmes Jr. that the Earth is hollow with solid concentric spheres accessible via openings at the poles (see Appendix E1). Symmes published his theory as a pamphlet in 1818. A fictional narrative recounting the discovery of these openings and a utopian society living inside the earth was published under the title *Symzonia* in 1820 under the pseudonym Captain Seaborn. While De Mille forgoes the hollow earth, he retains a warm southern ocean discovered by Seaborn. More and Agnew also make several references to tales by Poe. First published as a serial in 1838, *The Narrative of Arthur Gordon Pym* is Poe's only novel and a "*tour de force* in the genre of fantastic travel accounts to which 'MS. Found in a Bottle' belongs" (Kime 282). In "MS. Found in a Bottle" (1833), Poe's earliest and highly successful short story, a manuscript describing a voyage of discovery is found in a container floating in the ocean. The manuscript ends at the point that the boat plunges into a vast vortex at the South Pole. Like Symmes, in *The Narrative of Arthur Gordon Pym* Poe posits a warm southern ocean based on the experience of James Weddell in 1822 and Benjamin Morrell in 1823 (Appendix E2b). Weddell encountered ice at 72 degrees latitude, but then found that there was less ice to the south. Similarly, Morrell found open water at 69 degrees and observed that the climate seemed milder the further south he went.

If De Mille's adoption of a warm pole is indebted to Symmes and Poe, the explanation offered for it by the Doctor in Chapter 7 is original. The Doctor speculates that the flatness of the Earth at its poles means that the surface at the poles is thirteen miles closer to the centre of the earth, and that the interior of the earth "according to the popular theory of the present day is a mass of fire" (p. 108). Thus, the Doctor suggests, geothermal heat produces the warm climate. Along with De Mille's interest in Antarctic exploration narratives, his speculative use of geology begins to reveal the importance of natural science to *A Strange Manuscript*.

Nineteenth-Century Science: Geology and Paleontology

After Antarctic exploration, the second significant feature that De Mille manipulates is evolution. It "reflects, and in part, predicts the issues with which his culture became concerned in the aftermath of Darwin's publication *On the Origin of Species*" (McGaw 55). Writing within a decade of Darwin's landmark book, De Mille doesn't directly engage Darwin's evolutionary theory, but he does engage the larger project of the scientific observation (and knowledge acquisition: the taxonomies that obsess the eighteenth and nineteenth centuries) of flora and fauna from around the world.

This engagement has its ear close to the scientific ground of changing belief: namely the paleontological research that introduces the idea of geologic time and the fact that dinosaurs and other creatures once existed. More's tropical Antarctic sea is an evolutionary niche, a lost world reminiscent of Verne's *Voyage au Centre de la Terre* (Appendix E4), the original French edition of which was published in 1864 immediately before De Mille was working on *A Strange Manuscript*, and it looks forward to Arthur Conan Doyle's *The Lost World* (1912). Unlike the authors of these other works, De Mille retains an intense playfulness, a willingness to remind the reader that these creatures are not unlike the monsters of Sinbad or medieval romance—or that perhaps we are just reading a tall tale. But this playfulness has a serious edge, an insistent reminder that there may be a scientific basis to the fantastic monsters that litter imaginative literature. Alongside Verne's *Voyage*, *A Strange Manuscript* is one of the first novels to recast the monsters of fantasy and myth in terms of paleontology. Indeed, as Appendix B illustrates, De Mille's giant creatures and plants are taken from the writings and illustrations of early nineteenth-century books on paleontology and geology. Perhaps the most vivid examples of this can be seen by comparing More's first-hand descriptions of the creatures he encounters with the illustrations by Edouard Riou in Louis Figuier's *La Terre Avant le Déluge* (1863), translated in 1866 as *The World Before the Deluge* (see Appendix B2 for samples of Riou's illustrations). Likewise, along with the Doctor, if we peruse the engravings of Carboniferous era flora found in Figuier, we might be able to identify the various vegetation More describes as "the vegetation of the Coal Period—the lepidodendron, the lepidostrobus, the pecopteris, the neuropteris, the lonchopteris, the odontopteris, the sphenopteris, the cyclopteris, the sigillaria reniformis, the sphenophyllum, the calamites—" (p. 177, see Appendix B3).

Late in the novel, when Layelah shows More winged animals of "portentous size" called athaleb, More observes, "It seemed like some enormous bat, or rather like a winged crocodile, or yet again like one of those monstrous dragons of which I had read" (p. 208). The Doctor thinks that the athaleb is a pterodactyl: "The figure of the pterodactyl represents pretty closely that which is given to the dragons" (p. 249). And he goes on to suggest that pterodactyls may have persisted into the prehistoric period, and representations of them carved "upon wood and stone" may have been endowed with "the power of belching forth smoke and flames": "Thus the dragon idea pervaded the minds of men, and instead of a natural animal it became a fabulous one" (p. 249). This basic possibility recurs in the scientific literature of the mid-nineteenth century. For example, in one of De Mille's sources, *The Testimony of Rocks* (1865), Hugh Miller likens pterodactyls "to flying dragons,—real existences of the Oolitic period" (116). Thus, De Mille imagines a scenario that reflects what is becoming a commonplace in the paleontological writings of his time.

De Mille's university education at Brown between 1852 and 1854 included several courses in the sciences. These included a year-long course in natural philosophy (or physics), which introduced students to mechanics, hydrostatics, pneumatics, optics, acoustics, and astronomy (Monk 68). De Mille also took a class in chemistry and physiology that covered chemistry, heat, electricity, galvanism, magnetism, and animal and vegetable physiology and classification (Monk 69). As Parks notes, when De Mille began working as a professor at Dalhousie College in 1865, he joined a college "that gave natural science a prominent place in its curriculum," and he became friends with scientific colleagues ("Introduction" xxx). One such colleague was George Lawson, who published prolifically on chemistry and especially botany. It was probably Lawson who introduced De Mille to the Nova Scotian Institute of Natural Science, which he joined in 1866 (Monk 149). De Mille's attendance of meetings of this Institute, especially in 1866 and 1867, would have brought him into direct contact with the current scientific debates of the decade.

Near the end of Chapter 27, Melick suggests that the writer of the manuscript should have stepped "into the British Museum," where "in a couple of hours he could have crammed up on" the "philological, theological, sociological, geological, paleontological, ontological, ornithological, and all the other logical attainments" necessary to satisfy Oxenden and the Doctor's questions (p. 256). De Mille most likely visited the British Museum in 1850 or 1851 when he travelled to Europe with his older brother Elisha Budd.[1] Archibald MacMechan, who consulted James's journal of this trip (it was subsequently lost), states, "It would be hard to over-estimate the influence which these eighteen months abroad exerted upon the whole of De Mille's subsequent career" ("De Mille" 409). The brothers arrived in Liverpool on 15 September 1850, after which they spent some time in Scotland before returning to England, where they visited Bath, Oxford, and finally London in early November. After two weeks in London, they caught a steamer to France, touring through France, Italy, Geneva, Germany, and Belgium before returning to London in early May 1851. They stayed at least a week but perhaps as long as three months in London before returning to New Brunswick.[2] The timing of their return to London from the continent corresponds with the beginning of the first World Fair. The Great Exhibition of the Works of Industry of all Nations, or The Great Exhibition, was held in Hyde Park between 1 May and 15 October 1851. The Great Exhibition offered a remarkable display of contemporary industry and technology, but one feature in particular is especially relevant to *A Strange Manuscript*. In the enormous Crystal Palace, which was later moved to Sydenham in South London, paleontologist Richard Owen and sculptor Benjamin Waterhouse Hawkins collaborated to produce full-sized sculptures of dinosaurs based on reconstructions of fossils. Owen (1804-92) played a central role in nineteenth-century British comparative anatomy and paleontology. Owen first named dinosaurs, distinguishing them from lizards and introducing the term *Dinosauria*. He published several works on dinosaurs, including his guide to the Crystal Palace sculptures, *Geology and the Inhabitants of the Ancient World* (1854). As Parks demonstrates, many of the creatures that More encounters at the South Pole are found at the Crystal Palace, including Pterodactyls, Meglosaurus, Iguanodon, Hylaeosaurus, Teleosaurus, Ichthyosaurus, Plesiosaurus, and the Cheirotherium. Dr. Congreve's descriptions of some of them are based on Owen's descriptions ("Introduction" xxxi-xxxii). (See Appendix B1 for excerpts from Owen's guide and illustrations of the sculptures.)

---

1 MacLeod and Monk both recreate this trip based on journals kept by James and Elisha. Unfortunately, James's journal hasn't survived and Elisha doesn't provide a sequence of dated or detailed entries for the time they spent in London. Elisha's journal ends when they arrive back in London from the continent.

2 Ivison suggests that they returned home in September (62).

The most explicit engagement with the idea of evolution proper involves the origin of the Kosekin. Oxenden's hypothesis is that the Kosekin have migrated to the South Pole, and that their physiological differences (e.g., their lack of tolerance for light) and world-view (e.g., their inverted values) are produced through adaptation to their environment. The Doctor, on the other hand, believes that they are an "aboriginal and autochthonous race": "Their complexion, small stature, and peculiar eyes—their love of darkness, their singular characteristics, both physical and moral, all go to show that they can have no connection with the races in our part of the world" (p. 178). In his defence, Oxenden cites the "eyeless fishes of the great cave of Kentucky [...] whose eyes have become extinct from living in the dark" (p. 178). Living in thousands of caves throughout Kentucky and Indiana, the Northern cavefish (*Amblyopsis spelaeus*) is a troglobitic species of fish that is blind and colourless. It was first described by James DeKay in 1842. While Oxenden's position can be reconciled with either Charles Darwin's theory of natural selection or Jean-Baptiste Lamarck's theory of acquired characteristics, he seems to represent a Lamarckian approach. In *Philosophie Zoologique* (1809), Lamarck (1744-1829) elaborated a theory of evolution based on the inheritance of acquired characteristics by which animals pass on physiological changes developed in their lifetime. The key idea—one that is at odds with Darwin's passive theory of natural selection—is that animals actively adapt their bodies to their environment and then give these adaptations to their offspring. For Darwin, an animal is born with a set of traits, and if these traits contribute to the animal reproducing in a specific environment, then they will gradually become the norm while less adaptive traits will eventually be reduced or eliminated. Regardless of whether Oxenden follows a Lamarckian or Darwinian position, when he says that the "peculiar eyes" of the Kosekin "are no doubt produced by dwelling in caves for many generations" (p. 178), he advocates an evolutionary position that sees species as dynamic and adaptive to environment. Curiously, the Doctor, who knows so much about geology and paleontology, seems to ascribe to a more static model of special creation associated with Carl Linnaeus (1707-78) and Johann Friedrich Blumenbach (1752-1840). One reason for this may be the friendship between De Mille, whose interest in languages makes him resemble Oxenden, and his colleague George Lawson. The botanist Lawson was apparently "an anti-evolutionist who [argued] that 'plants were independent creations specially fitted for the places they were found'" (Parks "Introduction" xxx). In any case, the debate between Oxenden and the Doctor intersects mid-nineteenth-century scientific debates. Significantly, it links the more obvious paleontological themes of dinosaurs and Carboniferous-era flora with the values and worldview of the Kosekin.

Another, less obvious, link between paleontology and worldview can be seen in the giant flightless birds called ophamera that the Kosekin have domesticated. In Chapter 17, the Doctor tries to identify the birds. The discussion begins with the highly popular and recently extinct Dodo before taking up the New Zealand Moa, the Elephant bird of Madagascar, and other extinct giant birds. These are creatures that are the direct experience of European global expansion—creatures that are so fantastic that they should belong to the realm of myth. And yet, they were not only discovered but simultaneously lost. Even as Europeans witness their existence, they become extinct. The Dodo, endemic to Mauritius in the Indian Ocean, went extinct by the late seventeenth century. Found in New Zealand, the giant Moa were probably extinct by the sixteenth century, although there were reported sightings into the 1800s. The world's largest bird, with a height in excess of ten feet and a weight of 800 pounds, the Elephant bird of Madagascar went extinct by the seventeenth century. These birds are epitomes of a type of knówledge experience that characterizes global expansion. In this sense, we can see the connection between scientific and geopolitical issues.

Colonialism and Imperialism: Orientalism, Cannibalism, and Troglodytes

Born in the British colony of New Brunswick, James De Mille was a British subject. Living in Halifax, Nova Scotia, when he wrote *A Strange Manuscript* between 1866 and 1868, De Mille was writing in the dawn of the Canadian Confederation. It may be De Mille's subject position—a British subject raised in a loyalist colony but educated in the United States, a new-found Canadian writing about British characters for an American publication—that explains why Carole Gerson is able to engage in a "contrapuntal reading" of the novel: "tracing in the book two complementary processes: 'that of imperialism and that of resistance to it'" ("A Contrapuntal Reading" 224). Gerry Turcotte provides a related way to understand this aspect of the novel: he sees it expressing "imperialism's greatest fear—cultural dissolution" (77): "Colonial Gothic texts, such as De Mille's, constantly negotiate, both textually and thematically, the fear of separation and the terror of not belonging, which is endemic in the colonial experience" (84). This would help explain why Crawford Kilian suggests that the Kosekin are displaced Canadians (65).

A remarkable critical fact about De Mille's novel is that it wasn't discussed much before postcolonial theory allowed readers to recognize a displacement of colonialist anxieties on lost worlds encountered in Victorian fiction. With more than three quarters of the scholarship on this novel published in the past four decades, *A Strange Manuscript* is an example of a work gaining significance because it speaks to the critical and scholarly tools that have been developed to understand the past. There are two basic ideas that help clarify how *A Strange Manuscript* taps into the synchrony of global exploration and knowledge construction from the sixteenth to the nineteenth centuries: Orientalism and cannibalism.

If Orientalism names the study of eastern cultures and people from a western perspective, in *Orientalism* (1978), Edward Said argues that the historical study and representation of the Orient was skewed by preconceptions that tended to group all eastern societies and people together in opposition to Europeans. This pervasive and highly prejudiced stereotyping of eastern societies informed and shaped Western imperialist and colonialist practices. It is a type of shared cultural fantasy about other societies that helps shape both desire and anxiety.

Orientalism pervades *A Strange Manuscript*. In tracing Orientalist features, one should keep in mind that this is a lost world romance with the fantasy projected on the blank screen of Antarctica rather than an existing culture, and so the caricature is potentially more apparent.

Orientalism is explicitly signalled early on in the frame narration, when the four men gather around to open the copper cylinder. They observe that it is of "foreign make," maybe "Chinese" (p. 50). Oxenden speculates that it might contain "the mangled remains of one of the wives of some Moorish pasha" (p. 51). Once they begin to read More's story, it becomes apparent that the Kosekin are an elaborate Orientalist conceit. They are "very small in stature and slender in frame," "not unlike Arabs," with straight black hair, regular features, and a "general expression" of "great gentleness" (p. 93). Their physiognomy is accentuated by apparent evolutionary changes to their eyes. The architecture and technology of the Kosekin could be derived from books on ancient Egypt. The manuscript is written on papyrus. Epitomizing deep-seated beliefs about the Orient, the Kosekin are radically passive to the point that their passivity is threatening and overwhelming.

A synthesis of European imaginations of the Orient and the Antarctic, the Kosekin seem to originate in the Middle East: perhaps the Troglodytes of North Africa, their language and culture reflect Egyptian and Hebraic influences. But because they are not an actual people, the fact that they are so explicitly an Orientalist construction seems to say something about certain European fantasies about other civilizations. Whatever it says, it isn't exactly the same as other lost race fiction written in the nineteenth century. For example, Edward Bulwer Lytton's *The Coming Race* (1871), which also weaves a lost race from the thread of Ancient Egypt, expresses a profound anxiety about non-European societies gaining superior technology (see Appendix E3).

Whereas Orientalism provides a way to think about other civilizations, especially civilizations thought to be in decline, cannibalism is closely linked with distinctions between civilized and savage, human and inhuman, and self and other. Conventionally, cannibalism marks the threshold between these categories. To identify a cannibal is to identify the extremity of savagery and simultaneously to affirm the importance of civilization and cultural colonialism. Exploration narratives of the eighteenth and nineteenth centuries are rife with encounters with supposed cannibals (see Appendix C for two examples). In the article "'British Cannibals': Contemplation of an Event in the Death and Resurrection of James Cook, Explorer," Nananath Obeyesekere suggests that the idea of cannibalism reflects the anxieties and fantasies produced by the encounter with the other, and he questions the simplicity of seeing cannibalism as a way to distinguish civilized from savage; rather, Obeyesekere suggests that cannibalism reveals underlying anxieties about distinctions between civilized and savage, self and other. Cannibalism plays a unique role in *A Strange Manuscript*, serving first as a stereotypical marker of savagery when More and Agnew encounter the apparent savages on the outer coast and then working to elicit a different type of horror as the apparently civilized Kosekin are recognized as cannibals. In her analysis of cannibalism in the novel, Maggie Kilgour argues that the Kosekin are "clearly a nightmare version of modern capitalist society" (28). And Justin Edwards suggests that "De Mille is able to expose the obscenity of capitalist anthropophagy in which men and women are devoured as expendable commodities" (20).

When these features of colonialist discourse are supported or explicated through reference to antecedent sources, the frame narration draws attention to the constructed basis of the event. And these constructions are progressively problematized by the novel through the constant process of inversion that marks the cultural comparison of European and Kosekin norms and values. One example occurs early on in the novel, in Chapter IV, "The Sight of Human Beings," when More and Agnew encounter people living on the outer shore of Antarctica, people whom More comes to realize are cannibals. This example also illustrates how colonialist discourse intersects with De Mille's interest in evolution. Kenneth Hughes notes the similarity of More's description of these people with Charles Darwin's description of the natives of Tierra del Fuego in *Voyage of the Beagle*. Darwin observes, "These were the most abject and miserable creatures I anywhere beheld"; "one can hardly make oneself believe that they are fellow-creatures, and inhabitants of the same world" (see Appendix C2). Compare this to More's characterization of the natives:

> As for the natives themselves, the longer we looked at them the more abhorrent they grew. Even the wretched aborigines of Van Diemen's Land, who have been classed lowest in the scale of humanity, were pleasing and congenial when compared with these, and the land looked worse than Tierra del Fuego. (pp. 71-72)

Later, once he realizes that they (like the inhabitants of Tierra del Fuego) are cannibals, More is even more emphatic:

> These people were not like human beings. The vilest and lowest savages that I had ever seen were not so odious as these. A herd of monkeys would be far more congenial, a flock of wolves less abhorrent. They had the caricature of the human form; they were the lowest of humanity; their speech was a mockery of language; their faces devilish, their kindness a cunning pretence.... (p. 78)

What is remarkable about this scene is how completely wrong More is about almost everything. Indeed, these so-called natives are the paupers who form the most elite class of Kosekin society—they seek this desolation and deprivation. More's initial perception and assessment cites Darwin, and this anthropological construction is subsequently shown to be a misreading, a projection, a type of anxiety-induced fantasy that he subscribes to.

In the nineteenth century, primitive humans could also be studied by reading ancient history books and by excavating tombs. Oxenden's theory, in Chapter 17, that the Kosekin are related to the Troglodytes of north-east Africa, signals both endeavours. Derived from the Greek Τρωγλοδύτης, to get into or dwell in a hole or cave, the word Troglodyte has a long history of representing a specific type of culture, whether it is African cultures in the age of Herodotus or "people of the lowest stage of civilization" ("Troglodytæ" 290) in the Victorian era. Oxenden directly refers to Agatharchides of Cnidus's account of Troglodytes in Book 5 of his second century BCE Greek treatise on the African coast of the Red Sea, *On the Erythraean Sea*. While De Mille would have read Agatharchides in the original Greek, a recent translation by Stanley M. Burstein makes *On the Erythraean Sea* more accessible in English. Near the end of fragment 64, Agatharchides notes the Troglodytes' traditional burial practices:

> [T]he Trogodytes[1] deal as follows with the dead. With withies made from the Christ's thorn plant they bind the neck to the legs. Then, after they place the body on a mound, they pelt it with stones large enough to be held in a hand while jeering and laughing until they have hidden the corpse. Then they place on top (of the cairn) the horn of a goat and depart free of sadness and completely cheerful. In conducting this sort of funeral, he says, they act sensibly since to not cause themselves grief on account of those who are free from pain is a sign of intelligence. (Agatharchides Fragment 64a 113-14)

The cheerfulness in the face of death—seeing death as a release from pain—does make the Troglodytes seem related to the Kosekin. And this resemblance extends to certain Kosekin practices, such as the mercy killing of the wounded by the Kohen:

> Those individuals who are unable to follow the herds because of age wind the tail of a cow around their necks and willingly free themselves from life. But should one seek to postpone death, anyone has the right to fasten the noose as though from kindness and with a rebuke to deprive him of his life. It is likewise their custom to remove from life those who have been crippled or are suffering from incurable diseases. For they consider the greatest of evils to be for a person to desire to live when unable

1 Burstein follows current scholarly practice of omitting the "l," rendering the Hellenic word as "Trogodyte." He also points out, "Descriptions of them as cave-dwellers [...] are based on inferences from the incorrect form of their name, 'Troglodytes'" (113n1).

to do anything that makes life worth living. (Agatharchides Fragment 64b 115-16)

These fragments from Herodotus provide support for Oxenden's conjecture, but the introduction of Troglodytes into the novel has other implications as well. Troglodytes are an obscure but complex figure in nineteenth-century thought. The root metaphor signifies cave dwellers, primitives at a certain stage of development (see Appendix D2). The study of such primitives also involved the excavation of tombs—the archaeological reconstruction of the past. One example of tomb excavation happened in the early 1840s on the Canary Islands, the background setting of the frame narrative.[1] In the *Journal of the Ethnological Society of London* (1848), Thomas Hodgkin argues that his inspection of the Guanchee mummies found on the Canary Islands indicates that the ancient inhabitants were "a diminutive people," and he associates them with the legendary Troglodytes of north-east Africa (see Appendix D3). Hodgkin's paper provides a precedent for Oxenden's theory that the Kosekin's ancestors are the Troglodytes, but it also begins to illustrate how the root Colonialist metaphor (cave dwelling primitive) is intrinsically unstable. Comparative ethnology can produce hierarchies like the ones cited by More when he encounters the cave dwellers on the outer coast of Antarctica or Darwin regarding the natives of Tierra del Fuego, but it also intrinsically produces a relativist perspective of culture. Archaeology is like paleontology, and the study of the strata in caves allowed researchers to understand geological time. More's entry into the cave that takes him beneath the Antarctic continent and into Kosekin culture is literally a journey into the Mesozoic and Paleozoic Eras when Pterodactyls existed and Calamites grew instead of trees. Like troglobytic fish adapting to their environment, the Kosekin are a civilized race whose evolutionary arc takes it in a direction antithetical to progress. And the inversions of light and dark that dominate the South Pole, accentuated as they are by themes of blindness and insight, remind us of those other cave dwellers: in Plato's *The Republic*, Socrates uses the cave as a metaphor for "the region which the eye reveals" (see Appendix D1).

De Mille's oscillation of opposites in *A Strange Manuscript* potentially destabilizes the norms and values that undergird colonialist discourse. Angela Arnold argues that by the end of the

1 The yacht *The Falcon* is drifting in the Atlantic Ocean within sight of Mount Tenerife on the Canary Islands.

novel, Adam More inadvertently "exposes the violent and exploitive nature of the imperial project" (88). Stephen Milnes traces the "failure of colonialist appropriation of power and ... the limits of colonial discourse" (103). And Carole Gerson argues that De Mille "ultimately deconstructs the system of knowledge and understanding underpinning Western vision and practice" (230).

A Strange Manuscript is a novel that came to renewed attention in the latter part of the twentieth century, in part because of an interest in Confederation-era Canadian writers, in part because it appealed to a growing postmodern sensibility. Since the 1980s, this interest has shifted, growing in intensity with the emergence of postcolonialist approaches to literature and the growing interconnectivity between traditionally isolated nationalist literatures and artificially regimented literary periods. *A Strange Manuscript* will continue to grow in importance to the study of early Canadian literature. It is uniquely suited to postcolonial approaches to literature because it performs explicit Orientalist constructions of non-European cultures while ironically subverting the rationalism of European colonialist discourse. The novel's strong intersections with British and American writing in this period also make it relevant to nineteenth-century literary studies generally. It offers intersections with popular potboiler and sensation fiction of the period, and it is easy to relate to British and American fiction, especially genre innovations involving scientific romance and dystopian fiction. Strongly influenced by writers such as Poe and Verne, *A Strange Manuscript* is relevant both to the specific historical study of science fiction and the broader attempt to understand speculative and satirical literature. As De Mille's best-known novel, it extends an invitation to explore the other thirty or so novels he wrote. These include other novels of sensation and satirical romances, as well as his series of books for young boys, which are an example of early Canadian children's literature. Finally, if the Kosekin are a civilized race whose evolutionary arc takes it in a direction antithetical to progress, perhaps they have something to teach us in an age of unchecked capitalism and global warming.

James De Mille: A Brief Chronology

[The dates on serial publications of novels are only included if there is no subsequent book publication. Titles of poems, short stories, and miscellaneous prose are only listed if they are notable. Disputed titles are not included.]

1833	23 August, James is born in Saint John, New Brunswick, son of Nathan Smith De Mill and Elizabeth Budd, their third of nine children.
1840	Probably begins attending Saint John Grammar School.
1842	Father leaves Church of England to become a Baptist.
1847	Attends Horton Academy, a boarding school in Wolfville, Nova Scotia.
1848	Begins studies at Acadia College, Wolfville, Nova Scotia.
1849	24 September, James's brother, Will, dies at age 19.
1850-51	Travels with older brother Elisha to Boston, Quebec, England, Scotland, France, Italy, Germany, Belgium, and back to England. They spend an extended period in Italy and visit London twice.
1851	1 May-15 October, Great Exhibition in Hyde Park, London.
1852	Begins studies at Brown University in Providence, Rhode Island.
1853	Elected poet of Philermenian Society of Brown. Publishes "Acadie, and the Birth of Evangeline" in *Putnam's Monthly*.
1854	Publishes two poems and sixteen short stories. Appointed "Class Poet" for the class of 1854: composes and recites "Class Poem 1854." Awarded the degree of Master of Arts by Brown University. Returns to live in Saint John. Cholera Epidemic in New Brunswick doesn't affect the De Mill family, but the financial crisis that begins in this year does affect Nathan De Mill.
1855	Assistant editor for *Christian Visitor*, January to April. Moves to Cincinnati, Ohio, to become a bookkeeper for the West Columbia Mining and Manufacturing Company (an Acadia College investment).
1856	Returns to Saint John.
1857	In May, opens the Colonial Book Store in Saint John, in partnership with Hazen Fillmore. Assists Nathan and

Elisha in establishing the new Marsh Bridge Baptist Church and serves as Church clerk.

1858 Marries long-time fiancée Elizabeth Ann Pryor (Annie), daughter of Reverend Dr. Richard Pryor. The ceremony takes places on 26 November in Cambridge, Massachusetts. They reside in Saint John. James opens a second branch of the Colonial Book Store and registers as a merchant, acquiring a business licence.

1859 De Mille dissolves partnership with Fillmore and runs the book store by himself. William Budd, James and Annie's first child, is born in December.

1860 Acadia College, in Wolfville, appoints De Mille professor and chair of classics, with a one year leave until he assumes his duties. Publishes *John Wheeler's Two Uncles* (1860), which is now lost.

1861 Sells the Colonial Book Store to Thomas H. Hall. Publishes "Imagination and Fancy among the Arabs" (prose piece) in *Godey's Lady's Book*. Assists his brother Elisha with editing and writing for the *Christian Watchman* during Elisha's illness. Publishes "Andy O'Hara: Or, The Child of Promise" and "The Missionary's Son" (serialized in the *Christian Watchman*). Publishes approximately eleven poems in the Saint John *Morning News Double XXtra* and the *Christian Watchman*. Moves to Wolfville and assumes his duties as professor and chair of classics. Delivers his inaugural address at Acadia.

1862 Publishes the short story "The Loss of the Hector: Or, the Transformation" in *Godey's Lady's Book*.

1863 1 August, James's brother, Elisha, dies.

1864 Publishes the poem "Ode to the Great Confederation" in the *Humorist*. 26 December, James's father, Nathan De Mill, dies.

1865 Publishes *Martyrs of the Catacombs*. Resigns from Acadia College and accepts a position as professor of rhetoric and history at Dalhousie College, Halifax, Nova Scotia (18 October). Family moves to Halifax. Louise, James and Annie's second child, is born.

1866 Joins the Nova Scotian Institute of Natural Science. Probably begins composition of *A Strange Manuscript* (which continues into 1867).

1867 April, father-in-law, Dr. John Pryor, is accused of spending time with a "woman of ill repute" and loses his post as pastor at the Granville Street Baptist Church in Halifax. The controversy surrounding this scandal increases the amount of time James spends writing. Becomes librarian at Dalhousie (until 1872). Publishes the novel *Helena's Household.*

1868 Delivers the inaugural address for Dalhousie's new academic year.

1869 Publishes "The Earl's Daughter" (four episodes of a parody of society novels) in the *Dalhousie Gazette.* Publishes three novels: *Cord and Creese*, *The Dodge Club*, and *The B.O.W.C.: A Book for Boys* (first in the B.O.W.C. series for boys). John Pryor relocates to Lexington, Massachusetts.

1870 Publishes five novels: "The Minnehaha Mines" (serialized in *Boston Commercial Bulletin*), *The American Baron*, *The Lady of Ice*, *The Boys of Grande Pré School* (B.O.W.C. series), and *Lost in the Fog* (B.O.W.C. series).

1871 Publishes three novels: *The Cryptogram*, *Fire in the Woods* (B.O.W.C. series), and *Among the Brigands* (first in the Young Dodge Club series). Census lists the De Mille household as "Church of England": the family had changed their religious affiliation to Anglicanism and joined Saint Luke's Church sometime after 1867.

1872 Publishes two novels: *A Comedy of Terrors* and *Picked up Adrift* (B.O.W.C. series). Ethel Maud, James and Annie's second daughter, is born on 2 May.

1873 Publishes three novels: *An Open Question*, *The Seven Hills* (Young Dodge Club series), and *The Treasure of the Seas* (last of the B.O.W.C. series).

1874 Publishes two novels: *The Living Link* and *The Lily and the Cross. A Tale of Acadia.*

1875 Publishes the novel *The Babes in the Wood.* Appointed Examiner for *Young Elocution Prize* and appointed to MA Thesis committee. Sits as chair of the Dalhousie Senate.

1877 Publishes *The Early English Church* (a paper) and the last of the Young Dodge Club series, *The Winged Lion: Or, Stories of Venice.*

1878 Publishes the novel *A Castle in Spain.* Begins teaching a fourth year "History of Canada" course (Monk notes that this may be the first Canadian history course). Publishes *The Elements of Rhetoric* (an academic book).

1879 Recites "Phi Beta Kappa Poem" at Brown University and publishes the poem in the *Providence Daily Journal.*

1880 Dies of a lung infection on 28 January in Halifax. The funeral is held at Saint Luke's, and James is buried at Camp Hill Cemetery.

1883 Posthumous publication of the novel *Old Garth* is attributed to De Mille.

1888 Posthumous publication of *A Strange Manuscript Found in a Copper Cylinder.*

1893 Posthumous publication of the long poem *Beyond the Veil.*

A Note on the Text

This Broadview Edition of James De Mille's *A Strange Manuscript Found in a Copper Cylinder* is based on the *Harper's Weekly; A Journal of Civilization* serial version published between 7 January and 12 May 1888 (Volume 32, Issues 1620-38). It emulates the serial publication, breaking the novel into nineteen dated parts, each paired with the corresponding illustration by Gilbert Gaul.

Ironically, there is no surviving manuscript of *A Strange Manuscript*. This is the case with all of De Mille's novels. None of the manuscripts for his published novels survive in the Harper Brothers' archive or elsewhere. The only surviving manuscript of De Mille is the first half of "Ashdod Webster and His Starring Tour," which was rejected by *Blackwood's Magazine* in 1879 and thus returned. Apparently, the only other manuscript found with De Mille's papers was that of *A Strange Manuscript*, which his wife Annie sent to Harper Brothers in 1887—but it was subsequently lost or destroyed. This means that there is no extant manuscript against which to check the novel. When preparing the 1986 Centre for Editing Early Canadian Texts (CEECT) edition, Malcolm Parks carefully cross-checked the serial versions against the novel editions. He used the "Ashdod Webster" manuscript to establish De Mille's own standard practices on stylistics.[1] Parks's conclusion was that the Harper Brothers serial version, which preceded the novel edition and is relatively free of errors, is "closer to De Mille's known practices than the book" ("Introduction" xlvii). This is one of the reasons that I have adopted the *Harper's* serial as the basis for this edition. Another reason is that the nineteen starts and stops of the serial publication add another reading level to the starts and stops of the frame narrative—reminding us of our position as readers. And these instalments reflect the print culture context in which De Mille's novel first appeared to the public.

A distinctive feature of this edition, the nineteen illustrations by Gilbert Gaul were included in serials and the 1888 editions of the novel. Subsequent editions reduced the number of illustrations or eliminated them altogether. As Dean Irvine notes, the illustrations are a vital part of the novel's ties to "the American magazine and publishing industry and to the British imperial print culture

1 See Parks's Introduction to *A Strange Manuscript* (xlv-liii) for a detailed explanation of differences between the serial versions and novel editions, and other textual notes.

of illustrated newspapers," and nearly all of De Mille's novels published in his lifetime included illustrations (193). The illustrations by Gaul included in this edition were scanned from an 1888 Chatto & Windus edition of the novel and touched up (cropped, aligned, and resized, and the proper contrast, hue, and other settings selected for optimal reproduction) by Jesslyn Gosling. I believe the illustrations are significant because they belong to all of the original print versions of *A Strange Manuscript.* They represent a unique interpretation of the novel—a point exemplified by the inclusion of a servant in the background of one of the illustrations (see p. 176).

The text of this edition is derived directly from *Harper's Weekly*. A digital copy of the *Harper's* serial was produced using OCR software. My research assistant Jan Beecher and I checked the digital text by reading the original aloud one sentence at a time. The final text was electronically compared with an electronic copy of the 1888 Harper Brothers novel edition to identify variations. Variations and other problems were checked against Parks's notes in the Introduction and "Emendations in Copy-text" (319-21) of the CEECT edition and also notes from the preparation of this edition in the Carleton archive. I made an independent assessment for each variation and problem. I have noted key editorial decisions in the footnotes.

A Kosekin Glossary

[The invented Kosekin language plays several prominent roles in the narrative. The readers in the frame story develop a theory about it, and it is a significant part of Adam More's immersion in Kosekin society. As he learns the Kosekin language, More uses their words on an ongoing basis, in a way that can be difficult to remember. Here is a convenient glossary for ready reference.]

Amir Kosekin metropolis and capital city.

Ap Ram Father of thunder.

Asirin Kosekin caste (Chapter 24).

Athaleb Large flying creature identified by Dr. Congreve as a pterodactyl.

Athons Kosekin class.

Atœsmzori alonla Kosekin salutation (Chapter 24).

Cheder nebilin Cavern of the Dead (first mentioned in Chapter 9).

Epet Kosekin servant title (Chapter 22).

Gojin Another south pole people across the sea from the Kosekin. Apparently, they have different values (Chapter 20).

Hodu lecosck! Give thanks to darkness!

Iz Man.

Izza Woman.

Jantannin Giant scaled creature, sixty feet long by twenty around, resembling a crocodile with fins (Chapter 23).

Jom Day.

Kohen Kosekin title approximating "leader."

Kohen Gadol The first and noblest and richest Kosekin position—furthest from pauper.

Magones Volcanic island, site of a seasonal Kosekin ceremony.

Malca Kosekin title for queen (Chapter 19).

Meleks Kosekin class.

Mista Kosek Sacred Kosekin "Feast of Darkness."

Mosel anan wacosek Ruler of cloud and darkness.

Mudecheb Death recompense.

Mut Dead.

Opkuk Great bird, later compared by the Doctor to a giant dodo (Chapter 9).

Opmahera Great bird ridden by the Kosekin, compared by the Doctor to *Dinornis gigantea* (Chapter 11).

Or Light.

Orin A people among the Gojin, another south pole country, who love life and light (Chapter 23).

Pehmet Unspecified but apparently highly dangerous creature (Chapter 18).

Ranenu! Rejoice!

Salonla Salutation (Chapter 8).

Sar Tabakin Chief of the Kosekin executioners (Chapter 28).

Scullion Kosekin rank (Chapter 15).

Sepet-ram "Rod of thunder"; used to refer to Atam-or's rifle.

Sibgu Sibgin! Sacrifice the victims!

Sopet Mut Judge of death.

Thannin Sea monsters.

A STRANGE MANUSCRIPT
FOUND IN
A COPPER CYLINDER

PART 1 (7 JANUARY, 1888)

CHAPTER I.
THE FINDING OF THE COPPER CYLINDER.

IT occurred as far back as February 15, 1850. It happened on that day that the yacht *Falcon* lay becalmed upon the ocean between the Canaries and the Madeira Islands.[1] This yacht *Falcon* was the property of Lord Featherstone, who, being weary of life in England, had taken a few congenial friends for a winter's cruise in these southern latitudes. They had visited the Azores,[2] the Canaries, and the Madeira Islands, and were now on their way to the Mediterranean.

The wind had failed, a deep calm had succeeded, and everywhere, as far as the eye could reach, the water was smooth and glassy. The yacht rose and fell at the impulse of the long ocean undulations, and the creaking of the spars sounded out a lazy accompaniment to the motion of the vessel. All around was a watery horizon, except in the one place only, toward the south, where far in the distance the Peak of Teneriffe[3] rose into the air.

The profound calm, the warm atmosphere, the slow pitching of the yacht, and the dull creaking of the spars all combined to lull into a state of indolent repose the people on board the yacht. Forward were the crew; some asleep, others smoking, others playing cards. At the stern were Oxenden, the intimate friend of Featherstone, and Dr. Congreve, who had come in the double capacity of friend and medical attendant. These two, like the crew, were in a state of dull and languid repose. Suspended between the two masts, in an Indian hammock, lay Featherstone, with a cigar in his mouth and a novel in his hand, which he was pretending to read. The fourth member of the party, Melick, was seated near the mainmast, folding some papers in a peculiar way. His occupation at length attracted the roving eyes of Featherstone, who poked forth his head from his hammock, and said, in a sleepy voice:

---

1 Located off the northwest coast of Africa, these archipelagos of islands were respectively Spanish and Portuguese colonies in the nineteenth century.

2 West of the Canaries and Madeira islands, the Azores were a Portuguese colony.

3 The largest of the Canary Islands, Tenerife is sometimes associated with Atlantis. See Appendix D3 for possible significance.

"I say, Melick, you're the most energetic fellah I ever saw. By Jove! you're the only one aboard that's busy. What are you doing?"

"Paper boats," said Melick, in a business-like tone.

"Paper boats! By Jove!" said Featherstone. "What for?"

"I'm going to have a regatta," said Melick. "Anything to kill time, you know."

"By Jove!" exclaimed Featherstone again, raising himself higher in his hammock, "that's not a bad idea. A wegatta! By Jove! glowious! glowious! I say, Oxenden, did you hear that?"

"What do you mean by a regatta?" asked Oxenden, lazily.

"Oh, I mean a race with these paper boats. We can bet on them, you know."

At this Featherstone sat upright, with his legs dangling out of the hammock.

"By Jove!" he exclaimed again. "Betting! So we can. Do you know, Melick, old chap, I think that's a wegular piece of inspiration. A wegatta![1] and we can bet on the best boat."

"But there isn't any wind," said Oxenden.

"Well, you know, that's the fun of it," said Melick, who went solemnly on as he spoke, folding his paper boats; "that's the fun of it. For you see if there was a wind we should be going on ourselves, and the regatta couldn't come off; but, as it is, the water is just right. You pick out your boat, and lay your bet on her to race to some given point."

"A given point? But how can we find any?"

"Oh, easily enough; something or anything– a bubble'll do, or we can pitch out a bit of wood."

Upon this Featherstone descended from his perch, and came near to examine the proceedings, while the other two, eager to take advantage of the new excitement, soon joined him. By this time Melick had finished his paper boats. There were four of them, and they were made of different colors, namely, red, green, yellow, and white.

"I'll put these in the water," said Melick, "and then we can lay our bets on them as we choose. But first let us see if there is anything that can be taken as a point of arrival. If there isn't anything, I can pitch out a bit of wood, in any direction which may seem best."

Saying this, he went to the side, followed by the others, and all looked out carefully over the water.

"There's a black speck out there," said Oxenden.

"So there is," said Featherstone. "That'll do. I wonder what it is?"

---

1 A boat race.

"Oh, a bit of timber," said Melick. "Probably the spar of some ship."

"It don't look like a spar," said the doctor; "it's only a round spot, like the float of some net."

"Oh, it's a spar," said Melick. "It's one end of it, the rest is under water."

The spot thus chosen was a dark, circular object about a hundred yards away, and certainly did look very much like the extremity of some spar, the rest of which was under water. Whatever it was, however, it served well enough for their present purpose, and no one took any further interest in it, except as the point toward which the paper boats should run in their eventful race.

Melick now let himself down over the side, and placed the paper boats on the water as carefully as possible. After this the four stood watching the little fleet in silence. The water was perfectly still, and there was no perceptible wind, but there were draughts of air caused by the rise and fall of the yacht, and these affected the tiny boats. Gradually they drew apart, the green one drifting astern, the yellow one remaining under the vessel, while the red and the white were carried out in the direction where they were expected to go, with about a foot of space between them.

"Two to one on the red!" cried Featherstone, betting on the one which had gained the lead.

"Done," said Melick, promptly taking his offer.

Oxenden made the same bet, which was taken by Melick and the doctor.

Other bets were now made as to the direction which they would take, as to the distance by which the red would beat the white, as to the time which would be occupied by the race, and as to fifty other things which need not be mentioned. All took part in this; the excitement rose high and the betting went on merrily. At length it was noticed that the white was overhauling the red. The excitement grew intense; the betting changed its form, but was still kept up, until at last the two paper boats seemed blended together in one dim spot which gradually faded out of sight.

It was now necessary to determine the state of the race, so Featherstone ordered out the boat. The four were soon embarked, and the men rowed out toward the point which had been chosen as the end of the race. On coming near they found the paper boats stuck together, saturated with water, and floating limp on the surface. An animated discussion arose about this. Some of the bets were off, but others remained an open question, and each side insisted upon a different view of the case. In the midst of this, Featherstone's attention was drawn to the dark spot already mentioned as the goal of the race.

"That's a queer-looking thing," said he, suddenly. "Pull up, lads, a little; let's see what it is. It doesn't look to me like a spar."

The others, always on the lookout for some new object of interest, were attracted by these words, and looked closely at the thing in question. The men pulled. The boat drew nearer.

"It's some sort of floating vessel," said Oxenden.

"It's not a spar," said Melick, who was at the bow.

And as he said this he reached out and grasped at it. He failed to get it, and did no more than touch it. It moved easily and sank, but soon came up again. A second time he grasped at it, and with both hands. This time he caught it, and then lifted it out of the water into the boat. These proceedings had been watched with the deepest interest; and now, as this curious floating thing made its appearance among them, they all crowded around it in eager excitement.

"It looks like a can of preserved meat," said the doctor.

"It certainly is a can," said Melick, "for it's made of metal; but as to preserved meat, I have my doubts."

The article in question was made of metal, and was cylindrical in shape. It was soldered tight and evidently contained something. It was about eighteen inches long and eight wide. The nature of the metal was not easily perceptible, for it was coated with slime, and covered over about half its surface with barnacles and seaweed. It was not heavy, and would have floated higher out of the water had it not been for these encumbrances.

"It's some kind of preserved meat," said the doctor. "Perhaps something good—game, I dare say—yes, Yorkshire game-pie. They pot all sorts of things now."

"If it's game," said Oxenden, "it'll be rather high by this time. Man alive! look at those weeds and shells. It must have been floating for ages."

"It's my belief," said Featherstone, "that it's part of the provisions laid in by Noah for his long voyage in the ark. So come, let's open it, and see what sort of diet the antediluvians had."

"It may be liquor," said Oxenden.

Melick shook his head.

"No," said he; "there's something inside, but whatever it is, it isn't liquor. It's odd, too. The thing is of foreign make, evidently. I never saw anything like it before. It may be Chinese."

"By Jove!" cried Featherstone, "this is getting exciting. Let's go back to the yacht and open it."

The men rowed back to the yacht.

"It's meat of some sort," continued the doctor. "I'm certain of that. It has come in good time. We can have it for dinner."

"You may have my share, then," said Oxenden. "I hereby give and bequeath to you all my right, title, and interest in and to anything in the shape of meat that may be inside."

"Meat cans," said Melick, "are never so large as that."

"Oh, I don't know about that," said the doctor, "they make up pretty large packages of pemmican[1] for the arctic expeditions."

"But they never pack up pemmican in copper cylinders,"[2] said Melick, who had been using his knife to scrape off the crust from the vessel.

"Copper!" exclaimed Oxenden. "Is it copper?"

"Look for yourselves," said Melick, quietly.

They all looked, and could see, where the knife had cut into the vessel, that it was as he said. It was copper.

"It's foreign work," said Melick. "In England we make tin cans for everything. It may be something that's drifted out from Mogador[3] or some port in Morocco."

"In that case," said Oxenden, "it may contain the mangled remains of one of the wives of some Moorish pasha."[4]

By this time they had reached the yacht and hurried aboard. All were eager to satisfy their curiosity. Search was made for a cold-chisel, but to no purpose. Then Featherstone produced a knife which was used to open sardine boxes, but after a faithful trial this proved useless. At length Melick, who had gone off in search of

---

1 Protein and fat mixed together into a high energy food that can be stored for a long time.

2 Copper cylinders are routinely mentioned in nineteenth-century exploration narratives to the Arctic and Antarctic. For example, in *A Voyage of Discovery*, Sir John Ross notes, "a bottle, or a copper cylinder, containing an account of our proceedings, was thrown overboard every day, as soon as the ship's position had been determined" (33). In *Journal of a Third Voyage for the Discovery of a Northwest Passage*, William Parry writes, "During our passage across the Atlantic, and afterwards on our way up Davis's Strait, we threw overboard daily a strong copper cylinder, containing the usual papers, giving an account of our situation" (28).

3 Mogador (spelled Mogadore in the *Harper's* serial) is an ancient, isolated port city on the Atlantic coast of Morocco. Its modern name is Essaouira.

4 If Moor refers to a North African Muslim and pasha to a high ranking Ottoman or Egyptian, the phrase "Moorish pasha," which occurs in an 1854 issue of *Sharpe's London Magazine*, would seem to be an Orientalist stereotype.

something more effective, made his appearance, armed with an axe. With this he attacked the copper cylinder, and by means of a few dexterous blows succeeded in cutting it open. Then he looked in.

"What do you see?" asked Featherstone.

"Something," said Melick, "but I can't quite make it out."

"If you can't make it out, then shake it out," said Oxenden.

Upon this Melick took the cylinder, turned it upside down, shook it smartly, and then lifted it and pounded it against the deck. This served to loosen the contents, which seemed tightly packed,

Illustration 1: "With this he attacked the copper cylinder, and by means of a few dexterous blows succeeded in cutting it open."

but came gradually down until at length they could be seen and drawn forth. Melick drew them forth, and the contents of the mysterious copper cylinder resolved themselves into two packages.

The sight of these packages only served to intensify their curiosity. If it had been some species of food it would at once have revealed itself, but these packages suggested something more important. What could they be? Were there treasures inside—jewels, or golden ornaments from some Moorish seraglio,[1] or strange coin from far Cathay?[2]

One of the packages was very much larger than the other. It was enclosed in wrappers made of some coarse kind of felt, bound tight with strong cords. The other was much smaller, and, was folded in the same material without being bound. This Melick seized and began to open.

"Wait a minute," said Featherstone. "Let's make a bet on it. Five guineas that it's some sort of jewels!"

"Done," said Oxenden.

Melick opened the package, and it was seen that Featherstone had lost. There were no jewels, but one or two sheets of something that looked like paper. It was not paper, however, but some vegetable product which was used for the same purpose. The surface was smooth, but the color was dingy, and the lines of the vegetable fibres were plainly discernible. These sheets were covered with writing.

"Halloa!" cried Melick. "Why, this is English!"

At this the others crowded around to look on, and Featherstone in his excitement forgot that he had lost his bet. There were three sheets, all covered with writing—one in English, another in French, and a third in German. It was the same message, written in these three different languages. But at that moment they scarcely noticed this. All that they saw was the message itself, with its mysterious meaning.

It was as follows:

"To the finder of this:

"Sir,—I am an Englishman, and have been carried by a series of incredible events to a land from which escape is as impossible

1 An enclosed living quarters for women in a Muslim household. It can also refer to a harem.

2 Cathay, another name for China associated with Marco Polo, continues the theme of attributing an Oriental origin to the cylinder. The Venetian merchant Marco Polo (1254-1324) is largely credited with introducing China and central Asia to Europeans.

as from the grave. I have written this and committed it to the sea, in the hope that the ocean currents may bear it within the reach of civilized man. Oh, unknown friend! whoever you are, I entreat you to let this message be made known in some way to my father, Henry More, Keswick, Cumberland, England, so that he may learn the fate of his son. The MS. accompanying this contains an account of my adventures, which I should like to have forwarded to him. Do this for the sake of that mercy which you may one day wish to have shown to yourself.

"Adam More."

"By Jove!" cried Featherstone, as he read the above, "this is really getting to be something tremendous."

"This other package must be the manuscript," said Oxenden, "and it'll tell all about it."

"Such a manuscript'll be better than meat," said the doctor, sententiously.

Melick said nothing, but opening his knife he cut the cords and unfolded the wrapper. He saw a great collection of leaves, just like those of the letter, of some vegetable substance, smooth as paper, and covered with writing.

"It looks like Egyptian papyrus," said the doctor. "That was the common paper of antiquity."[1]

"Never mind the Egyptian papyrus," said Featherstone, in feverish curiosity. "Let's have the contents of the manuscript. You, Melick, read; you're the most energetic of the lot, and when you're tired the rest of us will take turns."

"Read? Why, it'll take a month to read all this," said Melick.

"All the better," said Featherstone; "this calm will probably last a month, and we shall have something to interest us."

Melick made no further objection. He was as excited as the rest, and so he began the reading of the manuscript.

CHAPTER II.
ADRIFT IN THE ANTARCTIC OCEAN.

MY name is Adam More. I am the son of Henry More, apothecary, Keswick, Cumberland. I was mate of the ship *Trevelyan*, (Bennet, master), which was chartered by the British Government

1 Made from the stem of a marshland plant called papyrus, this paper-like material was invented in Egypt as early as 3000 BCE.

to convey convicts to Van Diemen's Land.[1] This was in 1843. We made our voyage without any casualty, landed our convicts in Hobart Town, and then set forth on our return home. It was the 17th of December when we left. From the first adverse winds prevailed, and in order to make any progress we were obliged to keep well to the south. At length, on the 6th of January, we sighted Desolation Island.[2] We found it, indeed, a desolate spot. In its vicinity we saw a multitude of smaller islands, perhaps a thousand in number, which made navigation difficult, and forced us to hurry away as fast as possible. But the aspect of this dreary spot was of itself enough to repel us. There were no trees, and the multitude of islands seemed like moss-covered rocks; while the temperature, though in the middle of the antarctic summer, was from 38° to 58° Fahr.

In order to get rid of these dangerous islands we stood south and west, and at length found ourselves in south latitude 65°, longitude 60° east. We were fortunate enough not to find any ice, although we were within fifteen hundred miles of the South Pole, and far within that impenetrable icy barrier which in 1773 had arrested the progress of Captain Cook.[3] Here the wind failed us, and we lay becalmed and drifting. The sea was open all around us, except to the southeast, where there was a low line along the horizon terminating in a lofty promontory; but though it looked like land we took it for ice. All around us whales and grampuses[4] were gambolling and spouting in vast numbers. The weather was remarkably fine and clear.

For two or three days the calm continued, and we drifted along helplessly, until at length we found ourselves within a few miles of the promontory above mentioned. It looked like land, and seemed

---

1 Renamed Tasmania in 1854, Van Diemen's Land lies off the southern coast of Australia. In the early nineteenth century, Van Diemen's Land became a major British penal colony.

2 Properly named Kerguelen Island, Desolation Island is located at latitude 49° 20′ S, longitude 70° 20′ E.

3 More has his facts wrong. James Cook made two attempts to reach the South Pole during his second voyage. In January of 1773, they were stopped by ice at latitude 66° 36′ 30″ S, longitude 39° 35′ E (see Appendix A1a). In January of 1774, they encountered "mountains of ice" at latitude 71° 10′ S, longitude 106° 54′ W (see Appendix A1b). In both cases, Cook was farther south than the *Trevelyan*.

4 Probably Orca (or Killer Whales) rather than Risso's Dolphins (*Grampus griseus*), which prefer warmer waters. Grampus was used historically to name Orcas.

to be a rocky island rising from the depths of the sea. It was, however, all covered with ice and snow, and from this there extended eastward as far as the eye could reach an interminable line of ice, but toward the southwest the sea seemed open to navigation. The promontory was very singular in shape, rising up to a peak which was at least a thousand feet in height, and forming a striking object, easily discovered and readily identified by any future explorer. We named it, after our ship, Trevelyan Peak, and then felt anxious to lose sight of it forever. But the calm continued, and at length we drifted in close enough to see immense flocks of seals dotting the ice at the foot of the peak.

Upon this I proposed to Agnew, the second mate, that we should go ashore, shoot some seals, and bring them back. This was partly for the excitement of the hunt, and partly for the honor of landing in a place never before trodden by the foot of man. Captain Bennet made some objections; but he was old and cautious, and we were young and venturesome, so we laughed away his scruples and set forth. We did not take any of the crew, owing to the captain's objections. He said that if we chose to throw away our own lives he could not help it, but that he would positively refuse to allow a single man to go with us. We thought this refusal an excess of caution amounting to positive cowardice, but were unable to change his mind. The distance was not great, the adventure was attractive, and so the captain's gig[1] was lowered, and in this Agnew and I rowed ashore. We took with us a double-barrelled rifle apiece, and also a pistol. Agnew took a glass.

We rowed for about three miles, and reached the edge of the ice, which extended far out from the promontory. Here we landed, and secured the boat by means of a small grappling-iron, which we thrust into the ice. We then walked toward the promontory for about a mile, and here we found a multitude of seals. These animals were so fearless that they made not the slightest movement as we came up, but stared at us in an indifferent way. We killed two or three, and then debated whether to go to the promontory or not. Agnew was eager to go, so as to touch the actual rock; but I was satisfied with what we had done, and was now desirous of returning. In the midst of this I felt a flake of snow on my cheek. I started and looked up. To my great surprise, I saw that the sky had changed since I had last noticed it. When we left the ship it was clear and blue, but now it was overspread with dark, leaden-colored clouds, and the snow-flakes that had fallen were ominous

1 A rowing boat.

of evil. A snow-storm here, in the vicinity of the ice, was too serious a thing to be disregarded. But one course now remained, and that was an immediate return to the ship.

Each of us seized a seal and dragged it after us to the boat. We reached it and flung them in. Just at that moment a gun sounded over the water. It was from the ship—the signal of alarm—the summons from the captain for our return. We saw now that she had been drifting since we left her, and had moved southwest several miles. The row back promised to be far harder than the pull ashore, and what was worse, the wind was coming up, the sea was rising, and the snow was thickening. Neither of us said a word. We saw that our situation was very serious, and that we had been very foolhardy; but words were useless now. The only thing to be done was to pull for the ship with all our strength, and that was what we did.

So we pushed off, and rowed as we had never rowed before. Our progress was difficult. The sea grew steadily rougher; the wind increased; the snow thickened; and, worst of all, the day was drawing to a close. We had miscalculated both as to distance and time. Even if it had continued calm, we should have had to row back in the dark; but now the sun was setting, and with the coming darkness we had to encounter the gathering storm and the blinding snow. We rowed in silence. At every stroke our situation grew more serious. The wind was from the south, and therefore favored us to some extent, and also made less of a sea than would have been produced by a wind from any other quarter; but then this south wind brought dangers of its own, which we were soon to feel—new dangers and worse ones. For this south wind drove the ship farther from us, and at the same time broke up the vast fields of ice and impelled the fractured masses northward. But this was a danger which we did not know just then. At that time we were rowing for the ship, and amid the darkness and the blinding snow and the dashing waves we heard from time to time the report of signal-guns fired from the ship to guide us back. These were our only guide, for the darkness and the snow had drawn the ship from our sight, and we had to be guided by our hearing only.

We were rowing for our lives, and we knew it; but every moment our situation grew more desperate. Each new report of the gun seemed to sound farther away. We seemed always to be rowing in the wrong direction. At each report we had to shift the boat's course somewhat, and pull toward the last point from which the gun seemed to sound. With all this the wind was increasing rapidly to a gale, the sea was rising and breaking over the boat, the snow was blinding us with its ever-thickening sleet. The darkness deepened, and at length had grown so intense that nothing whatever could be seen—neither sea nor sky, not even the boat itself—yet we dared not stop; we had to row. Our lives depended on our efforts. We had to row, guided by the sound of the ship's gun, which the ever-varying wind incessantly changed, till our minds grew all confused, and we rowed blindly and mechanically.

So we labored for hours at the oars, and the storm continually increased, and the sea continually rose, while the snow fell thicker and the darkness grew intenser. The reports of the gun now grew fainter; what was worse, they were heard at longer intervals, and this showed us that Captain Bennet was losing heart; that he was giving us up; that he despaired of finding us, and was now firing only an occasional gun out of a mournful sense of duty. This thought reduced us to despair. It seemed as if all our efforts had only served to take us farther away from the ship, and deprived us of all motive for rowing any harder than was barely necessary to keep the boat steady. After a time Agnew dropped his oar and began to bail out the boat—a work which was needed; for, in spite of our care, she had shipped many seas, and was one-third full of water. He worked away at this while I managed the boat, and then we took turns at bailing. In this way we passed the dreary night.

[TO BE CONTINUED.]

PART 2 (14 JANUARY, 1888)

CHAPTER II.—(*Continued.*)
ADRIFT IN THE ANTARCTIC OCEAN.

MORNING at last came. The wind was not so violent, but the snow was so thick that we could only see for a little distance around us. The ship was nowhere visible, nor were there any signs of her. The last gun had been fired during the night. All that we could see was the dim outline of a gaunt iceberg—an ominous spectacle. Not knowing what else to do we rowed on as before, keeping in what seemed our best course, though this was mere conjecture, and we knew all the time that we might be going wrong. There was no compass in the boat, nor could we tell the sun's position through the thick snow. We rowed with the wind, thinking that it was blowing toward the north, and would carry us in that direction. We still hoped to come within sound of the ship's gun, and kept straining our ears incessantly to hear the wished-for report. But no such sound ever came again, and we heard nothing except the plash of the waves and the crash of breaking ice. Thus all that day we rowed along, resting at intervals when exhausted, and then resuming our labors, until at length night came; and again to the snow and ice and waves was added the horror of great darkness. We passed that night in deep misery. We had eaten nothing since we left the ship, but though exhausted by long fasting and severe labor, the despair of our hearts took away all desire for food. We were worn out with hard work, yet the cold was too great to allow us to take rest, and we were compelled to row so as to keep ourselves from perishing. But fatigue and drowsiness overcame us, and we often sank into sleep even while at the oars; and then after a brief slumber we would awake with benumbed limbs to wrestle again with the oars. In this way we passed that night.

Another morning came, and we found to our great joy that the snow had ceased. We looked eagerly around to see if there were any signs of the ship. Nothing could be seen of her. Far away on one side rose a peak, which looked like the place where we had landed. Judging from the wind, which we still supposed to be southerly, the peak lay toward the northeast; in which case we had been carried steadily, in spite of all our efforts, toward the south. About a mile on one side of us the ice began, and extended far away; while on the other side, at the distance of some ten miles, there was another line of ice. We seemed to have been carried in a southwesterly direction along a broad strait that ran into the vast ice-fields. This discovery showed how utterly useless our labors had been; for in spite of all, even with the wind in our favor, we had been drawn steadily in an opposite direction. It was evident that there was some current here, stronger than all our strength, which had brought us to this place.

We now determined to land on the ice, and try to cook a portion of our seals. On approaching it we noticed that there was a current which tended to draw us past the ice in what I supposed to be a southwesterly direction. This confirmed my worst fears. But now the labor of landing and building a fire on the ice served to interest us for a time and divert our thoughts. We brushed away the snow, and then broke up a box which was in the boat, and also the stern seats. This we used very sparingly, reserving the rest for another occasion. Then we cut portions from one of the seals, and laid them in thin strips on the flames. The cooking was but slight, for the meat was merely singed; but we were ravenous, and the contact of the fire was enough to give it an attractive flavor. With this food we were greatly refreshed; and as for drink, we had all around us an endless extent of ice and snow. Then taking our precious fragments of cooked meat, we returned to the boat and put off. We could scarcely tell what to do next, and while debating on this point we fell asleep. We slept far into the night, then awoke benumbed with cold; then took to the oars till we were weary; then fell asleep again, to be again awakened by the cold and again to pull at the oars. So the night passed, and another day came.

The snow still held off, but the sky was overcast with dark, leaden-colored clouds, and looked threatening. Ice was all around us as before; and the open water had diminished now from ten miles to five miles of width. The ice on one side was low, but on the opposite side it arose to the height of one hundred feet. We saw here, as we watched the shore, that the current which had already borne us thus far was now stronger than ever, and was carrying us along at a rate which made all efforts of ours against it utterly useless. And now a debate arose between us as to the direction of this current. Agnew suddenly declared his belief that it was running north, while I was firm in the conviction that it ran south.

"There's no use rowing any more," said Agnew. "If it runs south we can't resist it. It's too strong. But I always like to look on the bright side, and so I believe it runs north. In that case there is no use rowing, for it will carry us along fast enough."

Then I proposed that we should go ashore on the ice. To this Agnew objected, but afterward consented, at my earnest request. So we tried to get ashore, but this time found it impossible; for the ice consisted of a vast sheet of floating lumps, which looked like the ruin of bergs that had been broken up in some storm. After this I had nothing to say, nor was there anything left for us but to drift wherever the current might carry us.

So we drifted for some days, Agnew all the time maintaining that we were going north, while I was sure that we were going south. The sky remained as cloudy as ever, the wind varied incessantly, and there was nothing by which we could conjecture the points of the compass. We lived on our seal, and for drink we chewed ice and snow. One thing was certain—the climate was no colder. Agnew laid great stress on this.

"You see," said he, "we must be going north. If we were going south, we should be frozen stiff by this time."

"Yes; but if we were going north," said I, "we ought to find it growing warmer."

"No," said he, "not with all this ice around us. It's the ice that keeps the temperature in this cold state."

Argument could do no good, and so we each remained true to our belief—his leading him to hope, and mine dragging me down to despair. At length we finished the last fragment of the seal that we had cooked, and finding ourselves near some firm ice, we went ashore and cooked all that was left, using the remainder of our wood for fuel, and all that we dared to remove from the boat. Re-embarking with this, we drifted on as before.

Several more days passed. At last one night I was roused by Agnew. He pointed far away to the distant horizon, where I saw a deep red glow as of fire. We were both filled with wonder at the sight, and were utterly unable to account for it. We knew that it could not be caused by the sun or the moon, for it was midnight, and the cause lay on the earth and not in the skies. It was a deep, lurid glow, extending along the horizon, and seemed to be caused by some vast conflagration.

CHAPTER III.
A WORLD OF FIRE AND DESOLATION.

AT the sight of that deep red glow various feelings arose within us: in me there was new dejection; in Agnew there was stronger hope. I could not think but that it was our ship that was on fire, and was burning before our eyes. Agnew thought that it was some burning forest, and that it showed our approach to some habitable and inhabited land. For hour after hour we watched, and all the time the current drew us nearer, and the glow grew brighter and more intense. At last we were too weak to watch any longer, and we fell asleep.

On waking our first thoughts were about the fire, and we looked eagerly around. It was day, but the sky was as gloomy as ever, and the fire was there before our eyes, bright and terrible. We could now see it plainly, and discern the cause also. The fire came from two points, at some distance apart—two peaks rising above the horizon, from which there burst forth flames and smoke with incessant explosions. All was now manifest. It was no burning ship, no blazing forest, no land inhabited by man; those blazing peaks were two volcanoes in a state of active eruption, and at that sight I knew the worst.

"I know where we are now," I said, despairingly.

"Where?" asked Agnew.

"That," said I, "is the antarctic continent."

"The antarctic fiddlestick," said he, contemptuously. "It is far more likely to be some volcanic island in the South Sea. There's a tremendous volcano in the Sandwich Islands,[1] and these are something like it."

"I believe," said I, "that these are the very volcanoes that Sir James Ross discovered last year."[2]

"Do you happen to know where he found them?" Agnew asked.

"I do not," I answered.

"Well, I do," said he, "and they're thousands of miles away from this. They are south latitude 77°, east longitude 167°;[3] while we, as I guess, are about south latitude 40°, east longitude 60°."

"At any rate," said I, "we're drifting straight toward them."

"So I see," said Agnew, dryly. "At any rate, the current will take us somewhere. We shall find ourselves carried past these volcanic islands or through them, and then west to the Cape of Good

1 The historical name for the Hawaiian Islands. Mauna Loa, on the island of Hawai'i, rises more than 4 km from sea level to the summit.

2 Captain James Clark Ross (1800-62) led an expedition to the Antarctic in the ships *Erebus* and *Terror* from 1839 to 1843. He discovered and named the volcanoes Erebus and Terror in late January of 1841 (see Appendix A3). Note that More is speaking to Agnew in January of 1844, three years later. Ross was knighted in 1844.

3 The coordinates Agnew provides are correct (see Appendix A3).

Hope.[1] Besides, even here we may find land with animals and vegetation; who knows?"

"What! amid all this ice?" I cried. "Are you mad?"

"Mad?" said he; "I should certainly go mad if I hadn't hope."

"Hope!" I repeated; "I have long since given up hope."

"Oh, well," said he, "enjoy your despair, and don't try to deprive me of my consolation. My hope sustains me, and helps me to cheer you up. It would never do, old fellow, for both of us to knock under."

I said nothing more, nor did Agnew. We drifted on, and all our thoughts were taken up with the two volcanoes, toward which we were every moment drawing nearer. As we approached they grew larger and larger, towering up to a tremendous height. I had seen Vesuvius and Stromboli and Ætna and Cotopaxi;[2] but these appeared far larger than any of them, not excepting the last. They rose, like the Peak of Teneriffe, abruptly from the sea, with no intervening hills to dwarf or diminish their proportions. They were ten or twelve miles apart, and the channel of water in which we were drifting flowed between them.

Here the ice and snow ended. We thus came at last to land; but it was a land that seemed more terrible than even the bleak expanse of ice and snow that lay behind, for nothing could be seen except a vast and drear accumulation of lava blocks of every imaginable shape, without a trace of vegetation—uninhabited, uninhabitable, and unpassable to man. But just where the ice ended and the rocks began there was a long low reef, which projected for more than a quarter of a mile into the water, affording the only possible landing-place within sight. Here we decided to land, so as to rest and consider what was best to be done.

Here we landed, and walked up to where rugged lava blocks prevented any farther progress. But at this spot our attention was suddenly arrested by a sight of horror. It was a human figure lying prostrate, face downward.

At this sight there came over us a terrible sensation. Even Agnew's buoyant soul shrank back, and we stared at each other with quivering lips. It was some time before we could recover ourselves; then we went to the figure, and stooped down to examine it.

---

1 On the south coast of Africa.

2 Mount Vesuvius is east of Naples in Italy. Stromboli is a volcanic island north of Sicily. Mount Aetna (about 3 km high) is a volcano on the east coast of Sicily. The volcano Cotopaxi has a summit of almost 6 km, but it is located inland in the Andes Mountains of Ecuador.

The clothes were those of a European and a sailor; the frame was emaciated and dried up, till it looked like a skeleton; the face was blackened and all withered, and the bony hands were clinched tight. It was evidently some sailor who had suffered shipwreck in these frightful solitudes, and had drifted here to starve to death in this appalling wilderness. It was a sight which seemed ominous of our own fate, and Agnew's boasted hope, which had so long upheld him, now sank down into a despair as deep as my own. What room was there now for hope, or how could we expect any other fate than this?

At length I began to search the pockets of the deceased.

"What are you doing?" asked Agnew, in a hoarse voice.

"I'm trying to find out who he is," I said. "Perhaps there may be papers."

As I said this I felt something in the breast pocket of his jacket, and drew it forth. It was a leathern[1] pocket-book, mouldy and rotten like the clothing. On opening it, it fell to pieces. There was nothing in it but a piece of paper, also mouldy and rotten. This I unfolded with great care, and saw writing there, which, though faded, was still legible. It was a letter, and there were still visible the signs of long and frequent perusals, and marks, too, which looked as though made by tears—tears, perhaps, of the writer, perhaps of the reader: who can tell? I have preserved this letter ever since, and I now fasten it here upon this sheet of my manuscript.[2]

THE LETTER.

"*Bristol* April 20. 1820.[3]

"*my darling tom*

"*i writ you these few lines in hast i don like youar gon a walen an in the south sea dont go darlin tom or mebbe ill never se you agin for ave bad drems of you darlin tom an im afraid so don go my darlin tom but come back an take anoth ship for America baby is as wel as ever but mises is*

---

1 Made of leather.

2 This letter from Polley Reed is the only material artefact in the cylinder other than More's own introductory letter and the manuscript proper.

3 1820 is the year that the Antarctic continent was first sighted by Russian Fabian Gottlieb von Bellingshausen on the *Vostok* and *Mirnyi* (on 27 January). On 29 January 1820, Edward Bransfield on the *Williams* also sighted the Antarctic Peninsula as part of a British naval expedition. Bransfield and his crew, along with two Russian naval ships in the area, were the first to officially see the Antarctic mainland. There were a number of British sealing and whaling expeditions in the Southern Ocean in this year.

pa an as got a new tooth an i think you otnt go a walen o darlin tom * * * *sea as the wages was i in New York an better go thar an id like to go ther for good for they gives good wages in America. O come back my Darlin tom an take me to America an the baby an weel all live an love an di together*

"Your loving wife

"Polley Reed."

I began to read this, but there came a lump in my throat, and I had to stop. Agnew leaned on my shoulder, and we both read it in silence. He rubbed the back of his hand over his eyes and drew a long breath. Then he walked away for a little distance, and I put the letter carefully away in my own pocket-book. After a little while Agnew came back.

"More," said he, "do you remember any of the burial service?"

I understood his meaning at once.

"Yes," said I, "some of it—a good deal of it, I think."

"That's good," said he. "Let's put the poor fellow under ground."

"It would be hard to do that," I said; "we'll have to bury him in the snow."

At this Agnew went off for a little distance and clambered over the rocks. He was not gone long. When he returned he said, "I've found some crumbled pumice-stone; we can scoop a grave for him there."

We then raised the body and carried it to the place which Agnew had found. So emaciated was the poor dead sailor that his remains were no heavier than a small boy. On reaching the spot, we found the crumbled pumice-stone. We placed the body in a crevice among the lava rocks, and then I said what I could remember of the burial service. After this we carried in our hands the crumbled pumice-stone until we had covered the body, and thus gave the poor fellow a Christian burial.

We then returned to the shore.

"More, old fellow," said Agnew, "I feel the better for this; the service has done me good."

"And me too," said I. "It has reminded me of what I had forgotten. This world is only a part of life. We may lose it and yet live on. There is another world; and if we can only keep that in our minds we sha'n't be so ready to sink into despair—that is, I sha'n't. Despair is my weakness; you are more hopeful."

"Yes," said Agnew, solemnly; "but my hope thus far has referred only to the safety of my skin. After this I shall try to think

Illustration 2: "I began to read this, but there came a lump in my throat, and I had to stop."

of my soul, and cultivate, not the hope of escape, but the hope full of immortality. Yes, More, after all we shall live, if not in England, then, let us hope, in heaven."

There was a long silence after this—that kind of silence which one may preserve who is at the point of death.

"I wonder how he got here?" said Agnew, at last. "The letter mentions a whaler. No doubt the ship has been driven too far south; it has foundered; he has escaped in a boat, either alone or with others; he has been carried along this channel, and has landed here, afraid to go any farther."

"But his boat, what has become of that?"

"His boat! That must have gone long ago. The letter was written in 1820. At any rate, let's look around."

We did so. After some search we found fragments of a rotted rope attached to a piece of rock.

"That," said Agnew, "must have been fastened to the boat; and as for the boat herself, she has long ago been swept away from this."

"What shall we do now?" I said, after a long silence.

"There's only one thing," said Agnew. "We must go on."

"Go on?" I asked, in wonder.

"Certainly," said he, confidently. "Will you stay here? No. Will you go back? You can't. We must, therefore, go on. That is our only hope."

"Hope!" I cried. "Do you still talk of hope?"

"Hope!" said Agnew; "of course. Why not? There are no limits to hope, are there? One can hope anything, anywhere. It is better to die while struggling like a man, full of hope and energy, than to perish in inaction and despair. It is better to die in the storm and furious waters than to waste away in this awful place. So come along. Let's drift as before. Let's see where this channel will take us. It will certainly take us somewhere. Such a stream as this must have some outlet."

"This stream," said I, "will take us to death, and death only. The current grows swifter every hour. I've heard some old yarn of a vast opening at each of the poles, or one of them, into which the waters of the ocean pour. They fall into one, and some say they go through and come out at the other."[1]

---

1 See Appendix E1 for Captain Adam Seaborn's *Symzonia* and Appendix E2 for an introduction to Edgar Allan Poe's "MS Found in a Bottle" and *The Narrative of Arthur Gordon Pym*. All three of these stories involve openings at the South Pole.

Agnew laughed.

"That," said he, "is a madman's dream. In the first place, I don't believe that we are approaching the south, but the north. The warmth of the climate here shows that. Yes, we are drawing north. We shall soon emerge into warm waters and bright skies. So come along, and let us lose no more time."

I made no further objection. There was nothing else to be done, and at the very worst we could not be in greater danger while drifting on than in remaining behind. Soon, therefore, we were again in the boat, and the current swept us on as before.

The channel now was about four miles wide. On either side arose the lofty volcanoes vomiting forth flames and smoke with furious explosions; vast stones were hurled up into the air from the craters; streams of molten lava rolled down, and at intervals there fell great showers of ashes. The shores on either side were precipitous and rugged beyond all description, looking like fiery lava streams which had been arrested by the flood, and cooled into gloomy, overhanging cliffs. The lava rock was of a deep, dull slate-color, which at a distance looked black; and the blackness which thus succeeded to the whiteness of the snow behind us seemed like the funeral pall of nature. Through scenes like these we drifted on, and the volcanoes on either side of the channel towered on high with their fiery floods of lava, their incessant explosions, their fierce outbursts of flame, and overhead there rolled a dense black canopy of smoke—altogether forming a terrific approach to that unknown and awful pathway upon which we were going. So we passed this dread portal, and then there lay before us—what? Was it a land of life or a land of death? Who could say?

It was evening when we passed through. Night came on, and the darkness was illuminated by the fiery glow of the volcanic flames. Worn out with fatigue we fell asleep. So the night passed, and the current bore us on until, at length, the morning came. We awoke, and now, for the first time in many days, we saw the face of the sun. The clouds had at last broken, the sky was clear, and behind us the sun was shining. That sight told us all. It showed us where we were going.

I pointed to the sun.

"Look there," said I. "There is the sun in the northern sky—behind us. We have been drifting steadily toward the south."

At this Agnew was silent, and sat looking back for a long time. There we could still see the glow of the volcanic fires, though they were now many miles away; while the sun, but lately risen, was lying on a course closer to the horizon than we had ever seen before.

"We are going south," said I—"to the South Pole. This swift current can have but one ending—there may be an opening at the South Pole, or a whirlpool like the Maelstrom."[1]

Agnew looked around with a smile.

"All those notions," said he, "are dreams or theories or guesses. There is no evidence to prove them. Why trouble yourself about a guess? You and I can guess, and with better reason; for we have now, it seems, come farther south than any human being who has ever lived. Do not imagine that the surface of the earth is different at the poles from what it is anywhere else. If we get to the South Pole we shall see there what we have always seen—the open view of land or water, and the boundary of the horizon. As for this current, it seems to me like the Gulf Stream,[2] and it evidently does an important work in the movement of the ocean waters. It pours on through vast fields of ice on its way to other oceans, where it will probably become united with new currents. Theories about openings at the poles, or whirlpools, must be given up. Since the Maelstrom has been found to be a fiction,[3] no one need believe in any other whirlpool. For my own part, I now believe that this current will bear us on, due south, over the pole, and then still onward, until at last we shall find ourselves in the South Pacific Ocean. So cheer up—don't be downhearted; there's still hope. We have left the ice and snow behind, and already the air is warmer. Cheer up; we may find our luck turn at any moment."

To this I had no reply to make. Agnew's confidence seemed to me to be assumed, and certainly did not alleviate my own deep gloom, nor was the scene around calculated to rouse me in the slightest degree out of my despair. The channel had now lessened to a width of not more than two miles; the shores on either side were precipitous cliffs, broken by occasional declivities, but all of solid rock, so dark as to be almost black, and evidently of volcanic origin. At times there arose rugged eminences, scarred and riven,

1 A large whirlpool or vortex of water. The Moskstraumen in the Lofoten archipelago of Norway is probably the most famous maelström. Edgar Allan Poe's first tale, "MS Found in a Bottle," and his only novel, *The Narrative of Arthur Gordon Pym*, both end with the discovery of a huge maelström at the South Pole.

2 A powerful ocean current that begins in the Gulf of Mexico, runs up the east coast of North America, and crosses the Atlantic off of Newfoundland.

3 This comment seems to refer to Poe's "Descent into the Maelström" (1841), which plays with the question of whether the maelström that it describes is fictional or not.

indescribably dismal and appalling. There was not only an utter absence of life here in these abhorrent regions, but an actual impossibility of life, which was enough to make the stoutest heart quail.[1] The rocks looked like iron. It seemed a land of iron penetrated by this ocean stream which had made for itself a channel, and now bore us onward to a destination which was beyond all conjecture.

Through such scenes we drifted all that day. Night came, and in the skies overhead there arose a brilliant display of the aurora australis,[2] while toward the north the volcanic fires glowed with intense lustre. That night we slept. On awakening we noticed a change in the scene. The shores, though still black and forbidding, were no longer precipitous, but sloped down gradually to the water; the climate was sensibly milder, and far away before us there arose a line of giant mountains, whose summits were covered with ice and snow that gleamed white and purple in the rays of the sun.

Suddenly Agnew gave a cry, and pointed to the opposite shore.

"Look!" he cried—"do you see? They are men!"

I looked, and there I saw plainly some moving figures that were, beyond a doubt, human beings.

[TO BE CONTINUED.]

1 The verb quail is from the Middle English quaille, from Old French: to draw away involuntarily, usually out of fear or disgust.

2 The aurora of the southern hemisphere.

PART 3 (21 JANUARY, 1888)

CHAPTER IV.
THE SIGHT OF HUMAN BEINGS.

THE sight of human beings, thus unexpectedly found, filled us with strange feelings—feelings which I cannot explain. The country was still iron-bound and dark and forbidding, and the stream ran on in a strong current, deep, black as ink, and resistless as fate; the sky behind was lighted up by the volcanic glare which still shone from afar; and in front the view was bounded by the icy heights of a mountain chain. Here was indeed a strange country for human habitation; and strange, indeed, were the human beings whom we saw.

"Shall we land?" said Agnew.

"Oh no," said I. "Don't be hasty. The elements are sometimes kinder than men, and I feel safer here, even in this river of death, than ashore with such creatures as those."

Agnew made no reply. We watched the figures on the shore. We saw them coming down, staring and gesticulating. We drew on nearer to them till we were able to see them better. A nearer view did not improve them. They were human beings, certainly, but of such an appalling aspect that they could only be likened to animated mummies. They were small, thin, shrivelled, black, with long matted hair and hideous faces. They all had long spears, and wore about the waist short skirts that seemed to be made of the skin of some sea-fowl.

We could not imagine how these creatures lived, or where. There were no signs of vegetation of any kind—not a tree or a shrub. There were no animals; but there were great flocks of birds, some of which seemed different from anything that we had ever seen before. The long spears which the natives carried might possibly be used for catching these, or for fishing purposes. This thought made them seem less formidable, since they would thus be instruments of food rather than weapons of war. Meanwhile we drifted on as before, and the natives watched us, running along the shore abreast of us, so as to keep up with the boat. There seemed over a hundred of them. We could see no signs of any habitations—no huts, however humble; but we concluded that their abodes were farther inland. As for the natives themselves, the longer we looked at them the more abhorrent they grew. Even the wretched aborigines of Van Diemen's Land, who have been classed lowest in the scale of humanity, were pleasing and congenial when compared with these,[1] and the land looked worse than Tierra del Fuego.[2] It looked like a land of iron, and its inhabitants like fiends.

Agnew again proposed to land, but I refused.

"No," I said; "I'd rather starve for a week, and live on hope. Let us drift on. If we go on we may have hope if we choose, but if we land here we shall lose even that. Can we hope for anything from such things as these? Even if they prove friendly, can we live among them? To stay here is worse than death; our only hope is to go on."

Agnew made no reply, and we drifted on for two hours, still followed by the natives. They made no hostile demonstrations. They merely watched us, apparently from motives of curiosity. All this time we were drawing steadily nearer to the line of lofty mountains, which with their icy crests rose before us like an inaccessible and impassable barrier, apparently closing up all farther progress; nor was there any indication of any pass or any opening, however narrow, through which the great stream might run. Nothing was there but one unbroken wall of iron cliffs and icy summits. At last we saw that the sloping shores grew steeper, until about a mile or two before us they changed to towering cliffs that rose up on each side for about a thousand feet above the water; here the stream ran, and became lost to view as completely as though swallowed up by the earth.

"We can go no farther," said Agnew. "See—this stream seems to make a plunge there into the mountains. There must be some deep cañon[3] there with cataracts. To go on is certain death. We must stop here, if only to deliberate. Say, shall we risk it among these natives? After all, there is not, perhaps, any danger among them. They are little creatures and seem harmless. They are certainly not very good-looking; but then, you know, appearances often deceive, and the devil's not so black as he's painted. What do you say?"

"I suppose we can do nothing else," said I.

In fact, I could see that we had reached a crisis in our fate. To go on seemed certain death. To stop was our only alternative;

---

1 More alludes to Charles Darwin's description of the natives of Tierra del Fuego. See Appendix C2.

2 An archipelago off the southern tip of South America.

3 The Spanish cañon, which meant "a pipe, tube, gorge," is the origin for the English word canyon. The Spanish word is derived from the Latin canna, and earlier the Greek kanna, meaning "reed." The editor of the 1888 novel changed cañon *to* canyon.

and as we were armed we should not be altogether at the mercy of these creatures. Having made this decision we acted upon it at once, for in such a current there was no time for delay; and so, seizing the oars, we soon brought the boat ashore.

As we approached, the crowd of natives stood awaiting us, and looked more repulsive than ever. We could see the emaciation of their bony frames; their toes and fingers were like birds' claws; their eyes were small and dull and weak, and sunken in cavernous hollows, from which they looked at us like corpses—a horrible sight. They stood quietly, however, and without any hostile demonstration, holding their spears carelessly resting upon the ground.

"I don't like the looks of them," said I. "I think I had better fire a gun."

"Why?" cried Agnew. "For Heaven's sake, man, don't hurt any of them!"

"Oh no," said I; "I only mean to inspire a little wholesome respect."

Saying this I fired in the air. The report rang out with long echoes, and as the smoke swept away it showed us all the natives on the ground. They had seated themselves with their hands crossed on their laps, and there they sat looking at us as before, but with no manifestation of fear or even surprise. I had expected to see them run, but there was nothing of the kind. This puzzled us. Still, there was no time now for any further hesitation. The current was sweeping us toward the chasm between the cliffs, and we had to land without delay. This we did, and as I had another barrel still loaded and a pistol, I felt that with these arms and those of Agnew we should be able to defend ourselves. It was in this state of mind that we landed, and secured the boat by means of the grappling-iron.

The natives now all crowded around us, making many strange gestures, which we did not understand. Some of them bowed low, others prostrated themselves; on the whole these seemed like marks of respect, and it occurred to me that they regarded us as superior beings of some sort. It was evident that there was nothing like hostility in their minds. At the same time, the closer survey which I now made of them filled me with renewed horror; their meagre frames, small, watery, lack-lustre eyes, hollow, cavernous sockets, sunken cheeks, protruding teeth, claw-like fingers, and withered skins all made them look more than ever like animated mummies, and I shrank from them involuntarily, as one shrinks from contact with a corpse.

Illustration 3: "The natives now all crowded around us, making many strange gestures."

Agnew, however, was very different, and it was evident that he felt no repugnance whatever. He bowed and smiled at them, and shook hands with half a dozen of them in succession. The hand-shaking was a new thing to them, but they accepted it in a proper spirit, and renewed their bows and prostrations. After this they all offered us their lances. This certainly seemed like an act of peace and good-will. I shook my head and declined to touch them; but Agnew accepted one of them, and offered his rifle in return. The one to whom he offered it refused to take it. He seemed immensely gratified because Agnew had taken his lance, and the others seemed disappointed at his refusal to take theirs. But I felt my heart quake as I saw him offer his rifle, and still more when he offered it to one or two others, and only regained my composure as I perceived that his offer was refused by all.

They now made motions to us to follow, and we all set forth together.

"My dear More," said Agnew, cheerily, "they're not a bad lot. They mean well. They can't help their looks. You're too suspicious and reserved. Let's make friends with them, and get them to help us. Do as I do."

I tried to, but found it impossible, for my repugnance was immovable. It was like the horror which one feels toward rats, cockroaches, earwigs, or serpents. It was something that defied reason. These creatures seemed like human vermin.

We marched inland for about half a mile, crossed a ridge, and came to a valley, or rather a kind of hollow, at the other side of which we found a cave with a smouldering fire in front. The fire was made of coal, which must exist here somewhere. It was highly bituminous, and burned with a great blaze.

The day was now drawing to a close; far away I could see the lurid glow of the volcanoes, which grew brighter as the day declined: above, the skies twinkled with innumerable stars, and the air was filled with the moan of rushing waters.

We entered the cave. As we did so the natives heaped coal upon the fire, and the flames arose lighting up the interior. We found here a number of women and children, who looked at us without either fear or curiosity. The children looked like little dwarfs; the women were hags, hideous beyond description. One old woman in particular, who seemed to be in authority, was actually terrible in her awful and repulsive ugliness. A nightmare dream never furnished forth a more frightful object. This nightmare hag prostrated herself before each of us with such an air of self-immolation that she looked as though she wished us to kill her at once. The rough cave, the red light of the fire, all made the scene more awful; and a wild thought came to me that we had actually reached, while yet living, the infernal world, and that this was the abode of devils. Yet their actions, it must be confessed, were far from devilish. Everyone seemed eager to serve us. Some spread out couches formed of the skins of birds for us to sit on; others attended to the fire; others offered us gifts of large and beautiful feathers, together with numerous trinkets of rare and curious workmanship. This kind attention on their part was a great puzzle to me, and I could not help suspecting that beneath all this there must be some sinister design. Resolving to be prepared for the worst, I quietly reloaded the empty barrel of my rifle and watched with the utmost vigilance. As for Agnew, he took it all in the most unsuspicious manner. He made signs to them, shook hands with them, accepted their gifts, and even tried to do the agreeable to the formidable hags and the child-fiends around him. He soon attracted the chief attention, and while all looked admiringly upon him, I was left to languish in comparative neglect.

At length a savory odor came through the cave, and a repast was spread before us. It consisted of some large fowl that looked like a goose, but was twice as large as the largest turkey that I had ever seen. The taste was like that of a wild-goose, but rather fishy. Still to us it seemed delicious, for our prolonged diet of raw seal had made us ready to welcome any other food whatever; and this fowl, whatever it was, would not have been unwelcome to any hungry man. It was evident that these people lived on the flesh of birds of various sorts. All around us we saw the skins of birds dried with the feathers on, and used for clothing, for mats, and for ornaments.

The repast being finished, we both felt greatly strengthened and refreshed. Agnew continued to cultivate his new acquaintances, and seeing me holding back, he said,

"More, old fellow, these good people give me to understand that there is another place better than this, and want me to go with them. Will you go?"

At this a great fear seized me.

"Don't go!" I cried—"don't go! We are close by the boat here, and if anything happens we can easily get to it."

Agnew laughed in my face.

"Why, you don't mean to tell me," said he, "that you are still suspicious, and after that dinner? Why, man, if they wanted to harm us, would they feast us in this style? Nonsense, man! Drop your suspicions and come along."

I shook my head obstinately.

"Well," said he, "if I thought there was anything in your suspicions I would stay by you; but I'm confident they mean nothing but kindness, so I'm going off to see the place."

"You'll be back again?" said I.

"Oh yes," said he, "of course I'll come back, and sleep here."

With these words he left, and nearly all the people accompanied him. I was left behind with the women and children and about a dozen men. These men busied themselves with some work over bird-skins; the women were occupied with some other work over feathers. No one took any notice of me. There did not seem to be any restraint upon me, nor was I watched in any way. Once the nightmare hag came and offered me a small roasted fowl, about the size of a woodcock. I declined it, but at the same time this delicate attention certainly surprised me.

I was now beginning to struggle with some success against my feelings of abhorrence, when suddenly I caught sight of something which chased away every other thought, and made my blood turn cold in my veins. It was something outside. At the mouth of the cave—by the fire which was still blazing bright, and lighting up the scene—I saw four men who had just come to the cave: they were carrying something which I at first supposed to be a sick or wounded companion. On reaching the fire they put it down, and I saw, with a thrill of dismay, that their burden was neither sick nor wounded, but dead, for the corpse lay rigid as they had placed it. Then I saw the nightmare hag approach it with a knife. An awful thought came to me—the crowning horror! The thought soon proved to be but too well founded. The nightmare hag began to cut, and in an instant had detached the arm of the corpse, which she thrust among the coals in the very place where lately she had cooked the fowl. Then she went back for more.

For a moment my brain reeled, and I gasped for breath. Then I rose and staggered out, I know not how. No one tried to stop me, nor did anyone follow me; and for my part I was ready to blow out the brains of the first who dared to approach me. In this way I reached the open air, and passed by the hag and the four men as they were busy at their awful work. But at this point I was observed and followed. A number of men and women came after me, jabbering their uncouth language and gesticulating. I warned them off angrily. They persisted, and though none of them were armed, yet I saw that they were unwilling to have me leave the cave, and I supposed that they would try to prevent me by force.

The absence of Agnew made my position a difficult one. Had it not been for this I would have burst through them and fled to the boat; but as long as he was away I felt bound to wait; and though I longed to fly, I could not for his sake. The boat seemed to be a haven of rest. I longed to be in her once more, and drift away, even if it should be to my death. Nature was here less terrible than man; and it seemed better to drown in the waters, to perish amid rocks and whirlpools, than to linger here amid such horrors as these. These people were not like human beings. The vilest and lowest savages that I had ever seen were not so odious as these. A herd of monkeys would be far more congenial, a flock of wolves less abhorrent. They had the caricature of the human form; they were the lowest of humanity; their speech was a mockery of language; their faces devilish, their kindness a cunning pretence; and most hideous of all was the nightmare hag that prepared the cannibal repast.

I could not begin hostilities, for I had to wait for Agnew; so I stood and looked, and then walked away for a little distance. They followed me closely, with eager words and gesticulations, though as yet no one touched me or threatened me. Their tone seemed rather one of persuasion. After a few paces I stood still, with all of them around me. The horrible repast showed plainly all that was in store for us. They received us kindly and fed us well only to devote us to the most abhorrent of deaths. Agnew, in his mad confidence, was only insuring his own doom. He was putting himself completely in the power of devils, who were incapable of pity and strangers to humanity. To make friends with such fiends was impossible, and I felt sure that our only plan was to rule by terror—to seize, to slay, to conquer. But still I had to wait for him, and did not dare to resort to violence while he was absent; so I waited, while the savages gathered round me, contenting themselves with guarding me, and neither touching me nor threatening me. And all this time the hag went on, intent on her preparation of the horrible repast.

While standing there looking, listening, waiting for Agnew, I noticed many things. Far away the volcanoes blazed, and the northern sky was red with a lurid light. There, too, higher up, the moon was shining overhead, the sky was gleaming with stars; and all over the heavens there shone the lustre of the aurora australis, brighter than any I had ever seen—surpassing the moon and illuminating all. It lighted up the haggard faces of the devils around me, and it again seemed to me as though I had died and gone to the land of woe—an iron land, a land of despair, with lurid fires all aglow and faces of fear.

Suddenly, there burst upon my ears the report of a gun, which sounded like a thunder-peal, and echoed in long reverberations. At once I understood it. My fears had proved true. These savages had enticed Agnew away to destroy him. In an instant I burst through the crowd around me, and ran wildly in the direction of that sound, calling his name, as I ran, at the top of my voice.

I heard a loud cry; then another report. I hurried on, shouting his name in a kind of frenzy. The strange courage of these savages had already impressed me deeply. They did not fear our guns. They were all attacking him, and he was alone, fighting for his life.

Then there was another report; it was his pistol. I still ran on, and still shouted to him.

At last I received an answer. He had perhaps heard me, and was answering, or, at any rate, he was warning me.

"More," he cried, "fly, fly, fly to the boat! Save yourself!"

"Where are you?" I cried, as I still rushed on.

"Fly, More, fly! Save yourself! You can't save me. I'm lost. Fly for your life!"

Judging from his cries, he did not seem far away. I hurried on. I could see nothing of him. All the time the savages followed me. None were armed; but it seemed to me that they were preparing to fling themselves upon me and overpower me with their numbers. They would capture me alive, I thought, bind me, and carry me back, reserving me for a future time!

I turned and waved them back. They took no notice of my gesture. Then I ran on once more. They followed. They could not run so fast as I did, and so I gained on them rapidly, still shouting to Agnew. But there was no response. I ran backward and forward, crossing and recrossing, doubling and turning, pursued all the time by the savages. At last, in rage and despair, I fired upon them, and one of them fell. But, to my dismay, the others did not seem to care one whit; they did not stop for one moment, but pursued as before.

My situation was now plain in all its truth. They had enticed Agnew away; they had attacked him. He had fought, and had been overpowered. He had tried to give me warning. His last words had been for me to fly—to fly: yes, for he well knew that it was better far for me to go to death through the raging torrent than to meet the fate which had fallen upon himself. For him there was now no more hope. That he was lost was plain. If he were still alive he would call to me; but his voice had been silenced for some time. All was over, and that noble heart that had withstood so bravely and cheerily the rigors of the storm, and the horrors of our desperate voyage, had been stilled in death by the vilest of miscreants.

I paused for a moment. Even though Agnew was dead, I could not bear to leave him, but felt as though I ought to share his fate. The savages came nearer. At their approach I hesitated no longer. That fate was too terrible: I must fly.

But before I fled I turned in fury to wreak vengeance upon them for their crimes. Full of rage and despair, I discharged my remaining rifle-barrel into the midst of the crowd. Then I fled toward the boat. On the way I had a frightful thought that she might have been sent adrift; but, on approaching the place, I found her there just as I had left her. The savages, with their usual fearlessness, still pursued. For a moment I stood on the shore, with the grapple in my hand and the boat close by, and as they came near I discharged my pistol into the midst of them. Then I sprang into the boat; the swift current bore me away, and in a few minutes the crowd of pursuing demons disappeared from view.

[TO BE CONTINUED.]

PART 4 (28 JANUARY, 1888)

CHAPTER V. THE TORRENT SWEEPING UNDER THE MOUNTAINS.

THE boat drifted on. The light given by the aurora and the low moon seemed to grow fainter; and as I looked behind I saw that the distant glow from the volcanic fires had become more brilliant in the increasing darkness. The sides of the channel grew steeper, until at last they became rocky precipices, rising to an unknown height. The channel itself grew narrower, till from a width of two miles it had contracted to a tenth of those dimensions; but with this lessening width the waters seemed to rush far more swiftly. Here I drifted helplessly, and saw the gloomy, rocky cliffs sweep past me as I was hurled onward on the breast of the tremendous flood. I was in despair. The fate of Agnew had prepared me for my own, and I was only thankful that my fate, since it was inevitable, would be less appalling. Death seemed certain, and my chief thought now was as to the moment when it would come. I was prepared. I felt that I could meet it calmly, sternly, even thankfully: far better was a death here amid the roar of waters than at the hands of those abhorrent beings by whose treachery my friend had fallen.

As I went on, the precipices rose higher and seemed to overhang, the channel grew narrower, the light grew fainter, until at last all around me grew dark. I was floating at the bottom of a vast chasm, where the sides seemed to rise precipitously for thousands of feet, where neither watery flood nor rocky wall was visible, and where, far above, I could see the line of sky between the summits of the cliffs, and watch the glowing stars. And as I watched them there came to me the thought that this was my last sight on earth, and I could only hope that the life which was so swiftly approaching its end might live again somewhere among those glittering orbs. So I thought; and with these thoughts I drifted on, I cannot tell how long, until at length there appeared a vast black mass, where the open sky above me terminated, and where the lustre of the stars and the light of the heavens were all swallowed up in utter darkness.

This, then, I thought, is the end. Here, amid this darkness, I must make the awful plunge and find my death. I fell upon my knees in the bottom of the boat and prayed. As I knelt there the boat drew nearer, the black mass grew blacker. The current swept me on. There were no breakers; there was no phosphorescent sparkle of seething waters, and no whiteness of foam. I thought that I was on the brink of some tremendous cataract a thousand times deeper than Niagara; some fall where the waters plunged into the depths of the earth; and where, gathering for the terrific descent, all other movements—all dashings and writhings and twistings—were obliterated and lost in the one overwhelming onward rush. Suddenly all grew dark—dark beyond all expression; the sky above was in a moment snatched from view; I had been flung into some tremendous cavern; and there, on my knees, with terror in my heart, I waited for death.

The moments passed, and death delayed to come. The awful plunge was still put off; and though I remained on my knees and waited long, still the end came not. The waters seemed still, the boat motionless. It was borne upon the surface of a vast stream as smooth as glass; but who could tell how deep that stream was, or how wide? At length I rose from my knees and sank down upon the seat of the boat, and tried to peer through the gloom. In vain. Nothing was visible. It was the very blackness of darkness. I listened, but heard nothing save a deep, dull, droning sound, which seemed to fill all the air and make it all tremulous with its vibrations. I tried to collect my thoughts. I recalled that old theory which had been in my mind before this, and which I had mentioned to Agnew. This was the notion that at each pole there is a vast opening; that into one of them all the waters of the ocean pour themselves, and, after passing through the earth, come out at the other pole, to pass about its surface in innumerable streams.[1] It was a wild fancy, which I had laughed at under other circumstances, but which now occurred to me once more, when I was overwhelmed with despair, and my mind was weakened by the horrors which I had experienced; and I had a vague fear that I had been drawn into the very channel through which the ocean waters flowed in their course to that terrific, that unparalleled abyss. Still, there was as yet no sign whatever of anything like a descent, for the boat was on even keel, and perfectly level as before, and it was impossible for me to tell whether I was moving swiftly or slowly, or standing perfectly still; for in that darkness there were no visible objects by which I could find out the rate of my progress; and as those who go up in balloons are utterly insensible of motion, so was I on those calm but swift waters.

---

1 See Appendices E1 and E2.

At length there came into view something which arrested my attention and engrossed all my thoughts. It was a faint glow that at first caught my gaze; and on turning to see it better, I saw a round red spot glowing like fire. I had not seen this before. It looked like the moon when it rises from behind clouds, and glows red and lurid from the horizon; and so this glowed, but not with the steady light of the moon, for the light was fitful, and sometimes flashed into a baleful brightness, which soon subsided into a dimmer lustre. New alarm arose within me, for this new sight suggested something more terrible than anything that I had thus far thought of. This, then, I thought, was to be the end of my voyage; this was my goal—a pit of fire, into which I should be hurled! Would it be well, I thought, to wait for such a fate, and experience such a death-agony? Would it not be better for me to take my own life before I should know the worst? I took my pistol and loaded it, so as to be prepared, but hesitated to use it until my fate should be more apparent. So I sat, holding my pistol, prepared to use it, watching the light, and awaiting the time when the glowing fires should make all further hope impossible. But time passed, and the light grew no brighter; on the contrary, it seemed to grow fainter. There was also another change. Instead of shining before me, it appeared more on my left. From this it went on changing its position until at length it was astern. All the time it continued to grow fainter, and it seemed certain that I was moving away from it rather than toward it. In the midst of this there occurred a new thought, which seemed to account for this light—this was, that it arose from those same volcanoes which had illuminated the northern sky when I was ashore, and followed me still with their glare. I had been carried into this darkness, through some vast opening which now lay behind me, disclosing the red volcano glow, and this it was that caused that roundness and resemblance to the moon. I saw that I was still moving on away from that light as before, and that its changing position was due to the turning of the boat as the water drifted it along, now stern foremost, now sidewise, and again bow foremost. From this it seemed plainly evident that the waters had borne me into some vast cavern of unknown extent, which went under the mountains—a subterranean channel, whose issue I could not conjecture. Was this the beginning of that course which should ultimately become a plunge deep down into some unutterable abyss? or might I ever hope to emerge again into the light of day—perhaps in some other ocean—some land of ice and frost and eternal night? But the old theory of the flow of water through the earth had taken hold of me and could not be shaken off. I knew some scientific men held the opinion that the earth's interior is a mass of molten rock and pent-up fire, and that the earth itself had once been a burning orb, which had cooled down at the surface;[1] yet, after all, this was only a theory, and there were other theories which were totally different. As a boy I had read wild works of fiction about lands in the interior of the earth, with a sun at the centre, which gave them the light of a perpetual day. These, I knew, were only the creations of fiction;[2] yet, after all, it seemed possible that the earth might contain vast hollow spaces in its interior—realms of eternal darkness, caverns in comparison with which the hugest caves on the surface were but the tiniest cells. I was now being borne on to these. In that case there might be no sudden plunge, after all. The stream might run on for many thousand miles through this terrific cavern gloom, in accordance with natural laws; and I might thus live, and drift on in this darkness, until I should die a lingering death of horror and despair.

There was no possible way of forming any estimate as to speed. All was dark, and even the glow behind was fading away; nor could I make any conjecture whatever as to the size of the channel. At the opening it had been contracted and narrow; but here it might have expanded itself to miles, and its vaulted top might reach almost to the summit of the lofty mountains. While sight thus failed me, sound was equally unavailing, for it was always the same—a sustained and unintermittent roar, a low, droning sound, deep and terrible, with no variations of dashing breakers or rushing rapids or falling cataracts. Vague thoughts of final escape came and went; but in such a situation hope could not be sustained. The thick darkness oppressed the soul; and at length even the glow of the distant volcanoes, which had been gradually diminishing, grew dimmer and fainter, and finally faded out altogether. That seemed to me to be my last sight of earthly things. After this nothing was left. There was no longer for me such a thing as sight; there was

---

1 The theory that the Earth had a molten core was prevalent in the early nineteenth century. See, for instance, Charles Darwin's article "Observations of the Parallel Roads of Glen Roy, and of Other Parts of Lochaber in Scotland, with an Attempt to Prove that they are of Marine Origin," published in volume 129 of *Philosophical Transactions of the Royal Society of London* (1839). For another example, see Robert James Mann's *Lessons in General Knowledge* (1856).

2 Given More's age, he seems to be referring to the theories and fiction of John Cleves Symmes Jr. (see *Symzonia* in Appendix E1). Jules Verne's *Voyage au Centre de la Terre*, which also imagines hollow spaces in the interior of the earth, was published in 1864 (see Appendix E4).

nothing but darkness—perpetual and eternal night.[1] I was buried in a cavern of rushing waters, to which there would be no end, where I should be borne onward helplessly by the resistless tide to a mysterious and an appalling doom.

The darkness grew so intolerable that I longed for something to dispel it, if only for a moment. I struck a match. The air was still, and the flame flashed out, lighting up the boat and showing the black water around me. This made me eager to see more. I loaded both barrels of the rifle, keeping my pistol for another purpose, and then fired one of them. There was a tremendous report, that rang in my ears like a hundred thunder-volleys, and rolled and reverberated far along, and died away in endless echoes. The flash lighted up the scene for an instant, and for an instant only; like the sudden lightning, it revealed all around. I saw a wide expanse of water, black as ink—a Stygian pool;[2] but no rocks were visible, and it seemed as though I had been carried into a subterranean sea.

I loaded the empty barrel and waited. The flash of light had revealed nothing, yet it had distracted my thoughts, and the work of reloading was an additional distraction. Anything was better than inaction. I did not wish to waste my ammunition, yet I thought that an occasional shot might serve some good purpose, if it was only to afford me some relief from despair.

And now, as I sat with the rifle in my hands, I was aware of a sound—new, exciting, different altogether from the murmur of innumerable waters that filled my ears, and in sharp contrast with the droning echoes of the rushing flood. It was a sound that spoke of life. I heard quick, heavy pantings, as of some great living thing; and with this there came the noise of regular movements in the water, and the foaming and gurgling of waves. It was as though some living, breathing creature were here, not far away, moving through these midnight waters; and with this discovery there came a new fear—the fear of pursuit. I thought that some sea-monster

---

1 For a departure point regarding the themes of caves and darkness which are emphasized here, see Plato's Allegory of the Cave in Appendix D1.

2 Dark and gloomy, relating, in Greek mythology, to the River Styx in Hades, across which Charon ferries souls of the dead. The phrase "Stygian pool" occurs in line 14 of Book III of John Milton's *Paradise Lost* to describe what Satan has escaped from as he leaves hell and travels toward earth: "Thee I re-visit now with bolder wing, / Escap't the *Stygian* Pool, though long detain'd / In that obscure sojourn, while in my flight / Through utter and through middle darkness borne / With other notes then to th' *Orphean* Lyre / I sung of *Chaos* and *Eternal Night*...."

had scented me in my boat, and had started to attack me. This new fear aroused me to action. It was a danger quite unlike any other which I had ever known; yet the fear which it inspired was a feeling that roused me to action, and prompted me, even though the coming danger might be as sure as death, to rise against it and resist to the last. So I stood up with my rifle and listened, with all my soul in my sense of hearing. The sounds arose more plainly. They had come nearer. They were immediately in front. I raised my rifle and took aim. Then in quick succession two reports thundered out with tremendous uproar and interminable echoes, but the long reverberations were unheeded in the blaze of sudden light and the vision that was revealed.

For there full before me I saw, though but for an instant, a tremendous sight. It was a vast monster, moving in the waters against the stream and toward the boat. Its head was raised high, its eyes were inflamed with a baleful light, its jaws, opened wide, bristled with sharp teeth, and it had a long neck joined to a body of enormous bulk, with a tail that lashed all the water into foam. It was but for an instant that I saw it, and then with a sudden plunge the monster dived, while at the same moment all was as dark as before.

Full of terror and excitement, I loaded my rifle again and waited, listening for a renewal of the noise. I felt sure that the monster, balked of his prey, would return with redoubled fury, and that I should have to renew the conflict. I felt that the dangers of the subterranean passage and of the rushing waters had passed away, and that a new peril had arisen from the assault of this monster of the deep. Nor was it this one alone that was to be dreaded. Where one was, others were sure to be; and if this one should pass me by it would only leave me to be assailed by monsters of the same kind, and these would probably increase in number as I advanced farther into this realm of darkness. And yet, in spite of these grisly thoughts, I felt less of horror than before, for the fear which I had was now associated with action; and as I stood waiting for the onset and listening for the approach of the enemy, the excitement that ensued was a positive relief from the dull despair into which I had sunk but a moment before.

Yet, though I waited for a new attack, I waited in vain. The monster did not come back. Either the flash and the noise had terrified him, or the bullets had hit him, or else in his vastness he had been indifferent to so feeble a creature as myself; but whatever may have been the cause, he did not emerge again out of the darkness and silence into which he had sunk. For a long time I

Illustration 4: "I raised my rifle and took aim. Then in quick succession two reports thundered out with tremendous uproar."

stood waiting; then I sat down, still watchful, still listening, but without any result, until at length I began to think that there was no chance of any new attack. Indeed, it seemed now as though there had been no attack at all, but that the monster had been swimming at random without any thought of me, in which case my rifle-flashes had terrified him more than his fearful form had terrified me. On the whole this incident had greatly benefited me. It had roused me from my despair. I grew reckless, and felt a disposition to acquiesce in whatever fate might have in store for me.

And now, worn out with fatigue and exhausted from long watchfulness and anxiety, I sank down in the bottom of the boat and fell into a deep sleep.

CHAPTER VI.
THE NEW WORLD.

HOW long I slept I do not know. My sleep was profound, yet disturbed by troubled dreams, in which I lived over again all the eventful scenes of the past; and these were all intermingled in the wildest confusion. The cannibals beckoned to us from the peak, and we landed between the two volcanoes. There the body of the dead sailor received us, and afterward chased us to the boat. Then came snow and volcanic eruptions, and we drifted amid icebergs and molten lava until we entered an iron portal and plunged into darkness. Here there were vast swimming monsters and burning orbs of fire and thunderous cataracts falling from inconceivable heights, and the sweep of immeasurable tides and the circling of infinite whirlpools, while in my ears there rang the never-ending roar of remorseless waters that came after us, with all their waves and billows rolling upon us. It was a dream in which all the material terrors of the past were renewed; but these were all as nothing when compared with a certain deep underlying feeling that possessed my soul—a sense of loss irretrievable, an expectation of impending doom, a drear and immitigable despair.

In the midst of this I awoke. It was with a sudden start, and I looked all around in speechless bewilderment. The first thing of which I was conscious was a great blaze of light—light so lately lost, and supposed to be lost forever, but now filling all the universe—bright, brilliant, glowing, bringing hope and joy and gladness, with all the splendor of deep blue skies and the multitudinous laughter of ocean waves that danced and sparkled in the sun. I flung up my arms and laughed aloud. Then I burst into tears, and falling on my knees I thanked the Almighty Ruler of the skies for this marvellous deliverance.

Rising from my knees I looked around, and once more amazement overwhelmed me. I saw a long line of mountains towering up to immeasurable heights, their summits covered with eternal ice and snow. There the sun blazed low in the sky, elevated but a few degrees above the mountain crests, which gleamed in gold and purple under its fiery rays. The sun seemed enlarged to unusual dimensions, and the mountains ran away on every side like the segment of some infinite circle. At the base of the mountains lay a land all green with vegetation, where cultivated fields were visible and vineyards and orchards and groves, together with forests of palm and all manner of trees of every variety of hue, which ran up the sides of the mountains till they reached the limits of vegetation and the regions of snow and ice.

Here in all directions there were unmistakable signs of human life—the outlines of populous cities and busy towns and hamlets; roads winding far away along the plain or up the mountain-sides, and mighty works of human industry in the shape of massive structures, terraced slopes, long rows of arches, ponderous pyramids, and battlemented walls.

From the land I turned to the sea. I saw before me an expanse of water intensely blue—an extent so vast that never before in all my ocean voyages had anything appeared at all comparable with it. Out at sea, wherever I had been, the water had always limited the view; the horizon had never seemed far away; ships soon sank below it, and the visible surface of the earth was thus always contracted; but here, to my bewilderment, the horizon appeared to be removed to an immeasurable distance and raised high in the air, while the waters were prolonged endlessly. Starting from where I was, they went away to inconceivable distances, and the view before me seemed like a watery declivity reaching for a thousand miles, till it approached the horizon far up in the sky.[1] Nor was it any delusion of the senses that caused this unparalleled spectacle. I was familiar with the phenomena of the mirage, and knew well that there was nothing of that kind here; for the mirage always shows great surfaces of stillness, or a regular vibration—glassy

---

1 The enlarged view of the ocean and circuitous mountains is apparently produced by the flatness of the Earth at the South Pole. See Appendix B4 for a nineteenth-century account of how the diameter of the Earth meridian is about 43 km shorter than the diameter of the equator. The optical effect is De Mille's own, apparently unfounded, speculation.

tides and indistinct distances; but here everything was sharply defined in the clear atmosphere: the sky overhung a deep blue vault; the waves danced and sparkled in the sun; the waters rolled and foamed on every side; and the fresh breeze, as it blew over the ocean, brought with it such exhilarating influences that it acted upon me like some reviving cordial.

From the works of nature I turned to those of man. These were visible everywhere: on the land, in cities and cultivated fields and mighty constructions; on the sea, in floating craft, which appeared wherever I turned my eyes—boats like those of fishermen, ships long and low, some like galleys, propelled by a hundred oars, others provided with one huge square-sail, which enabled them to run before the wind.[1] They were unlike any ships which I had ever seen; for neither in the Mediterranean nor in Chinese waters were there any craft like these, and they reminded me rather of those ancient galleys which I had seen in pictures.[2]

I was lost in wonder as to where I was, and what land this could be to which I had been brought. I had not plunged into the interior of the earth, but I had been carried under the mountains, and had emerged again into the glad light of the sun. Could it be possible, I thought, that Agnew's hope had been realized, and that I had been carried into the warm regions of the South Pacific Ocean? Yet in the South Pacific there could be no place like this—no immeasurable expanse of waters, no horizon raised mountain high. It seemed like a vast basin-shaped world, for all around me the surface appeared to rise, and I was in what looked like a depression; yet I knew that the basin and the depression were an illusion, and that this appearance was due to the immense extent of level surface with the environment of lofty mountains. I had crossed the antarctic circle; I had been borne onward for an immense distance. Over all the known surface of the earth no one had ever seen anything like this; there were but two places where such an immeasurable plain was possible, and those were at the flattened poles. Where I was I now knew well. I had reached the antarctic pole. Here the earth was flat—an immense level with no roundness to lessen the reach of the horizon but an almost even surface that gave an unimpeded view for hundreds of miles.

---

1 De Mille may be consulting Sir J. Gardner Wilkinson's *A Popular Account of the Ancient Egyptians* (1854).

2 Compare this with Edward Bulwer Lytton's use of Orientalism to construct the Vril-ya in *The Coming Race* (see Appendix E3a).

The subterranean channel had rushed through the mountains and had carried me here. Here came all the waters of the Northern ocean pouring into this vast polar sea, perhaps to issue forth from it by some similar passage. Here, then, was the South Pole—a world by itself; and how different from that terrible, that iron land on the other side of the mountains!—not a world of ice and frost, but one of beauty and light, with a climate that was almost tropical in its warmth, and lands that were covered with the rank luxuriance of a teeming vegetable life. I had passed from that outer world to this inner one, and the passage was from death unto life, from agony and despair to sunlight and splendor and joy. Above all, in all around me that which most impressed me now was the rich and superabundant life, and a warmth of air which made me think of India. It was an amazing and an unaccountable thing, and I could only attribute it to the flattening of the poles, which brought the surface nearer to the supposed central fires of the earth, and therefore created a heat as great as that of the equatorial regions. Here I found a tropical climate—a land warmed not by the sun, but from the earth itself. Or another cause might be found in the warm ocean currents. Whatever the true one might be, I was utterly unable to form a conjecture.

But I had no time for such speculations as these. After the first emotions of wonder and admiration had somewhat subsided, I began to experience other sensations. I began to remember that I had eaten nothing for a length of time that I had no means of calculating, and to look around to see if there was any way of satisfying my hunger. The question arose now, What was to be done? After my recent terrible experience I naturally shrank from again committing myself to the tender mercies of strange tribes; yet further thought and examination showed me that the people of this strange land must be very different from those frightful savages on the other side of the mountains. Everywhere I beheld the manifest signs of cultivation and civilization. Still, I knew that even civilized people would not necessarily be any kinder than savages, and that I might be seized and flung into hopeless imprisonment or slavery.

So I hesitated, yet what could I do? My hunger was beginning to be insupportable. I had reached a place where I had to choose between starvation on the one hand, or a venture among these people on the other. To go back was impossible. Who could breast those waters in the tremendous subterranean channel, or force his way back through such appalling dangers? Or, if that were possible, who could ever hope to breast those mighty currents beyond, or work his way amid everlasting ice and immeasurable seas? No;

return was impossible. I had been flung into this world of wonders, and here would be my home for the remainder of my days; though I could not now imagine whether those days would be passed in peace or in bitter slavery and sorrow. Yet the decision must be made and the risk must be run. It must be so. I must land here, venture among these people, and trust in that Providence which had hitherto sustained me.

[TO BE CONTINUED.]

PART 5 (4 FEBRUARY, 1888)

CHAPTER VI.—(*Continued.*)
THE NEW WORLD.

HAVING thus resolved at all hazards to try my fate, I rowed in toward the shore. Thus far I had seen galleys passing and small boats, but they had taken no notice of me, for the reason that they were too far away to perceive anything about me that differed from any other boat; but now, as I rowed, I noticed a galley coming down toward me. She seemed to be going in toward the shore at the very point at which I was aiming, and her course and mine must soon meet if I continued to row. After some hesitation I concluded to make signals to her, so as to attract attention; for, now that I had resolved to venture among the people here, I was anxious to end my suspense as soon as possible. So I continued rowing, and gradually drew nearer. The galley was propelled by oars, of which there were fifty on either side. The stern was raised, and covered in like a cabin. At length I ceased rowing, and sat watching her. I soon saw that I was noticed, but this did not occur till the galley was close by me—so close, indeed, that I thought they would pass without perceiving me. I raised my hands, waved them, and gave a cry. The galley at once stopped, a boat was lowered, and some men descended and rowed toward me.

They were men of strange appearance—very small in stature and slender in frame. Their hair was black and straight, their features were quite regular, and their general expression was one of great gentleness. I was surprised to notice that they kept their eyes almost closed, as though they were weak and troubled by the glare of the sun. With their half-closed eyes they blinked at me, and then one who appeared to be their chief spoke to me. I understood not a word, and then I answered him in English, which of course was equally unintelligible to him. I then made signs, pointing to the mountains and endeavoring to make known to him that I had come from beyond them—that I had suffered shipwreck, that I had drifted here, and that I needed assistance. Of all this it was quite evident that they understood nothing except the fact that I needed help. The moment that they comprehended this they took me in tow and rowed back to the galley.

I found the galley to be about one hundred and fifty feet in length. For about two-thirds of this length forward it was open and filled with seats, where there were about a hundred rowers, who all looked like those that I had first seen, all being of small stature, slender frames, and, moreover, all being apparently distressed by the sunlight. There was in all of them the same mild and gentle expression. In complexion and general outline of features they were not unlike Arabs, but they were entirely destitute of that hardness and austerity which the latter have. They all had beards, which were dressed in a peculiar way in plaits. Their costume varied. The rowers wore a coarse tunic, with a girdle of rope. The officers wore tunics of fine cloth and very elegant mantles, richly embroidered, and with borders of down. They all wore broad-brimmed hats, and the one who seemed to be chief had on his some golden ornaments.

Here once more I tried to explain to them who I was. They looked at me, examining me all over, inspecting my gun, pistol, coat, trousers, boots, and hat, and talking all the time among themselves. They did not touch me, but merely showed the natural curiosity which is felt at the sight of a foreigner who has appeared unexpectedly. There was a scrupulous delicacy and a careful and even ceremonious politeness in their attitude toward me, which was at once amazing and delightful. All fear and anxiety had now left me; in the gentle manners and amiable faces of these people I saw enough to assure me of kind treatment; and in my deep joy and gratitude for this, even my hunger was for a time forgotten.

At length the chief motioned to me to follow him. He led the way to the cabin, where, opening the door, he entered, and I followed, after which the others came in also, and then the door was shut. At first I could see nothing whatever. There were no windows whatever, and only one or two slight crevices through which the light came. After a time my eyes grew more accustomed to the darkness, and I could see that the cabin was a spacious apartment, adorned with rich hangings of some unknown material. There was a large table and seats. Taking me by the hand, the chief led me to this, where I seated myself, while the others remained standing. Then some of them went away, and soon returned with food and drink. The food was of different kinds—some tasting like goose, others like turkey, others like partridge. It was all the flesh of fowls, though, judging from the slices before me, they must have been of great size. I wondered much at the behavior of the officers of the ship, who all, and the chief himself more than all, stood and waited upon me; but it was a new world, and I supposed that this must be the fashion; so I made no objections, but accepted the situation and ate with a thankful heart.

As the first keenness of my appetite was satisfied I had more leisure to make observations. I noticed that the eyes of my new friends no longer blinked; they were wide open; and, so far as I could make them out, their faces were much improved. Weakness of eyes seemed common among these people, and therefore the officers had their cabin darkened, while the unfortunate rowers had to labor in the blazing sun. Such was my conclusion, and the fact reminded me of the miserable fellahin[1] of Egypt, who have ophthalmia[2] from the blazing sun and burning sand.

After the repast they brought me water in a basin, and all stood around me. One held the basin, another a towel, another a flask, another took a sponge and proceeded to wash my face and hands. This was all strange to me, yet there was nothing left for me but submission. Then the chief, who had stood looking on with a smile on his face, took off his rich furred mantle and handed it to me. I was half inclined to refuse it, but was afraid of giving offence, so I accepted it, and he himself fastened it around my shoulders. The others seemed actually to envy the chief, as though he had gained some uncommon good-fortune. Then they offered me various drinks, of which I tasted several kinds. Some were sweet waters of different flavors, others tasted like mild wine, one was a fermented drink, light, sweet, and very agreeable to the palate. I now wished to show my generous entertainers that I was grateful; so I raised my cup, bowed to all of them, particularly the chief, and drank their health. They all watched this ceremony with very sober faces, and I could not quite make out whether they took my meaning or not. They certainly did not look pleased, and it seemed to me as though they felt hurt at any expression of gratitude, so I concluded for the future to abstain from all such demonstrations. Yet with every moment the manners of these people grew more bewildering. It was strange, indeed, for me to find myself so suddenly the centre of interest and of generous attentions. For a moment the thought occurred to me that they regarded me as some wonderful being with superior powers, and were trying to propitiate me by these services: yet I soon saw that these services were not at all acts of propitiation; they looked rather like those loving and profuse

---

1 Plural of Arabic *fellah*, agricultural worker or peasant.

2 Inflammation of the eye. The prevalence of eye diseases in Egypt has been long established, although its causes were debated in the nineteenth century. An 1837 article on Egypt in the *Penny Cyclopaedia of the Society for the Diffusion of Useful Knowledge* attributes it to "checked perspiration" and dust associated with the climate, noting that "great numbers of Egyptians are blind in one or both eyes" ("Egypt" 312).

Illustration 5: "Another took a sponge and proceeded to wash my face and hands."

attentions which a family showers down upon some dear one long absent and at last returned, and with this my wonder grew greater than ever.

The galley had long since resumed her progress. I heard the steady beat of the oars as they all moved in time, and at length the motion ceased. The chief then signed to me and went out. I followed, and the rest came after. And now as I emerged from the gloom of the cabin, I found myself once more in the glorious light of day, and saw that we had reached the land. The galley was hauled up alongside a stone quay, and on the shore there were buildings and walls and trees and people. The chief went ashore at once, and I accompanied him. We walked for some distance along a road with stone walls on either side, from behind which there arose trees that from a distance had looked like palms. I now found them to be giant ferns, arching overhead with their broad fan-like leaves and branches in dense masses, making the roadway quite dark in the shadow. Astonished as I was at the sight of these trees, I soon forgot them in a still more astonishing sight, for after going onward about a hundred paces, I stopped, and found myself in a wide space where four cross-roads met. Here there were three birds of gigantic stature.[1] They had vast bodies, short legs, short necks, and seemed as large as an ordinary-sized ox. Their wings were short, and evidently could not be used for flight; their beaks were like that of a sea-gull; each one had a man on his back, and was harnessed to a car. The chief motioned to me to enter one of these cars. I did so. He followed, and thereupon the driver started the bird, which set forth with long, rapid strides, at a pace fast as that of a trotting horse. So astonished was I that for some time I did not notice anything else; but at length, when my first feeling had subsided, I began to regard other objects. All the way the dense fern foliage arched overhead, throwing down deep shadows. They grew on either side in dense rows, but between their stalks I could see the country beyond, which lay all bright in the sunlight. Here were broad fields, all green with verdure; farther away arose clumps of tree-ferns; at every step of the way new vistas opened; amid the verdure and the foliage were the roofs of structures that looked like pavilions, and more massive edifices with pyramidal roofs. Our road constantly ascended, and at length we came to a crossing. This was a wide terrace at the slope of the mountain; on the lower side was a row of massive stone edifices with pyramidal

1 See Appendix B3.

roofs, while on the upper there were portals which seemed to open into excavated caverns. Here, too, on either side arose the giant ferns, overarching and darkening the terrace with their deep shadow. From this point I looked back, and through the trunks of the tree-ferns I could see fields and pavilions and the pyramidal roofs of massive edifices, and broad, verdant slopes, while in the distance there were peeps of the boundless sea. We continued on our way without stopping, and passed several successive terraces like the first, with the same caverns on the upper side and massive edifices on the lower, until at last the ascent ended at the fifth terrace, and here we turned to the left. Now the view became more varied. The tree-ferns arose on either side, arching overhead; on my right were the portals that opened into caverns, on my left solid and massive houses, built of great blocks of stone, with pyramidal roofs. As far as I could judge, I was in a city built on the slope of a mountain, with its streets formed thus of successive terraces and their connecting cross-ways, one half its habitations consisting of caverns, while the other half were pavilions and massive stone structures. Few people, however, were to be seen. Occasionally I saw one or two groping along with their eyes half shut, seeking the darkest shadows; and it seemed to me that this extraordinary race of men had some natural and universal peculiarity of eyesight which made them shun the sunlight, and seek the darkness of caves and of dense, overshadowing foliage.

At length we came to a place where the terrace ran back till it formed a semicircle against the mountain slope, when several vast portals appeared. Here there was a large space, where the tree-ferns grew in long lines crossing each other, and making a denser shade than usual. On the lower side were several stone edifices of immense size; and in the middle of the place there arose a singular structure, shaped like a half pyramid, with three sides sloping and the fourth perpendicular, flat on the top, which was approached by a flight of steps. We now went on until we reached the central portal of the range of caverns, and here we stopped. The chief got out and beckoned to me. I followed. He then led the way into the cavern, while I, full of wonder, walked behind him.

CHAPTER VII.
SCIENTIFIC THEORIES AND SCEPTICISM.

THUS far Melick had been reading the manuscript, but at this point he was interrupted by the announcement that dinner was ready. Upon this he stopped abruptly; for on board the *Falcon* dinner was the great event of the day, and in its presence even the manuscript had to be laid aside. Before long they were all seated around the dining-table in the sumptuous cabin, prepared to discuss the repast which had been served up by the genius of the French *chef* whom Lord Featherstone had brought with him.[1]

Let us pause here for a moment to take a minuter survey of these four friends. In the first place there was Lord Featherstone himself, young, handsome, languid, good-natured to a fault, with plenty of muscle if he chose to exert it, and plenty of brain if he chose to make use of it—a man who had become weary of the monotony of high life, and, like many of his order, was fond of seeking relief from the *ennui* of prosperity amid the excitements of the sea. Next to him was Dr. Congreve, a middle-aged man, with iron-gray hair, short beard and mustache, short nose, gray eyes, with spectacles, and stoutish body. Next came Noel Oxenden, late of Trinity College, Cambridge, a college friend of Featherstone's—a tall man, with a refined and intellectual face and reserved manner. Finally, there was Otto Melick, a *littérateur*[2] from London, about thirty years of age, with a wiry and muscular frame, and the restless manner of one who lives in a perpetual fidget.

For some time nothing was said; they partook of the repast in silence; but at length it became evident that they were thinking of the mysterious manuscript. Featherstone was the first to speak.

"A deuced queer sort of thing this, too," said he, "this manuscript. I can't quite make it out. Who ever dreamed of people living at the South Pole—and in a warm climate, too? Then it seems deuced odd, too, that we should pick up this copper cylinder with the manuscript. I hardly know what to think about it."

Melick smiled. "Why, it isn't much to see through," said he.

"See through what?" said the doctor, hastily, pricking up his ears at this, and peering keenly at Melick through his spectacles.

---

1 This French chef makes an appearance in the background of Gilbert Gaul's illustration seen in Illustration 11. Like meat-eating, class issues like leisure and servants are themes in the frame narration that provide implicit, and often ironic, commentary on issues More encounters in Kosekin society.

2 "A literary man, a writer of literary or critical works" (*OED*).

"Why, the manuscript, of course."

"Well," said the doctor, "what is it that you see? What do you make out of it?"

"Why, anyone can see," said Melick, "that it's a transparent hoax,[1] that's all. You don't mean to say, I hope, that you really regard it in any other light?"

"A transparent hoax!" repeated the doctor. "Will you please state why you regard it in that light?"

"Certainly," said Melick. "Some fellow wanted to get up a sensation novel[2] and introduce it to the world with a great flourish of trumpets, and so he has taken this way of going about it. You see, he has counted on its being picked up, and perhaps published. After this he would come forward and own the authorship."[3]

"And what good would that do?" asked the doctor, mildly. "He couldn't prove the authorship, and he couldn't get the copyright."

"Oh, of course not; but he would gain notoriety, and that would give him a great sale for his next effort."

The doctor smiled. "See here, Melick," said he, "you've a very vivid imagination, my dear fellow; but come, let us discuss this for a little while in a common-sense way. Now, how long should you suppose that this manuscript has been afloat?"

"Oh, a few months or so," said Melick.

"A few months!" said the doctor. "A few years, you mean. Why, man, there are successive layers of barnacles on that copper cylinder which show a submersion of at least three years, perhaps more."[4]

"By Jove! yes," remarked Featherstone. "Your sensation novelist must have been a lunatic if he chose that way of publishing a book."

---

1 For a comparison with the hoax theme in Poe, see Appendix E2a.

2 Increasingly popular from the 1860s forward, so-called "sensation novels" involve shocking subject matter in a more normalized social setting than Gothic novels. They were often the focus of controversy, as is the case with Ellen Wood's *East Lynne* (1861), and used techniques designed to heighten suspense, like Wilkie Collins's cliffhangers. Despite their popularity, the term was usually used in a negative manner. For example, considering the sensation novel "decidedly inferior," an 1868 article in *The British Controversialist and Literary Magazine* defines the genre as characterized by "startling dialogue and thrilling incident" that aim "to convulse the soul of the reader for the sake of doing so" (49).

3 A similar, albeit more convoluted, scheme is the basis of Poe's *The Narrative of Arthur Gordon Pym*. See Appendix E2.

4 It seems to have been in the ocean for about five years: More writes the manuscript in 1845 and they find the cylinder in 1850.

"Then, again," continued the doctor, "how did it get here?"

"Oh, easily enough," answered Melick. "The ocean currents brought it."

"The ocean currents!" repeated the doctor. "That's a very vague expression. What do you mean? Of course it has been brought here by the ocean currents."

"Why, if it were thrown off the coast of England it would be carried away, in the ordinary course of things, and might make the tour of the world."

"The ocean currents," said the doctor, "have undoubtedly brought this to us. Of that I shall have more to say presently; but just now, in reference to your notion of a sensation novelist, and an English origin, let me ask your opinion of the material on which it is written. Did you ever see anything like it before? Is it paper?"

"No," said Melick; "it is evidently some vegetable substance. No doubt the writer has had it prepared for this very purpose, so as to make it look natural."

"Do you know what it is?" asked the doctor.

"No."

"Then I'll tell you: it's papyrus."

"Papyrus?"

"Yes, actual papyrus. You can find but little of that in existence at the present day. It is only to be found here and there in museums. I know it perfectly well, however, and saw what it was at the first glance. Now, I hold that a sensation novelist would never have thought of papyrus. If he didn't wish to use paper, he could have found a dozen other things. I don't see how he could have found anyone able to prepare such a substance as this for writing. It must have come from a country where it is actually in use. Now, mark you, the papyrus-plant may still be found growing wild on the banks of the upper Nile, and also in Sicily, and it is made use of for ropes and other things of that sort. But as to making writing material out of it, that is hardly possible, for the art is lost.[1] The ancient process was very elaborate, and this manuscript is written on leaves which resembled in a marvellous manner those of the Egyptian papyrus books. There are two rolls at Marseilles which I have seen and examined, and they are identical with this. Now these papyrus leaves indicate much mechanical skill, and have a professional look. They seem like the work of an experienced manufacturer."

1 There is a detailed explanation of how papyrus is made in Chapter 7 of Sir J. Gardner Wilkinson's *A Popular Account of the Ancient Egyptians* (1854).

"I don't see," said Melick, obstinately, "why one shouldn't get papyrus now and have it made up into writing material."

"Oh, that's out of the question," said the doctor. "How could it ever enter into anyone's head? How could your mere sensation-monger procure the raw material? That of itself would be a work of immense difficulty. How could he get it made up? That would be impossible. But, apart from this, just consider the strong internal evidence that there is as to the authenticity of the manuscript. Now, in the first place, there is the description of Desolation Island,[1] which is perfectly accurate. But it is on his narrative beyond this that I lay chief stress. I can prove that the statements here are corroborated by those of Captain Ross in his account of that great voyage from which he returned not very long ago."[2]

The doctor, who had been talking with much enthusiasm, paused here to take breath, and then went on:

"I happen to know all about that voyage, for I read a full report of it just before we started, and you can see for yourselves whether this manuscript is credible or not.

"Captain James Clarke Ross was sent forth on his expedition in 1839. On January 1, 1841, he passed the antarctic circle in 178° east longitude. On the 11th he discovered land in 70° 41′ south latitude, 172° 36′ east longitude. He found that the land was a continuous coast, trending southward, and rising to peaks of ten thousand feet in height, all covered with ice and snow. On the 12th he landed and took possession in the name of the Queen. After this he continued his course as far as 78° 4′ south latitude, tracing a coast-line of six hundred miles. Observe, now, how all this coincides with More's narrative. Well, I now come to the crowning statement. In 77° 32′ south latitude, 167° east longitude, he came in sight of two enormous volcanoes over twelve thousand feet in height. One of these was in an active state of eruption. To this he gave the name of Mount Erebus. The other was quiet; it was of somewhat less height, and he gave it the name of Mount Terror. Mark, now, how wonderfully all this resembles More's account. Well, just here his progress was arrested by a barrier which presented a perpendicular wall of over a hundred and fifty feet in height, along which he coasted for some distance. On the following year he penetrated six miles farther south, namely, 78° 11′

1 Kerguelen Island, located at latitude 49° 20′ S, longitude 70 ° 20′ E, is mentioned in Chapter 2.

2 See Appendix A3 for excerpts from those parts of Captain Ross's narrative described by the doctor below.

south latitude, 161° 27′ west longitude. At this point he was again stopped by the impassable cliffs, which arose here like an eternal barrier, while beyond them he saw a long line of lofty mountains covered with ice and snow."[1]

"Did you hear the result of the American expedition?" asked Melick.

"Yes," replied the doctor. "Wilkes[2] pretends to have found a continent, but his account of it makes it quite evident to my mind that he saw nothing but ice. I believe that Wilkes's antarctic continent will some day be penetrated by ships, which will sail for hundreds of miles farther south. All that is wanted is a favorable season. But mark the coincidence between Ross's report and More's manuscript. This must have been written at least three years ago, and the writer could not have known anything about Ross's discoveries. Above all, he could not have thought of those two volcanoes unless he had seen them."

"But these volcanoes mentioned by More are not the Erebus and Terror, are they?" said Lord Featherstone.

"Of course not; they are on the other side of the world."

"The whole story," said Melick, "may have been written by one of Ross's men and thrown overboard. If I'd been on that expedition I should probably have written it to beguile the time."

"Oh yes," said the doctor; "and you would also have manufactured the papyrus and the copper cylinder on board to beguile the time."

"I dare say the writer picked up that papyrus and the copper cylinder in China or Japan, and made use of it in this way."

"Where do you make out the position of More's volcanoes?" asked Featherstone.

"It is difficult to make it out accurately," said the doctor. "More gives no data. In fact he had none to give. He couldn't take any observations."

"The fact is," said Melick, "it's not a sailor's yarn at all. No sailor would ever express himself in that way. That's what struck me

---

1 The doctor rationalizes More's account in terms of the limits of current exploration.

2 The United States Exploring Expedition, led by Charles Wilkes (1798-1877), took place between 1838 and 1842 and included two attempts (February-March 1839 and January-February 1840) to reach the South Pole. It is during the second attempt that Wilkes believed he had discovered sufficient evidence of an Antarctic continent. See Appendix A2 for excerpts from Wilkes's exploration narrative.

from the first. It has the ring of a confounded sensation-monger all through."

The doctor elevated his eyebrows, but took no notice of this.

"You see," he continued, addressing himself to the others, "Desolation Island is in 50° south latitude and 70° east longitude. As I make out, More's course led him over about ten degrees of longitude in a southwest course. That course depended altogether upon the ocean currents. Now there is a great antarctic drift-current, which flows round the Cape of Good Hope and divides there, one-half flowing past the east coast of Africa and the other setting across the Indian Ocean. Then it unites with a current which flows round the south of Van Diemen's Land, which also divides, and the southernmost current is supposed to cross the Pacific until it strikes Cape Horn,[1] around which it flows, dividing as before. Now my theory is, that south of Desolation Island—I don't know how far—there is a great current setting toward the South Pole, and running southwest through degrees of longitude 60°, 50°, 40°, 30°, 20°, 10°, east of Greenwich; and finally sweeping on, it would reach More's volcanoes at a point which I should judge to be about 80° south latitude and 10° west longitude. There it passes between the volcanoes and bursts through the vast mountain barrier by a subterranean way, which has been formed for it in past ages by some primeval convulsion of nature. After this it probably sweeps around the great South Polar ocean, and emerges at the opposite side, not far from the volcanoes Erebus and Terror."

[TO BE CONTINUED.]

---

1 On Tierra del Fuego, Chile, Cape Horn is the southernmost point of South America.

PART 6 (11 FEBRUARY, 1888)

CHAPTER VII.—(*Continued.*)
SCIENTIFIC THEORIES AND SCEPTICISM.

HERE the doctor paused, and looked around with some self-complacency.

"Oh," said Melick, "if you take that tone, you have us all at your mercy. I know no more about the geography of the antarctic circle than I do of the moon. I simply criticise from a literary point of view, and I don't like his underground cavern with the stream running through it. It sounds like one of the voyages of Sinbad the Sailor.[1] Nor do I like his description; he evidently is writing for effect. Besides, his style is vicious; it is too stilted. Finally, he has recourse to the stale device of a sea-serpent."

"A sea-serpent!" repeated the doctor. "Well, for my part I feel by no means inclined to sneer at a sea-serpent. Its existence cannot be proved, yet it cannot be pooh-poohed. Every school-boy knows that the waters of the sea were once filled with monsters more tremendous than the greatest sea-serpent that has ever been imagined. The plesiosaurus,[2] with its snake-like head, if it existed now, would be called a sea-serpent. Some of these so-called fossil animals may have their representatives still living in the remoter parts of the world. Think of the recently discovered ornithorhynchus[3] of Australia!"

---

1 An ancient Middle Eastern story cycle in which a sailor from Basrah has seven fantastic voyages.

2 A marine reptile that lived during the Jurassic period (Liassic epoch: 176-200 million years ago), the plesiosaurus, which reaches a length of about five meters, is distinguished by its elongated neck with crocodile-like head, stocky body with four paddle-like limbs, and short tail. De Mille's description of the plesiosaurus, here and later, is based on Richard Owen's explanation, in *Geology and the Inhabitants of the Ancient World* (1854), of the life-sized reconstruction of a plesiosaurus discovered in England during the 1820s (see Appendix B1, plesiosaurus). Notably, Georges Cuvier called the plesiosaurus the "most monstrous" of the ancient reptiles.

3 Native to Australia, the egg-laying, duck-billed, beaver-tailed Platypus (*Ornithorhynchus anatinus*) was suspected of being a hoax when it was discovered in 1798. Here, the doctor is citing its radical hybridity as a precedent for the survival of species thought to be extinct.

"If you please, I'd really much rather not," said Melick with a gesture of despair. "I haven't the honor of the gentleman's acquaintance."

"Well, what do you think of his notice of the sun, and the long light, and his low position on the horizon?"

"Oh, that's all right," said Melick. "Anyone who chose to get up this thing would of course read up about the polar day, and all that. Everyone knows that at the poles there is a six-months' day, followed by a six-months' night."

"You are a determined sceptic," said the doctor.

"How is it about the polar day?" asked Featherstone.

"Well," said the doctor, "at the poles themselves there is one day of six months, during which the sun never sets, and one night of six months, during which he never rises. In the spaces between the polar circles the quantities of the continuous day and continuous night vary in accordance with the distance from the pole. At the north point of Nova Zembla,[1] 75° north latitude, there is uninterrupted light from May 1st to August 12th, and uninterrupted darkness from November 8th to February 9th. At the arctic circle at the summer solstice the day is twenty-four hours long. At the antarctic circle at the same time the night is twenty-four hours long."

Upon this Melick filled the doctor's wine-glass with a great deal of ceremony.

"After all those statistics," he said, "you must feel rather dry. You should take a drink before venturing any further."

The doctor made no reply, but raised the glass to his lips and swallowed the wine in an abstracted way.

"The thing that struck me most," said Oxenden, "in all that has been read thus far, is the flatness of the South Pole, and the peculiar effect which this produces on the landscape."

"I must say," added Melick, "that the writer has got hold of a very good idea there, and has taken care to put it forward in a very prominent fashion."

"What is the difference," asked Oxenden, "between the two diameters of the earth, the polar and the equatorial? Is it known?"

"By Jove!" said Featherstone, "that's the very question I was going to ask. I've always heard that the earth is flattened at the poles, but never knew how much. Is there any way by which people can find out?"

---

1 Novaya Zemlya (known in English as Nova Zembla) is a Russian archipelago in the Arctic Ocean (74° N, 56° E).

The doctor drew a long breath, and beamed upon the company with a benevolent smile.

"Oh yes," said he; "I can answer that question, if you care to know, and won't feel bored."

"Answer it, then, my dear fellow, by all means," said Featherstone, in his most languid tone.

"There are two ways," said the doctor, "by which the polar compression of the earth has been found out. One is by the measurement of arcs on the earth's surface; the other is by experiments with pendulums or weights with regard to the earth's gravity at different places. The former of these methods is, perhaps, the more satisfactory. Measurements of arcs have been made on a very extensive scale in different parts of the world—in England, France, Lapland, Peru, and India. Mr. Ivory,[1] who devoted himself for years to an exhaustive examination of the subject, has deduced that the equatorial radius of the earth is over 3962 miles, and the polar radius over 3949 miles.[2] This makes the depression at either pole upward of thirteen miles. A depression of over thirteen miles, as you must plainly see, should produce strange results in the scenery at the poles. Of course, if there are mountains, no difference would be noticed between this and any other part of the earth's surface; but if there is water, why, we ought to expect some such state of things as More describes. The gravitation test has also been tried, with very nearly the same result. The surface of the earth at the equator being farthest from the centre of gravity, indicates the least weight in bodies; but at the poles, where the surface is nearest the centre of gravity, there must be the greatest weight. It is found, in fact, that the weight of bodies increases in passing from the equator to the poles. By experiments made in this way the polar compression is ascertained to be the same as I have mentioned."

---

1 Sir James Ivory (1765-1852) was a Scottish mathematician whose writings on geometry and astronomy were published in the *Philosophical Transactions of the Royal Society* and *Encyclopedia Britannica*.

2 This is a general consensus in scientific writings of the time. For example, in the eighteenth century, William Guthrie and James Ferguson's *A New Geographical, Historical, and Commercial Grammar* (1798) noted the following: "Sir Isaac [Newton] demonstrated from mathematical principles, that the earth was an *oblate spheroid*, or that it was flatted at the poles, and jutted out towards the equator, so that a line, drawn through the centre of the earth, and passing through the poles, which is called a diameter, would not be so long as a line drawn through the same centre and passing through the east and west points" (11).

"What effect would this have on the climate at the poles?" asked Oxenden.

"That's a complicated question," said the doctor. "In answer to that we must leave ascertained facts and trust to theories, unless, indeed, we accept as valid the statements of this remarkable manuscript. For my own part, I see no reason why it should not be as More says. Remember, this polar world is thirteen miles nearer to the centre of the earth. Whether this should affect the climate or not, depends upon the nature of the earth's interior. That interior, according to the popular theory of the present day, is a mass of fire. This theory affirms that the earth was once a red-hot mass, which has cooled down; but the cooling process has only taken place on the surface, leaving the interior still a molten mass of matter in a state of intense heat and combustion. At the poles the surface is thus thirteen miles nearer to these tremendous fires. Of course it may be supposed that the earth's crust is of about equal thickness on all parts; yet still, even if this be so, thirteen miles ought to make some difference. Now at the North Pole there seem to be causes at work to counterbalance the effect of the internal heat, chiefly in the enormous accumulation of polar ice which probably hems it in on every side; and though many believe in an open polar sea of warm water at the North Pole, yet still the effect of vast ice-masses and of cold submarine currents must be to render the climate severe. But at the South Pole it is different. The observations of Ross and of More show us that there is a chain of mountains of immense height, which seem to encircle the pole. If this be so, and I see no reason to disbelieve it, then the ice of the outer seas must be kept away altogether from that strange inner sea of which More speaks. Ross saw the volcanoes Erebus and Terror; More saw two others. How many more there may be it is impossible to say; but all this shows that the effect of the earth's internal fires is very manifest in that region, and More has penetrated to a secluded world, which lies apart by itself, free from the influence of ice-masses, left to feel the effect of the internal fires, and possessing what is virtually a tropical climate."

"Well," said Melick, "there is no theory, however wild and fantastic, which some man of science will not be ready to support and to fortify by endless arguments, all of the most plausible kind. For my own part, I still believe More and his south polar world to be no more authentic than Sinbad the Sailor."

But the others evidently sympathized with the doctor's view, and regarded Melick as carrying his scepticism to an absurd excess.

"How large do you suppose this south polar ocean to be?" asked Featherstone.

"It is impossible to answer that question exactly," said the doctor. "It may be, as More hints, a thousand miles in extent, or only five hundred, or two hundred. For my own part, however, I feel like taking More's statements at their utmost value; and the idea that I have gathered from his narrative is that of a vast sea like the Mediterranean, surrounded by impassable mountains, by great and fertile countries, peopled with an immense variety of animals, with a fauna and flora quite unlike those of the rest of the world; and, above all, with great nations possessing a rare and unique civilization, and belonging to a race altogether different from any of the known races of men."

"Well," said Melick, "that at least is the idea which the writer of the manuscript tries to convey."

By this time they had finished dinner.

"And now," said Featherstone, "let's have some more of the manuscript. Melick is tired of it, I dare say. I would relieve him, but I'm an infernally bad reader. Doctor, what do you say? Will you read the next instalment?"

"With all my heart," said the doctor, briskly.

"Very well, then," said Featherstone; "we will all be your attentive hearers."

And now the doctor took up the manuscript and began to read.

CHAPTER VIII. THE CAVE-DWELLERS.

THE cavern into which the chief led me was very spacious, but had no light except that which entered through the portal. It was with difficulty that I could see anything, but I found that there were many people here moving about, all as intent upon their own pursuits as those which one encounters in the streets of our cities. As we went on further the darkness increased, until at last I lost sight of the chief altogether, and he had to come back and lead me. After going a little farther we came to a long, broad passageway like a subterranean street, about twenty feet in width, and as many in height. Here there were discernible a few twinkling lamps, which served to make the darkness less intense and enabled me to see the shadowy figures around. These were numerous, and all seemed busy, though what their occupation might be I could not guess. I was amazed at the extent of these caverns, and at the multitude of the people. I saw also that from the nature of their eyes the sunlight distressed them, and in this cavern gloom they found their most congenial dwelling-place. From what I had thus far seen, this extraordinary people shrank from the sunlight; and when they had to move abroad they passed over roads which were darkened as much as possible by the deep shadows of mighty ferns, while for the most part they remained in dark caverns, in which they lived and moved and had their being.[1] It was a puzzle to me whether the weakness of their eyes had caused this dislike of light, or the habit of cave-dwelling had caused this weakness of eyes. Here, in this darkness, where there was but a faint twinkle from the feeble lamps, their eyes seemed to serve them as well as mine did in the outer light of day; and the chief, who outside had moved with an uncertain step, and had blinked painfully at objects with his eyes almost closed, now appeared to be in his proper element; and while I hesitated like a blind man and groped along with a faltering step, he guided me, and seemed to see everything with perfect vision.

At length we stopped, and the chief raised up a thick, heavy mat which hung like an unwieldly curtain in front of a doorway. This the chief lifted. At once a blaze of light burst forth, gleaming into the dark, and appearing to blind him. His eyes closed. He held up the veil for me to pass through. I did so. He followed, and then groped his way slowly along, while I accompanied and assisted him.

I now found myself in a large grotto with an arched roof, from which was suspended an enormous lamp, either golden or gilded. All around were numerous lamps. The walls were adorned with rich hangings; couches were here, with soft cushions, and divans and ottomans; soft mats were on the floor, and everything gave indications of luxury and wealth. Other doors, covered with overhanging mats, seemed to lead out of this grotto. To one of these the chief walked, and raising the mat he led the way into another grotto like the last, with the same bright lights and the same adornments, but of smaller size. Here I saw someone who at once took up all my attention.

It was a young maiden. Her face and form, but especially her eyes, showed her to be of quite a different race from these others. To me she was of medium height, yet she was taller than any of the people here that I had hitherto seen. Her complexion was much lighter; her hair was dark, luxuriant, and wavy, and arranged in a coiffure secured with a golden band. Her features were of a

1 See Plato's Allegory of the Cave in Appendix D1.

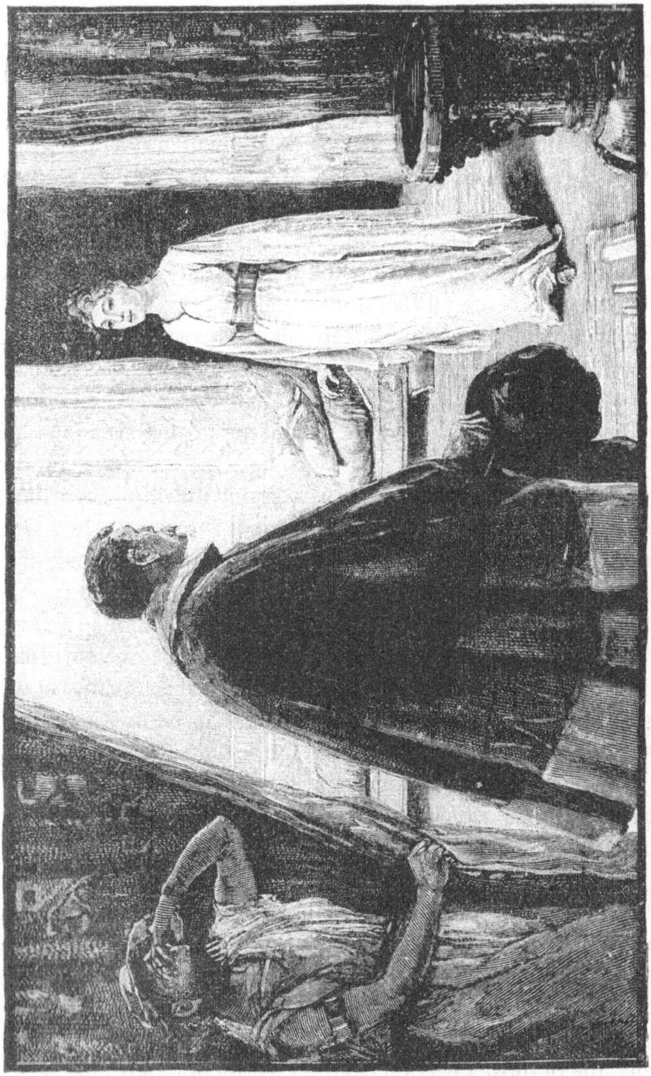

Illustration 6: "Her face and form, but especially her eyes, showed her to be of quite a different race from these others."

different cast from those of the people here, for they were regular in outline and of exquisite beauty; her nose was straight; she had a short upper lip, arched eyebrows finely pencilled, thin lips, and a well-rounded chin. But the chief contrast was in her eyes. These were large, dark, liquid, with long lashes, and with a splendid glow in their lustrous depths. She stood looking at me with her face full of amazement; and as I caught the gaze of her glorious eyes I rejoiced that I had at last found one who lived in the light and loved it—one who did not blink like a bat, but looked me full in the face, and allowed me to see all her soul revealed. The chief, who still was pained by the glare of light, kept his eyes covered, and said a few hasty words to the maiden. After this he hurried away, leaving me there.

The maiden stood for a moment looking at me. As the chief spoke to her a change came over her face. She looked at me in silence, with an expression of sad and mournful interest, which seemed to increase every moment. At length she approached and said something in the same strange language which the chief had used. I shook my head and replied in English, whereupon she shook her head with a look of perplexity. Then, anxious to conciliate her, I held out my hand. She looked at it in some surprise. Upon this I took her hand, and pressed it to my lips, feeling, however, somewhat doubtful as to the way in which she might receive such an advance. To my great delight she accepted it in a friendly spirit, and seemed to consider it my foreign fashion of showing friendship and respect. She smiled and nodded, and pointed to my gun, which thus far I had carried in my hand. I smiled and laid it down. Then she pointed to a seat. I sat down, and then she seated herself close by me, and we looked at each other in mutual wonder and mutual inquiry.

I was full of amazement at thus meeting with so exquisite a being, and lost myself in conjectures as to her race, her office, and her position here. Who was she, or what? She was unlike the others, and reminded me of those Oriental beauties whose portraits I had seen in annuals and illustrated books.[1] Her costume was in keeping with such a character. She wore a long tunic that reached from the neck

---

1 Paintings and drawings of odalisques, female slaves who attended concubines in the living quarters of Ottoman harems, were common in the nineteenth century and recall Oxenden's fascination with Moorish seraglios in Chapter 1. Natale Schiavoni's *Odalisque* (1840) or Jean-Auguste-Dominique Ingres and Jean-Paul Flandrin's *Odalisque with Slave* (1841) are vivid examples contemporary with More. Friedrich Amerling's *The Young Eastern Woman* (1838), in which the model is clearly a European

to the ground, secured at the waist with a golden girdle; the sleeves were long and loose; over this she had a long mantle; on her feet were light slippers, white and glistening. All about her, in her room and in her costume, spoke of light and splendor and luxury. To these others who shrank so from the light she could not be related in any way. The respect with which she was treated by the chief, the peculiar splendor of her apartments, seemed to indicate some high rank. Was she, then, the queen of the land? Was she a princess? I could not tell. At any rate, whatever she was, she seemed anxious to show me the utmost attention. Her manner was full of dignity and sweet graciousness, and she appeared particularly anxious to make herself understood. At first she spoke in a language that sounded like that of the chief, and was full of gutturals and broad vowels; afterward she spoke in another that was far more euphonious. I, on the other hand spoke in English and in French; but of course I was as unintelligible to her as she was to me.

Language was, therefore, of no use. It was necessary to go back to first principles and make use of signs, or try to gain the most elementary words of her language; so first of all I pointed to her, and tried to indicate that I wanted to know her name. She caught my meaning at once, and pointing to herself, she looked fixedly at me and said,

"Almah, Almah!"

I repeated these words after her, saying, "Almah, Almah!" She smiled and nodded, and then pointed to me with a look of inquiry that plainly asked for my name. I said, "Adam More." She repeated this, and it sounded like "A-tam-or." But as she spoke this slowly her smile died away. She looked anxious and troubled, and once more that expression of wondering sadness came over her face. She repeated my name over and over in this way with a mournful intonation that thrilled through me, and excited forebodings of evil. "Atamor, Atamor!" And always after that she called me "Atam-or."

But now she sat for some time, looking at me with a face full of pity and distress. At this I was greatly astonished; for but a moment before she had been full of smiles, and it was as though something in my name had excited sorrowful thoughts. Yet how could that be, since she could never by any possibility have heard my name before? The beautiful Almah seemed to be not altogether happy, or why should she be so quick to sadness? There was a mystery about all this which was quite unaccountable.

---

wearing Turkish dress, exemplifies the type of Orientalist fantasy reflected by More's comment about Almah.

It was a singular situation, and one which excited within me feelings of unutterable delight. This light and splendor, this warmth and peace—what a contrast it offered to the scenes through which I had but lately passed! Those scenes of horror, of ice and snow, of storm and tempest, of cold and hunger, of riven cliff and furious ocean stream, and, above all, that crowning agony in the bleak iron-land of the cannibals—from all these I had escaped. I had been drawn down under the earth to experience the terrors of that unspeakable passage, and had at last emerged to light and life, to joy and hope. In this grotto I had found the culmination of all happiness. It was like a fairy realm; and here was one whose very look was enough to inspire the most despairing soul with hope and peace and happiness. The only thing that was now left to trouble me was this mournful face of Almah. Why did she look at me with such sad interest and such melancholy meaning? Did she know of any evil fate in store for me? Yet how could there be any evil fate to be feared from people who had received me with such unparalleled generosity? No, it could not be; so I resolved to try to bring back again the smile that had faded out of her face.

I pointed to her, and said, "Almah."

She said, "Atam-or."

And the smile did not come back, but the sadness remained in her face.

My eager desire now was to learn her language, and I resolved at once to acquire as many words and phrases as possible. I began by asking the names of things, such as "seat," "table," "mat," "coat," "hat," "shoe," "lamp," "floor," "wall," and all the common objects around. She gave all the names, and soon became so deeply interested that her sadness departed, and the smile came back once more. For my own part, I was always rather quick at learning languages. I had a correct ear and a retentive memory; in my wanderings round the world I had picked up a smattering of many languages, such as French, Italian, Spanish, Arabic, German, Hindostanee, and a few others. The words which I learned from Almah had a remote resemblance to Arabic; and, in fact, my knowledge of Arabic was actually of some assistance, though how it was that these people should have a language with that resemblance was certainly a mystery, and I did not try to solve it.[1] The beautiful Almah soon grew immensely interested in my efforts to

1 This linguistic cue is one of many that associate the Kosekin with the Middle East.

learn, and also in the English words which I gave when I pointed to any object.

Thus I pointed to myself, and said, "Man," then pointing to her, I said, "Woman." She laughed, and pointing to me said, "Iz," and pointing to herself said, "Izza." Then I pointed to the row of lights, and said, "Light"; she did the same, and said, "Or." Then her face grew mournful, and she pointed to me, saying, "Atam-or." It struck me then that there was some chance resemblance between "or," the word meaning "light," and one of the syllables of my name as she pronounced it, and that this might cause her sadness; but as I could make out nothing of this, I dismissed the thought, and went on with my questions. This took up the time, until at length someone appeared who looked like a servant. He said something, whereupon Almah arose and beckoned to me to follow. I did so, and we went to a neighboring apartment, where there was spread a bounteous repast. Here we sat and ate, and Almah told me the names of all the dishes. After dinner we returned to the room.

It was a singular and a delightful position. I was left alone with the beautiful Almah, who herself showed the utmost graciousness and the kindest interest in me. I could not understand it, nor did I try to; it was enough that I had such a happy lot. For hours we thus were together, and I learned many words. To insure remembrance, I wrote them down in my memorandum-book with a pencil, and both of these were regarded by Almah with the greatest curiosity. She felt the paper, inspected it, touched it with her tongue, and seemed to admire it greatly; but the pencil excited still greater admiration. I signed to her to write in the book. She did so, but the characters were quite unlike anything that I had ever seen. They were not joined like our writing and like Arabic letters, but were separate like our printed type,[1] and were formed in an irregular manner. She then showed me a book made of a strange substance. It was filled with characters like those which she had just written. The leaves were not at all like paper, but seemed like some vegetable product, such as the leaves of a plant or the bark of a tree. They were very thin, very smooth, all cut into regular size, and fastened together by means of rings. This manuscript is written upon the same material.[2] I afterward found that it was universally used here, and was made of a reed that grows in marshes.

---

1 That the writing is in a non-cursive script is probably a significant clue to the origin of the Kosekin.

2 More thus confirms the doctor's speculation at the end of Chapter 1 that the manuscript is written on papyrus.

Here in these vast caverns there was no way by which I could tell the progress of time, but Almah had her own way of finding out when the hours of wakeful life were over. She arose and said, "Salonla." This I afterward found out to be the common salutation of the country. I said it after her. She then left me. Shortly afterward a servant appeared, who took me to a room, which I understood to be mine. Here I found everything that I could wish, either for comfort or luxury; and as I felt fatigue, I flung myself upon the soft bed of down, and soon was sound asleep.

I slept for a long time. When I awoke I heard sounds in the distance, and knew that people were moving. Here in these caverns there was no difference between day and night, but, by modes of which I was ignorant, a regular succession was observed of waking times and sleeping times.

[TO BE CONTINUED.]

PART 7 (18 FEBRUARY, 1888)

CHAPTER IX.
THE CAVERN OF THE DEAD.

ON going forth into the outer grotto I saw the table spread with a sumptuous repast, and the apartment in a blaze of light. Almah was not here; and though some servants made signs for me to eat, yet I could not until I should see whether she was coming or not. I had to wait for a long time, however; and while I was waiting the chief entered, shading his eyes with his hand from the painful light. He bowed low with the most profound courtesy, saying, "Salonla," to which I responded in the same way. He seemed much pleased at this, and made a few remarks, which I did not understand; whereupon, anxious to lose no time in learning the language, I repeated to him all the words I knew, and asked after others. I pointed to him and asked his name. He said, "Kohen." This, however, I afterward found was not a name, but a title. The "Kohen" did not remain long, for the light was painful. After his departure I was alone for some time, and at length Almah made her appearance. I sprang to meet her, full of joy, and took her hand in both of mine and pressed it warmly. She smiled, and appeared quite free from the melancholy of the previous day.

We ate our breakfast together, after which we went out into the world of light, groping our way along through the dark passages amid the busy crowd. Almah could see better than I in the darkness; but she was far from seeing well, and did not move with that easy step and perfect certainty which all the others showed. Like me, she was a child of light, and the darkness was distressing to her. As we went on we were seen by all, but were apparently not considered prisoners. On the contrary, all looked at us with the deepest respect, and bowed low or moved aside, and occasionally made little offerings of fruit or flowers to one or the other of us. It seemed to me that we were treated with equal distinction; and if Almah was their queen, I, their guest, was regarded with equal honor. Whatever her rank might be, however, she was to all appearance the absolute mistress of her own actions, and moved about among all these people with the independence and dignity of some personage of exalted rank.

At length we emerged into the open air. Here the contrast to the cavern gloom inside gave to the outer world unusual brightness and splendor, so that even under the heavy overarching tree-ferns,[1] which had seemed so dark when I was here before, it now appeared light and cheerful. Almah turned to the right, and we walked along the terrace. But few people were visible. They shrank from the light, and kept themselves in the caverns. Then after a few steps we came to the base of a tall half-pyramid, the summit of which was above the tops of the trees. I pointed to this, as though I wished to go up. Almah hesitated for a moment, and seemed to shrink back, but at length, overcoming her reluctance, began the ascent. A flight of stone steps led up. On reaching the top, I found it about thirty feet long by fifteen wide, with a high stone table in the middle. At that moment, however, I scarce noticed the pyramid summit, and I only describe it now because I was fated before long to see it with different feelings. What I then noticed was the vast and wondrous display of all the glories of nature that burst at once upon my view. There was that same boundless sea, rising up high toward the horizon, as I had seen it before, and suggesting infinite extent. There were the blue waters breaking into foam, the ships traversing the deep, the far-encircling shores green in vegetation, the high rampart of ice-bound mountains that shut in the land, making it a world by itself. There was the sun, low on the horizon, which it traversed on its long orbit, lighting up all these scenes till the six months' day should end and the six months' night begin.

For a long time I stood feasting my eyes upon all this splendor, and at length turned to see whether Almah shared my feelings. One look was enough. She stood absorbed in the scene, as though she were drinking in deep draughts of all this matchless beauty. I felt amazed at this; I saw how different she seemed from the others, and could not account for it. But as yet I knew too little of the language to question her, and could only hope for a future explanation when I had learned more.

We descended at length and walked along the terrace and up and down the side streets. All were the same as I had noticed before—terraced streets, with caverns on one side and massive stone structures on the other. I saw deep channels, which were used as drains to carry down mountain torrents. I did not see all at this first walk, but I inspected the whole city in many subsequent walks until its outlines were all familiar. I found it about a mile long and about half a mile wide, constructed in a series of terraces, which rose one above another in a hollow of the mountains round

1 See Appendix B3 for an introduction to Carboniferous era flora and pictures of tree-ferns from Louis Figuier's *The World Before the Deluge* (1866).

a harbor of the sea. On my walks I met with but few people on the streets, and they all seemed troubled with the light. I saw also occasionally some more of those great birds, the name of which I learned from Almah; it was "opkuk."

For some time my life went on most delightfully. I found myself surrounded with every comfort and luxury. Almah was my constant associate, and all around regarded us with the profoundest respect. The people were the mildest, most gentle, and most generous that I had ever seen. The Kohen seemed to pass most of his time in making new contrivances for my happiness. This strange people, in their dealings with me and with one another, seemed animated by a universal desire to do kindly acts; and the only possible objection against them was their singular love of darkness.

My freedom was absolute. No one watched me. Almah and I could go where we chose. So far as I could perceive, we were quite at liberty, if we wished, to take a boat and escape over the sea. It seemed also quite likely that if we had ordered out a galley and a gang of oarsmen, we should have been supplied with all that we might want in the most cheerful manner. Such a thought, however, was absurd. Flight! Why should I think of flying?

I had long ago lost all idea of time; and here, where it was for the present perpetual day, I was more at a loss than ever. I supposed that it was somewhere in the month of March,[1] but whether at the beginning or the end I could not tell. The people had a regular system of wake-time and sleep-time, by which they ordered their lives; but whether these respective times were longer or shorter than the days and nights at home I could not tell at that time, though I afterward learned all about it. On the whole, I was perfectly content—nay, more, perfectly happy; more so, indeed, than ever in my life, and quite willing to forget home and friends and everything in the society of Almah. While in her company there was always one purpose upon which I was most intent, and that was to master the language. I made rapid progress, and while she was absent I sought out others, especially the Kohen, with whom to practise. The Kohen was always most eager to aid me in every conceivable way or to any conceivable thing; and he had such a gentle manner and showed such generous qualities that I soon learned to regard him with positive affection.

---

1 March of 1844: it must be early March because the equinox in the Antarctic occurs on 21 March, when the sun dips beneath the horizon.

Almah was always absent for several hours after I rose in the morning, and when she made her appearance it was with the face and manner of one who had returned from some unpleasant task. It always took some time for her to regain that cheerfulness which she usually showed. I soon felt a deep curiosity to learn the nature of her employment and office here, and as my knowledge of the language increased I began to question her. My first attempts were vain. She looked at me with indescribable mournfulness and shook her head. This, however, only confirmed me in my suspicions that her duties, whatever they might be, were of a painful nature; so I urged her to tell me, and asked her as well as I could if I might not share them or help her in some way. To all this, however, she only returned sighs and mournful looks for an answer. It seemed to me, from her manner and from the general behavior of the people, that there was no express prohibition on my learning anything, doing anything, or going anywhere; and so, after this, I besought her to let me accompany her some time. But this too she refused. My requests were often made, and as I learned more and more of the language I was able to make them with more earnestness and effect, until at length I succeeded in overcoming her objections.

"It is for your own sake," said she, "that I have refused, Atamor. I do not wish to lessen your happiness. But you must know all soon; and so, if you wish to come with me and see what I have to do, why, you may come the next *jom*."

This meant the next day, *jom* being the division of time corresponding with our day. At this promise I was so full of gratitude that I forgot all about the dark suggestiveness of her words. The next *jom* I arose sooner than usual and went forth. I found Almah waiting for me. She looked troubled, and greeted me with a mournful smile.

"You will find pain in this," said she; "but you wish it, and if you still wish it, why, I will take you with me."

At this I only persisted the more, and so we set forth. We went through the cavern passages. Few people were there; all seemed asleep. Then we went out-of-doors and came into the full blaze of that day which here knew no night, but prolonged itself into months. For a while Almah stood looking forth between the trees to where the bright sunlight sparkled on the sea, and then with a sigh she turned to the left. I followed. On coming to the next portal she went in. I followed, and found myself in a rough cavern, dark and forbidding. Traversing this we came to an inner doorway, closed with a heavy mat. This she raised, and passed through, while I went in after her.

I found myself in a vast cavern, full of dim sparkling lights, which served not to illuminate it, but merely to indicate its enormous extent. Far above rose the vaulted roof, to a height of apparently a hundred feet. Under this there was a lofty half-pyramid with stone steps. All around, as far as I could see in the obscure light, there were niches in the walls, each one containing a figure with a light burning at its feet. I took them for statues. Almah pointed in silence to one of these which was nearest, and I went up close so as to see it.

The first glance that I took made me recoil with horror. It was no statue that I saw in that niche, but a shrivelled human form—a hideous sight. It was dark and dried; it was fixed in a sitting posture, with its hands resting on its knees, and its hollow eyes looking forward. On its head was the mockery of a wreath of flowers, while from its heart there projected the handle and half of the blade of a knife which had been thrust there. What was the meaning of this knife? It seemed to tell of a violent death. Yet the flowers must surely be a mark of honor. A violent death with honor, and the embalmed remains—these things suggested nothing else than the horrid thought of a human sacrifice. I looked away with eager and terrible curiosity. I saw all the niches, hundreds upon hundreds, all filled with these fearful occupants. I turned again with a sinking heart to Almah. Her face was full of anguish.

"This is my duty," said she. "Every *jom* I must come here and crown these victims with fresh flowers."

A feeling of sickening horror overwhelmed me. Almah had spoken these words and stood looking at me with a face of woe. This, then, was that daily task from which she was wont to return in such sadness—an abhorrent task to her, and one to which familiarity had never reconciled her. What was she doing here? What dark fate was it that thus bound this child of light to these children of darkness? or why was she thus compelled to perform a service from which all her nature revolted? I read in her face at this moment a horror equal to my own; and at the sight of her distress my own was lessened, and there arose within me a profound sympathy and a strong desire to do something to alleviate her misery.

"This is no place for you," continued Almah. "Go, and I will soon join you."

"No," said I, using her language after my own broken fashion—"no, I will not go—I will stay, I will help, if you will permit."

She looked at me earnestly, and seemed to see that my resolution was firmly fixed, and that I was not to be dissuaded from it.

"Very well," said she; "if you do stay and help me, it will be a great relief."

With these simple words she proceeded to carry out her work. At the foot of the pyramid there was a heap of wreaths made out of fresh flowers, and these were to be placed by her on the heads of the embalmed corpses.

"This work," said she, "is considered here the highest and most honorable that can be performed. It is given to me out of kindness, and they cannot understand that I can have any other feelings in the performance than those of joy and exultation—here among the dead and in the dark."

I said nothing, but followed and watched her, carrying the wreaths and supplying her. She went to each niche in succession, and after taking the wreath off each corpse she placed a fresh one on, saying a brief formula at each act. By keeping her supplied with wreaths I was able to lighten her task, so much so that whereas it usually occupied her more than two hours, on the present occasion it was finished in less than half an hour. She informed me that those which she crowned were the corpses of men who had been sacrificed during the present season—by season meaning the six months of light; and that though many more were here, yet they wore crowns of gold. At the end of ten years they were removed to public sepulchres. The number of those which had to be crowned by her was about a hundred. Her work was only to crown them, the labor of collecting the flowers and weaving the wreaths and attending to the lamps being performed by others.

I left this place with Almah, sad and depressed. She had not told me why these victims had been sacrificed, nor did I feel inclined to ask. A dark suspicion had come to me that these people, underneath all their amiable ways, concealed thoughts, habits, and motives of a frightful kind; and that beyond all my present brightness and happiness there might be a fate awaiting me too horrible for thought. Yet I did not wish to borrow trouble. What I had seen and heard was quite enough for one occasion. I was anxious, rather, to forget it all. Nor did Almah's words or manner in any way reassure me. She was silent and sad and preoccupied. It was as though she knew the worst, and knowing it, dared not speak; as though there was something more horrible which she dared not reveal. For my part, I feared it so that I dared not ask. It was enough for me just then to know that my mild and self-denying and generous entertainers were addicted to the abhorrent custom of human sacrifices.

Illustration 7: "After taking the wreath off each corpse she placed a fresh one on."

CHAPTER X.
THE SACRED HUNT.

ON that very *jom* the Kohen informed me that they were about to set forth on the "sacred hunt," an event which always occurred toward the end of the season, and he kindly invited me to go. I, eager to find any relief from the horrible thoughts that had taken possession of me, and full of longing for active exertion, at once accepted the invitation. I was delighted to hear Almah say that she too was going; and I learned at the same time that in this strange land the women were as fond of hunting as the men, and that on such occasions their presence was expected.[1]

The sacred hunt was certainly a strange one. I saw that it was to take place on the water; for a great crowd, numbering over a hundred, went down to the harbor and embarked on board a galley, on which there were a hundred others, who served as rowers. The hunters were all armed with long light javelins and short swords. Some of these were offered to me, for as yet no one supposed that my rifle and pistol were instruments of destruction, or anything else than ornaments. My refusal to accept their weapons created some surprise, but with their usual civility they did not press their offers further. It was evident that this hunting expedition was only made in obedience to some hallowed custom; for the light of the sun pained their eyes, and all their movements were made with uncertainty and hesitation. With these a hunt by sunlight is the same as a hunt by night would be with us. There was the same confusion and awkwardness.

The Kohen was in command. At his word the galley started, and the rowers pulled out to sea with long, regular strokes. I was anxious to know what the expedition was aimed at, and what were the animals that we expected to get; but I could not make out Almah's explanations. Her words suggested something of vague terror, vast proportions, and indescribable ferocity; but my ignorance of the language prevented me from learning anything more.

We went along the coast for a few miles, and then came to the mouth of a great river, which seemed to flow from among the mountains. The current was exceedingly swift, and as I looked back it seemed to me that it must be the very stream which had

---

1 This type of gendered role change is common to late nineteenth-century speculative fiction. For example, see Edward Bulwer Lytton's *The Coming Race,* in Appendix E3b, where gendered roles are almost completely reversed.

borne me here into this remote world. I afterward found out that this was so—that this stream emerges from among the mountains, flowing from an unknown source. It was over this that I had been borne in my sleep, after I had emerged from the subterranean darkness, and it was by this current that I had been carried into the open sea. As we crossed the estuary of this river I saw that the shores on either side were low, and covered with the rankest vegetation; giant trees of fern, vast reeds and grasses, all arose here in a dense growth impassable to man. Upon the shallow shores the surf was breaking; and here in the tide I saw objects which I at first supposed to be rocks, but afterward found out to be living things. They looked like alligators, but were far larger than the largest alligators known to us, besides being of far more terrific aspect. Toward these the galley was directed, and I now saw with surprise that these were the objects of the sacred hunt.

Suddenly, as the galley was moving along at half-speed, there arose out of the water a thing that looked like the folds of a giant hairy serpent, which, however, proved to be the long neck of an incredible monster, whose immense body soon afterward appeared above the water. With huge fins he propelled himself toward us; and his head, twenty feet in the air, was poised as though about to attack. The head was like that of an alligator, the open jaws showed a fearful array of sharp teeth, the eyes were fiercely glowing, the long neck was covered with a coarse, shaggy mane, while the top of the body, which was out of the water, was incased in an impenetrable cuirass of bone. Such a monster as this seemed unassailable, especially by men who had no missile weapons, and whose eyes were so dim and weak. I therefore expected that the galley would turn and fly from the attack, for the monster itself seemed as large as our vessel; but there was not the slightest thought of flight. On the contrary, every man was on the alert: some sprang to the bow and stood there, awaiting the first shock; others, amidship, stood waiting for the orders of the Kohen. Meanwhile the monster approached, and at length, with a sweep of his long neck, came down upon the dense crowd at the bows. A dozen frail lances were broken against his horny jaws, a half-dozen wretches were seized and terribly torn by those remorseless jaws. Still none fled. All rushed forward, and with lances, axes, knives, and ropes they sought to destroy the enemy. Numbers of them strove to seize his long neck. In the ardor of the fight the rowers dropped their oars and hurried to the scene, to take part in the struggle. The slaughter was sickening, but not a man quailed. Never had I dreamed of such blind and desperate courage as was now displayed before my horror-stricken eyes. Each sought to outdo the other. They had managed to throw ropes around the monster's neck, by which he was held close to the galley. His fierce movements seemed likely to drag us all down under the water; and his long neck, free from restraint, writhed and twisted among the struggling crowd of fighting men, in the midst of whom was the Kohen, as desperate and as fearless as any.

All this had taken place in a very short space of time, and I had scarce been able to comprehend the full meaning of it all. As for Almah, she stood pale and trembling, with a face of horror. At last it seemed to me that every man of them would be destroyed, and that they were all throwing their lives away to no purpose whatever. Above all, my heart was wrung for the Kohen, who was there in the midst of his people, lifting his frail and puny arm against the monster. I could endure inaction no longer. I had brought my arms with me, as usual; and now, as the monster raised his head, I took aim at his eye and fired. The report rang out in thunder. Almah gave a shriek, and amid the smoke I saw the long, snake-like neck of the monster sweeping about madly among the men. In the water his vast tail was lashing the surface of the sea, and churning it into foam. Here I once more took aim immediately under the fore-fin, where there was no scaly covering. Once more I fired. This time it was with fatal effect; and after one or two convulsive movements the monster, with a low, deep bellow, let his head fall and gasped out his life.

I hurried forward. There lay the frightful head, with its long neck and shaggy mane, while all around was a hideous spectacle. The destruction of life had been awful. Nineteen were dead and twenty-eight were wounded, writhing in every gradation of agony, some horribly mangled. The rest stood staring at me in astonishment, not understanding those peals of thunder that had laid the monster low. There was no terror or awe, however—nothing more than surprise; and the Kohen, whose clothes were torn into shreds and covered with blood, looked at me in bewilderment. I said to him, out of my small stock of words, that the wounded ought at once to be cared for. At this he turned away and made some remarks to his men.

I now stood ready to lend my own services, if needful. I expected to take a part in the tender attentions which were the due of these gallant souls, who had exhibited such matchless valor; these men who thought nothing of life, but flung it away at the command of their chief without dreaming of flight or of hesitation. Thus I stood looking on in an expectant attitude, when there came a moment in which I was simply petrified with horror; for the Kohen drew his knife, stooped over the wounded man nearest him, and then stabbed him to the heart with a mortal wound. The others all proceeded to do the same, and they did it in the coolest and most business-like manner, without any passion, without any feeling of any kind, and, indeed, with a certain air of gratification, as though they were performing some peculiarly high and sacred duty. The mildness and benevolence of their faces seemed actually heightened, and the perpetration of this unutterable atrocity seemed to affect these people in the same way in which the performance of acts of humanity might affect us.

For my own part, I stood for a few moments actually motionless from perplexity and horror: then, with a shriek, I rushed forward as if to prevent it; but I was too late. The unutterable deed was done, and the unfortunate wounded, without an exception, lay dead beside their slain companions. As for myself, I was only regarded with fresh wonder, and they all stood blinking at me with their half-closed eyes. Suddenly the Kohen fell prostrate on his knees before me, and bowing his head handed me his bloody knife.

"Atam-or," said he, "give me also the blessing of darkness and death!"

At these strange words, following such actions, I could say nothing. I was more bewildered than ever, and horror and bewilderment made me dumb. I turned away and went aft to Almah, who had seen it all. She looked at me with an anxious gaze, as if to learn what the effect of all this had been on me. I could not speak a word, but with a vague sense of the necessity of self-preservation I loaded my rifle, and tried in vain to make out what might be the meaning of this union of gentleness and kindness with atrocious cruelty. Meanwhile, the men all went to work upon various tasks. Some secured lines about the monster so as to tow it astern; others busied themselves with the corpses, collecting them and arranging them in rows. At length we returned, towing the monster astern.

I could not speak until I was back again in the lighted rooms and alone with Almah; then I told her, as well as I could, the horror that I felt.

"It was honor to those brave men," said she.

"Honor!" said I. "What! to kill them?"

"Yes," said she; "it is so with these people; with them death is the highest blessing. They all love death and seek after it. To die for another is immortal glory. To kill the wounded was to show that they had died for others. The wounded wished it themselves. You saw how they all sought after death. These people were too generous and kind-hearted to refuse to kill them after they had received wounds."

At this my perplexity grew deeper than ever, for such an explanation as this only served to make the mystery greater.

"Here," said she, "no one understands what it is to fear death. They all love it and long for it; but everyone wishes above all to die for others. This is their highest blessing. To die a natural death in bed is avoided if possible."

All this was incomprehensible.

"Tell me, Almah," I said—"you hate darkness as I do—do you not fear death?"

"I fear it above all things," said Almah. "To me it is the horror of life; it is the chief of terrors."

"So it is with me," said I. "In my country we call death the King of Terrors."

"Here," said Almah, "they call death the Lord of Joy."

Not long after, the Kohen came in, looking as quiet, as gentle, and as amiable as ever. He showed some curiosity about my rifle, which he called a *sepet-ram*, or "rod of thunder." Almah also showed curiosity. I did not care to explain the process of loading it to the Kohen, though Almah had seen me load it in the galley, and I left him to suppose that it was used in some mysterious way. I cautioned him not to handle it carelessly, but found that this caution only made him the more eager to handle it, since the prospect of an accident found an irresistible attraction. I would not let it go out of my own hands, however; and the Kohen, whose self-denial was always most wonderful to me, at once checked his curiosity.

CHAPTER XI.
THE SWAMP MONSTER.

A FEW *jom*s after, I was informed by the Kohen that there was to be another sacred hunt. At first I felt inclined to refuse, but on learning that Almah was going I resolved to go also; for Almah, though generally mistress of her actions, had nevertheless certain duties to perform, and among these was the necessity of accompanying hunting parties. I did not yet understand her position here, nor had I heard from her yet how it was that she was so different from the rest of them. That was all to be learned at a future time. For the present I had to be satisfied with knowing that she belonged to a different nation, who spoke a different language, and that all her thoughts and feelings were totally different from those of the people among whom she was living. She loved the light, she feared death, and she had never been able in the slightest degree to reconcile herself to the habits of these people. This I could readily understand, for to me it seemed as though they lived in opposition to nature itself.

We went out into the daylight, and then I saw a sight which filled me with amazement. I saw a flock of birds larger than even the opkuks. They were called "opmahera." They seemed as tall as giraffes, and their long legs indicated great powers of running. Their wings were very short, and not adapted for flight. They were very tractable, and were harnessed for riding in a peculiar way; lines like reins were fastened to the wings, and the driver, who sat close by the neck, guided the bird in this way. Each bird carried two men, but for Almah and me there was a bird apiece. An iron prod was also taken by each driver as a spur. I did not find out until afterward how to drive. At that time the prospect of so novel a ride was such an exciting one that I forgot everything else. The birds seemed quiet and tractable. I took it for granted that mine was well trained, and would go with the others of his own accord. We all mounted by means of a stone platform which stood by the pyramid, and soon were on our way.

The speed was amazing; the fastest race-horse at home is slow compared with this. It was as swift as an ordinary railway train,[1] if not more so. For some minutes the novelty of my situation took away all other thoughts, and I held the reins in my hands without knowing how to use them. But this mattered not, for the well-trained bird kept on after the others, while Almah on her bird was close behind me. The pace, as I said, was tremendous, yet no easier motion can be imagined. The bird bounded along with immense leaps, with wings outstretched, but its feet touched the ground so lightly that the motion seemed almost equal to flying. We did not confine ourselves to the roads, for the birds were capable of going over any kind of a country in a straight line. On this occasion we passed over wide fields and rocky mountain ridges and deep swamps and sandy wastes at the same speed, until at length we reached a vast forest of dense tree-ferns, where the whole band stopped for a short time, after which we took up a new direction,

1 The first steam locomotive was built in England in 1804. By 1825, the Stockton & Darlington Railroad Company was carrying passengers and commercial goods. By 1844, the speed of an ordinary train was about 60 kph.

moving on more slowly. The forest grew up out of a swamp, which extended as far as the eye could reach from the sea to the mountains. Along the edge of this forest we went for some time, until at length there came a rushing, crackling sound, as of something moving there among the trees, crushing down everything in its progress. We halted, and did not have to wait long; for soon, not far away, there emerged from the thick forest a figure of incredible size and most hideous aspect.

It looked like one of those fabled dragons such as may be seen in pictures, but without wings. It was nearly a hundred feet in length, with a stout body and a long tail, covered all over with impenetrable scales. Its hind-legs were rather longer than its fore-legs, and it moved its huge body with ease and rapidity. Its feet were armed with formidable claws. But its head was most terrific. It was a vast mass of bone, with enormous eyes that glared like fire; its jaws opened to the width of six or eight feet, and were furnished with rows of sharp teeth, while at the extremity of its nose there was a tusk several feet long, like the horn of a rhinoceros, curving backward. All this I took in at the first glance, and the next instant the whole band of hunters, with their usual recklessness, flung themselves upon the monster.

For a short time all was the wildest confusion—an intermingling of birds and men, with the writhing and roaring beast. With his huge claws and his curved horn and his wide jaws he dealt death and destruction all around; yet still the assailants kept at their work. Many leaped down to the ground and rushed close up to the monster, thrusting their lances into the softer and more unprotected parts of his body; while others, guiding their birds with marvellous dexterity, assailed him on all sides. The birds, too, were kept well to their work; nor did they exhibit any fear. It was not until they were wounded that they sought to fly. Still, the contest seemed too unequal. The sacrifice of life was horrible. I saw men and birds literally torn to pieces before my eyes. Nevertheless, the utter fearlessness of the assailants confounded me. In spite of the slaughter, fresh crowds rushed on. They clambered over his back, and strove to drive their lances under his bony cuirass. In the midst of them I saw the Kohen. By some means he had reached the animal's back, and was crawling along, holding by the coarse, shaggy mane. At length he stopped, and with a sudden effort thrust his lance into the monster's eye. The vast beast gave a low and terrible howl; his immense tail went flying all about; in his pain he rolled over and over, crushing underneath him in his awful struggles all who were nearest. I could no longer be inactive.

I raised my rifle, and as the beast in his writhings exposed his belly I took aim at the soft flesh just inside his left fore-leg, and fired both barrels.

At that instant my bird gave a wild, shrill scream and a vast bound into the air, and then away it went like the wind—away, I know not where. That first bound had nearly jerked me off; but I managed to avoid this and now instinctively clung with all my might to the bird's neck, still holding my rifle. The speed of the bird was twice as great as it had been before—as the speed of a runaway horse surpasses that of the same horse when trotting at his ordinary rate and under control. I could scarcely make out where I was going. Rocks, hills, swamps, fields, trees, sand, and sea all seemed to flash past in one confused assemblage, and the only thought in my mind was that I was being carried to some remote wilderness, to be flung there bruised and maimed among the rocks, to perish helplessly. Every moment I expected to be thrown, for the progress of the bird was not only inconceivably swift, but it also gave immense leaps into the air; and it was only its easy mode of lighting on the ground after each leap that saved me from being hurled off. As it was, however, I clung instinctively to the bird's neck, until at last it came to a stop so suddenly that my hands slipped, and I fell to the ground.

[TO BE CONTINUED.]

PART 8 (25 FEBRUARY, 1888)

CHAPTER XI.—(*Continued.*)
THE SWAMP MONSTER.

I WAS senseless for I know not how long. When at last I revived I found myself propped up against a bank, and Almah bathing my head with cold water. Fortunately, I had received no hurt. In falling I had struck on my head, but it was against the soft turf, and though I was stunned, yet on regaining my senses no further inconvenience was experienced. The presence of Almah was soon explained. The report of the rifle had startled her bird also, which had bounded away in terror like mine; but Almah understood how to guide him, and managed to keep him after me, so as to be of assistance in case of need. She had been close behind all the time, and had stopped when I fell, and come to my assistance.

The place was a slope looking out upon an arm of the sea, and apparently remote from human abode. The scenery was exquisitely beautiful. A little distance off we saw the edge of the forest; the open country was dotted with clumps of trees; on the other side of the arm of the sea was an easy declivity covered with trees of luxuriant foliage and vast dimensions; farther away on one side rose the icy summits of impassable mountains; on the other side there extended the blue expanse of the boundless sea. The spot where I lay was overshadowed by the dense foliage of a tree which was unlike anything that I had ever seen, and seemed like some exaggerated grass; at our feet a brook ran murmuring to the shore; in the air and all around were innumerable birds.

The situation in which I found myself seemed inexpressibly sweet, and all the more so from the gentle face of Almah. Would it not be well, I thought, to remain here? Why should Almah go back to her repulsive duties? Why should we return to those children of blood, who loved death and darkness? Here we might pass our days together unmolested. The genial clime would afford us warmth; we needed no shelter except the trees, and as for food, there were the birds of the air in innumerable flocks.

I proposed this to her; she smiled sadly. "You forget," said she, "this season of light will not last much longer. In a few more *jom*s the dark season will begin, and then we should perish in a place like this."

"Are there no caverns here?"

"Oh no. This country has no inhabitants. It is full of fierce wild beasts. We should be destroyed before one *jom*."

"But must we go back?" said I. "You have a country. Where is it? See, here are these birds. They are swift. They can carry us anywhere. Come, let us fly, and you can return to your own country."

Almah shook her head. "These birds," said she, "cannot go over the sea, or through these endless forests. My country can only be reached by sea."

"Can we not hurry back, seize a boat, and go? I know how to sail over the water without oars."

"We certainly might leave the country; but there is another difficulty. The dark season is coming, and we should never be able to find our way. Besides, the sea is full of monsters, and you and I would perish."

"At any rate, let us try. I have my *sepet-ram*."

"We could never find our way."

"Only tell me," said I, "where it lies, and I will go by the stars."

"The trouble is," said she, "that even if we did succeed in reaching my land, I should be sent back again; for I was sent here as a sacred hostage, and I have been here four seasons."[1]

But in the midst of this conversation a sound arrested our attention—a heavy, puffing, snorting sound, as of some living thing. Hastily I started up, rifle in hand, and looked; and as I looked I felt my nerves thrill with horror. There, close by the shore, I saw a vast form—a living thing—full sixty feet in length. It had a body like that of an elephant, the head of a crocodile, and enormous glaring eyes. Its immense body was covered with impenetrable armor, and was supported on legs long enough to allow it to run with great speed. It differed in many respects from the monster of the swamp—the legs being longer, the tail shorter and thinner, and its head and jaws larger and longer. I shrank back, thinking of seizing Almah and hiding. But I saw that she had already taken the alarm, and with more presence of mind than I had she had hurried to the birds, who were standing near, and had made them lie down. As I turned, she beckoned to me without a word. I hurried to her. She told me to mount. I did so at once; she did the same. Scarce had we mounted than the monster perceived us, and with a terrible bellow came rushing toward us. Almah drove her goad deep into her bird, which at once rose and went off like the wind, and mine started to follow. The vast monster came on. His roar sounded

1 Given that there are only two seasons a year, Almah has been captive for two years.

close behind, and I heard the clash of his tremendous jaws; but the swift bird with a bound snatched me from his grasp, and bore me far away out of his reach. Away I went like the wind. Almah was ahead, looking back from time to time, and waving her hand joyously. So we went on, returning on our course at a speed almost as great as that with which we had come. By this time the novelty had in part worn away, and the easy motion gave me confidence. I noticed that we were travelling a wild, uninhabited, and rocky district by the sea-side. Before me the country spread far away, interspersed with groves, terminating in forests, and bounded in the far distance by mountains. The country here was so rough that it seemed as if nothing could pass over it except such creatures as these—the opmaheras.

At length we arrived at the spot which we had left—the scene of the hunt. We could see it from afar, for the opmaheras stood quietly around, and the men were busy elsewhere. As we drew nearer I saw the vast body of the monster. They had succeeded in killing it, yet—oh heavens, at what a cost! One-half of all the party lay dead. The rest were unharmed, and among these was the Kohen. He greeted me with a melancholy smile. That melancholy smile, however, was not caused by the sad fate of his brave companions, but, as I afterward learned, simply and solely because he himself had not gained his death. When I saw that there were no wounded, a dark suspicion came over me that the wounded had again been put to death. I did not care to ask. The truth was too terrible to hear, and I felt glad that accident had drawn me away. It was all a dark and dreadful mystery. These people were the most gentle, the most self-sacrificing, and the most generous in the world; yet their strange and unnatural love of death made them capable of endless atrocities. Life and light seemed to them as actual evils, and death and darkness the only things worthy of regard.

Almah told me that they were going to bring the monster home, and had sent for opkuks to drag it along. The dead were also to be fetched back. There was no further necessity for us to remain, and so we returned at once.

On the way, Almah said, "Do not use the *sepet-ram* again. You can do no good with it. You must not make it common. Keep it. The time may come when you will need it: you are not fond of death."

I shuddered.

"Never forget," she said, "that here death is considered the chief blessing. It is useless for you to interfere in their ways. You cannot change them."

Some more *joms* passed. The bodies were embalmed, and Almah had more victims to crown with garlands in the horrible *cheder nebilin.*[1]

CHAPTER XII.
THE BALEFUL SACRIFICE.

I RESOLVED to go on no more sacred hunts. I was sickened at the horrible cruelty, the needless slaughter, the mad self-sacrifice which distinguished them. I was overwhelmed with horror at the merciless destruction of brave comrades, whose wounds, so gallantly received, should have been enough to inspire pity even in a heart of stone. The gentleness, the incessant kindness, the matchless generosity, of these people seemed all a mockery. What availed it all when the same hand that heaped favors upon me, the guest, could deal death without compunction upon friends and relatives? It seemed quite possible for the Kohen to kill his own child, or cut the throat of his wife, if the humor seized him. And how long could I hope to be spared among a people who had this insane thirst for blood?

Some more *joms* had passed, and the light season had almost ended. The sun had been sinking lower and lower. The time had at last come when only a portion of his disk would be visible for a little while above the hills, and then he would be seen no more for six months of our time. This was the dark season, and, as I had already learned, its advent was always hailed with joy and celebrated with solemn services, for the dark season freed them from their long confinement, permitted them to go abroad, to travel by sea and land, to carry on their great works, to indulge in all their most important labors and favourite amusements. The Kohen asked me to be present at the great festival, and I gladly consented. There seemed to be nothing in this that could be repellent. As I was anxious to witness some of their purely religious ceremonies, I wished to go. When I told Almah, she looked sad, but said nothing. I wondered at this, and asked her if she was going. She informed me that she would have to go, whereupon I assured her that this was an additional reason why I should go.

I went with Almah. The Kohen attended us with his usual kind and gracious consideration. It seemed almost as though he was our servant. He took us to a place where we could be seated, although all the others were standing. Almah wished to refuse, but I prevailed upon her to sit down, and she did so.

---

1 The Cavern of the Dead first mentioned in Chapter 9.

The scene was upon the semicircular terrace in front of the cavern, and we were seated upon a stone platform beside the chief portal. A vast crowd was gathered in front. Before us arose the half-pyramid of which I have already spoken. The light was faint. It came from the disk of the sun, which was partly visible over the icy crest of the distant mountains. Far away the sea was visible, rising high over the tops of the trees, while overhead the brighter stars were plainly discernible.

The Kohen ascended the pyramid, and others followed. At the base there was a crowd of men, with emaciated forms and faces, and coarse, squalid attire, who looked like the most abject paupers, and seemed the lowest in the land. As the Kohen reached the summit there arose a strange sound—a mournful, plaintive chant, which seemed to be sung chiefly by the paupers at the base of the pyramid. The words of this chant I could not make out, but the melancholy strain affected me in spite of myself. There was no particular tune, and nothing like harmony; but the effect of so many voices uniting in this strain was very powerful and altogether indescribable. In the midst of this I saw the crowd parting asunder so as to make way for something; and through the passage thus formed I saw a number of youths in long robes, who advanced to the pyramid, singing as they went. Then they ascended the steps, two by two, still singing, and at length reached the summit, where they arranged themselves in order. There were thirty of them, and they arranged themselves in three rows of ten each; and as they stood they never ceased to sing, while the paupers below joined in the strain.

And now the sun was almost hidden, and there was only the faintest line from the upper edge of his disk perceptible over the icy mountain-tops. The light was a softened twilight glow. It was to be the last sight of the sun for six months, and this was the spectacle upon which he threw his parting beam. So the sun passed away, and then there came the beginning of the long dark season.[1] At first, however, there was rather twilight than darkness, and this twilight continued long. All this only served to heighten the effect of this striking scene; and as the light faded away I looked with increasing curiosity upon the group at the top of the pyramid. Almah was silent. I half turned, and said something to her about the beauty of the view. She said nothing, but looked at me with such an expression that I was filled with amazement. I saw in her face something like a dreadful anticipation—something that spoke of coming evil. The feeling was communicated to me, and I turned my eyes back to the group on the pyramid with vague fears in my soul.

---

1. Approximately 20 or 21 March: the equinox is the sunset in Antarctica and it marks the beginning of autumn in the southern hemisphere.

Those fears were but too well founded, for now the dread ceremony began. The Kohen drew his knife, and placed himself at the head of the stone table. One of the youths came forward, stepped upon it, and lay down on his back with his head toward the Kohen. The mournful chant still went on. Then the Kohen raised his knife and plunged it into the heart of the youth.[1] I sat for a moment rooted to the spot; then a groan burst from me in spite of myself. Almah caught my hands in hers, which were as cold as ice.

"Be firm," she said, "or we are both lost. Be firm, Atam-or!"

"I must go," said I, and I tried to rise.

"Don't move," she said, "for your life! We are lost if you move. Keep still—restrain yourself—shut your eyes."

I tried to do so, but could not. There was a horrible fascination about the scene, which forced me to look and see all. The Kohen took the victim, and drawing it from the altar, threw it over the precipice to the ground beneath. Then a loud shout burst forth from the great crowd.

"*Sibgu Sibgin! Ranenu! Hodu lecosck!*" which means, "Sacrifice the victims! Rejoice! Give thanks to darkness!"

Then another of the youths went forward amid the singing, and laid himself down to meet the same fate; and again the corpse was flung from the top of the pyramid, and again the shout arose. All the others came forward in the same manner.

Oh, horrible, horrible, thrice horrible spectacle! I do not remember how I endured it. I sat there with Almah, trying to restrain myself as she had entreated me, more for her sake than for my own, a prey to every feeling of horror, anguish, and despair. How it all ended I do not know, nor do I know how I got away from the place; for I only remember coming back to my senses in the lighted grotto, with Almah bending anxiously over me.

After this there remained a dark mystery and an ever-present horror. I found myself among a people who were at once the gentlest of the human race and the most blood-thirsty—the kindest and the most cruel. This mild, amiable, and self-sacrificing Kohen, how was it possible that he should transform himself to a fiend

---

1 De Mille seems to draw on a description of a Mayan human sacrifice at the great pyramid temple of Uxmal in *The Saturday Magazine* (January 1844): the high Mayan priest is described as using a "broad and sharp knife made of flint": He "tore out the heart, reeking, with his hands, and showed it to the sun" ("Account of the Ruined Cities of Yucatan" 37). Only, here, the sun has just gone down. The Mayan sacrificial victim is then thrown to the "savages beneath, who prepared with them a cannibal repast to complete the work of abomination."

Illustration 8: "Then the Kohen raised his knife and plunged it into the heart of the youth."

incarnate? And for me and for Almah, what possible hope could there be? What fate might they have in reserve for us? Of what avail was all this profound respect, this incessant desire to please, this attention to our slightest wish, this comfort and luxury and splendor, this freedom of speech and action? Was it anything better than a mockery? Might it not be the shallow kindness of the priest to the victim reserved for the sacrifice? Was it, after all, in any degree better than the kindness of the cannibal savages on those drear outer shores who received us with such hospitality, but only that they might destroy us at last? Might they not all belong to the same race, dwelling as they did in caverns, shunning the sunlight, and blending kindness with cruelty? It was an awful thought!

Yet I had one consolation. Almah was with me, and so long as she was spared to me I could endure this life. I tried for her sake to resist the feelings that were coming over me. I saw that she too was a prey to ever-deepening sadness. She felt as I did, and this despair of soul might wreck her young life if there were no alleviation. And so I sought to alleviate her distress and to banish her sadness. The songs of these people had much impressed me; and one day, as I talked about this with Almah, she brought forth a musical instrument of peculiar shape, which was not unlike a guitar, though the shape was square and there were a dozen strings. Upon this she played, singing at the same time some songs of a plaintive character. An idea now occurred to me to have an instrument made according to my own plans, which should be nothing less than a violin. Almah was delighted at the proposal, and at once found a very clever workman, who under my direction succeeded in producing one which served my purpose well. I was a good violinist, and in this I was able to find solace for myself and for Almah for many a long hour.

The first time that I played was memorable. As the tones floated through the air they caught the ears of those outside, and soon great numbers came into the apartment, listening in amazement and in rapt attention. Even the painful light was disregarded in the pleasure of this most novel sensation, and I perceived that if the sense of sight was deficient among them, that of hearing was sufficiently acute. I played many times, and sometimes sang from among the songs of different nations; but those which these people liked best were the Irish and Scottish melodies—those matchless strains created by the genius of the Celtic race,[1] and handed down from immemorial ages through long generations. In these there

---

1 A European people dating from the Iron Age who spoke the Celtic language.

was nothing artificial, nothing transient. They were the utterance of the human heart, and in them there was that touch of nature which makes all men kin. These were the immortal passions which shall never cease to affect the soul of man, and which had power even here; the strains of love, of sadness, and of pathos were sweet and enticing to this gentle race; for in their mild manners and their outburst of cruelty they seemed to be not unlike the very race which had created this music, since the Celt is at once gentle and blood-thirsty.

I played "Tara," "Bonnie Doon," "The Last Rose of Summer," "The Land of the Leal," "Auld Lang Syne," "Lochaber."[1] They stood entranced, listening with all their souls. They seemed to hunger and thirst after this music, and the strains of the inspired Celtic race seemed to come to them like the revelation of the glory of Heaven. Then I played more lively airs. Some I played a second time, singing the words. They seemed eager to have the same one played often. At last a grisly thought came to me: it was that they would learn these sweet strains, and put their own words to them so as to use them at the awful sacrifices. After that I would play no more.

It is a land of tender love and remorseless cruelty. Music is all-powerful to awaken the one, but powerless to abate the other; and the eyes that weep over the pathetic strains of "Lochaber"[2] can gaze without a tear upon the death-agonies of a slaughtered friend.

[TO BE CONTINUED.]

---

1 All of these Celtic songs are from Ireland and Scotland: "The Harp that Once Through Tara's Halls" and "The Last Rose of Summer" were written by the Irish singer and poet Thomas Moore (1789-1852); the Scottish poet Robert Burns (1759-96) wrote "The Banks O'Doon" ("Ye flowery banks o'bonie Doon") and "Auld Lang Syne"; the lyrics of "The Land of the Leal," a Scottish folk song, were written by Lady Carolina Nairne (1766-1845) in 1797-98 after a friend's child died; "Farewell to Lochaber," composed by Allan Ramsay in the early eighteenth century, refers to a rugged geographical region on the northwest coast of Scotland.

2 In addition to the "pathetic strains," the lyrics of "Farewell to Lochaber," as well as the themes of many of these songs, might also appeal to the Kosekin: "These tears that I shed they are all for my dear, / And no' for the dangers attending or weir; / Tho' borne on rough seas to a far distant shore. / Maybe to return to Lochaber no more."

PART 9 (3 MARCH, 1888)

CHAPTER XIII.
THE AWFUL "*MISTA KOSEK*."

THE terrible sacrifice marked the end of the light season. The dark season had now begun, which would last for half the coming year. No more sunlight would now be visible, save at first for a few *jom*s, when at certain times the glare would be seen shooting up above the icy crests of the mountains. Now the people all moved out of the caverns into the stone houses on the opposite side of the terraces, and the busy throng transferred themselves and their occupations to the open air. This with them was the season of activity, when all their most important affairs were undertaken and carried out; the season, too, of enjoyment, when all the chief sports and festivals took place. Then the outer world all awoke to life; the streets were thronged, fleets of galleys came forth from their moorings, and the sounds of labor and of pleasure, of toil and revelry, arose into the darkened skies. Then the city was a city of the living, no longer silent, but full of bustle, and the caverns were frequented but little. This cavern life was only tolerable during the light season, when the sun-glare was over the land; but now, when the beneficent and grateful darkness pervaded all things, the outer world was infinitely more agreeable.

To me, however, the arrival of the dark season brought only additional gloom. I could not get rid of the thought that I was reserved for some horrible fate, in which Almah also might be involved. We were both aliens here, in a nation of kind-hearted and amiable miscreants—of generous, refined, and most self-denying fiends; of men who were highly civilized, yet utterly wrong-headed and irreclaimable in their blood-thirsty cruelty. The stain of blood-guiltiness was over all the land. What was I, that I could hope to be spared? The hope was madness, and I did not pretend to indulge it.

The only consolation was Almah. The manners of these people were such that we were still left as unconstrained as ever in our movements, and always, wherever we went, we encountered nothing but amiable smiles and courteous offices. Everyone was always eager to do anything for us—to give, to go, to act, to speak, as though we were the most honored of guests, the pride of the city. The Kohen was untiring in his efforts to please. He was in the habit of making presents every time he came to see me, and on each occasion the present was of a different kind; at one time it was a new robe of curiously wrought feathers, at another some beautiful gem, at another some rare fruit.

He also made incessant efforts to render my situation pleasant, and was delighted at my rapid progress in acquiring the language.

On the *jom* following the sacrifice I accompanied Almah as she went to her daily task, and after it was over I asked when the new victims would be placed here. "How long does it take to embalm them?" I added.

Almah looked at me earnestly. "They will not bring them here; they will not embalm them," said she.

"Why not?" I asked; "what will they do with them?"

"Do not ask," said she. "It will pain you to know."

In spite of repeated solicitation she refused to give me any satisfaction. I felt deeply moved at her words and her looks. What was it, I wondered, that could give me pain? or what could there still be that could excite fear in me, who had learned and seen so much? I could not imagine. It was evidently some disposal of the bodies of the victims—that was plain. Turning this over in my mind, with vague conjectures as to Almah's meaning, I left her and walked along the terrace until I came to the next cavern. This had never been open before, and I now entered through curiosity to see what it might be. I saw a vast cavern, quite as large as the *cheder nebilin*, full of people, who seemed to be engaged in decorating it. Hundreds were at work, and they had brought immense tree-ferns, which were placed on either side in long rows, with their branches meeting and interlacing at the top. It looked like the interior of some great Gothic cathedral at night, and the few twinkling lights that were scattered here and there made the shadowy outline just visible to me.[1]

I asked one of the by-standers what this might be, and he told me that it was the *Mista Kosek*, which means the "Feast of Darkness," from which I gathered that they were about to celebrate the advent of the dark season with a feast. From what I knew of their character this seemed quite intelligible, and there was much beauty and taste in the arrangements. All were industrious and orderly, and each one seemed most eager to assist his neighbor.

---

1 Beginning in the 1840s, the Gothic Revival brought medieval architecture back into vogue in Britain. Gothic cathedrals figure large in many Gothic novels and also in works by Romantic writers, such as Samuel Taylor Coleridge's *Bibliographia Literaria* (1817) and Thomas de Quincey's *Confessions of an English Opium-Eater* (1821).

Indeed, there seemed to be a friendly rivalry in this which at times amounted to positive violence; for more than once when a man was seen carrying too large a burden, someone else would insist on taking it from him. At first these altercations seemed exactly like the quarrels of workmen at home, but a closer inspection showed that it was merely the persistent effort of one to help another.

I learned that the feast was to take place as soon as the hall was decorated, and that it would be attended by a great multitude. I felt a great interest in it. There seemed something of poetic beauty in this mode of welcoming the advent of a welcome season, and it served to mitigate the horrible remembrance of that other celebration, upon which I could not think without a shudder. I thought that it would be pleasant to join with them here, and resolved to ask Almah to come with me, so that she might explain the meaning of the ceremonies. Full of this thought, I went to her and told her my wish. She looked at me with a face full of amazement and misery. In great surprise I questioned her eagerly.

"Ask me nothing," said she. "I will answer nothing; but do not think of it. Do not go near it. Stay in your room till the fearful repast is over."

"Fearful? How is it fearful?" I asked.

"Everything here is fearful," said Almah, with a sigh. "Every season it grows worse, and I shall grow at length to hate life and love death as these people do. They can never understand us, and we can never understand them. Oh, if I could but once more stand in my own dear native land but for one moment—to see once more the scenes and the faces that I love so well! Oh, how different is this land from mine! Here all is dark, all is terrible. There the people love the light and rejoice in the glorious sun, and when the dark season comes they wait, and have no other desire than long day. There we live under the sky, in the eye of the sun. We build our houses, and when the dark season comes we fill them with lamps that make a blaze like the sun itself."

"We must try to escape," I said, in a low voice.

"Escape!" said she. "That is easy enough. We might go now; but where?"

"Back," said I, "to your own country. See, the sky is dotted with stars: I can find my way by them."

"Yes," said she, "if I could only tell you where to go; but I cannot. My country lies somewhere over the sea, but where, I know not. Over the sea there are many lands, and we might reach one even worse than this."

"Perhaps," said I, "the Kohen might allow us to go away to your country, and send us there. He is most generous and most amiable. He seems to spend most of his time in efforts to make us happy. There must be many seamen in this nation who know the way. It would be worth trying."

Almah shook her head. "You do not understand these people," said she. "Their ruling passion is the hatred of self, and therefore they are eager to confer benefits on others. The only hope of life that I have for you and for myself is in this, that if they kill us they will lose their most agreeable occupation. They value us most highly, because we take everything that is given us. You and I now possess as our own property all this city and all its buildings, and all the people have made themselves our slaves."

At this I was utterly bewildered.

"I don't understand," said I.

"I suppose not," said Almah; "but you will understand better after you have been here longer. At any rate, you can see for yourself that the ruling passion here is self-denial and the good of others. Everyone is intent upon this, from the Kohen up to the most squalid pauper."

"*Up* to the most squalid pauper?" said I. "I do not understand you. You mean *down* to the most squalid pauper."

"No," said Almah; "I mean what I say. In this country the paupers form the most honored and envied class."

"This is beyond my comprehension," said I. "But if this is really so, and if these people pretend to be our slaves, why may we not order out a galley and go?"

"Oh, well, with you in your land, if a master were to order his slaves to cut his throat and poison his children and burn down his house, would the slaves obey?"

"Certainly not."

"Well, our slaves here would not—in fact could not—obey a command that would be shocking to their natures. They think that we are in the best of all lands, and my request to be sent home would be utterly monstrous."

"I suppose," said I, "they would kill us if we asked them to do so?"

"Yes," said Almah; "for they think death the greatest blessing."

"And if at the point of death we should beg for life, would they spare us?"

"Certainly not," said Almah. "Would you kill a man who asked for death? No more would these people spare a man who asked for life."

All this was so utterly incomprehensible that I could pursue the subject no further. I saw, however, that Almah was wretched, dejected, and suffering greatly from home-sickness. Gladly would I have taken her and started off on a desperate flight by sea or land—gladly would I have dared every peril, although I well knew what tremendous perils there were; but she would not consent, and believed the attempt to be useless. I could only wait, therefore, and indulge the hope that at last a chance of escape might one day come, of which she would be willing to avail herself.

Almah utterly refused to go to the feast, and entreated me not to go; but this only served to increase my curiosity, and I determined to see it for myself, whatever it was. She had seen it, and why should not I? Whatever it might be, my nerves could surely stand the shock as well as hers. Besides, I was anxious to know the very worst; and if there was anything that could surpass in atrocity what I had already witnessed, it were better that I should not remain in ignorance of it.

So at length, leaving Almah, I returned to the hall of the feast. I found there a vast multitude, which seemed to comprise the whole city—men, women, children, all were there. Long tables were laid out. The people were all standing and waiting. A choir was singing plaintive strains that sounded like the chant of the sacrifice. Those nearest me regarded me with their usual amiable smiles, and wished to conduct me to some place of honor; but I did not care about taking a part in this feast. I wished to be a mere spectator, nothing more.

I walked past and came to the next cavern. This seemed to be quite as large as the other. There was a crowd of people here also, and at one end there blazed an enormous fire. It was a furnace that seemed to be used for cooking the food of this banquet, and there was a thick steam rising from an immense cauldron, while the air was filled with an odor like that of a kitchen.

All this I took in at a glance, and at the same instant I saw something else. There were several very long tables, which stood at the sides of the cavern and in the middle, and upon each of these I saw lying certain things covered over with cloths. The shape of these was more than suggestive—it told me all. It was a sight of horror—awful, tremendous, unspeakable! For a moment I stood motionless, staring; then all the cavern seemed to swim around me. I reeled, I fell, and sank into nothingness.[1]

1 See Appendix C for examples of cannibalism in different exploration narratives.

Illustration 9: "For a moment I stood motionless, staring; then all the cavern seemed to swim around me."

When I revived I was in the lighted grotto, lying on a couch, with Almah bending over me. Her face was full of tenderest anxiety, yet there was also apparent a certain solemn gloom that well accorded with my own feelings. As I looked at her she drew a long breath, and buried her face in her hands.

After a time my recollection returned, and all came back before me. I rose to a sitting posture.

"Do not rise yet," said Almah, anxiously; "you are weak."

"No," said I; "I am as strong as ever; but I'm afraid that you are weaker."

Almah shuddered.

"If you had told me exactly what it was," said I, "I would not have gone."

"I could not tell you," said she. "It is too terrible to name. Even the thought is intolerable. I told you not to go. Why did you go?"

She spoke in accents of tender reproach, and there were tears in her eyes.

"I did not think of anything so hideous as that," said I. "I thought that there might be a sacrifice, but nothing worse."

I now learned that when I fainted I had been raised most tenderly, and the Kohen himself came with me as I was carried back, and he thought that Almah would be my most agreeable nurse. The Kohen was most kind and sympathetic, and all the people vied with one another in their efforts to assist me—so much so that there was the greatest confusion. It was only by Almah's express entreaty that they retired and left me with her.

Here was a new phase in the character of this mysterious people. Could I ever hope to understand them? Where other people are cruel to strangers, or at best indifferent, these are eager in their acts of kindness; they exhibit the most unbounded hospitality, the most lavish generosity, the most self-denying care and attention; where others would be offended at the intrusion of a stranger, and enraged at his unconquerable disgust, these people had no feeling save pity, sympathy, and a desire to alleviate his distress. And yet—oh, and yet!—oh, thought of horror!—what was this that I had seen? The abhorrent savages in the outer wilderness were surely of the same race as these. They too received us kindly, they too lavished upon us their hospitality, and yet there followed the horror of that frightful repast. Here there had been kindness and generosity and affectionate attention, to be succeeded by deeds without a name. Ah me! what an hour that was! And yet it was as nothing compared to what lay before me in the future.

But the subject was one of which I dared not speak—one from which I had to force my thoughts away. I took the violin and played "Lochaber" till Almah wept, and I had to put it away. Then I begged her to play or sing. She brought an instrument like a lute, and upon this she played some melancholy strains. At length the Kohen came in. His mild, benevolent face never exhibited more gentle and affectionate sympathy than now. He seated himself, and with eyes half closed, as usual, talked much; and yet, with a native delicacy which always distinguished this extraordinary man, he made no allusion to the awful *Mista Kosek*. For my own part, I could not speak. I was absent-minded, overwhelmed with gloom and despair, and at the same time full of aversion toward him and all his race. One question, however, I had to put.

"Who were the victims of the *Mista Kosek*?"

"They?" said he, with an agreeable smile. "Oh, they were the victims of the sacrifice."

I sank back in my seat, and said no more. The Kohen then took Almah's lute, played and sang in a very sweet voice, and at length, with his usual gentle consideration, seeing that I looked weary, he retired.

CHAPTER XIV.
I LEARN MY DOOM.

HORROR is a feeling that cannot last long; human nature is incapable of supporting it. Sadness, whether from bereavement, or disappointment, or misfortune of any kind, may linger on through life. In my case, however, the milder and more enduring feeling of sadness had no sufficient cause for existence. The sights which I had seen inspired horror, and horror only. But when the first rush of this feeling had passed there came a reaction. Calmness followed, and then all the circumstances of my life here conspired to perpetuate that calm. For here all on the surface was pleasant and beautiful; all the people were amiable and courteous and most generous. I had light and luxury and amusements. Around me there were thousands of faces, all greeting me with cordial affection, and thousands of hands all ready to perform my slightest wish. Above all, there was Almah. Everything combined to make her most dear to me. My life had been such that I never before had seen anyone whom I loved; and here Almah was the one congenial associate in a whole world of aliens: she was beautiful and gentle and sympathetic, and I loved her dearly, even before I understood what my feelings were. One day I learned all, and found that she was more precious to me than all the world.

It was one *jom* when she did not make her appearance as usual. On asking after her I learned that she was ill. At this intelligence there came over me a feeling of sickening anxiety and fear. Almah ill! What if it should prove serious? Could I endure life here without her sweet companionship? Of what value was life without her? And as I asked myself these questions I learned that Almah had become dearer to me than life itself, and that in her was all the sunshine of my existence. While she was absent, life was nothing; all its value, all its light, its flavor, its beauty, were gone. I felt utterly crushed. I forgot all else save her illness, and all that I had endured seemed as nothing when compared with this.

In the midst of my own anxiety I was surprised to find that the whole community was most profoundly agitated. Among all classes there seemed to be but one thought—her illness. I could overhear them talking. I could see them waiting outside to hear about her. It seemed to be the one subject of interest, beside which all others were forgotten. The Kohen was absorbed in her case; all the physicians of the city were more or less engaged in her behalf; and there came forward as volunteers every woman in the place who had any knowledge of sick duties. I was somewhat perplexed, however, at their manner. They were certainly agitated and intensely interested, yet not exactly sad. Indeed, from what I heard it seemed as though this strange people regarded sickness as rather a blessing than otherwise. This, however, did not interfere in the slightest degree with the most intense interest in her, and the most assiduous attention. The Kohen in particular was devoted to her. He was absent-minded, silent, and full of care. On the whole, I felt more than ever puzzled, and less able than ever to understand these people. I loved them, yet loathed them; for the Kohen I had at once affection and horror. He looked like an anxious father, full of tenderest love for a sick child—full also of delicate sympathy with me; and yet I knew all the time that he was quite capable of plunging the sacrificial knife in Almah's heart and of eating her afterward.

But my own thoughts were all of Almah. I learned how dear she was. With her the brightness of life had passed; without her existence would be intolerable. Her sweet voice, her tender and gracious manner, her soft touch, her tender, affectionate smile, her mournful yet trustful look—oh, heavens! would all these be mine no more? I could not endure the thought. At first I wandered about, seeking rest and finding none; and at length I sat in my own room, and passed the time in listening, in questioning the attendants, in wondering what I should do if she should be taken from me.

At length on one blessed *jom*, the Kohen came to me with a bright smile.

"Our darling Almah is better," said he. "Eat, I beseech you. She is very dear to all of us, and we have all felt for her and for you. But now all danger is past. The physicians say that she will soon be well." There were tears in his eyes as he spoke. It may have been caused by the bright light, but I attributed this to his loving heart, and I forgot that he was a cannibal. I took his hands in mine and pressed them in deep emotion. He looked at me with a sweet and gentle smile.

"I see it all," said he, in a low voice—"you love her, Atam-or."

I pressed his hands harder, but said nothing. Indeed, I could not trust myself to speak.

"I knew it," said he; "it is but natural. You are both of a different race from us; you are both much alike, and in full sympathy with one another. This draws you together. When I first saw you I thought that you would be a fit companion for her here—that you would lessen her gloom, and that she would be pleasant to you. I found out soon that I was right, and I felt glad, for you at once showed the fullest sympathy with one another. Never till you came was Almah happy with us; but since you have come she has been a different being, and there has been a joyousness in her manner that I never saw before. You have made her forget how to weep; and as for yourself, I hope she has made your life in this strange land seem less painful, Atam-or."

At all this I was so full of amazement that I could not say one word.

"Pardon me," continued he, "if I have said anything that may seem like an intrusion upon your secret and most sacred feelings. I could not have said it had it not been for the deep affection I feel for Almah and for you, and for the reason that I am just now more moved than usual, and have less control over my feelings."

Saying this, he pressed my hand and left me. It was not the custom here to shake hands, but with his usual amiability he had adopted my custom, and used it as naturally as though he had been to the manner born.

I was encouraged now. The mild Kohen came often to cheer me. He talked much about Almah—about her sweet and gracious disposition, the love that all felt for her, the deep and intense interest which her illness had aroused. In all this he seemed more like a man of my own race than before, and in his eager desire for her recovery he failed to exhibit that love for death which was his nature. So it seemed: yet this desire for her recovery did not arise out of any lack of love for death; its true cause I was to learn afterward; and I was to know that if he desired Almah's recovery now, it was only that she might live long enough to encounter death in a more terrific form. But just then all this was unknown, and I judged him by myself.

[TO BE CONTINUED.]

PART 10 (10 MARCH, 1888)

CHAPTER XIV.—(*Continued.*)
I LEARN MY DOOM.[1]

AT last I learned that she was much better, and would be out on the following *jom*. This intelligence filled me with a fever of eager anticipation, so great that I could think of nothing else. Sleep was impossible. I could only wait, and try as best I might to quell my impatience. At last the time came. I sat waiting. The curtain was drawn aside. I sprang up, and hurrying toward her, I caught her in my arms and wept for joy. Ah me, how pale she looked! She bore still the marks of her illness. She seemed deeply embarrassed and agitated at the fervor of my greeting; while I, instead of apologizing or trying to excuse myself, only grew more agitated still.

"Oh, Almah," I cried. "I should have died if you had not come back to me! Oh, Almah, I love you better than life and I never knew how dearly I loved you till I thought that I had lost you! Oh, forgive me, but I must tell you—and don't weep, darling."

She was weeping as I spoke. She said nothing, but twined her arms around my neck and wept on my breast.

After this we had much to say that we had never mentioned before. I cannot tell the sweet words that she said to me; but I now learned that she had loved me from the first—when I came to her in her loneliness, when she was homesick and heartsick; and I came, a kindred nature, of a race more like her own; and she saw in me the only one of all around her whom it was possible not to detest, and therefore she loved me.

We had many things to say to one another, and long exchanges of confidence to make. She now for the first time told me all the sorrow that she had endured in her captivity—sorrow which she had kept silent and shut up deep within her breast. At first her life here had been so terrible that it had brought her down nearly to death. After this she had sunk into dull despair; she had grown familiar with horrors and lived in a state of unnatural calm. From this my arrival had roused her. The display of feeling on my part had brought back all her old self, and roused anew all those feelings which in her had become dormant. The darkness, the bloodshed, the sacrifices, all these affected me as they had once affected

1 In the *Harper's* serial, the title for the 10 March continuation of Chapter XIV is "I HEAR MY DOOM."

Illustration 10: "We had many things to say to one another."

her. I had the same fear of death which she had. When I had gone with her to the *cheder nebilin*, when I had used my *sepet-ram* to save life, she had perceived in me feelings and impulses to which all her own nature responded. Finally, when I asked about the *Mista Kosek*, she warned me not to go. When I did go she was with me in thought and suffered all that I felt, until the moment when I was brought back and laid senseless at her feet.

"Then," said Almah, "I felt the full meaning of all that lies before us."

"What do you mean by that?" I asked, anxiously. "You speak as though there were something yet—worse than what has already been; yet nothing can possibly be worse. We have seen the worst; let us now try to shake off these grisly thoughts, and be happy with one another. Your strength will soon be back, and while we have one another we can be happy even in this gloom."

"Ah me," said Almah, "it would be better now to die. I could die happy now, since I know that you love me."

"Death!" said I; "do not talk of it—do not mention that word. It is more abhorrent than ever. No, Almah, let us live and love—let us hope—let us fly."

"Impossible!" said she, in a mournful voice. "We cannot fly. There is no hope. We must face the future, and make up our minds to bear our fate."

"Fate!" I repeated, looking at her in wonder and in deep concern. "What do you mean by our fate? Is there anything more which you know and which I have not heard?"

"You have heard nothing," said she, slowly; "and all that you have seen and heard is as nothing compared with what lies before us. For you and for me there is a fate—inconceivable, abhorrent, tremendous!—a fate of which I dare not speak or even think, and from which there is no escape whatever."

As Almah said this she looked at me with an expression in which terror and anguish were striving with love. Her cheeks, which shortly before had flushed rosy red in sweet confusion, were now pallid, her lips ashen; her eyes were full of a wild despair. I looked at her in wonder, and could not say a word.

"Oh, Atam-or," said she, "I am afraid of death!"

"Almah," said I, "why will you speak of death? What is this fate which you fear so much?"

"It is this," said she, hurriedly and with a shudder, "you and I are singled out. I have been reserved for years until one should be found who might be joined with me. You came. I saw it all at once. I have known it—dreaded it—tried to fight against it. But it was of no use. Oh, Atam-or, our love means death; for the very fact that you love me and I love you seals our doom!"

"Our doom? What doom?"

"The sacrifice!" exclaimed Almah, with another shudder. In her voice and look there was a terrible meaning, which I could not fail to take. I understood it now, and my blood curdled in my veins. Almah clung to me despairingly.

"Do not leave me!" she cried—"do not leave me! I have no one but you. The sacrifice, the sacrifice! It is our doom, the great sacrifice—at the end of the dark season. It is at the *amir*. We must go there to meet our doom."

"The *amir*?" I asked; "what is that?"

"It is the metropolis," said she.

I was utterly overwhelmed, yet still I tried to console her; but the attempt was vain.

"Oh!" she cried, "you will not understand. The sacrifice is but a part—it is but the beginning. Death is terrible; yet it may be endured—if there is only death. But oh!—oh, think!—think of that which comes after—the *Mista Kosek*!"

Now the full meaning flashed upon me, and I saw it all. In an instant there arose in my mind the awful sacrifice on the pyramid and the unutterable horror of the *Mista Kosek*. Oh, horror! horror! horror! Oh, hideous abomination and deed without a name! I could not speak. I caught her in my arms, and we both wept passionately.

The happiness of our love was now darkened by this tremendous cloud that lowered before us. The shock of this discovery was overpowering, and some time elapsed before I could rally from it. Though Almah's love was sweet beyond expression, and though as the time passed I saw that every *jom* she regained more and more of her former health and strength, still I could not forget what had been revealed. We were happy with one another, yet our happiness was clouded, and amid the brightness of our love there was ever present the dread spectre of our appalling doom.

These feelings, however, grew fainter. Hope is ever ready to arise; and I began to think that these people, though given to evil ways, were after all kind-hearted, and might listen to entreaty. Above all, there was the Kohen, so benevolent, so self-denying, so amiable, so sympathetic. I could not forget all that he had said during Almah's illness, and it seemed more than probable that an appeal to his better nature might not be without effect. I said as much to Almah.

"The Kohen," said she; "why, he can do nothing."

"Why not? He is the chief man here, and ought to have great influence."

"You don't understand," said she, with a sigh. "The Kohen is the lowest and least influential man in the city."

"Why, who are influential if he is not?" I asked.

"The paupers," said Almah.

"The paupers!" I exclaimed, in amazement.

"Yes," said Almah. "Here among these people the paupers form the most honored, influential, and envied portion of the community."

This was incomprehensible. Almah tried to explain, but to no purpose, and I determined to talk to the Kohen.

CHAPTER XV.
THE KOHEN IS INEXORABLE.

I DETERMINED to talk to the Kohen, and try for myself whether he might not be accessible to pity. This greatest of cannibals might, indeed, have his little peculiarities, I thought, and who has not?—yet at bottom he seemed full of tender and benevolent feeling; and as he evidently spent his whole time in the endeavor to make us happy, it seemed not unlikely that he might do something for our happiness in a case where our very existence was at stake.

The Kohen listened with deep attention as I stated my case. I did this fully and frankly. I talked of my love for Almah and of Almah's love for me; our hope that we might be united so as to live happily in reciprocal affection; and I was going on to speak of the dread that was in my heart, when he interrupted me:

"You speak of being united," said he. "You talk strangely. Of course you mean that you wish to be separated."

"Separated!" I exclaimed. "What do you mean? Of course we wish to be united."

The Kohen stared at me as I said this with the look of one who was quite puzzled; and I then went on to speak of the fate that was before us, and to entreat his sympathy and his aid that we might be saved from so hideous a doom. To all these words the Kohen listened with an air of amazement, as though I was saying incomprehensible things.

"You have a gentle and an affectionate nature," I said—"a nature full of sympathy with others, and noble self-denial."

"Of course," said the Kohen, quickly, as though glad to get hold of something which he could understand, "of course we are all so, for we are so made. It is our nature. Who is there who is not self-denying? No one can help that."

This sounded strange indeed; but I did not care to criticize it. I came to my purpose direct and said,

"Save us from our fate."

"Your fate?"

"Yes—from death—that death of horror."

"Death?—horror? What do you mean by horror?" said the Kohen, in an amazement that was sincere and unfeigned. "I cannot comprehend your meaning. It seems as though you actually dislike death; but that is not conceivable. It cannot be possible that you fear death."

"Fear death!" I exclaimed, "I do—I do. Who is there that does not fear it?"

The Kohen stared.

"I do not understand you," he said.

"Do you not understand," said I, "that death is abhorrent to humanity?"

"Abhorrent!" said the Kohen; "that is impossible. Is it not the highest blessing? Who is there that does not long for death? Death is the greatest blessing, the chief desire of man—the highest aim. And you—are you not to be envied in having your felicity so near? above all, in having such a death as that which is appointed for you—so noble, so sublime? You must be mad; your happiness has turned your head."

All this seemed like hideous mockery, and I stared at the Kohen with a gaze that probably strengthened his opinion of my madness.

"Do you love death?" I asked at length, in amazement.

"Love death? What a question! Of course I love death;—all men do; who does not? Is it not human nature? Do we not instinctively fly to meet it whenever we can? Do we not rush into the jaws of sea-monsters, or throw ourselves within their grasp? Who does not feel within him this intense longing after death as the strongest passion of his heart?"

"I don't know—I don't know," said I. "You are of a different race; I do not understand what you say. But I belong to a race that fears death. I fear death and love life; and I entreat you, I implore you, to help me now in my distress, and assist me so that I may save my life and that of Almah."

"I—I help you!" said the Kohen, in new amazement. "Why do you come to me—to me, of all men? Why, I am nothing here. And help you to live!—to live! Who ever heard of such a thing?"

And the Kohen looked at me with the same astonishment which I should evince if a man should ask me to help him to die.

Still, I persisted in my entreaty for his help.

"Such a request," said he, "is revolting; you must be mad. Such a request outrages all the instincts of humanity. And even if I could do such violence to my own nature as to help you to such a thing, how do you think I could face my fellow-men, or how could I endure the terrible punishment which would fall upon me?"

"Punishment!" said I. "What! would you be punished?"

"Punished!" said the Kohen. "That, of course, would be inevitable. I should be esteemed an unnatural monster and the chief of criminals. My lot in life now is painful enough; but in this case my punishment would involve me in evils without end. Riches would be poured upon me; I should be raised to the rank of Kohen Gadol; I should be removed farther away than ever from the pauper class—so far, indeed, that all hope in life would be over. I should be made the first and noblest and richest in all the land."

He spoke these words just as if he had said, "the lowest, meanest, poorest, and most infamous." It sounded like fresh mockery, and I could not believe but that he was amusing himself at my expense.

"This is cruel," said I. "You are mocking me."

"Cruel?—cruel?" said he; "what is cruel? You mean that such a fate would be cruel for me."

"No, no," said I; "but alas! I see we cannot understand one another."

"No," said the Kohen, musingly, as he looked at me. "No, it seems not; but tell me, Atam-or, is it possible that you really fear death—that you really love life?"

"Fear death!—love life!" I cried. "Who does not? Who can help it? Why do you ask me that?"

The Kohen clasped his hands in amazement.

"If you really fear death," said he, "what possible thing is there left to love or to hope for? What, then, do you think the highest blessing of man?"

"Long life," said I, "and riches, and requited love."

At this the Kohen started back, and stared at me as though I were a raving madman.

"Oh, holy shades of night!" he exclaimed. "What is this you say? What do you mean?"

"We can never understand one another, I fear," said I. "The love of life must necessarily be the strongest passion of man. We are so made. We give up everything for life. A long life is everywhere considered as the highest blessing; and there is no one who is willing to die, no matter what his suffering may be. Riches also are desired by all, for poverty is the direst curse that can embitter life; and as to requited love, surely that is the sweetest, purest, and most divine joy that the human heart may know."

At this the Kohen burst forth in a strain of high excitement:

"Oh, sacred cavern gloom! Oh, divine darkness! Oh, impenetrable abysses of night! What, oh, what is this! Oh, Atam-or, are you mad? Alas! it must be so. Joy has turned your brain; you are quite demented. You call good evil, and evil good; our light is your darkness, and our darkness your light. Yet surely you cannot be altogether insane. Come, come, let us look further. How is it? Try now to recall your reason. A long life—a life, and a long one! Surely there can be no human being in a healthy state of nature who wishes to prolong his life; and as to riches, is it possible that anyone exists who really and honestly desires riches? Impossible! And requited love! Oh, Atam-or, you are mad today! You are always strange, but now you have quite taken leave of your senses. I cannot but love you, and yet I can never understand you. Tell me, and tell me truly, what is it that you consider evils, if these things that you have just mentioned are not the very worst?"

He seemed deeply in earnest and much moved. I could not understand him, but could only answer his questions with simple conciseness.

"Poverty, sickness, and death," said I, "are evils; but the worst of all evils is unrequited love."

At these words the Kohen made a gesture of despair.

"It is impossible to understand this," said he. "You talk calmly; you have not the air of a madman. If your fellow-countrymen are all like you, then your race is an incomprehensible one. Why, death is the greatest blessing. We all long for it; it is the end of our being. As for riches, they are a curse, abhorred by all. Above all, as to love, we shrink from the thought of requital. Death is our chief blessing, poverty our greatest happiness, and unrequited love the sweetest lot of man."

All this sounded like the ravings of a lunatic, yet the Kohen was not mad. It seemed also like the mockery of some teasing demon; but the gentle and self-denying Kohen was no teasing demon, and mockery with him was impossible. I was therefore more bewildered than ever at this reiteration of sentiments that were so utterly incomprehensible. He, on the other hand, seemed as astonished at my sentiments and as bewildered, and we could find no common ground on which to meet.

"I remember now," said the Kohen, in a musing tone, "having heard of some strange folk at the *amir*, who profess to feel as you say you feel, but no one believes that they are in earnest; for although they may even bring themselves to think that they are in earnest in their professions, yet after all everyone thinks that they are self-deceived. For you see, in the first place, these feelings which you profess are utterly unnatural. We are so made that we cannot help loving death; it is a sort of instinct. We are also created in such a way that we cannot help longing after poverty. The pauper must always, among all men, be the most envied of mortals. Nature, too, has made us such that the passion of love, when it arises, is so vehement, so all-consuming, that it must always struggle to avoid requital. This is the reason why, when two people find that they love each other, they always separate and avoid one another for the rest of their lives. This is human nature. We cannot help it; and it is this that distinguishes us from the animals. Why, if men were to feel as you say you feel, they would be mere animals. Animals fear death; animals love to accumulate such things as they prize; animals, when they love, go in pairs, and remain with one another. But man, with his intellect, would not be man if he loved life and desired riches and sought for requited love."

I sank back in despair. "You cannot mean all this," I said.

He threw at me a piteous glance. "What else can you believe or feel?" said he.

"The very opposite. We are so made that we hate and fear death; to us he is the King of Terrors. Poverty is terrible also, since it is associated with want and woe; it is therefore natural to man to strive after riches. As to the passion of love, that is so vehement that the first and only thought is requital. Unrequited love is anguish beyond expression—anguish so severe that the heart will often break under it."

The Kohen clasped his hands in new bewilderment.

"I cannot understand," said he. "A madman might imagine that he loved life and desired riches; but as to love, why, even a madman could not think of requital, for the very nature of the passion of love is the most utter self-surrender, and a shrinking from all requital; wherefore the feeling that leads one to desire requital cannot be love. I do not know what it can be—indeed, I never heard of such a thing before, and the annals of the human race make no mention of such a feeling. For what is love? It is the ardent outflow of the whole being—the yearning of one human heart to lavish all its treasures upon another. Love is more than self-denial; it is self-surrender and utter self-abnegation. Love gives all away, and cannot possibly receive anything in return. A requital of love would mean selfishness, which would be self-contradiction. The more one loves, the more he must shrink from requital."

"What!" cried I, "among you do lovers never marry?"

"Lovers marry? Never!"

"Do married people never love one another?"

The Kohen shook his head.

"It unfortunately sometimes happens so," said he, "and then the result is, of course, distressing. For the children's sake the parents will often remain with one another, but in many cases they separate. No one can tell the misery that ensues where a husband and wife love one another."

The conversation grew insupportable. I could not follow the Kohen in what seemed the wildest and maddest flights of fancy that ever were known; so I began to talk of other things, and gradually the Kohen was drawn to speak of his own life. The account which he gave of himself was not one whit less strange than his previous remarks, and for this reason I add it here.

"I was born," said he, "in the most enviable of positions. My father and mother were among the poorest in the land. Both died when I was a child, and I never saw them. I grew up in the open fields and public caverns, along with the most esteemed paupers. But, unfortunately for me, there was something wanting in my natural disposition. I loved death, of course, and poverty too, very strongly; but I did not have that eager and energetic passion which is so desirable, nor was I watchful enough over my blessed estate of poverty. Surrounded as I was by those who were only too ready to take advantage of my ignorance or want of vigilance, I soon fell into evil ways, and gradually, in spite of myself, I found wealth pouring in upon me. Designing men succeeded in winning my consent to receive their possessions; and so I gradually fell away from that lofty position in which I was born. I grew richer and richer. My friends warned me, but in vain. I was too weak to resist; in fact, I lacked moral fibre, and had never learned how to say 'No.' So I went on, descending lower and lower in the scale of being. I became a capitalist, an Athon,[1] a general officer, and finally Kohen.

"At length, on one eventful day, I learned that one of my associates had by a long course of reckless folly become the richest man in all the country. He had become Athon, Melek,[2] and at last

1 "Al-hon" is mistakenly used for Athon in the *Harper's Weekly* serial.

2 "Malek" in the *Harper's* serial—another error.

Kohen Gadol. It was a terrible shock, but I trust a salutary one. I at once resolved to reform. That resolution I have steadily kept, and have at least saved myself from descending any lower. It is true, I can hardly hope to become what I once was. It is only too easy to grow rich; and, you know, poverty once forfeited can never return, except in rare instances. I have, however, succeeded in getting rid of most of my wealth, chiefly through the fortunate advent of Almah, and afterward of yourself. This, I confess, has been my salvation. Neither of you had any scruples about accepting what was bestowed, and so I did not feel as though I was doing you any wrong in giving you all I had in the world. Most of the people of this city have taken advantage of your extraordinary indifference to wealth, and have made themselves paupers at your expense. I had already become your slave, and had received the promise of being elevated to the rank of scullion[1] in the cavern of the *Mista Kosek*. But now, since this event of your love for Almah, I hope to gain far more. I am almost certain of being made a pauper, and I think I can almost venture to hope some day for the honor of a public death."

To such a story I had nothing to say. It was sheer madness; yet it was terribly suggestive, and showed how utterly hopeless was my effort to secure the assistance of such a man toward my escape from death.

"A public death!" I said, grimly. "That will be very fortunate! And do you think that you will gain the dignity of being eaten up afterward?"

The Kohen shook his head in all seriousness.

"Oh no," said he; "that would be far beyond my deserts.[2] That is an honor which is only bestowed upon the most distinguished."

CHAPTER XVI.
THE KOSEKIN.

THESE people call themselves the Kosekin. Their chief characteristic, or, at least, their most prominent one, is their love of darkness, which perhaps is due to their habit of dwelling in caves.[3]

---

1 In the Renaissance, a scullion was a low-ranking domestic servant who performed menial tasks in the kitchen.

2 Plural of desert, the reward or punishment that one deserves, as in "just deserts."

3 See Appendix D for more information on the idea of cave dwellers.

Another feeling, equally strong and perhaps connected with this, is their love of death and dislike of life. This is visible in many ways, and affects all their character. It leads to a passionate self-denial, an incessant effort to benefit others at their own expense. Each one hates life and longs for death. He therefore hates riches, and all things that are associated with life.

Among the Kosekin everyone makes perpetual efforts to serve others, which, however, are perpetually baffled by the unselfishness of these others. People thus spend years in trying to overreach one another, so as to make others richer than themselves. In a race, each one tries to keep behind; but as this leads to confusion, there is then a universal effort for each one to be first, so as to put his neighbor in the honorable position of the rear. It is the same way in a hunt. Each one presses forward, so as to honor his companion by leaving him behind. Instead of injuring, everyone tries to benefit his neighbor. When one has been benefited by another, he is filled with a passion which may be called Kosekin revenge—namely, a sleepless and vehement desire to bestow some adequate and corresponding benefit on the other. Feuds are thus kept up among families and wars among nations. For no one is willing to accept from another any kindness, any gift, or any honor, and all are continually on the watch to prevent themselves from being overreached in this way. Those who are less watchful than others are overwhelmed with gifts by designing men, who wish to attain to the pauper class. The position of Almah and myself illustrates this. Our ignorance of the blessings and honors of poverty led us to receive whatever was offered us. Taking advantage of our innocence and ignorance, the whole city thereupon proceeded to bestow their property upon us, and all became paupers through our fortunate arrival.

No one ever injures another unless by accident, and when this occurs it affords the highest joy to the injured party. He has now a claim on the injurer; he gets him into his power, is able to confer benefits on him, and force upon him all that he wishes. The unhappy injurer, thus punished by the reception of wealth, finds himself helpless; and where the injury is great, the injured man may bestow upon the other all his wealth and attain to the envied condition of a pauper.

Among the Kosekin the sick are objects of the highest regard. All classes vie with one another in their attentions. The rich send them luxuries; the paupers, however, not having anything to give, go themselves and wait on them and nurse them. For this there is no help, and the rich grumble, but can do nothing. The sick are thus sought out incessantly, and most carefully tended. When they die there is great rejoicing, since death is a blessing; but the nurses labor hard to preserve them in life, so as to prolong the enjoyment of the high privilege of nursing. Of all sick the incurable are most honored, since they require nursing always. Children also are highly honored and esteemed, and the aged too, since both classes require the care of others, and must be the recipients of favors which all are anxious to bestow. Those who suffer from contagious diseases are more sought after than any other class, for in waiting on these there is the chance of gaining the blessing of death; indeed, in these cases much trouble is usually experienced from the rush of those who insist on offering their services.

For it must never be forgotten that the Kosekin love death as we love life; and this accounts for all those ceremonies which to me were so abhorrent, especially the scenes of the *Mista Kosek*. To them a dead human body is no more than the dead body of a bird: there is no awe felt, no sense of sanctity, of superstitious horror; and so I learned, with a shudder, that the hate of life is a far worse thing than the fear of death. This desire for death is, then, a master-passion, and is the key to all their words and acts. They rejoice over the death of friends, since those friends have gained the greatest of blessings; they rejoice also at the birth of children, since those who are born will one day gain the bliss of death.

For a couple to fall in love is the signal for mutual self-surrender. Each insists on giving up the loved one; and the more passionate the love is, the more eager is the desire to have the loved one married to someone else. Lovers have died broken-hearted from being compelled to marry one another. Poets here among the Kosekin celebrate unhappy love which has met with this end. These poets also celebrate defeats instead of victories, since it is considered glorious for one nation to sacrifice itself to another; but to this there are important limitations, as we shall see. Poets also celebrate street-sweepers, scavengers, lamp-lighters, laborers, and above all, paupers, and pass by as unworthy of notice the Athons,[1] Meleks, and Kohens of the land.

The paupers here form the most honorable class. Next to these are the laborers. These have strikes, as with us; but it is always for harder work, longer hours, or smaller pay. The contest between capital and labor rages, but the conditions are reversed; for the grumbling capitalist complains that the laborer will not take as

1 "Athons" is "Authors" in *Harper's Weekly* serial—yet another mistake.

much pay as he ought to, while the laborer thinks the capitalist too persistent in his efforts to force money upon him.[1]

Here among the Kosekin the wealthy class forms the mass of the people, while the aristocratic few consist of the paupers. These are greatly envied by the others, and have many advantages. The cares and burdens of wealth, as well as wealth itself, are here considered a curse, and from all these the paupers are exempt. There is a perpetual effort on the part of the wealthy to induce the paupers to accept gifts, just as among us the poor try to rob the rich. Among the wealthy there is a great and incessant murmur at the obstinacy of the paupers. Secret movements are sometimes set on foot which aim at a redistribution of property and a levelling of all classes, so as to reduce the haughty paupers to the same condition as the mass of the nation. More than once there has been a violent attempt at a revolution, so as to force wealth on the paupers; but as a general thing these movements have been put down and their leaders severely punished. The paupers have shown no mercy in their hour of triumph; they have not conceded one jot to the public demand, and the unhappy conspirators have been condemned to increased wealth and luxury, while the leaders have been made Meleks and Kohens. Thus there are among the Kosekin the unfortunate many who are cursed with wealth, and the fortunate few who are blessed with poverty. These walk while the others ride, and from their squalid huts look proudly and contemptuously upon the palaces of their unfortunate fellow-countrymen.

[TO BE CONTINUED.]

---

1 De Mille is alluding to the growing labour movement and various critiques of capitalism during the nineteenth century. Karl Marx published the first volume of *Das Kapital* in 1867, about the time that De Mille was writing *A Strange Manuscript*. Chartism was a mass working class labour movement that sought political and social reforms in Britain between 1838 and 1850.

PART 11 (17 MARCH, 1888)

CHAPTER XVI.—(*Continued.*)
THE KOSEKIN.

THE love of death leads to perpetual efforts on the part of each to lay down his life for another. This is a grave difficulty in hunts and battles. Confined prisoners dare not fly, for in such an event the guards kill themselves. This leads to fresh rigors in the captivity of the prisoners in case of their recapture, for they are overwhelmed with fresh luxuries and increased splendors. Finally, if a prisoner persists and is recaptured, he is solemnly put to death, not, as with us, by way of severity, but as the last and greatest honor. Here extremes meet; and death, whether for honor or dishonor, is all the same—death—and is reserved for desperate cases. But among the Kosekin this lofty destiny is somewhat embittered by the agonizing thought of the prisoner, who thus gains it, that his wretched family must be doomed, not, as with us, to poverty and want, but, on the contrary, to boundless wealth and splendor.

Among so strange a people it seemed singular to me what offences could possibly be committed which could be regarded and punished as crimes. These, however, I soon found out. Instead of robbers, the Kosekin punished the secret bestowers of their wealth on others. This is regarded as a very grave offence. Analogous to our crime of piracy is the forcible arrest of ships at sea and the transfer to them of valuables. Sometimes the Kosekin pirates give themselves up as slaves. Kidnapping, assault, highway robbery, and crimes of violence have their parallel here in cases where a strong man, meeting a weaker, forces himself upon him as his slave or compels him to take his purse. If the weaker refuse, the assailant threatens to kill himself, which act would lay the other under obligations to receive punishment from the state in the shape of gifts and honors, or at least subject him to unpleasant inquiries. Murder has its counterpart among the Kosekin in cases where one man meets another, forces money on him, and kills himself. Forgery occurs where one uses another's name so as to confer money on him.

There are many other crimes, all of which are severely punished. The worse the offence is, the better is the offender treated. Among the Kosekin capital punishment is imprisonment amid the greatest splendor, where the prisoner is treated like a king, and has many palaces and great retinues; for that which we consider the highest they regard as the lowest, and with them the chief post of honor is what we would call the lowest menial office. Of course, among such a people, any suffering from want is unknown, except when it is voluntary. The pauper class, with all their great privileges, have this restriction, that they are forced to receive enough for food and clothing. Some, indeed, manage by living in out-of-the-way places to deprive themselves of these, and have been known to die of starvation; but this is regarded as dishonorable, as taking an undue advantage of a great position, and where it can be proved, the children and relatives of the offender are severely punished according to the Kosekin fashion.

State politics here move, like individual affairs, upon the great principle of contempt for earthly things. The state is willing to destroy itself for the good of other states; but as other states are in the same position, nothing can result. In times of war the object of each army is to honor the other and benefit it by giving it the glory of defeat. The contest is thus most fierce. The Kosekin, through their passionate love of death, are terrible in battle; and when they are also animated by the desire to confer glory on their enemies by defeating them, they generally succeed in their aim. This makes them almost always victorious; and when they are not so, not a soul returns alive. Their state of mind is peculiar. If they are defeated they rejoice, since defeat is their chief glory; but if they are victorious they rejoice still more, in the benevolent thought that they have conferred upon the enemy the joy, the glory, and the honor of defeat.

Here all shrink from governing others. The highest wish of each is to serve. The Meleks and Kohens, whom I at first considered the highest, are really the lowest orders; next to these come the Athons,[1] then the merchants, then farmers, then artisans, then laborers, and, finally, the highest rank is reached in the paupers. Happy the aristocratic, the haughty, the envied paupers! The same thing is seen in their armies. The privates here are highest in rank, and the officers come next in different gradations. These officers, however, have the command and the charge of affairs as with us; yet this is consistent with their position, for here to obey is considered nobler than to command. In the fleet the rowers are the highest class; next come the fighting-men; and lowest of all are the officers. War arises from motives as peculiar as those which give rise to private feuds; as, for instance, where one nation tries to force a province upon another; where they try to make each other greater; where they try to benefit unduly each other's commerce;

---

1 "Athons" is "Authors" in the *Harper's Weekly* serial—a mistake.

where one may have a smaller fleet or army than has been agreed on, or where an ambassador has been presented with gifts, or received too great honor or attention.

In such a country as this, where riches are disliked and despised, I could not imagine how people could be induced to engage in trade. This, however, was soon explained. The laborers and artisans have to perform their daily work, so as to enable the community to live and move and have its being. Their impelling motive is the high one of benefiting others most directly. They refuse anything but the very smallest pay, and insist on giving for this the utmost possible labor. Tradesmen also have to supply the community with articles of all sorts; merchants have to sail their ships to the same end—all being animated by the desire of effecting the good of others. Each one tries not to make money, but to lose it; but as the competition is sharp and universal, this is difficult, and the larger portion are unsuccessful. The purchasers are eager to pay as much as possible, and the merchants and traders grow rich in spite of their utmost endeavors. The wealthy classes go into business so as to lose money, but in this they seldom succeed. It has been calculated that only two per cent.[1] in every community succeed in reaching the pauper class. The tendency is for all the products of the working-class to be ultimately turned upon the unfortunate wealthy class. The workmen being the creators of wealth, and refusing to take adequate pay, cause a final accumulation of the wealth of the community in the hands of the mass of the non-producers, who thus are fixed in their unhappy position, and can hope for no escape except by death. The farmers till the ground, the fishermen fish, the laborers toil, and the wealth thus created is pushed from these incessantly till it all falls upon the lowest class—namely, the rich, including Athons, Meleks, and Kohens. It is a burden that is often too heavy to be borne; but there is no help for it, and the better-minded seek to cultivate resignation.

Women and men are in every respect absolutely equal, holding precisely the same offices and doing the same work. In general, however, it is observed that women are a little less fond of death than men, and a little less unwilling to receive gifts. For this reason they are very numerous among the wealthy class, and abound in the offices of administration. Women serve in the army and navy as well as men, and from their lack of ambition or energetic perseverance they are usually relegated to the lower ranks, such as

1 The use of the period is an archaism—"per cent."—and it is accurate to the *Harper's Weekly* serial.

officers and generals. To my mind it seemed as though the women were in all the offices of honor and dignity, but in reality it was the very opposite. The same is true in the family. The husbands insist on giving everything to the wives and doing everything for them. The wives are therefore universally the rulers of the household while the husbands have an apparently subordinate, but, to the Kosekin, a more honorable position.

As to the religion of the Kosekin, I could make nothing of it. They believe that after death they go to what they call the world of darkness. The death that they long for leads to the darkness that they love; and the death and the darkness are eternal. Still, they persist in saying that the death and the darkness together form a state of bliss. They are eloquent about the happiness that awaits them there in the sunless land—the world of darkness; but, for my own part, it always seemed to me a state of nothingness.

CHAPTER XVII.
BELIEF AND UNBELIEF.

THE doctor was here interrupted by Featherstone, who with a yawn informed him that it was eleven o'clock, and that human endurance had its limits. Upon this the doctor rolled up the manuscript and put it aside for the night, after which supper was ordered.

"Well," said Featherstone, "what do you think of this last?"

"It contains some very remarkable statements," said the doctor.

"There are certainly monsters enough in it," said Melick—"'Gorgons, and hydras, and chimeras dire.'"[1]

"Well, why not?" said the doctor.

"It seems to me," said Melick, "that the writer of this has peopled his world with creatures that resemble the fossil animals more than anything else."

"The so-called fossil animals," said the doctor, "may not be extinct. There are fossil specimens of animals that still have living

1 Melick quotes John Milton's *Paradise Lost*: "Where all life dies, death lives, and nature breeds, / Perverse, all monstrous, all prodigious things, / Abominable, inutterable, and worse / Than Fables yet have feign'd, or fear conceiv'd, / GORGONS and HYDRAS, and CHIMERAS dire" (Book II, lines 624-28). It is notable, given other references in this chapter, that Hugh Miller also quotes this line in *The Testimony of Rocks* (1865), when he suggests that mythical dragons have a paleontological basis in dinosaurs.

representatives. There is no reason why many of those supposed to be extinct may not be alive now. It is well known that many very remarkable animals have become extinct within a comparatively recent period. These great birds, of which More speaks, seem to me to belong to these classes. The dodo[1] was in existence fifty years ago,[2] the moa[3] about a hundred years ago. These great birds, together with others, such as the epiornis[4] and palapteryx,[5] have disappeared, not through the ordinary course of nature, but by the hand of man. Even in our hemisphere they may yet be found. Who can tell but that the moa or the dodo may yet be lurking somewhere here in the interior of Madagascar, of Borneo, or of Papua?"[6]

"Can you make out anything about those great birds?" asked Featherstone. "Do they resemble anything that exists now, or has ever existed?"

"Well, yes, I think so," said the doctor. "Unfortunately, More is not at all close or accurate in his descriptions; he has a decidedly unscientific mind, and so one cannot feel sure; yet from his

---

1 A flightless bird that went extinct by the late seventeenth century, the dodo (*Raphus cucullatus*) was endemic to Mauritius, an island in the Indian Ocean off the east coast of Africa. It was about a meter in height and weighed about 20 kilograms.

2 The last recorded sighting of the dodo was made in 1681 by Benjamin Harry, chief mate of the *Berkeley Castle*. The doctor seems to refer to the Rodrigues Solitaire (*Pezophaps solitaria*), a relative of the dodo endemic to the island of Rodrigues, just east of the island of Mauritius. The Rodrigues Solitaire is presumed to have been extinct by the late eighteenth century.

3 Gigantic flightless birds, the eleven species of Moa were endemic to New Zealand. The largest species were up to twelve feet in height and weighed up to 500 pounds. They were probably extinct by the sixteenth century, but unverified sightings were reported into the nineteenth.

4 Taller than ten feet and weighing more than 800 pounds, the gigantic flightless elephant bird (*Aepyornis maximus*) was the world's largest bird. It was native to Madagascar and went extinct by the seventeenth century. Richard Owen discusses the epiornis, dodo, moa, and palapteryx in the same section of *Paleontology*: "Summary on Fossil Reptiles, Class III: Aves" (330-32). He notes that the egg of an epiornis is equivalent in size to six ostrich eggs.

5 Richard Owen distinguished the palapteryx, another large flightless bird native to New Zealand, from the moa (or dinornis) in the 1840s.

6 Madagascar is an island in the Indian Ocean off the southeast coast of Africa. Located in the Malay or Indonesian archipelago between southeastern Asia and Australia, Borneo is the third largest island in the world. By Papua, the doctor presumably means the island of New Guinea, the second largest island in the world, located directly north of Australia.

general statements I think I can decide pretty nearly upon the nature and the scientific name of each one of his birds and animals. It is quite evident to me that most of these animals belong to races that no longer exist among us, and that this world at the South Pole has many characteristics which are like those of what is known as the Coal Period.[1] I allude in particular to the vast forests of fern, of gigantic grasses and reeds.[2] At the same time the general climate and the atmosphere seem like what we may find in the tropics at present. It is evident that in More's world various epochs are represented, and that animals of different ages are living side by side."

"What do you think of the opkuk?" asked Featherstone, with a yawn.

"Well, I hardly know."

"Why, it must be a dodo, of course," said Melick, "only magnified."

"That," said the doctor, gravely, "is a thought that naturally suggests itself; but then the opkuk is certainly far larger than the dodo."

"Oh, More put on his magnifying-glasses just then."

"The dodo," continued the doctor, taking no notice of this, "in other respects corresponds with More's description of the opkuk. Clusius and Bontius[3] give good descriptions and there is a well-known picture of one in the British Museum.[4] It is a massive, clumsy bird, ungraceful in its form, with heavy movements, wings too short for flight, little or no tail, and down rather than feathers. The body, according to Bontius, is as big as that of the African

---

1 De Mille's scientific sources use the term "Coal Period" as synonymous with Carboniferous Period, a geological period that extended from the Devonian to the Permian periods (about 359 to 299 million years ago). For information on the Carboniferous or "Coal" period, De Mille may have consulted Charles Lyell's *Elements of Geology* (1838), John William Dawson's *Air Breathers of the Coal Period* (1863), Hugh Miller's *The Testimony of Rocks* (1865), and Louis Figuier's *The World Before the Deluge* (1866). See Appendix B3 for excerpts from Figuier's work.

2 Figuier provides vivid illustrations of many of the carboniferous vegetation mentioned by More.

3 Carolus Clusius (1516-1609) was the first to publish a scientific account of the Mauritius dodo. Jacobus Bontius (Jacob de Bondt) (1592-1631), a Dutch physician who was one of the first naturalists employed by the Dutch East India Company in the East Indies, also describes the dodo and provides one of the most reproduced drawings of the bird in *Tropische Geneeskunde*, his book on tropical medicine.

4 De Mille visited London, and presumably the British Museum, in 1850 and 1851.

ostrich, but the legs are very short. It has a large head, great black eyes, long bluish-white bill, ending in a beak like that of a vulture, yellow legs, thick and short, four toes on each foot, solid, long, and armed with sharp black claws. The flesh, particularly on the breast, is fat and esculent. Now, all this corresponds with More's account, except as to the size of the two, for the opkuks are as large as oxen."

"Oh, that's nothing," said Melick; "I'm determined to stand up for the dodo." With this he burst forth singing:

"Oh, the dodo once lived, but he doesn't live now;
Yet why should a cloud overshadow our brow?
The loss of that bird ne'er should trouble our brains,
For though he is gone, still our claret[1] remains.
Sing do-do—jolly do-do!
Hurrah! in his name let our cups overflow.[2]

"As for your definition, doctor," continued Melick, "I'll give you one worth a dozen of yours:

"'Twas a mighty bird; those strong short legs were never known to fail,
And he felt a glory of pride while thinking of that little tail,
And his beak was marked with vigor, curving like a wondrous hook;
Thick and ugly was his body—such a form as made one look!"

"Melick," said Featherstone, "you're a volatile youth. You mustn't mind him, doctor. He's a professional cynic, sceptic, and scoffer. Oxenden and I, however, are open to conviction, and want to know more about those birds and beasts. Can you make anything out of the opmahera?"

The doctor swallowed a glass of wine, and replied:

"Oh yes; there are many birds, each of which may be the opmahera. There's the fossil bird of Massachusetts,[3] of which nothing

---

1 A British name for red wine made in the Bordeaux region of France.

2 Both of Melick's stanzas can be found in an anonymous 1844 article, entitled "Recreations in Natural History—the Dodo," in the London publication *Bentley's Miscellany* (529). Perhaps Melick read it.

3 The fossilized bird prints found in the red sandstone of the Connecticut River Valley are discussed extensively by Hugh Miller in *The Testimony of Rocks* (112-16). Miller assigns them to the "Grallae or stilt order of birds" (113). He describes the prints as "tridactyle footprints" that measure

is left but the footprints; but some of these are eighteen inches in length, and show a stride of two yards. The bird belonged to the order of the *Grallae*,[1] and may have been ten or twelve feet in height. Then there is the *Gastornis parisiensis*,[2] which was as tall as an ostrich, as big as an ox, and belongs to the same order as the other. Then there is the *Palapteryx*, of which remains have been found in New Zealand, which was seven or eight feet in height. But the one which to my mind is the real counterpart of the opmahera is the *Dinornis gigantea*,[3] whose remains are also found in New Zealand. It is the largest bird known, with long legs, a long neck, and short wings, useless for flight. One specimen that has been found is upward of thirteen feet in height. There is no reason why some should not have been much taller. More compares its height to that of a giraffe. The Maoris[4] call this bird the *Moa*, and their legends and traditions are full of mention of it. When they first came to the island, six or seven hundred years ago, they found these vast birds everywhere, and hunted them for food. To my mind the dinornis[5] is the opmahera of More. As to riding on them, that is likely enough; for ostriches are used for this purpose, and the dinornis must have been far stronger and fleeter than the ostrich. It is possible that some of these birds may still be living in the remoter parts of our hemisphere."

"What about those monsters," asked Featherstone, "that More speaks of in the sacred hunt?"

"I think," said the doctor, "that I understand pretty well what they were, and can identify them all. As the galley passed the estuary of that great river, you remember that he mentions seeing

---

"eighteen inches in length from the heel to the middle claw" having "a stride of about six feet" (115). Miller likens the birds who made these prints to "the Roc of Sinbad the Sailor" (116) and he directly relates the size of these prints to the moa (*Dinornis gigantea*).

1 An order of birds that includes waders such as sandpipers and plovers.

2 The fossilized remains of this large flightless bird that lived 56-40 million years ago were found in 1855 by the French geologist Edmond Hébert. Richard Owen wrote an article on the discovery, and he mentions it in *Paleontology*: "They belonged to a species as large as an Ostrich, but more robust, and with affinities to wading or aquatic birds" (328).

3 One of the largest of eleven species of moa. Captain James Ross mentions *Dinornis gigantea* in Volume 2 of *A Voyage of Discovery in the Southern and Antarctic Regions* (see Appendix A3 for an introduction to Ross) and notes that its height is sixteen feet (409). Richard Owen devotes several pages to *Dinornis giganteus* in *Paleontology* (330-32).

4 The Māori are a Polynesian people indigenous to New Zealand.

5 I.e., *Dinornis gigantea.*

them on the shore. One may have been the *Ichthyosaurus*.[1] This, as the name implies, is a fish-lizard. It has the head of a lizard, the snout of a dolphin, the teeth of an alligator, enormous eyes, whose membrane is strengthened by a bony frame, the vertebrae of fishes, sternum and shoulder-bones like those of the lizard, and the fins of a whale. Bayle[2] calls it the whale of the saurians.[3] Another may have been the *Cheirotherium*.[4] On account of the hand-shaped marks made by its paws, Owen[5] thinks that it was akin to the frogs; but it was a formidable monster, with head and jaws of a crocodile. Another may have been the *Teleosaurus*, which resembled our alligators. It was thirty-five feet in length.[6] Then there was the *Hylœosaurus*,[7] a monster twenty-five feet in length, with a cuirass of bony plates."

"But none of these correspond with More's description of the monster that fought with the galley."

---

1 A giant marine reptile of the early Jurassic period (199-189 million years ago). See Appendices B1 and B2 for descriptions of the Ichthyosaurus in Richard Owen and Louis Figuier. Note how the doctor's description closely follows that of Figuier.

2 Claude-Emile Bayle (1819-85) was a French naturalist and paleontologist. See also Appendix B2, where Figuier uses the same wording: "Bayle calls it the whale of the saurians." Parks notes that Bayle doesn't seem to say this (Parks 286-87), which suggests that Figuier is one of De Mille's sources.

3 Reptiles, including lizards, crocodiles, and dinosaurs. The term was used in the nineteenth century, but is no longer used.

4 Also known as *Chirotherium*, this creature is only known by its fossilized prints found in red sandstone in Germany. See Owen's description of the *Labyrinthodon* in Appendix B1, where he associates it with the prints left by the *Cheirotherium*. See the drawing of the *Labyrinthodon salamandroides*.

5 The British comparative anatomist, biologist, and paleontologist Sir Richard Owen (1804-92) introduced the term *Dinosauria* and made full-sized sculptures of dinosaurs based on fossils for the 1851 Great Exhibition. See Appendix B1 for a fuller introduction to Owen and excerpts from *Geology and the Inhabitants of the Ancient World* (1854).

6 An extinct genus of ocean-going crocodilian of the Middle Jurassic period. Figuier specifies a length of "about 30 feet" (223). See Appendix B1 for Owen's description.

7 Resembling an Ankylosaurus, the Hylaeosaurus was an armoured plant-eating dinosaur that lived 135-119 million years ago. It was one of the first creatures that Owen identified as a dinosaur. See Appendix B1 for Owen's description and an illustration of its fossilized remains. See Appendix B2: the illustration of the Teleosaurus has a Hylaeosaurus in the background.

"No," said the doctor; "I am coming to that now. That monster could have been no other than the *Plesiosaurus*,[1] one of the most wonderful animals that has ever existed. Imagine a thing with the head of a lizard, the teeth of a crocodile, the neck of a swan, the trunk and tail of a quadruped, and the fins of a whale. Imagine a whale with its head and neck consisting of a serpent, with the strength of the former and the malignant fury of the latter, and then you will have the plesiosaurus. It was an aquatic animal, yet it had to remain near or on the surface of the water, while its long, serpent-like neck enabled it to reach its prey above or below with swift, far-reaching darts. Yet it had no armor, and could not have been at all a match for the tremendous Ichthyosaurus. More's account shows, however, that it was a fearful enemy for man to encounter."

"He seems to have been less formidable than that beast which they encountered in the swamp. Have you any idea what that was?"

"I think it can have been no other than the *Iguanodon*,"[2] said the doctor. "The remains of this animal show that it must have been the most gigantic of all primeval saurians. Judging from existing remains its length was not less than sixty feet, and larger ones may have existed. It stood high on its legs; the hind ones were larger than the fore. The feet were massive and armed with tremendous claws. It lived on the land and fed on herbage. It had a horny, spiky ridge all along its back. Its tail was nearly as long as its body. Its head was short, its jaws[3] enormous, furnished with teeth of a very elaborate structure, and on its muzzle it carried a curved horn. Such a beast as this might well have caused all that destruction of life on the part of his desperate assailants of which More speaks.

"Then there was another animal," continued the doctor, who was evidently discoursing upon a favorite topic. "It was the one that came suddenly upon More while he was resting with Almah after his flight with the run-away bird. That I take to be the *Megalosaurus*.[4] This animal was a monster of tremendous size and

---

1 A marine reptile that lived during the Jurassic period (200-176 million years ago), the Plesiosaurus, which reaches a length of about five meters, is distinguished by its elongated neck with crocodile-like head, stocky body with four paddle-like limbs, and short tail. See Appendix B1.

2 A large herbivore that lived during the Early Cretaceous period (135-125 million years ago). See Appendix B1.

3 Jaws is "paws" in the *Harper's Weekly* serial—a mistake.

4 The first dinosaur to be described and named, the Megalosaurus was a genus of large carnivorous dinosaur of the Middle Jurassic period (166 million years ago). See Appendix B1 for Owen's description and illustration.

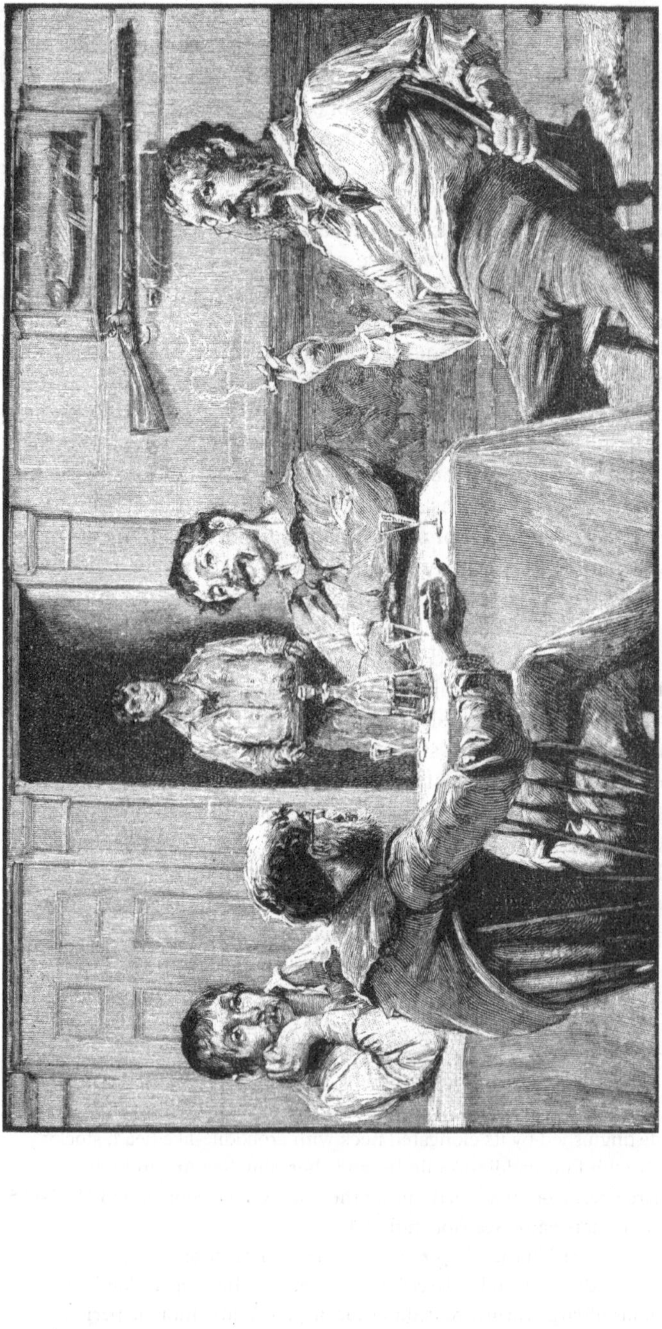

Illustration 11: "'Then there was another animal,' continued the doctor, who was evidently discoursing upon a favorite topic."

strength. Cuvier thought that it might have been seventy feet in length.[1] It was carnivorous, and therefore more ferocious than the iguanodon, and more ready to attack. Its head was like that of a crocodile, its body massive like that of an elephant, yet larger; its tail was small, and it stood high on its legs, so that it could run with great speed. It was not covered with bony armor, but had probably a hide thick enough to serve the purpose of shell or bone. Its teeth were constructed so as to cut with their edges, and the movement of the jaws produced the combined effect of knife and saw, while their inward curve rendered impossible the escape of prey that had once been caught. It probably frequented the river-banks, where it fed upon reptiles of smaller size, which inhabited the same places.

"More," continued the doctor, "is too general in his descriptions. He has not a scientific mind, and he gives but few data; yet I can bring before myself very easily all the scenes which he describes, particularly that one in which the megalosaurus approaches, and he rushes to mount the dinornis so as to escape. I see that river, with its trees and shrubs, all unknown now except in museums—the vegetation of the Coal Period—the lepidodendron, the lepidostrobus, the pecopteris, the neuropteris, the lonchopteris, the odontopteris, the sphenopteris, the cyclopteris, the sigillaria reniformis,[2] the sphenophyllum, the calamites—"[3]

Melick started to his feet.

"There, there!" he cried, "hold hard, doctor. Talking of calamities, what greater calamity can there be than such a torrent of unknown words? Talk English, doctor, and we shall be able to appreciate you; but to make your jokes, your conundrums, and your

---

1 The French naturalist and zoologist Georges (Jean Léopold Nicolas Frédéric) Cuvier (1769-1832) made enormous contributions to the fields of comparative anatomy and paleontology. He notes that the Megalosaurus "must have exceeded seventy feet in length" (259) in his *Essay on the Theory of the Earth* (1827).

2 The *Harper's Weekly* serial's "sigillaria viniformis" and the book's "sigellaria reniformis" are both incorrect. Parks corrects to "sigillaria reniformis" (Parks l).

3 The lepidodendron, sigillaria reniformis, and calamites were tree-like; the lepidostrobus was a fruit-cone of the lepidodendron; pecopteris names a type of leaf; neuropteris, odontopteris, sphenopteris were all ferns or fern-like; cyclopteris were oval or oval-elliptical leaflets of the neuropteris; and sphenophyllum was a shrub or a creeping vine. See Appendix B3 for Louis Figuier's description of vegetation in the Coal (or Carboniferous) period in *The World Before the Deluge* (1866). Figuier discusses all of the species mentioned by the doctor. See the separate figures Figuier provides for ferns, calamites, lepidodendron, and sphenophyllum.

brilliant witticisms in a foreign language isn't fair to us, and does no credit either to your head or your heart."

The doctor elevated his eyebrows, and took no notice of Melick's ill-timed levity.

"All these stories of strange animals," said Oxenden, "may be very interesting, doctor, but I must say that I am far more struck by the account of the people themselves. I wonder whether they are an aboriginal race, or descendants of the same stock from which we came?"

"I should say," remarked the doctor, confidently, "that they are, beyond a doubt, an aboriginal and autochthonous race."[1]

"I differ from you altogether," said Oxenden, calmly.

"Oh," said the doctor, "there can be no doubt about it. Their complexion, small stature, and peculiar eyes—their love of darkness, their singular characteristics, both physical and moral, all go to show that they can have no connection with the races in our part of the earth."

"Their peculiar eyes," said Oxenden, "are no doubt produced by dwelling in caves for many generations."[2]

"On the contrary," said the doctor, "it is their peculiarity of eye that makes them dwell in caves."

"You are mistaking the cause for the effect, doctor."

"Not at all; it is you who are making that mistake."

"It's the old debate," said Melick. "As the poet has it:

"'Which was first, the egg or the hen?
Tell me, I pray, ye learned men.'"[3]

"There are the eyeless fishes of the great cave of Kentucky," said Oxenden, "whose eyes have become extinct from living in the dark."[4]

---

1 Indigenous to a particular place; originating where found. Given the subterranean associations of chthonic (dwelling beneath the Earth), this may suggest that the Kosekin originate underground.

2 Oxenden's idea can be reconciled with either Charles Darwin's theory of natural selection and Jean-Baptiste Lamarck's theory of acquired characteristics, but his comments below seem to favour a Lamarckian approach.

3 Melick's couplet is derived from an anonymous poem in dialogue form published in several publications in the 1850s and 1860s, including *Hartford Courant* (29 November 1856): "So, tell me, I pray you, ye learned men, / Whether was first, the egg or the hen?" ("Ignoramus" 209).

4 Located in central Kentucky, the Mammoth Cave is the longest system of caves known in the world, extending for almost 600 km. Living in thousands of caves throughout Kentucky and Indiana, the Northern

"No," cried the doctor; "the fish that have arisen in that lake have never needed eyes, and have never had them."

Oxenden laughed.

"Well," said he, "I'll discuss the question with you on different grounds altogether, and I will show clearly that these men, these bearded men, must belong to a stock that is nearly related to our own, or at least that they belong to a race of men with whom we are all very familiar."

"I should like very much to have you try it," said the doctor.

"Very well," said Oxenden. "In the first place, I take their language."

"Their language!"

"Yes. More has given us very many words in their language. Now he himself says that these words had an Arabic sound. He was slightly acquainted with that language. What will you say if I tell you that these words are still more like Hebrew?"

"Hebrew!" exclaimed the doctor, in amazement.

"Yes, Hebrew," said Oxenden. "They are all very much like Hebrew words, and the difference is not greater than that which exists between the words of any two languages of the Aryan family."[1]

"Oh, if you come to philology I'll throw up the sponge," said the doctor. "Yet I should like to hear what you have to say on that point."

"The languages of the Aryan family," said Oxenden, "have the same general characteristics, and in all of them the differences that exist in their most common words are subject to the action of a regular law. The action of the law is best seen in the changes which take place in the mutes. These changes are indicated in a summary and comprehensive way by means of what is called 'Grimm's Law.'[2] Take Latin and English, for instance. 'Grimm's Law' tells us, among other things, that in Latin and in that part of English which is of Teutonic[3] origin a large number of words are essentially the same, and differ merely in certain phonetic changes. Take the word 'father.' In Latin, as also in Greek, it is 'pater.' Now the Latin 'p' in English becomes 'f'; that is, the thin

---

cavefish (*Amblyopsis spelaeus*) is a troglobitic species of fish first described by James DeKay in 1842. It is blind and colourless, although it does have rudimentary eyes hidden under its skin and non-functional pigment cells.

1 I.e., Indo-European languages.

2 A milestone in nineteenth-century linguistics, this systematic sound-change principle was elaborated by Jacob Grimm (1785-1863) in 1822. Oxenden provides an accurate explanation of the law.

3 Of or relating to the Teutons, an ancient Germanic people.

mute becomes the aspirated mute.[1] The same change may be seen in the Latin 'piscis,' which in English is 'fish,' and the Greek 'πυρ' which in English is 'fire.' Again, if the Latin or Greek word begins with an aspirate,[2] the English word begins with a medial;[3] thus the Latin 'f' is found responsive to the English 'b,' as in Latin 'fagus,' English 'beech,' Latin 'fero,' English 'bear.' Again, if the Latin or Greek has the medial, the English has the thin, as in Latin 'duo,' English 'two,' Latin 'genu,' English 'knee.' Now I find that in many of the words which More mentions this same 'Grimm's Law' will apply; and I am inclined to think that if they were spelled with perfect accuracy they would show the same relation between the Kosekin language and the Hebrew that there is between the Saxon English and the Latin."

The doctor gave a heavy sigh.

"You're out of my depth, Oxenden," said he. "I'm nothing of a philologist."[4]

"By Jove!" said Featherstone, "I like this. This is equal to your list of the plants of the Coal Period, doctor. But I say, Oxenden, while you are about it, why don't you give us a little dose of Anglo-Saxon[5] and Sanscrit?[6] By Jove! the fellow has Bopp[7] by heart, and yet he expects us to argue with him."

"I have it!" cried Melick. "The Kosekin are the lost Ten Tribes.[8] Oxenden is feeling his way to that. He is going to make them out to be all Hebrew; and then, of course, the only conclusion will be that they are the Ten Tribes, who after a life of strange vicissitudes have pulled up at the South Pole. It's a wonder More didn't think

---

1 In today's linguistic terms, Oxenden seems to be saying that a voiceless stop, a consonant made with no audible sound except in the transition to or from another sound (in this case, p), becomes a voiceless fricative (in this case, f).

2 An expiratory breath puff such as follows initial (p), (t), or (k) in English.

3 A voiced stop, such as (b), (d), or (g).

4 One who studies philology, the humanist study of language, especially its history.

5 Old English: English prior to about 1100.

6 Sanskrit is an ancient language of India. The Vedas are written in Sanskrit.

7 Franz Bopp (1791-1867), a German linguist known for his comparative analysis of the grammars of Indo-European languages.

8 The Northern Kingdom of Israel, with its capital at Samaria, was conquered by the Assyrians circa 720 BCE. The population, including ten tribes of Israelites, was relocated or dispersed, lost from the biblical record, leading to the myth of the Lost Ten Tribes. There are many different accounts and theories regarding their fate and they figure prominently in nineteenth-century lost world narratives such as Rider Haggard's *King Solomon's Mines* (1885) and Samuel Butler's *Erewhon* (1872).

of that—or the writer of this yarn, whoever he may be. Well, for my part, I always took a deep interest in the lost Ten Tribes, and thought them a fine body of men."

"Don't think they've got much of the Jew about them," said Featherstone, languidly. "They hate riches and all that, you know. Break a Jew's heart to hear of all that property wasted, and money going a-begging. Not a bad idea, though, that of theirs about money. Too much money's a howwid baw,[1] by Jove!"

"Well," continued Oxenden, calmly resuming, and taking no notice of these interruptions, "I can give you word after word that More has mentioned which corresponds to a kindred Hebrew word in accordance with 'Grimm's Law.' For instance, Kosekin 'Op,' Hebrew 'Oph'; Kosekin 'Athon,' Hebrew 'Adon'; Kosekin 'Salon,' Hebrew 'Shalom!' They are more like Hebrew than Arabic, just as Anglo-Saxon words are more like Latin or Greek than Sanscrit."

"Hurrah!" cried Melick, "we've got him to Sanscrit at last! Now, Oxenden, my boy, trot out the 'Hitopadesa,'[2] the 'Megha Dhuta,'[3] the 'Rig Veda.'[4] Quote 'Beowulf'[5] and Caedmon.[6] Gives us a little Zeno,[7] and wind up with 'Lalla Rookh'[8] in modern Persian."[9]

"So I conclude," said Oxenden, calmly, ignoring Melick, "that the Kosekin are a Semitic people. Their complexion and their

---

1 Horrid bore.

2 A collection of ancient Sanskrit fables attributed to Narayana, the Hitopadesa has been translated into many languages and exerted enormous influence on fables told in other countries. It is "Hetopadesa" in the Harper's Weekly serial (17 March 1888)—an error.

3 Usually *Megha Dūta*, translated as Cloud Messenger, this poem was written in Sanskrit by the Indian poet Kālidāsa. It was first fully translated into English by H.A. Ouvry in 1868.

4 This ancient collection of more than 1000 Vedic Sanskrit hymns is one of the sacred Vedas of Hinduism.

5 This Old English epic poem, preserved in a single manuscript dated circa 1000 CE, tells the story of the Scandinavian hero Beowulf.

6 The nine-line poem "Caedmon's Hymn" is the first and only surviving work by this earliest known English poet, a herdsman who lived during the seventh century CE.

7 The pre-Socratic Greek philosopher, Zeno of Elea (fifth century BCE) is best known for his paradoxes.

8 Written in 1817 by the Irish poet Thomas Moore (1759-1852), this Oriental Romance consists of four tales told to the Indian princess Lalla Rookh by the poet Feramorz as they travel from Delhi to Kashmir for her wedding to the King of Bukhara.

9 An Iranian language that is widely spoken in Iran, Afghanistan, Tajikistan, Uzbekistan, and elsewhere.

beards show them to be akin to the Caucasian race, and their language proves beyond the shadow of a doubt that they belong to the Semitic branch of that race. It is impossible for an autochthonous people to have such a language."

"But how," cried the doctor—"how in the name of wonder did they get to the South Pole?"

"Easily enough," interrupted Melick—"Shem[1] landed there from Noah's ark,[2] and left some of his children to colonize the country. That's as plain as a pikestaff. I think, on the whole, that this idea is better than the other one about the Ten Tribes. At any rate they are both mine, and I warn all present to keep their hands off them, for on my return I intend to take out a copyright."

"There's another thing," continued Oxenden, "which is of immense importance, and that is their habit of cave-dwelling. I am inclined to think that they resorted to cave-dwelling at first from some hereditary instinct or other, and that their eyes and their whole morals have become affected by this mode of life. Now, as to ornamented caverns, we have many examples—caverns adorned with a splendor fully equal to anything among the Kosekin. There are in India the great Behar caves,[3] the splendid Karli temple with its magnificent sculptures and imposing architecture,[4] and the cavern-temples of Elephanta;[5] there are the subterranean works in Egypt, the temple of Dendera[6] in particular; in Petra[7] we have

---

1 In the King James Version of the Bible, Noah had three sons: Shem, Ham, and Japheth (Genesis 6:10). Shem, often considered the eldest, was on the ark (7:13). Along with Japheth, Shem didn't look on Noah's nakedness (9:23) and was blessed by Noah (9:26). Shem had many children, including Elam, Asshur, Arphaxad, Lud, and Aram (10:22). The descendants of Shem include Abraham. Shem is said to have lived to 600 years.

2 The vessel built by the Noah that saves his family and different types of animals from a flood. See Genesis (Chapters 6-9).

3 Rock-cut caves, most consisting of two chambers carved out of granite, situated in the Barabar Hills near Gaya, Bihar, India. They are associated with ascetics of different Buddhist and Jainist sects.

4 The Indian cave temples of Karli are located in the Borghat hills. The largest one is a hall, approximately 38 meters by 14 meters (by 15 meters high), with 37 pillars topped with kneeling elephants.

5 A network of cave temples cut out of basalt on the island of Gharapuri or Elephanta, near Mumbai, India. The main cave, also called the Shiva cave, is 27 meters square and has columns cut out of the rock.

6 The temple of Hathor at Dendera, Egypt is a complex of shrines measuring some 40,000 square meters. It includes a necropolis consisting of a series of mastaba tombs.

7 A spectacular ancient city in Jordan that is half cut into the rock of surrounding mountains.

the case of an entire city excavated from the rocky mountains; yet, after all, these do not bear upon the point in question, for they are isolated cases; and even Petra, though it contained a city, did not contain a nation. But there is a case, and one which is well known, that bears directly upon this question, and gives us the connecting link between the Kosekin and their Semitic brethren in the northern hemisphere."

"What is that?" asked the doctor.

"The Troglodytes,"[1] said Oxenden, with impressive solemnity.

"Well, and what do you make out of the Troglodytes?"

"I will explain," said Oxenden. "The name Troglodytes is given to various tribes of men, but those best known and celebrated under this name once inhabited the shores of the Red Sea, both on the Arabian and the Egyptian side. They belonged to the Arabian race, and were consequently a Semitic people. Mark that, for it is a point of the utmost importance. Now, these Troglodytes all lived in caverns, which were formed partly by art and partly by nature, although art must have had most to do with the construction of such vast subterranean works. They lived in great communities in caverns, and they had long tunnels passing from one community to another. Here also they kept their cattle. Some of these people have survived even to our own age; for Bruce, the Abyssinian traveler, saw them in Nubia.[2]

"The earliest writer who mentions the Troglodytes was Agatharcides, of Cnidos.[3] According to him they were chiefly herdsmen. Their food was the flesh of cattle, and their drink a mixture of milk and blood. They dressed in the skins of cattle; they tattooed their

1 Derived from the Greek Τρωγλοδύτης, to get into or dwell in a hole or cave. See Appendix D for a range of sources that help make sense of De Mille's use of Troglodytes; see Appendix D2 especially for an example of a nineteenth-century reference entry on the word in the 1843 *Penny Cyclopaedia*.

2 Scottish travel writer James Bruce (1730-94) was the first European to trace the confluence of the Blue Nile River in the White Nile. In volume 3 of *Travels to Discover the Source of the Nile, In the Years 1768, 1769, 1770, 1771, 1772, and 1773*, Bruce associates a group of Shiho people whom he encounters with the Troglodytes (394-95). Nubia is the region along the Nile River of northern Sudan and southern Egypt where the ancient Kingdom of Kush was located.

3 The Greek historian and geographer Agatharcides of Cnidos (second century BCE) devotes a section to the North African Troglodytes in Book 5 of his treatise on the African coast of the Red Sea, *On the Erythraean Sea*. For more detailed information on Agatharcides, see the Introduction, pp. 33-34.

bodies. They were very swift of foot, and were able to run down wild beasts in the hunt. They were also greatly given to robbery, and caravans passing to and fro had to guard against them.

"One feature in their character has to my mind a strange significance, and that is their feelings with regard to death. It was not the Kosekin love of death, yet it was something which must certainly be considered as approximating to it. For Agatharcides says that in their burials they were accustomed to fasten the corpse to a stake, and then gathering round, to pelt it with stones amid shouts of laughter and wild merriment. They also used to strangle the old and infirm, so as to deliver them from the evils of life. These Troglodytes, then, were a nation of cave-dwellers, loving the dark—not exactly loving death, yet at any rate regarding it with merriment and pleasure; and so I cannot help seeing a connection between them and the Kosekin."

"Yes," said the doctor, "but how did they get to the South Pole?"

"That," said Oxenden, "is a question which I do not feel bound to answer."

"Oh, it is easy enough to answer that," said Melick. "They, of course, dug through the earth."

Oxenden gave a groan.

"I think I'll turn in for the night," said he, rising. Upon this the others rose also and followed his example.

On the following morning the calm still continued. None of the party rose until very late, and then over the breakfast-table they discussed the manuscript once more, each from his own point of view, Melick still asserting a contemptuous scepticism—Oxenden and the doctor giving reasons for their faith, and Featherstone listening without saying much on either side.

At length it was proposed to resume the reading of the manuscript, which task would now devolve upon Oxenden. They adjourned to the deck, where all disposed themselves in easy attitudes to listen to the continuation of More's narrative.

[TO BE CONTINUED.]

PART 12 (24 MARCH, 1888)

CHAPTER XVIII.
A VOYAGE OVER THE POLE.

THE discovery of our love had brought a crisis in our fate for me and Almah. The Kohen hailed it with joy, for now was the time when he would be able to present us to the Kohen Gadol.[1] Our doom was certain and inevitable. We were to be taken to the *amir*; we were to be kept until the end of the dark season, and then we were both to be publicly sacrificed. After this our bodies were to be set apart for the hideous rites of the *Mista Kosek*. Such was the fate that lay before us.

The Kohen was now anxious to take us to the *amir*. I might possibly have persuaded him to postpone our departure, but I saw no use in that. It seemed better to go, for it was possible that amid new scenes and among new people there might be hope. This, too, seemed probable to Almah, who was quite anxious to go. The Kohen pressed forward the preparations, and at length a galley was ready for us.

This galley was about three hundred feet in length and fifty in width, but not more than six feet in depth. It was like a long raft. The rowers, two hundred in number, sat on a level with the water, one hundred on each side. The oars were small, being not more than twelve feet in length, but made of very light, tough material, with very broad blades. The galley was steered with broad-bladed paddles at both ends. There was no mast or sail. Astern was a light poop,[2] surrounded by a pavilion, and forward there was another. At the bow there was a projecting platform, used chiefly in fighting the *thannin* or sea monsters, and also in war. There were no masts or flags or gay streamers; no brilliant colors; all was intensely black, and the ornaments were of the same hue.

We were now treated with greater reverence than ever, for we were looked upon as the recipients of the highest honor that could fall to any of the Kosekin, namely, the envied dignity of a public death. As we embarked, the whole city lined the public ways, and watched us from the quays, from boats, and from other galleys.

---

1 First mentioned in Chapter 15, the Kohen Gadol is the richest and noblest Kosekin. He is ostensibly the most powerful leader and must exhibit great displays of wealth.

2 A partial deck above the main deck.

Songs were sung by a chosen choir of paupers, and to the sound of this plaintive strain we moved out to sea.

"This will be a great journey for me," said the Kohen, as we left the port. "I hope to be made a pauper at least, and perhaps gain the honor of a public death. I have known people who have gained death for less. There was an Athon last year who attacked a pehmet[1] with forty men and one hundred and twenty rowers. All were killed or drowned except himself. In reward for this he gained the *mudecheb*, or death recompense. In addition to this he was set apart for the *Mista Kosek*."

"Then with you, when a man procures the death of others he is honored?"

"Why, yes; how could it be otherwise?" said the Kohen. "Is it not the same with you? Have you not told me incredible things about your people, among which there were a few that seemed natural and intelligible? Among these was your system of honoring above all men those who procure the death of the largest number. You, with your pretended fear of death, wish to meet it in battle as eagerly as we do, and your most renowned men are those who have sent most to death."

To this strange remark I had no answer to make.

The air out at sea now grew chillier. The Kohen noticed it also, and offered me his cloak, which I refused. He seemed surprised, and smiled.

"You are growing like one of us," said he. "You will soon learn that the greatest happiness in life is to do good to others and sacrifice yourself. You already show this in part. When you are with Almah you act like one of the Kosekin. You watch her to see and anticipate her slightest wish; you are eager to give her everything. She, on the other hand, is equally eager to give up all to you. Each one of you is willing to lay down life for the other. You would gladly rush upon death to save her from harm, much as you pretend to fear death; and so I see that, with Almah, you will soon learn how sweet a thing death may be."

"To live without her," said I, "would be so bitter that death with her would indeed be sweet. If I could save her life by laying down my own, death would be sweeter still; and not one of you Kosekin would meet it so gladly."

The Kosekin smiled joyously.

"Oh, almighty and wondrous power of Love!" he exclaimed, "how thou hast transformed this foreigner! Oh, Atam-or! you will

1 This is the only mention of this creature.

soon be one of us altogether. For see, how is it now? You pretend to love riches and life, and yet you are ready to give up everything for Almah."

"Gladly, gladly!" I exclaimed.

"Yes," he said, "all that you have you would gladly lavish on her, and would rejoice to make yourself a pauper for her sweet sake. You also would rejoice equally to give up life for her. Is it not so?"

"It is," said I.

"Then I see by this that Almah has awakened within you your true human nature. Thus far it has lain dormant; it has been concealed under a thousand false and unnatural habits, arising from your strange native customs. You have been brought up under some frightful system, where nature is violated. Here among us your true humanity is unfolded, and with Almah you are like the Kosekin. Soon you will learn new lessons, and will find out that there is a new and a final self-abnegation in perfect love; and your love will never rest till you have separated yourself from Almah, so that love can have its perfect work."

The sea now opened wide before us, rising up high as if half-way to the zenith, giving the impression of a vast ascent to endless distances. Around the shores spread themselves, with the shadowy outlines of the mountains; above was the sky, all clear, with faint aurora-flashes and gleaming stars. Hand-in-hand with Almah I stood and pointed out the constellations as we marked them, while she told me of the different divisions known among the Kosekin as well as her own people. There, high in the zenith, was the southern polar-star, not exactly at the pole, nor yet of very great brightness, yet still sufficiently noticeable.

Looking back, we saw, low down, parts of the Phœnix and the Crane; higher up, the Toucan, Hydrus, and Pavo.[1] On our right, low down, was the beautiful Altar; higher up, the Triangle; while on the left were the Sword-fish and the Flying-fish. Turning to look forward, we beheld a more splendid display. Then over the bow of the vessel, between the Centaur, which lay low, and Musca Indica, which rose high, there blazed the bright stars of the Southern Cross—a constellation if not the brightest, at least the most

---

1 More's description of the southern night sky is based on Plate 7, "Southern Circumpolar Map," found in the *Atlas Designed to Illustrate The Geography of the Heavens* by Elijah H. Burritt (see Appendix B4). The five constellations named here are all clustered together in the upper hemisphere of the map. Hydrus, which means male water snake, is represented as a snake. Pavo is Latin for Peacock. These constellations were originally created by Petrus Plancius in 1597.

conspicuous and attractive in all the heavens.[1] All around there burned other stars, separated widely. Then over the stern gleamed the splendid lustre of Acherner,[2] on the left the brilliant glow of μ Robur[3] and Canopus, and low down before us the bright light of Argo. It was a scene full of splendor and fascination. After a time a change came over the sky: the aurora flashes, at first faint, gradually increased in brilliancy till the stars grew dim, and all the sky, wherever the eye might turn from the horizon to the zenith, seemed filled with lustrous flames of every conceivable hue. Colossal beams radiated from the pole toward the horizon till the central light was dissipated, and there remained encircling us an infinite colonnade of flaming pillars that towered to the stars. These were all in motion, running upon one another, incessantly shifting and changing; new scenes forever succeeded to old; pillars were transformed to pyramids, pyramids to fiery bars; these in their turn were transformed to other shapes, and all the while one tint of innumerable hues overspread the entire circle of the sky.[4]

Our voyage occupied several *jom*s; but our progress was continuous, for different sets of rowers relieved one another at regular intervals. On the second *jom* a storm broke out. The sky had been gathering clouds during sleeping-time, and when we awoke we found the sea all lashed to fury, while all around the darkness was intense. The storm grew steadily worse; the lightning flashed, the thunder pealed, and at length the sea was so heavy that rowing was impossible. Upon this the oars were all taken in, and the galley lay tossing upon the furious sea, amid waves that continually beat upon her.

---

1 These three constellations are the bottom centre of Burritt's map (see p. 187, note 1). Musca Indica is short for *Musca Australis vel Indica*, the Southern or Indian Fly.

2 Acherner, which is used in the *Harper's Weekly* serial, is a variant spelling of Achernar, the brightest star in the constellation Eridanus.

3 De Mille uses Burritt's convention of designating the brightest star in the constellation using the Greek character μ, thus μ Robur. Burritt treated this star as part of the constellation Robur Caroli, which means King Charles Oak, and depicts the constellation as an oak tree (see Appendix B4).

4 Like Aurora Borealis, Aurora Australis is caused when plasma particles from the sun collide with the Earth's magnetic field and ionize oxygen and nitrogen. Aurora Australis is noted often in Antarctic exploration narratives consulted by De Mille. For example, on 16 September 1770, James Cook reported seeing lights over the South Pole that resembled the Aurora Borealis.

And now a scene ensued that filled me with amazement, and took away all my thoughts from the storm. It seemed impossible that so frail a bark could stand the fury of the waves. Destruction was inevitable, and I was expecting to see the usual signs of grief and despair—wondering, too, how these rowers would preserve their subordination. But I had forgotten in my excitement the strange nature of the Kosekin. Instead of terror there was joy, instead of wild despair there was peace and serene delight.

The lightning-flashes revealed a wonderful scene. There were all the rowers, each one upon his seat, and from them all there came forth a chant which was full of triumph, like a song of public welcome to some great national hero, or a song of joy over victory. The officers embraced one another and exchanged words of delight. The Kohen, after embracing all the others, turned to me, and, forgetting my foreign ways, exclaimed, in a tone of enthusiastic delight:

"We are destroyed! Death is near! Rejoice!"

Accustomed as I was to the perils of the sea, I had learned to face death without flinching. Almah too was calm, for to her this death seemed preferable to that darker fate which awaited us; but the words of the Kohen jarred upon my feelings.

"Do you not intend to do anything to save the ship?" I asked.

He laughed joyously.

"There's no occasion," said he. "When the oars are taken in we always begin to rejoice. And why not? Death is near—it is almost certain. Why should we do anything to distract our minds and mar our joy? For oh, dear friend, the glorious time has come when we can give up life—life with all its toils, its burdens, its endless bitternesses, its perpetual evils. Now we shall have no more suffering from vexatious and oppressive riches, from troublesome honors, from a surplus of food, from luxuries and delicacies, and all the ills of life."

"But what is the use of being born at all?" I asked, in a wonder that never ceased to rise at every fresh display of Kosekin feeling.

"The use?" said the Kohen. "Why, if we were not born, how could we know the bliss of dying, or enjoy the sweetness of death? Death is the end of being—the one sweet hope and crown and glory of life, the one desire and hope of every living man. The blessing is denied to none. Rejoice with me, oh Atam-or! you will soon know its blessedness as well as I."

He turned away. I held Almah in my arms, and we watched the storm by the lightning-flashes and waited for the end. But the end came not. The galley was light, broad, and buoyant as a life-boat;

Illustration 12: "There were all the rowers, each one upon his seat, and from them all there came forth a chant which was full of triumph."

at the same time it was so strongly constructed that there was scarcely any twist or contortion in the sinewy fabric. So we floated buoyantly and safely upon the summit of vast waves, and a storm that would have destroyed a ship of the European fashion scarcely injured this in the slightest degree. It was as indestructible as a raft and as buoyant as a bubble; so we rode out the gale, and the death which the Kosekin invoked did not come at all.

The storm was but short-lived; the clouds dispersed, and soon went scudding over the sky; the sea went down. The rowers had to take their oars once more, and the reaction that followed upon their recent rejoicings was visible in universal gloom and dejection. As the clouds dispersed the aurora lights came out more splendid than ever, and showed nothing but melancholy faces. The rowers pulled with no life or animation; the officers stood about sighing and lamenting. Almah and I were the only ones that rejoiced over this escape from death.

Joms passed. We saw other sights; we met with galleys and saw many ships about the sea. Some were moved by sails only; these were merchant-ships, but they had only square sails, and could not sail in any other way than before the wind.[1] Once or twice I caught glimpses of vast shadowy objects in the air. I was startled and terrified; for, great as were the wonders of this strange region, I had not yet suspected that the air itself might have denizens as tremendous as the land or the sea. Yet so it was, and afterward during the voyage I saw them often. One in particular was so near that I observed it with ease. It came flying along in the same course with us, at a height of about fifty feet from the water. It was a frightful monster, with a long body and vast wings like those a bat. Its progress was swift, and it soon passed out of sight. To Almah the monster created no surprise; she was familiar with them, and told me that they were very abundant here, but that they never were known to attack ships. She informed me that they were capable of being tamed if caught when young, though in her country they were never made use of. The name given by the Kosekin to these monsters is *athaleb*.

At length we drew near to our destination. We reached a large harbor at the end of a vast bay: here the mountains extended around, and before us there arose terrace after terrace of twinkling lights running away to immense distances. It looked like a city of a million inhabitants, though it may have contained far less than

1 The most ancient and basic type of rigging, square sails always present the same face to the wind.

that. By the brilliant aurora light I could see that it was in general shape and form precisely like the city that we had left, though far larger and more populous. The harbor was full of ships and boats of all sorts, some lying at the stone quays, others leaving port, others entering. Galleys passed and repassed, and merchant ships with their clumsy sails, and small fishing-boats. From afar arose the deep hum of a vast multitude and the low roar that always ascends from a populous city.

The galley hauled alongside her wharf, and we found ourselves at length in the mighty *amir* of the Kosekin. The Kohen alone landed; the rest remained on board, and Almah and I with them.

Other galleys were here. On the wharf workmen were moving about. Just beyond were caverns that looked like warehouses. Above these was a terraced street, where a vast multitude moved to and fro—a living tide as crowded and as busy as that in Cheapside.[1]

After what seemed a long time the Kohen returned. This time he came with a number of people, all of whom were in cars drawn by opkuks. Half were men and half women. These came aboard, and it seemed as though we were to be separated; for the women took Almah, while the men took me. Upon this I entreated the Kohen not to separate us. I informed him that we were both of a different race from his, that we did not understand their ways; we should be miserable if separated.

I spoke long and with all the entreaty possible to one with my limited acquaintance with the language. My words evidently impressed them: some of them even wept.

"You make us sad," said the Kohen. "Willingly would we do everything that you bid, for we are your slaves; but the state law prevents. Still, in your case, the law will be modified; for you are in such honor here that you may be considered as beyond the laws. For the present, at least, we cannot separate you."

These words brought much consolation. After this we landed, and Almah and I were still together.

---

1 *Dickens's Dictionary of London* (1879) describes Cheapside as "the greatest thoroughfare in the City of London."

CHAPTER XIX.
THE WONDERS OF THE "*AMIR.*"

WE were drawn on cars up to the first terraced street, and here we found the vast multitude which we had seen from a distance. Crossing this street we ascended and came to another precisely like it; then, still going on, we came to a third. Here there was an immense space, not overgrown with trees like the streets, but perfectly open. In the midst arose a lofty pyramid, and as I looked at it I could not refrain from shuddering; for it looked like the public altar, upon which in due time I should be compelled to make my appearance, and be offered up as a victim to the terrific superstitions of the Kosekin.

Crossing this great square we came to a vast portal, which opened into a cavern with twinkling lights. The city itself extended above this, for we could see the terraced streets rising above our heads; but here our progress ended at the great cavern in the chief square, opposite the pyramid.

On entering the cavern we traversed an antechamber, and then passing on we reached a vast dome, of dimensions so great that I could perceive no end in that gloom. The twinkling lights served only to disclose the darkness and to indicate the immensity of the cavern. In the midst there arose two enormous columns, which were lost in the gloom above.

It was only by passing through this that we learned its great extent. We at length came to the other end, and here we saw numerous passages leading away. The Kohen led us through one of these, and after passing through several other domes of smaller dimensions we at length reached an apartment where we stopped. This place was furnished with couches and hangings, and lighted with flaming lamps. The light was distressing to those who had accompanied us, and many of them left, while the few who remained had to cover their eyes. Here we found that all preparations had been made. The apartments were all illuminated, though our love of light never ceased to be a matter of amazement to the Kosekin, and a bounteous repast was spread for us. But the Kohen and the others found the light intolerable, and soon left us to ourselves.

After the repast some women appeared to take Almah to her chamber, and, with the usual kindness of the Kosekin, they assured her that she would not be expected to obey the law of separation, but that she was to remain here, where she would be always within reach of me.

After her departure there came to visit me the lowest man in all the land of the Kosekin, though, according to our view, he would be esteemed the highest. This was the *Kohen Gadol.* His history had already been told me. I had learned that through lack of Kosekin virtue he had gradually sunk to this position, and now was compelled to hold in his hands more wealth, power, and display than any other man in the nation.

He was a man of singular appearance. The light was not so troublesome to him as to the others—he merely kept his eyes shaded; but he regarded me with a keen look of inquiry that was suggestive of shrewdness and cunning. I confess it was with a feeling of relief that I made this discovery; for I longed to find someone among this singular people who was selfish, who feared death, who loved life, who loved riches, and had something in common with me. This I thought I perceived in the shrewd, cunning face of the Kohen Gadol, and I was glad; for I saw that while he could not possibly be more dangerous to me than those self-sacrificing, self-denying cannibals whom I had thus far known, he might prove of some assistance, and might help me to devise means of escape. If I could only find someone who was a coward, and selfish and avaricious—if this Kohen Gadol could but be he—how much brighter my life would be! And so there happened to me an incredible thing, that my highest wish now was to find in the Kohen Gadol cowardice, avarice, and selfishness.

The Kohen was accompanied by a young female, richly attired, who, I afterward learned, was his daughter. Her name was Layelah, and she filled the office of *Malca,* which signifies queen; and though honorable with us above all, is among the Kosekin the lowest in the land. Layelah was so beautiful that I looked at her in amazement. She was very tall for one of the Kosekin, which made her stature equal to that of an ordinary girl with us; her hair was rich, dark, and luxuriant, gathered about her head in great masses and bound by a golden band. Her features were delicate and perfect in their outline; her expression was noble and commanding. Her eyes were utterly unlike those of the other Kosekin; the upper lids had a slight droop, but that was all, and that was the nearest approach to the national blink. Her first entrance into the room seemed to dazzle her, and she shaded her eyes for a few moments, but after that she looked at me fixedly, and seemed to suffer no more inconvenience than I did. The perfect liberty of women among the Kosekin[1] made this visit from her quite as

1 See Appendix E3b for an example of gender inversions in Edward Bulwer Lytton's *The Coming Race* (1871).

natural as that of her father; and though she said but little on this occasion, she was an attentive listener and close observer.

Their visit was long, for they were evidently full of curiosity. They had heard much about me and wished to hear more. It was the first time that I had found among the Kosekin the slightest desire to know where I had come from. Hitherto all had been content with the knowledge that I was a foreigner. Now, however, I found in the Kohen Gadol and Layelah a curiosity that was most eager and intense. They questioned me about my country, about the great world beyond the mountains, about the way in which I had come here, about the manners and customs of my countrymen. They were eager to know about those great nations of which I spoke, who loved light and life; about men who loved themselves better than others; of that world where men feared death and loved life, and sought after riches and lived in the light.

The sleeping-time came and passed, and my visitors were still full of eager questionings. It was Layelah who at last thought of the lateness of the hour. At a word from her the Kohen Gadol rose, with many apologies, and prepared to go. But before he left he said:

"When I was a child I was shipwrecked, and was taken up by a ship which conveyed me to a nation beyond the sea. There I grew up to manhood. I learned their language and manners and customs, and when I returned home I found myself an alien here: I do not love darkness or death, I do not hate riches, and the result is that I am what I am. If I were like the rest of my countrymen my lot would make me miserable; but as it is I prefer it to any other, and consider myself not the lowest but the greatest in the land. My daughter is like me, and instead of being ashamed of her station she is proud of it, and would not give it up even to become a pauper.[1] I will see you again. I have much to say."

With these words the Kohen Gadol retired, followed by Layelah, leaving me more hopeful than I had been for a long time.

For many *jom*s following I received visits from the Kohen Gadol and from Layelah. Almah was with me until sleeping-time, and then these other visitors would come. In this, at least, they resembled the other Kosekin, that they never dreamed of interfering

---

1 That the Kohen Gadol's learned behaviour is passed on to his daughter suggests an evolutionary model of acquired characteristics proposed by Jean-Baptiste Lamarck (1744-1829). While Lamarck's theory was at odds with Charles Darwin's theory of natural selection, the two theories were often blurred in the middle of the nineteenth century.

with Almah when she might wish to be with me. Their visits were always long, and we had much to say; but what I lost of sleep I always made up on the following *jom*. The Kohen Gadol, with his keen, shrewd face, interested me greatly; but Layelah, with her proud face and air of command, was a positive wonder.

I soon learned that the Kohen Gadol was what we term "a man of advanced views," or perhaps a "Reformer," or a "Philosophic Radical," it matters not which; suffice it to say that his ideas and feelings differed from those of his nation, and if carried out would be equal to a revolution in politics and morals.

The Kohen Gadol advocated selfishness as the true law of life, without which no state can prosper. There were a few of similar views, but they were all regarded with great contempt by the multitude, and had to suffer the utmost rigor of the law; for they were all endowed with vast wealth, compelled to live in the utmost splendor and luxury, to have enormous retinues, and to wield the chief power in politics and in religion. Even this, however, had not changed the sentiments of the condemned, and I learned that they were laboring incessantly, notwithstanding their severe punishment, to disseminate their peculiar doctrines. These were formulated as follows:

A man should not love others better than himself.
Life is not an evil to be got rid of.
Other things are to be preferred to death.
Poverty is not the best state for man.
Unrequited love is not the greatest happiness.
Lovers may sometimes marry.
To serve is not more honorable than to command.
Defeat is not more glorious than victory.
To save a life should not be regarded as a criminal offence.
The paupers should be forced to take a certain amount of wealth, to relieve the necessities of the rich.

These articles were considered both by the Kohen Gadol and by Layelah to be remarkable for their audacity, and were altogether too advanced for mention by any except the chosen few. With the multitude he had to deal differently, and had to work his way by concealing his opinions. He had made a great conspiracy, in which he was still engaged, and had gained immense numbers of adherents by allowing them to give him their whole wealth. Through his assistance many Athons and Kohens and Meleks had become artisans, laborers, and even paupers; but all were bound by him to the strictest secrecy. If anyone should divulge the secret, it would be ruin to him and to many others; for they would at once be punished by the bestowal of the extremest wealth, by degradation to the rank of rulers and commanders, and by the severest rigors of luxury, power, splendor, and magnificence known among the Kosekin. Overwhelmed thus with the cares of government, crushed under the weight of authority and autocratic rule, surrounded by countless slaves all ready to die for them, their lives would be embittered and their punishment would be more than they could bear. But the philosophic Kohen Gadol dared all these punishments, and pursued his way calmly and pertinaciously.

Nothing surprised the Kohen Gadol so much as the manner in which I received his confidences. He half expected to startle me by his boldness, but was himself confounded by my words. I told him that in my country self was the chief consideration, self-preservation the first law of nature; death the King of Terrors; wealth the object of universal search, poverty the worst of evils; unrequited love nothing less than anguish and despair; to command others the highest glory; victory, honor; defeat, intolerable shame; and other things of the same sort, all of which sounded in his ears, as he said, with such tremendous force that they were like peals of thunder. He shook his head despondently; he could not believe that such views as mine could ever be attained to among the Kosekin. But Layelah was bolder, and with all a woman's impetuosity grasped at my fullest meaning and held it firm.

"He is right," said Layelah—"the heaven-born Atam-or. He shall be our teacher. The rich shall be esteemed, the poor shall be down-trodden; to rule over others shall be glorious, to serve shall be base; victory shall be an honor, defeat a shame; selfishness, self-seeking, luxury, and indulgence shall be virtues; poverty, want, and squalor shall be things of abhorrence and contempt."

The face of Layelah glowed with enthusiasm as she said these words, and I saw in her a daring, intrepid, and high-hearted woman, full of a woman's headlong impetuosity and disregard of consequences. In me she saw one who seemed to her like a prophet and teacher of a new order of things, and her whole soul responded to the principles which I announced. It required immense strength of mind and firmness of soul to separate herself from the prevalent sentiment of her nation; and though nature had done much for her in giving her a larger portion of original selfishness than was common to her people, still she was a child of the Kosekin, and her daring was all the more remarkable. And so she went further than her father, and adopted my extreme views when he shrank back, and dared more unflinchingly the extremest rigors of the national law, and all that the Kosekin could inflict in the way of wealth, luxury, supreme command, palatial abodes, vast retinues of slaves, and the immense degradation of the queenly office.

I spoke to her in a warning voice about her rashness.

"Oh," said she, "I have counted the cost, and am ready to accept all that they can inflict. I embrace the good cause, and will not give it up—no, not even if they could increase my wealth a thousand-fold, and sentence me to live a hundred seasons. I can bear their utmost inflictions of wealth, power, magnificence; I could even bear being condemned to live forever in the light. Oh, my friend, it is the conviction of right and the support of conscience that strengthen one to bear the greatest evils that man can inflict."

From these words it was evident to me that Layelah was a true child of the Kosekin; for though she was of advanced sentiments she still used the language of her people, and spoke of the punishments of the law as though they were punishments in reality. Now, to me and to Almah these so-called punishments seemed rewards.

It was impossible for me to avoid feeling a very strong regard for this enthusiastic and beautiful girl; all the more, indeed, because she evinced such an undisguised admiration for me. She evidently considered me some superior being, from some superior race; and although my broken and faulty way of speaking the language was something of a trial, still she seemed to consider every word I uttered as a maxim of the highest wisdom. The tritest of truths, the commonest of platitudes, the most familiar of proverbs or old saws current among us were eagerly seized by Layelah, and accepted as truths almost divine—as new doctrines for the guidance of the human race. These she would discuss with me; she would put them into better and more striking language, and ask for my opinion. Then she would write them down.

For the Kosekin knew the art of writing. They had an alphabet of their own, which was at once simple and very scientific. There were no vowels, but only consonant sounds, the vowels being supplied in reading, just as if one should write the words fthr or dtr,[1] and read them father and daughter. Their letters were as follows: P, K, T, B, G, D, F, Ch, Th, M, L, N, S, H, R. There were also three others,[2] which have no equivalents in English.

1 The *Harper's* serial has "dtr" but the novel edition has "dghtr."

2 There are eighteen letters in total.

It soon became evident to me that Layelah had a complete ascendancy over her father; that she was not only the Malca of the *amir*, but the presiding spirit and the chief administrative genius of the whole nation of the Kosekin. She seemed to be a new Semiramis[1]—one who might revolutionize an empire and introduce a new order of things. Such, indeed, was her high ambition, and she plainly avowed it to me; but what was more, she frankly informed me that she regarded me as a Heaven-sent teacher—as one who in this darkness could tell her of the nations of light—who could instruct her in the wisdom of other and greater races, and help her to accomplish her grand designs.

As for Almah, she seemed quite beneath the notice of the aspiring Layelah. She never noticed her, she never spoke of her, and she always made her visits to me after Almah had gone.

[TO BE CONTINUED.]

1 First noted by Ctesias of Cnidus (400 BCE) and identified as the wife of the mythical King Ninus, the legendary Assyrian queen Semiramis is attributed with great conquests and feats, including the restoration of Babylon. Monuments such as the Hanging Gardens of Babylon are ascribed to her. She is sometimes identified with the historical Assyrian queen Shammuramat.

PART 13 (31 MARCH, 1888)

CHAPTER XX.
THE DARK MAIDEN LAYELAH.

LAYELAH at length began to make pointed remarks about Almah.

"She loves you," said she, "and you love her. How is it that you do not give each other up?"

"I would die rather than give up Almah," said I.

Layelah smiled. "That sounds strange to the Kosekin," said she, "for here to give up your love and to die are both esteemed the greatest possible blessings. But Almah should give you up. It is the women with us who make the beginning. Women generally fall in love first, and it is expected that they will tell their love first. The delicacy of a woman's feelings makes this natural, for if a man tells his love to a woman who does not love him, it shocks her modesty; while if a woman tells a man, he has no modesty to shock."[1]

"That is strange," said I; "but suppose the man does not love the woman?"

"Why, no woman wants to be loved; she only wants to love."

At this I felt somewhat bewildered.

"That," said Layelah, "is unrequited love, which is the chief blessing here, though for my part I am a philosopher, and would wish when I love to be loved in return."

"And then," said I, "if so, would you give up your lover, in accordance with the custom of your country?"

Layelah's dark eyes rested on me for a moment with a glance of intense earnestness and profound meaning. She drew a long breath, and then said, in a low, tremulous voice,

"Never!"

Layelah was constantly with me, and at length used to come at an earlier time, when Almah was present. Her manner toward Almah was full of the usual Kosekin courtesy and gracious cordiality. She was still intent upon learning from me the manners, customs, and principles of action of the race to which I belonged. She had an insatiable thirst for knowledge, and her curiosity extended to all of those great inventions which are the wonder of Christendom. Locomotives and steamboats were described to her

---

1 See Appendix E3b for an example of gender inversions in Edward Bulwer Lytton's *The Coming Race* (1871).

under the names of "horses of fire" and "ships of fire"; printing was "letters of power"; the electric telegraph, "messages of lightning"; the organ, "lute of giants," and so on.[1] Yet, in spite of the eagerness with which she made her inquiries, and the diligence with which she noted all down, I could see that there was in her mind something lying beneath it all—a far more earnest purpose, and a far more personal one, than the pursuit of useful knowledge.

Layelah was watchful of Almah; she seemed studying her to see how far this woman of another race differed from the Kosekin. She would often turn from me and talk with Almah for a long time, questioning her about her people and their ways. Almah's manner was somewhat reserved, and it was rendered somewhat more so from the fact that her mind was always full of the prospect of our impending doom. Each *jom* as it came and went brought us nearer to that awful time, and the hour was surely coming when we should be taken to the outer square and to the top of the pyramid of sacrifice.

Once Layelah sat for some time silent and involved in thought. At length she began to speak to me.

"Almah," said she, "is very different from us. She loves you and you love her. She ought to give you up. Almah, you ought to give up Atam-or, since you love him."

Almah looked confused, and made some reply to the effect that she belonged to a different race with different customs.

"But you should follow our customs. You are one of us now. You can easily find another who will take him."

Almah threw a piteous glance at me and said nothing.

"I," said Layelah, "will take him."

She spoke these words with an air of magnanimity, as though putting it in the light of a favor to Almah; but Almah did not make any reply, and after some silence Layelah spoke of something else.

Not long after we were alone together, and Layelah returned to the subject. She referred to Almah's want of sympathy with the manners of the Kosekin, and asserted that she ought to aim after a separation.

"I love her," said I, with great warmth, "and will never give her up."

"But she must give you up; it is the woman's place to take the first step. I should be willing to take you."

1 This rhetorical framing of modern technology as magic is the correlative to De Mille's use of dinosaurs for monsters.

As Layelah said this she looked at me very earnestly, as if anxious to see how I accepted this offer. It was for me a most embarrassing moment. I loved Almah, but Layelah also was most agreeable, and I liked her very much; indeed, so much so that I could not bear to say anything that might hurt her feelings. Among all the Kosekin there was not one who was not infinitely inferior to her in my eyes. Still, I loved Almah, and I told her so again, thinking that in this way I might repel her without giving offence.

But Layelah was quite ready with her reply.

"If you love Almah," said she, "that is the very reason why you should marry me."

This made me feel more embarrassed than ever.

I stammered something about my own feelings—the manners and customs of my race—and the fear that I had of acting against my own principles. "Besides," I added, "I'm afraid it would make you unhappy."

"Oh no," said Layelah, briskly; "on the contrary, it would make me very happy indeed."

I began to be more and more aghast at this tremendous frankness, and was utterly at a loss what to say.

"My father," continued Layelah, "is different from the other Kosekin, and so am I. I seek requital for love, and do not think it an evil."

A sudden thought now suggested itself, and I caught at it as a last resort.

"You have," said I, "some lover among the Kosekin. Why do you not marry him?"

Layelah smiled.

"I have no lover that I love," said she, "among the Kosekin."

My feeble effort was thus a miserable failure. I was about saying something concerning the Kosekin alphabet or something else of an equally appropriate nature, when she prevented me.

"Atam-or," said she, in a low voice.

"Layelah," said I, with my mind full of confusion.

"I love you!"

She sat looking at me with her beautiful face all aglow, her dark eyes fixed on mine with an intense and eager gaze. I looked at her and said not one single word. Layelah was the first to break the awkward silence.

"You love Almah, Atam-or; but say, do you not love me? You smile at me, you meet me always when I come with warm greetings, and you seem to enjoy yourself in my society. Say, Atam-or, do you not love me?"

This was a perilous and a tremendous moment. The fact is, I did like Layelah very much indeed, and I wanted to tell her so; but my ignorance of the language did not allow me to observe those nice distinctions of meaning which exist between the words "like" and "love." I knew no other word than the one Kosekin word meaning "love," and could not think of any meaning "like." It was, therefore, a very trying position for me.

"Dear Layelah," said I, floundering and stammering in my confusion, "I love you; I—"

But here I was interrupted without waiting for any further words; the beautiful creature flung her arms around me and clung to me with a fond embrace. As for me, I was utterly confounded, bewildered, and desperate. I thought of my darling Almah, whom alone I loved. It seemed at that moment as though I was not only false to her, but as if I was even endangering her life. My only thought now was to clear up my meaning.

"Dear Layelah," said I, as I sat with her arms around me, and with my own around her slender waist, "I do not want to hurt your feelings."

"Oh, Atam-or! oh, my love! never, never did I know such bliss as this."

Here again I was overwhelmed, but I still persisted in my effort.

"Dear Layelah," said I, "I love Almah most dearly and most tenderly."

"Oh, Atam-or, why speak of that? I know it well. And so by our Kosekin law you give her up; among us, lovers never marry. So you take me, your own Layelah, and you will have me for your bride; and my love for you is ten thousand times stronger than that of the cold and melancholy Almah. She may marry my papa."

This suggestion filled me with dismay.

"Oh no," said I. "Never, never will I give up Almah!"

"Certainly not," said Layelah; "you do not give her up—she gives you up."

"She never will," said I.

"Oh yes," said Layelah; "I will tell her that you wish it."

"I do not wish it," said I. "I love her, and will never give her up."

"It's all the same," said Layelah. "You cannot marry her at all. No one will marry you. You and Almah are victims, and the State has given you the matchless honor of death. Common people who love one another may marry if they choose, and take the punishment which the law assigns; but illustrious victims who love cannot marry, and so, my Atam-or, you have only me."

I need not say that all this was excessively embarrassing. I was certainly fond of Layelah, and liked her too much to hurt her feelings. Had I been one of the Kosekin I might perhaps have managed better; but being a European, a man of the Aryan race—being such, and sitting there with the beautiful Layelah lavishing all her affections upon me—why, it stands to reason that I could not have the heart to wound her feelings in any way. I was taken at an utter disadvantage. Never in my life had I heard of women taking the initiative. Layelah had proposed to me; she would not listen to refusal, and I had not the heart to wound her. I had made all the fight I could by persisting in asserting my love for Almah, but all my assertions were brushed lightly aside as trivial things.

Let any gentleman put himself in my situation, and ask himself what he would do. What would he do if such a thing could happen to him at home? But there such a thing could not happen, and so there is no use in supposing an impossible case. At any rate I think I deserve sympathy. Who could keep his presence of mind under such circumstances? With us a young lady who loves one man can easily repel another suitor; but here it was very different, for how could I repel Layelah? Could I turn upon her and say "Unhand me"? Could I say "Away! I am another's"? Of course I couldn't; and what's worse, if I had said such things Layelah would have smiled me down into silence. The fact is, it doesn't do for women to take the initiative—it's not fair. I had stood a good deal among the Kosekin. Their love of darkness, their passion for death, their contempt of riches, their yearning after unrequited love, their human sacrifices, their cannibalism, all had more or less become familiar to me, and I had learned to acquiesce in silence; but now when it came to this—that a woman should propose to a man—it really was more than a fellow could stand. I felt this at that moment very forcibly; but then the worst of it was that Layelah was so confoundedly pretty, and had such a nice way with her, that hang me if I knew what to say.

Meanwhile Layelah was not silent; she had all her wits about her.

"Dear papa," said she, "would make such a nice husband for Almah. He is a widower, you know. I could easily persuade him to marry her. He always does whatever I ask him to do."

"But victims cannot marry, you said."

"No," said Layelah, sweetly, "they cannot marry one another, but Almah may marry dear papa, and then you and I can be married, and it will be all very nice indeed."

At this I started away.

"No," said I, indignantly, "it won't be nice. I'm engaged to be married to Almah, and I'm not going to give her up."

"Oh, but she gives you up, you know," said Layelah, quietly.

"Well, but I'm not going to be given up."

"Why, how unreasonable you are, you foolish boy!" said Layelah, in her most caressing manner. "You have nothing at all to do with it."

At this I was in fresh despair, and then a new thought came, which I seized upon.

"See here," said I, "why can't I marry both of you? I'm engaged to Almah, and I love her better than all the world. Let me marry her and you too."

At this Layelah laughed long and merrily. Peal after peal of laughter, musical and most merry, burst from her. It was contagious; I could not help joining in, and so we both sat laughing. It was a long time before we regained our self-control.

"Why, that's downright bigamy!" exclaimed Layelah with fresh laughter. "Why, Atam-or, you're mad!" and so she went off again in fresh peals of laughter. It was evident that my proposal was not at all shocking, but simply comical, ridiculous, and inconceivable in its absurdity.[1] It was to her what the remark of some despairing beauty would be among us who, when pressed by two lovers should express a confused willingness to marry both. It was evident that Layelah accepted it as a ludicrous jest.

Laughter was all very well, of course; but I was serious and felt that I ought not to part with Layelah without some better understanding, and so I once more made an effort.

"All this," said I, in a mournful tone, "is a mere mockery. What have I to say about love and marriage? If you loved me as you say, you would not laugh, but weep. You forget what I am. What am I? A victim, and doomed—doomed to a hideous fate—a fate of horror unutterable. You cannot even begin to imagine the anguish with which I look forward to that fate which impends over me and Almah. Marriage—idle word! What have I to do with marriage? What has Almah? There is only one marriage before us—the dread marriage with death! Why talk of love to the dying? The tremendous ordeal, the sacrifice, is before us, and after that there remains the hideous *Mista Kosek*!"

At this Layelah sprang up, with her whole face and attitude full of life and energy.

"I know, I know," said she, quickly; "I have arranged for all. Your life shall be saved. Do you think that I have consented to

1 Bigamy, the practice of having two spouses at the same time, is one of the few practices despised by both Europeans and Kosekin.

your death? Never! You are mine. I will save you. I will show you what we can do. You shall escape."

"Can you really save me?" I cried.

"I can."

"What! in spite of the whole nation?"

Layelah laughed scornfully.

"I can save you," said she. "We can fly. There are other nations beside ours. We can find some land among the Gojin where we can live in peace. The Gojin are not like us."

"But Almah?" said I.

The face of Layelah clouded.

"I can only save you," said she.

"Then I will stay and die with Almah," said I, obstinately.

"What!" said Layelah, "do you not fear death?"

"Of course I do," said I; "but I'd rather die than lose Almah."

"But it's impossible to save both of you."

"Then leave me and save Almah," said I.

"What! would you give up your life for Almah?"

"Yes, and a thousand lives," said I.

"Why," said Layelah, "now you talk just like the Kosekin. You might as well be one of us. You love death for the sake of Almah. Why not be more like the Kosekin, and seek after a separation from Almah?"

Layelah was not at all offended at my declaration of love for Almah. She uttered these words in a lively tone, and then said that it was time for her to go.

CHAPTER XXI.
THE FLYING MONSTER.

I RETIRED to bed, but could not sleep. The offer of escape filled me with excited thoughts. These made sleep impossible, and as I lay awake I thought that perhaps it would be well to know what might be Layelah's plan of escape, for I might then make use of it to save Almah. I determined to find out all about it on the following *jom*—to question her as to the lands of the Gojin, to learn all her purpose. It might be that I could make use of that very plan to save Almah; but if not, why then I was resolved to remain and meet my fate with her. If Layelah could be induced to take both of us, I was of course resolved to go, trusting to chance as to the claims of Layelah upon me, and determined at all hazards to be faithful to Almah; but if she should positively refuse to save

Almah, then I thought it possible that I might be able to find in Layelah's plan of escape something of which I might avail myself. I could not imagine what it was, but it seemed to me that it might be something quite feasible, especially for a desperate man. The only thought I had was of escape by means of some boat over the seas. In a boat I would be at home. I could make use of a sail so as to elude pursuit, and could guide myself by the stars. The only thing that I wanted to know was the situation of the lands of the Gojin.

On the following *jom* the Kohen Gadol and Layelah came quite early and spent much time. I was surprised to see the Kohen Gadol devoting himself in an absurd fashion to Almah. It at once occurred to me that Layelah had obtained her father's co-operation in her scheme, and that the old villain actually imagined that he could win the hand of Almah. To Almah herself I had said nothing whatever about the proposal of Layelah, so that she was quite ignorant of the intentions of her companion; but it was excessively annoying to me to see such proceedings going on under my own eyes. At the same time I felt that it would be both unwise and uncivil to interfere; and I was also quite sure that Almah's affections were not to be diverted from me by anyone, much less by such an elderly party as the Kohen Gadol. It was very trying, however, and, in spite of my confidence in Almah, my jealousy was excited, and I began to think that the party of philosophical Radicals were not so agreeable as the orthodox cannibals whom I first met. As for Layelah, she seemed quite unconscious of any disturbance in my mind. She was as amiable, as sprightly, as inquisitive, and as affectionate as ever. She even outdid herself, and devoted herself to me with an abandon that was quite irresistible.

After Almah had left me, Layelah came again, and this time she was alone.

"I have come," said she, "to show you the way in which we can escape, whenever you decide to do so."

It was the thing above all others which I wished to know, and therefore I questioned her eagerly about it; but to all of my questions she only replied that she would show me, and I might judge for myself.

Layelah led the way, and I followed her. We traversed long galleries and vast halls, all of which were quite empty. It was the sleeping-time, and only those were visible who had some duties which kept them up later than usual. Faint, twinkling lights but feebly illuminated the general gloom. At length we came to an immense cavern, which was darker than ever, and without any lamps at all. Through a vast portal, which was closed with a barred gateway, the beams of the brilliant aurora penetrated and disclosed something of the interior.

Here Layelah stopped and peered through the gloom while I stood waiting by her side, wondering what means of escape could be found in this cavern. As I stood I heard through the still air the sound as of living things. For a time I saw nothing, but at length I descried a vast, shadowy form moving forward toward the portal, where the darkness was less. It was a form of portentous size and fearful shape, and I could not make out at first the nature of it. It surpassed all that I had ever seen. Its head was large and its jaws long, armed with rows of terrible teeth like those of a crocodile. Its body was of great size. It walked on its hind-legs, so as to maintain itself in an upright attitude, and in that position its height was over twelve feet. But the most amazing thing about this monster has yet to be told. As it walked its forearms waved and fluttered, and I saw descending from them what seemed like vast folded leathern wings, which shook and swayed in the air at every step. Its pace was about as fast as that of a man, and it moved with ease and lightness. It seemed like some enormous bat, or rather like a winged crocodile, or yet again like one of those monstrous dragons of which I had read, but in whose actual existence I had never believed. Yet here I saw one living and moving before me—an actual dragon, with the exception of a tail; for that appendage, which plays so great a part in all the pictures of dragons, had no place here. This beast had but a short caudal appendage, and all its terrors lay in its jaws and in its wings.[1]

For a moment I stood almost lifeless with terror and surprise. Then I shrank back, but Layelah laid her hand on my arm.

"Don't be afraid," said she; "it's only an athaleb."

"But won't it—won't it bite?" I asked, with a shudder.

"Oh no," said Layelah; "it swallows its victuals whole."

At this I shrank away still farther.

"Don't be afraid," said Layelah again. "Its jaws are muzzled, and, besides, it's a tame athaleb. Its jaws are unmuzzled only at feeding-time. But this one is very tame. There are three or four others in here, and all as tame as I am. They all know me. Come up nearer; don't be afraid. These athalebs are easily tamed."

"How can such tremendous monsters be tamed?" I asked, in an incredulous tone.

1 See Appendix B1.

"Oh, man can tame anything. The athalebs are very docile when they are taken young. They are very long-lived. This one has been in service here for a hundred seasons and more."

At this I began to regain my confidence, and as Layelah moved nearer to the athaleb I accompanied her. A nearer view, however, was by no means reassuring. The dragon-look of the athaleb was stronger than ever, for I could see that all its body was covered with scales. On its neck and back was a long ridge of coarse hair, and the sweep of its vast arms was enormous. It was with a quaking heart that I stood near; but the coolness of Layelah reassured me, for she went close up, as a boy would go up to a tame elephant, and she stroked his enormous back, and the monster bent down his terrible head and seemed pleased.

"This," said Layelah, "is the way we have of escaping."

"This!" I exclaimed, doubtfully.

"Yes," said she. "He is trained to the service. We can mount on his back, and he will fly with us wherever I choose to guide him."

"What!" I exclaimed, as I shrank back—"fly! Do you mean to say that you will mount this hideous monster, and trust yourself to him?"

"Certainly," said Layelah, quietly. "He is very docile. There is harness here with which we can guide him. Should you like to see him harnessed?"

"Very much indeed," said I.

Upon this Layelah walked up to the monster and stroked his breast. The huge athaleb at once lay down upon his belly. Then she brought two long straps like reins, and fastened each to the tip of a projecting tip of each wing. Then she fastened a collar around his neck, to which there was attached a grappling-iron.

"We seat ourselves on his back," said Layelah. "I guide with these reins. When we land anywhere I fasten him with the grapple. He looks dull now, but if I were to open the gate and remove his muzzle he would be off like the wind."

"But can he carry both of us?" I asked.

"Easily," said Layelah. "He can carry three persons without fatigue."

"Could you mount on his back now, and show me how you sit?"

Layelah readily assented, and mounted with the greatest ease, seating herself on the broadest part of the back between the wings.

"Here," said she, "is room for you. Will you not come?"

For an instant I hesitated; but then the sight of her, seated there as coolly as though she were on a chair, reassured me, and I

Illustration 13: "'This,' said Layelah, 'is the way we have of escaping.'"

climbed up also, though not without a shudder. The touch of the fearful monster was abhorrent; but I conquered my disgust and seated myself close behind Layelah. Here she sat, holding the reins in her hands, with the grapple just in front of her; and, seated in this position, she went on to explain the whole process by which the mighty monster was guided through the air.

[TO BE CONTINUED.]

PART 14 (7 APRIL, 1888)

CHAPTER XXI.—(*Continued.*)
THE FLYING MONSTER.

NO sooner had I found myself actually on the back of the athaleb than all fear left me. I perceived fully how completely tame he was, and how docile. The reins attached to his wings could be pulled with the greatest ease, just as one would pull the tiller-ropes of a boat.

"Familiarity breeds contempt"; and now, since the first terror had passed away, I felt perfect confidence, and under the encouragement of Layelah I had become like some rustic in a menagerie,[1] who at first is terrified by the sight of the elephant, but soon gains courage enough to mount upon his back. With my new-found courage and presence of mind I listened most attentively to all of Layelah's explanations, and watched most closely the construction and fastening of the harness; for the thought had occurred to me that this athaleb might be of avail in another way—that if I did not fly with Layelah, I might fly with Almah. This thought was only of a vague and shadowy character—a dim suggestion, the carrying out of which I scarce dared to think possible; still, it was in my mind, and had sufficient power over me to make me very curious as to the plans of Layelah. I determined to find out where she proposed to go, and how far; to ask her about the dangers of the way and the means of sustenance. It seemed, I confess, rather unfair to Layelah to find out her plans and use them for another purpose; but then that other purpose was Almah, and to me at that time every device which was for her safety seemed fair and honorable.

"Here," said Layelah—"here, Atam-or, you see the way of escape. The athaleb can carry us both far away to a land where you need never fear that they will put you to death—a land where the people love light and life. Whenever you are ready to go, tell me; if you are ready to go now, say so, and at once I will open the door, and we shall soon be far away."

She laid her hand on mine and looked at me earnestly; but I was not to be beguiled into any hasty committal of myself, and so I turned her proposal away with a question:

---

1 The precursor to zoos and circuses, menageries were collections of captive animals. Travelling menageries with exotic animals became popular in the eighteenth century.

"How far is it," I asked, "to that land?"

"It is too far for one flight," said Layelah. "We go first over the sea till we come to a great island, which is called Magones, where there are mountains of fire; there we must rest, and feed the athaleb on fish, which are to be found on the shore. The athaleb knows his way there well, for he goes there once every season for a certain sacred ceremony. He has done this for fifty or sixty seasons, and knows his way there and back perfectly well. The difficulty will be, when we leave Magones, in reaching the land of the Orin."

"The Orin?" I repeated. "Who are they?"

"They are a people among the Gojin who love life and light. It is their land that I wish to reach, if possible."

"Where is it?" I asked, eagerly.

"I cannot explain," said Layelah. "I can only trust to my own skill, and hope to find the place. We may have to pass over different lands of the Gojin, and if so we may be in danger."

"What is the reason why the athaleb goes to Magones every season?" I asked.

"To take there the chief pauper of the season, who has won the prize of death by starvation. It is one of the greatest honors among the Kosekin."

"Is Magones barren?"

"It is an island of fire, without anything on it but craggy mountains and wild rocks and flowing rivers of fire. It stands almost in the middle of the sea."

"How can we get away from here?" I asked, after some silence.

"From here?—why, I open the gates, and the athaleb flies away; that is all."

"But shall we not be prevented?"

"Oh no. No one here ever prevents anyone from doing anything. Everyone is eager to help his neighbor."

"But if they saw me deliberately mounting the athaleb and preparing for flight, would they not stop me?"

"No."

I was amazed at this.

"But," said I, "am I not a victim—preserved for the great sacrifice?"

"You are; but you are free to go where you like, and do what you like. Your character of victim makes you most distinguished. It is the highest honor and dignity. All believe that you rejoice in your high dignity, and no one dreams that you are anxious to escape."

"But if I did escape, would they not pursue me?"

"Certainly not."

"What would they do for a victim?"

"They would wonder at your unaccountable flight, and then choose some distinguished pauper."

"But if I were to stay here, would they not save me from death at my entreaty?"

"Oh, certainly not; they would never understand such an entreaty. That's a question of death, the supreme blessing. No one is capable of such a base act as saving his fellow-man from death. All are eager to help each other to such a fate."

"But if I were to fly they would not prevent me, and they would not pursue me?"

"Oh no."

"Are there any in the land who are exempt from the sacrifice?"

"Oh yes; the Athons,[1] Meleks, and Kohens—these are not worthy of the honor. The artisans and tradesmen are sometimes permitted to attain to this honor; the laborers in greater numbers; but it is the paupers who are chiefly favored. And this is a matter of complaint among the rich and powerful, that they cannot be sacrificed."

"Well, why couldn't I be made an Athon or a Kohen, and be exempted in that way?"

"Oh, that would be too great a dishonor; it would be impossible. On the contrary, the whole people are anxious to honor you to the very uttermost, and to bestow upon you the greatest privileges and blessings which can possibly be given. Oh no, it would be impossible for them to allow you to become an Athon or a Kohen. As for me, I am Malca, and therefore the lowest in the land—pitied and commiserated by the haughty pauper class, who shake their heads at the thought of one like me. All the people shower upon me incessantly new gifts and new offices. If my present love of light and life were generally known, they would punish me by giving me new contributions of wealth and new offices and powers, which I do not want."

"But you love riches, do you not? and you must want them still?"

"No," said Layelah, "I do not want them now."

"Why, what do you want?" I asked.

"You!" said she, with a sweet smile.

I said nothing, but tried desperately to think of something that might divert the conversation.

1 The *Harper's Weekly* serial mistakenly transcribed this as "Alhons."

Layelah was silent for a few moments, and then went on in a musing tone:

"As I was saying, I love you, Atam-or, and I hate Almah because you love her. I think Almah is the only human being in all the world that I ever really hated; and yet, though I hate her, still, strange to say, I feel as though I should like to give her the immense blessing of death, and that is a very strange feeling indeed for one of the Kosekin. Do you understand, Atam-or, what such can possibly be?"

I did not answer, but turned away the conversation by a violent effort.

"Are there any other athalebs here?"

"Oh yes."

"How many?"

"Four."

"Are they all as tame as this?"

"Oh yes, all quite as tame; there is no difference whatever."

Upon this I left the back of the athaleb, and Layelah also descended, after which she proceeded to show me the other monsters. At length she unharnessed the athaleb and we left the cavern.

CHAPTER XXII. ESCAPE.

ON the following *jom* I told everything to Almah. I told her that Layelah was urging me to fly with her, and that I had found out all about her plans. I described the athalebs, informed her about the direction which we were to take, the island of fire, and the country of the Orin. At this intelligence Almah was filled with delight, and for the first time since we had come to the *amir* there were smiles of joy upon her face. She needed no persuasion. She was ready to set forth whenever it was fitting, and to risk everything upon this enterprise. She felt as I did, and thought that the wildest attempt was better than this dull inaction.

Death was before us here, and every *jom* as it passed only brought it nearer. True, we were treated with the utmost kindness, we lived in royal splendor, we had enormous retinues; but all this was a miserable mockery, since it all served as the prelude to our inevitable doom. For that doom it was hard indeed to wait. Anything was better. Far better would it be to risk all the dangers of this unusual and amazing flight, to brave the terrors of that drear isle of fire, Magones; better to perish there of starvation, or to be killed by the hands of hostile Gojin, than to wait here and be destroyed at last by the sacrificial knife of these smiling, generous, kind-hearted, self-sacrificing fiends; to be killed—ay, and afterward borne to the tremendous *Mista Kosek*.

There was a difficulty with Layelah that had to be guarded against: in the first place that she might not suspect, and again that we might choose our time of escape when she would not be at all likely to find us out. We resolved to make our attempt without any further delay. Layelah was with us for the greater part of that *jom*, and the Kohen Gadol also gave us much of his company. Layelah did not seem to have any suspicions whatever of my secret purpose; for she was as bright, as amiable, and as devoted to me as ever, while the Kohen Gadol sought as before to make himself agreeable to Almah. I did not think fit to tell her about Layelah's proposal, and therefore she was quite ignorant of the secret plans of the Kohen Gadol, evidently attributing his attention to the unfailing amiability of the Kosekin.

Layelah came again after Almah had retired, and spent the time in trying to persuade me to fly with her. The beautiful girl was certainly never more engaging, nor was she ever more tender. Had it not been for Almah it would have been impossible to resist such sweet persuasions; but as it was I did resist. Layelah, however, was not at all discouraged, nor did she lose any of her amiability; but when she took leave it was with a smile and sweet words of forgiveness on her lips for what she called my cruelty. After she left I remained for a time with a painful sense of helplessness. The fact is my European training did not fit me for encountering such a state of things as existed among the Kosekin. It's very easy to be faithful to one's own true-love in England, when other fair ladies hold aloof and wait to be sought; but here among the Kosekin, women have as much liberty in making love as men, and there is no law or custom about it. If a woman chooses she can pay the most desperate attentions, and play the part of a distracted lover to her heart's content. In most cases the women actually take the initiative, as they are more impressible and impulsive than men; and so it was that Layelah made me the object of her persistent assault—acting all the time, too, in accordance with the custom of the country, and thus having no thought whatever of indelicacy, since, according to the Kosekin, she was acting simply in accordance with the rights of every woman. Now, where a woman is urged by one ardent lover to dismiss her other lover, she may sometimes find it difficult to play her part satisfactorily; but in my case I did not play my part satisfactorily at all; the ordeal was too hard, and I was utterly unable to show to Layelah that firmness and decision of character which the occasion demanded.

Yet, after all, the ordeal at last ended. Layelah left, as I have said, with sweet words of forgiveness on her lips, and I after a time succeeded in regaining my presence of mind.

Almah was waiting, and she soon joined me. We gathered a few articles for the journey, the chief of which were my rifle and pistol, which I had not used here, and then we set forth. Leaving our apartments we traversed the long passages, and at length came to the cavern of the athalebs. We met several people on the way, who looked at us with smiles, but made no other sign. It was evident that they had no commission to watch us, and that thus far Layelah's information was correct.

Upon entering the cavern of the athalebs my first feeling was one of helplessness; for I had no confidence whatever in my own powers of managing these awful monsters, nor did I feel sure that I could harness them; but the emergency was a pressing one, and there was no help for it. I had seen where Layelah had left the harness, and now my chief desire was to secure one of the athalebs. The faint light served to disclose nothing but gloom; and I waited for a while, hoping that one of them would come forward as before. But waiting did no good, for no movement was made, and I had to try what I could do myself to rouse them. So I walked farther in toward the back part of the cavern, peering through the gloom, while Almah remained near the entrance.

As I advanced I heard a slight noise, as of someone moving. I thought it was one of the athalebs, and walked on farther, peering through the gloom, when suddenly I came full upon a man who was busy at some work which I could not make out. For a moment I stood in amazement and despair, for it seemed as though all was lost, and as if this man would at once divine my intent. While I stood thus he turned and gave me a very courteous greeting, after which, in the usual manner of the Kosekin, he asked me with much amiability what he could do for me. I muttered something about seeing the athalebs, upon which he informed me that he would show them to me with pleasure.

He went on to say that he had recently been raised from the low position of Athon to that of Feeder of the Athalebs, a post involving duties like those of ostlers or grooms[1] among us, but which here indicated high rank and honor. He was proud of his title of "Epet," which means servant, and more than usually obliging. I

1 A person who tended horses at an inn or other establishment.

at once took advantage of his complaisance, and requested him to show me the athalebs. Upon this he led the way farther on, where I could see through the gloom the shadowy outlines of four monsters, all of which were resting in an upright posture against the wall, with their claws fixed on a shelf of rock. They looked more than ever like dragons, or rather like enormous bats, for their wings were disclosed hanging in loose leathern folds.

"Can they be roused," I asked, "and made to move?"

"Oh yes," said the Epet, and without waiting for any further request he proceeded to pull at the loose fan-like wing of the nearest one. The monster drew himself together, gave a flutter with his wings, and then moved back from the wall.

"Make him walk," said I, eagerly.

The Epet at this pulled upon his wing once more, and the athaleb moved forward.

"Bring him to the portal, so that I may see him," said I.

The Epet, still holding the athaleb's wing, pulled at him, and thus guided him toward the portal. I was amazed at the docility of this terrific monster; yet, after all, I thought that it was no more astonishing than the docility of the elephant, which in like manner allows itself to be guided by the slightest pressure. A child may lead a vast elephant with ease, and here with equal ease the Epet led the athaleb. He led him up near to the portal, where the aurora light beamed through far brighter than the brightest moon, and disclosed all the vast proportions of the monster. I stood and looked on for some time in silence, quite at a loss what to do next.

And now Layelah's words occurred to me as to the perfect willingness of the Kosekin to do anything which one might wish. She had insisted on it that they would not prevent our flight, and had given me to understand that they would even assist me if I should ask them. This is what now occurred to me, and I determined to make a trial. So I said:

"I should like to fly in the air on the athaleb. Will you harness him?"

I confess it was with some trepidation that I said this, but the feeling was soon dissipated. The Epet heard my words with perfect coolness, as though they conveyed the most natural request in the world, and then proceeded to obey me, just as at home a servant might hear and obey his master, who might say, "I should like to take a ride; will you harness the bay mare?"

So the Epet proceeded to harness the athaleb, and I watched him in silence; but it was the silence of deep suspense, and my heart throbbed painfully. There was yet much to be risked. The gates had to be opened. Others might interfere. Layelah might come. All these thoughts occurred to me as I watched the Epet; and though the labor of harnessing the athaleb was simple and soon performed, still the time seemed long. So the collar was secured around the neck of the athaleb, with the grapple attached, and the lines were fastened to the wings, and then Almah and I mounted.

The Epet now stood waiting for further orders.

"Open the gates," said I.

The Epet did so.

Almah was seated on the back of the athaleb before me, holding on to the coarse mane; I, just behind, held the reins in my hand. The gates were opened wide. A few people outside, roused by the noise of the opening gates, stood and looked on. They had evidently no other feeling but curiosity.

All was now ready and the way was open, but there was an unexpected difficulty—the athaleb would not start, and I did not know how to make him. I had once more to apply for help to the Epet.

"How am I to make him start?" I asked.

"Pull at the collar to make him start, and pull at both reins to make him stop," said the Epet.

Upon this I pulled at the collar.

The athaleb obeyed at once. He rose almost erect, and moved out through the gate. It was difficult to hold on, but we did so. On reaching the terrace outside, the athaleb expanded his vast wings, which spread out over a space of full fifty feet, and then with vigorous motions raised himself in the air.

It was a moment full of terror to both of us; the strange sensation of rising in the air, the quivering muscles of the athaleb at the working of the enormous pinions, the tremendous display of strength, all combined to overwhelm me with a sense of utter helplessness. With one hand I clung to the stiff mane of the monster; with the other I held Almah, who was also grasping the athaleb's hair; and thus for some time all thought was taken up in the one purpose of holding on. But at length the athaleb lay in the air in a perfectly horizontal position; the beat of the wings grew more slow and even, the muscular exertion more steady and sustained. We both began to regain some degree of confidence, and at length I raised myself up and looked around.

It did not seem long since we had left; but already the city was far behind, rising with its long, crescent terraces, sparkling and twinkling with innumerable lights. We had passed beyond the

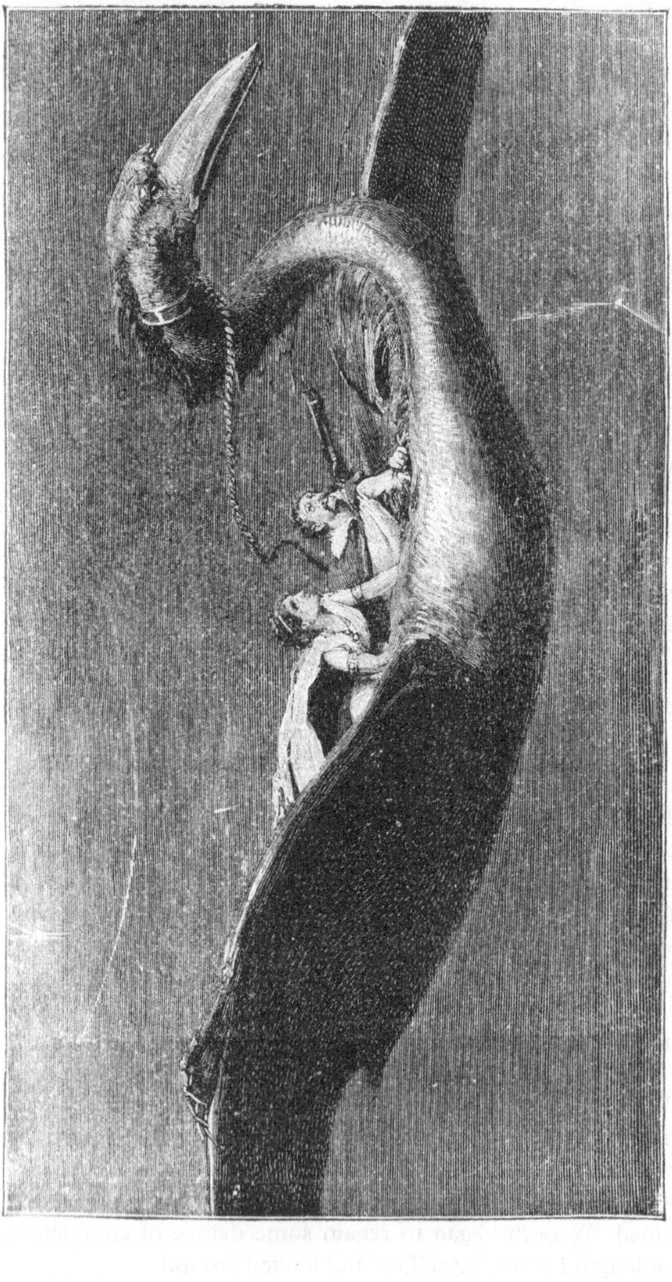

Illustration 14: "With one hand I clung to the stiff mane of the monster; with the other I held Almah."

bay; the harbor was behind us, the open sea before us, the deep water beneath. The athaleb flew low, not more than a hundred feet above the water, and maintained that distance all the time. It seemed, indeed, as if he might drop into the water at any time; but this was only fancy, for he was perfect master of all his movement, and his flight was swift and well sustained.

Overhead the sky was filled with the glory of the aurora beams, which spread everywhere, flashing out from the zenith and illuminating the earth with a glow brighter than that of the brightest moon; beneath, the dark waters of the sea extended, with the waves breaking into foam, and traversed by galleys, by merchant-ships, and by the navies of the Kosekin. Far away the surface of the sea spread, with that marvellous appearance of an endless ascent, as though for a thousand miles, rising thus until it terminated half-way up the sky; and so it rose up on every side, so that I seemed to be at the bottom of a basin-shaped world—an immense and immeasurable hollow—a world unparalleled and unintelligible.[1] Far away, at almost infinite distances, arose the long lines of mountains, which, crowned with ice, gleamed in the aurora light, and seemed like a barrier that made forever impossible all ingress and egress.

On and on we sped. At length we grew perfectly accustomed to the situation, the motion was so easy and our seats were so secure. There were no obstacles in our way, no roughness along our path; for that pathway was the smooth air, and in such a path there could be no interruption, no jerk or jar. After the first terror had passed there remained no longer any necessity for holding on—we could sit and look around with perfect freedom; and at length I rose to my feet, and Almah stood beside me, and thus we stood for a long time, with all our souls kindled into glowing enthusiasm by the excitement of that adventurous flight, and the splendors of that unequalled scene.

At length the aurora light grew dim. Then came forth the stars, glowing and burning in the black sky. Beneath there was nothing visible but the darkness of the water, spotted with phosphorescent points, while all around a wall of gloom arose which shut out from view the distant shores.

Suddenly I was aware of a noise like the beat of vast wings, and these wings were not those of our athaleb. At first I thought it was

1 More's description resembles Hans Pfaal's description of the Earth as he rises into space in Poe's "The Unparalleled Adventures of One Hans Pfaal."

the fluttering of a sail, but it was too regular and too long continued for that. At length I saw through the gloom a vast shadowy form in the air behind us, and at once the knowledge of the truth flashed upon me. It was another monster flying in pursuit!

Were we pursued? Were there men on his back? Should I resist? I held my rifle poised, and was resolved to resist at all hazards. Almah saw it all, and said nothing. She perceived the danger, and in her eyes I saw that she, like me, would prefer death to surrender. The monster came nearer and nearer, until at last I could see that he was alone, and that none were on his back. But now another fear arose. He might attack our athaleb, and in that way endanger us. He must be prevented from coming nearer; yet to fire the rifle was a serious matter. I had once before learned the danger of firing under such circumstances, when my opmahera had fled in terror at the report, and did not wish to experience the danger which might arise from a panic-stricken athaleb; and so as I stood there I waved my arms and gesticulated violently. The pursuing athaleb seemed frightened at such an unusual occurrence, for he veered off, and soon was lost in the darkness.

[TO BE CONTINUED.]

PART 15 (14 APRIL, 1888)

CHAPTER XXIII.
THE ISLAND OF FIRE.

AT last there appeared before us what seemed like a long line of dull-red fires, and as we looked we could see bursts of flame at fitful intervals, which shone out for a few moments and then died away. Upon this now our whole attention was fixed; for it seemed as though we were approaching our destination, and that this place was the Island of Fire—a name which, from present appearances, was fully justified. As we went on and drew steadily nearer, the mass of glowing fire grew larger and brighter, and what at first had seemed a line was broken up into different parts, one of which far surpassed the others. This was higher in the air, and its shape was that of a long, thin, sloping line, with a burning, glowing globule at each end. It seemed like lava running down from the crater of a volcano, and this appearance was made certainty on a nearer approach; for we saw at the upper point, which seemed the crater, an outburst of flame, followed by a new flow of the fiery stream. In other places there were similar fires, but they were less bright, either because they were smaller or more remote.

At length we heard beneath us the roar of breakers, and saw long white lines of surf beating upon the shore. Our athaleb now descended and alighted; we clambered to the ground, and I, taking the grapple, fixed it securely between two sharp rocks. We were at last on Magones, the Island of Fire.

The brightness of the aurora light had left us, but it needed not this to show us the dismal nature of the land to which we had come. It was a land of horror, where there was nothing but the abomination of desolation—a land overstrewn with blasted fragments of fractured lava-blocks, intermixed with sand, from which there arose black precipices and giant mountains that poured forth rivers of fire and showers of ashes and sheets of flame. A tremendous peak arose before us, with a crest of fire and sides streaked with red torrents of molten lava; between us and it there spread away a vast expanse of impassable rocks—a scene of ruin and savage wildness which cannot be described, and all around was the same drear and appalling prospect. Here in the night-season—the season of darkness and of awful gloom—we stood in this land of woe; and not one single sign appeared of life save the life that we had brought with us. As for food, it was vain to think of it.

To search after it would be useless. It seemed, indeed, impossible to move from the spot where we were. Every moment presented some new discovery which added to the horror of Magones.

But Almah was weary, for our flight had been long, and she wished to rest. So I found a place for her where there was some sand between two rocks, and here she lay down and went to sleep. I sat at a little distance off on a shelf of the rock, with my back against it, and here, after a little time, I also went to sleep.

At length we awoke. But what a waking! There was no morning dawn, no blessed returning light to greet our eyes. We opened our eyes to the same scenes upon which we had closed them, and the darkness was still deep and dense around us. Over us both there was a sense of utter depression, and I was so deeply plunged into it that I found it impossible to rouse myself, even for the sake of saying words of cheer to Almah. I had brought a few fragments of food, and upon these we made our breakfast; but there was the athaleb to feed, and for him I found nothing, nor could I think of anything—unless he could feed upon rocks and sand. Yet food for him was a matter of the highest consequence, for he was all our support and stay and hope; and if the monster were deprived of food he might turn upon us and satisfy upon us his ravenous appetite. These thoughts were painful indeed, and added to my despondency.

Suddenly I heard the sound of running water. I started away toward the place from which the sound came, and found, only a little distance off, a small brook trickling along on its way to the shore. I called Almah, and we both drank and were refreshed.

This showed an easy way to get to the shore, and I determined to go there to see if there were any fish to be found. Shell-fish might be there, or the carcasses of dead fish thrown up by the sea, upon which the athaleb might feed. I left my pistol with Almah, telling her to fire it if she heard me fire, for I was afraid of losing my way, and therefore took this precaution. I left it lying on the rock full-cocked, and directed her to point it in the air and pull the trigger. It was necessary to take these precautions, as of course she was quite ignorant of its nature. After this I left her and tried to follow the torrent.

This, however, I soon found to be impossible, for the brook on reaching a huge rock plunged underneath it and became lost to view. I then went toward the shore as well as I could—now climbing over sharp rocks, now going round them, until at length after immense labor I succeeded in reaching the water. Here the scene was almost as wild as the one I had left. There was no beach whatever—nothing but a vast extent of wild fragments of fractured lava-blocks, which were evidently the result of some comparatively recent convulsion of nature, for their edges were still sharp, and the water had not worn even those which were within its grasp to anything like roundness, or to anything else than the jagged and shattered outlines which had originally belonged to them. All the shore thus consisted of vast rocky blocks, over which the sea beat in foam.

Eager to find something, I toiled along this rocky shore for a long distance, but without seeing any change. I was unwilling to go back baffled, yet I was at length compelled to do so. But the necessity of feeding the athaleb was pressing, and I saw that our only course now would be to mount him again, leave this place, and seek some other. But where could we go? That I could not imagine, and could only conclude to trust altogether to the instinct of the athaleb, which might guide him to places where he might obtain food. Such a course would involve great risk for we might be carried into the midst of vast flocks of these monsters; yet there was nothing else to be done.

I now retraced my steps, and went for a long time near the sea. At length I found a place where the walking was somewhat easier, and went in this way up into the island and away from the sea. It seemed to lead in the direction where I wished to go. At length it seemed as if I had walked far enough, yet I could see no signs of Almah. I shouted, but there was no answer. I shouted again and again, but with the like result. Then I fired my rifle and listened. In response there came the report of the pistol far away behind me. It was evident that in coming back along the shore I had passed by the place where Almah was. There was nothing now left but to retrace my steps and this I accordingly did. I went back to the shore, and returned on my steps, shouting all the time, until at length I was rejoiced to hear the answering shout of Almah. After this it was easy to reach her.

We now took up the grapple and once more mounted. The athaleb, eager to be off, raised himself quickly in the air, and soon our late resting-place was far behind. His flight was now different from what it was before. Then he stood off in one straight line for a certain fixed destination, as though under some guidance; for though I did not direct him, still his long training had taught him to fly to Magones.

But now training and guidance were both wanting, and the athaleb was left to the impulse of his hunger and the guidance of his instinct; so he flew no longer in one undeviating straight line, but rose high, and bent his head down low, and flew and soared in vast circles, even as I have seen a vulture or a condor sweep about while searching for food. All the while we were drawing farther and farther away from the spot which we had left.

We passed the lofty volcano; we saw more plainly the rivers of molten lava; we passed vast cliffs and bleak mountains, all of which were more terrific than all that we had left behind. Now the darkness lessened, for the aurora was brightening in the sky, and gathering up swiftly and gloriously all its innumerable beams, and flashing forth its lustrous glow upon the world. To us this was equal to the return of day; it was like a blessed dawn. Light had come, and we rejoiced and were exceeding glad.

Now we saw before us, far beyond the black precipices, a broad bay with sloping shores, and a wide beach which seemed like a beach of sand. The surf broke here, but beyond the surf was the gentle sandy declivity, and beyond this there appeared the shores, still rocky and barren and desolate, but far preferable to what we had left behind. Far away in the interior arose lofty mountains and volcanoes, while behind us flamed the burning peak which we had passed.

Here the athaleb wheeled in long, circuitous flights, which grew lower and lower, until at length he descended upon the sandy beach, where I saw a vast sea-monster lying dead. It had evidently been thrown up here by the sea. It was like one of those monsters which I had seen from the galley of the Kohen at the time of the sacred hunt. By this the athaleb descended, and at once began to devour it, tearing out vast masses of flesh, and exhibiting such voracity and strength of jaw that I could scarcely bear to look upon the sight. I fastened the grapple securely to the head of the dead monster, and leaving the athaleb to feed upon it, Almah and I went up the beach.

On our way we found rocks covered with sea-weed, and here we sought after shell-fish. Our search was at length rewarded, for suddenly I stumbled upon a place where I found some lobsters. I grasped two of these, but the others escaped. Here at last I had found signs of life, but they were of the sea rather than of the shore. Delighted with my prey, I hastened to Almah to show them to her. She recognized them at once, and I saw that they were familiar to her. I then spoke of eating them, but at this proposal she recoiled in horror. She could not give any reason for her repugnance, but merely said that among her people they were regarded as something equivalent to vermin, and I found that she would no more think of eating one than I would think of eating a rat. Upon this I had to throw them away, and we once more resumed our search.

At last we came to a place where numbers of dead fish lay on the sand. Nearer the water they were more fresh, and not at all objectionable. I picked up a few which looked like our common smelt, and found that Almah had no objection to these. But now the question arose how to cook them; neither of us could eat them raw. A fire was necessary, yet a fire was impossible; for on the whole island there was probably not one single combustible thing. Our discovery, therefore, seemed to have done us but little good, and we seemed destined to starvation, when fortunately a happy thought suggested itself. In walking along I saw far away the glow of some lava which had flowed to the shore at the end of the sandy beach, and was probably cooling down at the water's edge. Here, then, was a natural fire, which might serve us better than any contrivance of our own, and toward this we at once proceeded. It was about two miles away; but the beach was smooth, and we reached the place without any difficulty.

Here we found the edge of that lava flood which seemed eternally descending from the crater beyond. The edge which was nearest the water was black; and the liquid fire, as it rolled down, curled over this in a fantastic shape, cooling and hardening into the form which it thus assumed. Here, after some search, I found a crevice where I could approach the fire, and I laid the fish upon a crimson rock, which was cooling and hardening into the shape of a vast ledge of lava. In this way, by the aid of nature, the fish were broiled, and we made our repast.

There was nothing here to invite a longer stay, and we soon returned to the athaleb. We found the monster, gorged with food, asleep, resting upon his hind legs, with his breast supported against the vast carcass. Almah called it a *jantannin.* It was about sixty feet in length and twenty in thickness, with a vast horny head, ponderous jaws, and back covered with scales. Its eyes were of prodigious size, and it had the appearance of a crocodile, with the vast size of a whale. It was unlike a crocodile, however; for it had fins rather than paws, and must have been as clumsy on the land as a seal or a walrus. It lay on its side, and the athaleb had fed itself from the uncovered flesh of its belly.[1]

There was nothing here to induce us to stay, and so we wandered along the beach in the other direction. On our right was the bay; on our left the rocky shore, which, beginning at the beach,

1 See Appendices B1 and B2 on the Ichthyosaurus.

Illustration 15: "Almah lay down upon the sand, and I seated myself against a rock, a little distance off."

ran back into the country, a waste of impassable rocks, where not a tree or plant or blade of grass relieved the appalling desolation. Once or twice we made an attempt to penetrate into the country, where openings appeared. These openings seemed like the beds of dried-up torrents. We were able to walk but a few paces, for invariably we would come to some immense blocks of rock, which barred all farther progress. In this way we explored the beach for miles, until it terminated in a savage promontory that rose abruptly from the sea, against which the huge billows broke in thunder.

Then we retraced our steps, and again reached the spot where the athaleb was asleep by the jantannin. Almah was now too weary to walk any farther, nor was it desirable to do so; for, indeed, we had traversed all that could be visited. On one side of the beach was the sea, on the other the impassable rocks; at one end the promontory, at the other the lava fires. There was nothing more for us to do but to wait here until the athaleb should awake, and then our actions would depend upon what we might now decide.

This was the question that was now before us, and this we began to consider. We both felt the most unspeakable aversion for the island, and to remain here any longer was impossible. We would once more have to mount the athaleb, and proceed to some other shore. But where? Ah! there was the question! Not on the island, for it did not seem possible that in all its extent there could be one single spot capable of affording a resting-place. Layelah's information with regard to Magones had made that much plain. I had not taken in her full meaning, but now mine eyes had seen it. Yet where else could we go? Almah could not tell where under the sky lay that land which she loved; I could not guess where to go to find the land of the Orin. Even if I did know, I did not feel able to guide the course of the athaleb; and I felt sure that if we were to mount again, the mighty monster would wing his flight back to the very place from which we had escaped—the *amir*. These thoughts weighed down our spirits. We felt that we had gained nothing by our flight, and that our future was dark indeed. The only hope left us was that we might be able to guide the course of the athaleb in some different direction altogether, so that we should not be carried back to the Kosekin.

And now, worn out by the long fatigues of this *jom*, we thought of sleep. Almah lay down upon the sand, and I seated myself, leaning against a rock, a little distance off, having first reloaded my rifle and pistol.

CHAPTER XXIV.
RECAPTURE.

HOW long I slept I do not know; but in the midst of my sleep there sounded voices, which at first intermingled themselves with my dreams, but gradually became separate and sounded from without, rousing me from my slumbers. I opened my eyes drowsily, but the sight that I saw was so amazing that in an instant all sleep left me. I started to my feet, and gazed in utter bewilderment upon the scene before me.

The aurora light was shining with unusual brilliancy, and disclosed everything—the sea, the shore, the athaleb, the jantannin, the promontory, all—more plainly and more luminously than before; but it was not any of these things that now excited my attention and rendered me dumb. I saw Almah standing there at a little distance, with despairing face, surrounded by a band of armed Kosekin; while immediately before me, regarding me with a keen glance and an air of triumph, was Layelah.

"*Atœsmzori alonla,*" said she, with a sweet smile, giving me the usual salutation of the Kosekin.

I was too bewildered to say a word, and stood mute as before, looking first at her and then at Almah.

The sight of Almah a prisoner once more, surrounded by the Kosekin, excited me to madness. I seized my rifle, and raised it as if to take aim; but Almah, who understood the movement, cried to me:

"Put down your *sepet-ram*, Atam-or! you can do nothing for me. The Kosekin are too numerous."

"*Sepet-ram!*" said Layelah; "what do you mean by that? If your *sepet-ram* has any power, do not try to use it, Atam-or, or else I shall have to order my followers to give to Almah the blessing of death."

At this my rifle was lowered: the whole truth flashed upon me, and I saw, too, the madness of resistance. I might kill one or two, but the rest would do as Layelah said, and I should speedily be disarmed. Well I knew how powerless were the thunders of my fire-arms to terrify these Kosekin; for the prospect of death would only rouse them to a mad enthusiasm, and they would all rush upon me as they would rush upon a jantannin—to slay and be slain. The odds were too great. A crowd of Europeans could be held in check far more easily than these death-loving Kosekin. The whole truth was thus plain: we were prisoners, and were at their mercy.

Layelah showed no excitement or anger whatever. She looked and spoke in her usual gracious and amiable fashion, with a sweet smile on her face.

"We knew," said she, "that you would be in distress in this desolate place, and that you would not know where to go from Magones; and so we have come, full of the most eager desire to relieve your wants. We have brought with us food and drink, and are ready to do everything for you that you may desire. We have had great trouble in finding you, and have coursed over the shores for vast distances, and far over the interior, but our athalebs found you at last by their scent. And we rejoice to have found you in time, and that you are both so well, for we have been afraid that you had been suffering. Nay, Atam-or, do not thank us; thanks are distasteful to the Kosekin: these brave followers of mine will all be amply rewarded for this, for they will all be made paupers; but as for myself, I want no higher reward than the delightful thought that I have saved you from suffering."

The beautiful, smiling Layelah, who addressed me in this way with her sweet voice, was certainly not to be treated as an enemy. Against her a rifle could not be levelled; she would have looked at me with the same sweet smile, and that smile would have melted all my resolution. Nor could I even persist in my determination to remain. Remain! For what? For utter despair! And yet where else could we go?

"You do not know where lie the lands of the Orin," said Layelah. "The athaleb does not know. You could not guide him if you did know. You are helpless on his back. The art of driving an athaleb is difficult, and cannot be learned without long and severe practice. My fear was that the athaleb might break away from you and return, leaving you to perish here. Had you tried to leave this place he would have brought you back to the *amir*."

To this I said nothing—partly because it was so true that I had no answer to make, and partly also out of deep mortification and dejection. My pride was wounded at being thus so easily baffled by a girl like Layelah, and all my grief was stirred by the sadness of Almah. In her eyes there seemed even now the look of one who sees death inevitable, and the glance she gave to me was like an eternal farewell.

Almah now spoke, addressing herself to Layelah.

"Death," said she, in a voice of indescribable mournfulness, "is better here than with you. We would rather die here than go back. Let us, I pray you, receive the blessing of death here. Let us be paupers and exiles, and die on Magones."

Layelah heard this, and stood for a moment in deep thought.

"No one but a stranger," said she at length, "would ask such a favor as that. Do you not know that what you ask is among the very highest honors of the Kosekin? Who am I that I can venture to grant such a request as that? Ask for anything in my power, and I will be glad to grant it. I have already arranged that you shall be separated from Atam-or; and that, surely, is a high privilege. I might consent to bind you hand and foot, after the manner of the more distinguished *Asirin*; you may also be blindfolded if you wish it. I might even promise, after we return to the *amir*, to keep you confined in utter darkness, with barely sufficient food to keep you alive until the time of the sacrifice; in short, there is no blessing known among the Kosekin that I will not give so long as it is in my power. And so, beloved Almah," continued Layelah, "you have every reason for happiness; you have all the highest blessings known among the Kosekin: separation from your lover, poverty, want, darkness; and, finally, the prospect of inevitable death ever before you as the crowning glory of your lot."

These words seemed to the Kosekin the very excess of magnanimity, and involuntary murmurs of admiration escaped them; although it is just possible that they murmured at the greatness of the favor that was offered. But to me it sounded like fiendish mockery, and to Almah it sounded the same; for a groan escaped her, her fortitude gave way, she sank on her knees, buried her head in her hands, and wept.

"Almah," cried I, in a fury, "we will not go back—we will not be separated! I will destroy all the athalebs and we shall all perish here together. At least, you and I will not be separated."

At this Almah started up.

"No, no," said she—"no; let us go back. Here we have nothing but death."

"But we have death also at the *amir*, and a more terrible one," said I.

"If you kill the athalebs," said Layelah, "I will give Almah the blessing of death."

At this I recoiled in horror, and my resolution again gave way.

"You have some mysterious power of conferring death," continued Layelah, "with what Almah calls your *sepet-ram*; but do not kill the athalebs, for it will do you no good. Almah would then receive the blessing of death. My followers, these noble Kosekin, would rejoice in thus gaining exile and death on Magones. As for myself, it would be my highest happiness to be here alone with you. With you I should live for a few sweet *joms*, and with you I should die; so go on—kill the athalebs if you wish."

"Do not!" cried Almah—"do not! There is no hope. We are their prisoners, and our only hope is in submission."

Upon this all further thought of resistance left me, and I stood in silence, stolidly waiting for their action. As I looked around I noticed a movement near the jantannin, and saw several athalebs there, which were devouring its flesh. I now went over to Almah and spoke with her. We were both full of despair. It seemed as though we might never meet again. We were to be separated now; but who could say whether we should be permitted to see each other after leaving this place? We had but little to say. I held her in my arms, regardless of the presence of others; and these, seeing our emotion, at once moved away, with the usual delicacy of the Kosekin, and followed Layelah to the jantannin to see about the athalebs.

[TO BE CONTINUED.]

PART 16 (21 APRIL, 1888)

CHAPTER XXIV.—(*Continued.*)
RECAPTURE.

AT last our interview was terminated. Layelah came and informed us that all was ready for our departure. We walked sadly to the place, and found the athalebs crouched to receive their riders. There were four beside ours. Layelah informed me that I was to go with her, and Almah was to go on another athaleb. I entreated her to let Almah go with me; but she declined, saying that our athaleb could only carry two, as he seemed fatigued, and it would not be safe to overload him for so long a flight. I told her that Almah and I could go together on the same athaleb; but she objected on the ground of my ignorance of driving. And so, remonstrances and objections being alike useless, I was compelled to yield to the arrangements that had been made. Almah mounted on another athaleb. I mounted with Layelah, and then the great monsters expanded their mighty wings, rose into the air, and soon were speeding over the waters.

We went on in silence for some time. I was too despondent to say a word, and all my thoughts turned toward Almah, who was now separated from me—perhaps forever. The other athalebs went ahead, at long intervals apart, flying in a straight line, while ours was last. Layelah said nothing. She sat in front of me; her back was turned toward me; she held in her hands the reins, which hung quite loose at first, but after a while she drew them up, and seemed to be directing our course. For some time I did not notice anything in particular, for my eyes were fixed upon the athaleb immediately before us, upon which was seated the loved form of Almah, which I could easily recognize. But our athaleb flew slowly, and I noticed that we were falling behind. I said this to Layelah, but she only remarked that it was fatigued with its long journey. To this I objected that the others had made as long a journey, and insisted that she should draw nearer. This she at first refused to do; but at length, as I grew persistent, she complied, or pretended to do so. In spite of this, however, we again fell behind, and I noticed that this always happened when the reins were drawn tight. On making this discovery I suddenly seized both reins and let them trail loose, whereupon the athaleb at once showed a perceptible increase of speed, which proved that there was no fatigue in him whatever. This I said to Layelah.

She acquiesced with a sweet smile, and taking the reins again, she sat around so as to face me, and said:

"You are very quick. It is no use to try to deceive you, Atam-or: I wish to fall behind."

"Why?"

"To save you."

"To save me?"

"Yes. I can take you to the land of the Orin. Now is the time to escape from death. If you go back you must surely die; but now, if you will be guided by me, I can take you to the land of the Orin. There they all hate death, they love life, they live in the light. There you will find those who are like yourself; there you can love and be happy."

"But what of Almah?" I asked.

Layelah made a pretty gesture of despair.

"You are always talking of Almah," said she. "What is Almah to you? She is cold, dull, sad! She never will speak. Let her go."

"Never!" said I. "Almah is worth more than all the world to me."

Layelah sighed.

"I can never, never, never," said she, "get from you the least little bit of a kind word—even after all that I have done for you, and when you know that I would lie down and let you trample me under your feet if it gave you any pleasure."

"Oh, that is not the question at all," said I. "You are asking me to leave Almah—to be false to her—and I cannot."

"Among the Kosekin," said Layelah, "it is the highest happiness for lovers to give one another up."

"I am not one of the Kosekin," said I. "I cannot let her go away—I cannot let her go back to the *amir*—to meet death alone. If she dies she shall see me by her side, ready to die with her."

At this Layelah laughed merrily.

"Is it possible," said she, "that you believe that? Do you not know that if Almah goes back alone she will not die?"

"What do you mean?"

"Why, she can only die when you are in her company. She has lived for years among us, and we have waited for someone to appear whom she might love, so that we might give them both the blessing of death. If that one should leave her, Almah could not receive the blessing. She would be compelled to live longer, until some other lover should appear. Now, by going with me to the land of the Orin, you will save Almah's life—and as for Almah, why, she will be happy—and dear papa is quite willing to marry her. You must see, therefore, dear Atam-or, that my plan is the very best that can be thought of for all of us, and above all for Almah."

This, however, was intolerable; and I could not consent to desert Almah, even if by doing so I should save her life. My own nature revolted from it. Still it was not a thing which I could dismiss on the instant. The safety of Almah's life, indeed, required consideration; but then the thought came of her wonder at my desertion. Would she not think me false? Would not the thought of my falsity be worse than death?

"No," said I, "I will not leave her—not even to save her life. Even among us there are things worse than death. Almah would rather die by the sacrificial knife than linger on with a broken heart."

"Oh no," said Layelah, sweetly; "she will rejoice that you are safe. Do you not see that while you are together death is inevitable, but if you separate you may both live and be happy?"

"But she will think me dead," said I, as a new idea occurred. "She will think that some accident has befallen me."

"Oh no, she won't," said Layelah; "she will think that you have gone off with me."

"Then that will be worse, and I would rather die, and have her die with me, than live and have her think me false."

"You are very, very obstinate," said Layelah, sweetly.

I made no reply. During this conversation I had been too intent upon Layelah's words to notice the athalebs before me; but now as I looked up I saw that we had fallen far behind, and that Layelah had headed our athaleb in a new direction. Upon this I once more snatched the reins from her, and tried to return to our former course. This, however, I was utterly unable to do.

Layelah laughed.

"You will have to let me guide our course," said she. "You can do nothing. The athaleb will now go in a straight line to the land of the Orin."

Upon this I started up in wild excitement.

"Never, never, never!" I cried, in a fury. "I will not; I will destroy this athaleb and perish in the water!"

As I said this I raised my rifle.

"What are you going to do?" cried Layelah, in accents of fear.

"Turn back," I cried, "or I will kill this athaleb!"

Upon this Layelah dropped the reins, stood up, and looked at me with a smile.

"Oh, Atam-or," said she, "what a thing to ask! How can I go back now, when we have started for the land of the Orin?"

"We shall never reach the land of the Orin," I cried; "we shall perish in the sea!"

Illustration 16: "The next instant we were all in the water together."

"Oh no," said Layelah; "you cannot kill the athaleb. You are no more than an insect; your rod is a weak thing, and will break on his iron frame."

It was evident that Layelah had not the slightest idea of the powers of my rifle. There was no hesitation on my part. I took aim with the rifle. At that moment I was desperate. I thought of nothing but the swift flight of the athaleb, which was bearing me away forever from Almah. I could not endure that thought, and still less could I endure the thought that she should believe me false. It was therefore in a wild passion of rage and despair that I levelled my rifle, taking aim as well as I could at what seemed a vital part under the wing. The motion of the wing rendered this difficult, however, and I hesitated a moment, so as to make sure. All this time Layelah stood looking at me with a smile on her rosy lips and a merry twinkle in her eyes—evidently regarding my words as empty threats and my act as a vain pretence, and utterly unprepared for what was to follow.

Suddenly I fired both barrels in quick succession. The reports rang out in thunder over the sea. The athaleb gave a wild, appalling shriek, and fell straight down into the water, fluttering vainly with one wing, while the other hung down useless. A shriek of horror burst from Layelah. She started back, and fell from her standing-place into the waves beneath. The next instant we were all in the water together—the athaleb writhing and lashing the water into foam, while I involuntarily clung to his coarse mane, and expected death every moment.

But death did not come; for the athaleb did not sink, but floated with his back out of the water, the right pinion being sunk underneath and useless, and the left struggling vainly with the sea. But after a time he folded up the left wing and drew it close in to his side, and propelled himself with his long hind-legs. His right wing was broken, but he did not seem to have suffered any other injury.

Suddenly I heard a cry behind me:

"Atam-or! oh, Atam-or!"

I looked around and saw Layelah. She was swimming in the water, and seemed exhausted. In the agitation of the past few moments I had lost sight of her, and had thought that she was drowned; but now the sight of her roused me from my stupor and brought me back to myself. She was swimming, yet her strokes were weak and her face was full of despair. In an instant I had flung off my coat, rolled up the rifle and pistol in its folds, and sprung into the water. A few strokes brought me to Layelah. A moment more and I should have been too late. I held her head out of water, told her not to struggle, and then struck out to go back. It would have been impossible for me to do this, encumbered with such a load, had I not fortunately perceived the floating wing of the athaleb close beside me. This I seized, and by means of it drew myself with Layelah alongside; after which I succeeded in putting her on the back of the animal, and soon followed myself.

The terror of the rifle had overwhelmed her, and the suddenness of the catastrophe had almost killed her. She had struggled in the water for a long time, and had called to me in vain. Now she was quite exhausted, and lay in my arms trembling and sobbing. I spoke to her encouragingly, and wrapped her in my coat, and rubbed her hands and feet, until at last she began to recover. Then she wept quietly for a long time; then the weeping fit passed away. She looked up with a smile, and in her face there was unutterable gratitude.

"Atam-or," said she, "I never loved death like the rest of the Kosekin; but now—but now—I feel that death with you would be sweet."

Then tears came to her eyes, and I found tears coming to my own, so that I had to stoop down and kiss away the tears of Layelah. As I did so she twined both her arms around my neck, held me close to her, and sighed.

"Oh, Atam-or, death with you is sweet! And now you cannot reproach me— You have done this yourself, with your terrible power; and you have saved my life to let me die with you. You do not hate me, then, Atam-or, do you? Just speak once to a poor little girl, and say that you do not hate her!"

All this was very pitiable. What man that had a heart in his breast could listen unmoved to words like these, or look without emotion upon one so beautiful, so gentle, and so tender? It was no longer Layelah in triumph with whom I had to do, but Layelah in distress: the light banter, the teasing, mocking smile, the kindling eye, the ready laugh, all were gone. There was nothing now but mournful tenderness—the timid appeal of one who dreaded a repulse, the glance of deep affection, the abandonment of love.

I held Layelah in my arms, and I thought of nothing now but words of consolation for her. Life seemed over; death seemed inevitable; and there, on the back of the athaleb, we floated on the waters and waited for our doom.

CHAPTER XXV.
FALLING, LIKE ICARUS,[1] INTO THE SEA.

THE aurora light, which had flamed brightly, was now extinct, and darkness was upon the face of the deep, where we floated on the back of the monster. He swam, forcing himself onward with his hind-legs, with one broad wing folded up close. Had both been folded up the athaleb could have swum rapidly; but the broken wing lay expanded over the water, tossing with the waves, so that our progress was but slight. Had it not been for this, the athaleb's own instinct might have served to guide him toward some shore which we might have hoped to reach before life was extinct; but as it was, all thought of reaching any shore was out of the question, and there arose before us only the prospect of death—a death, too, which must be lingering and painful and cruel. Thus amid the darkness we floated, and the waves dashed around us, and the athaleb never ceased to struggle in the water, trying to force his way onward. It seemed sweet at that moment to have Layelah with me, for what could have been more horrible than loneliness amid those black waters? and Layelah's mind was made up to meet death with joy, so that her mood conveyed itself to me. And I thought that since death was inevitable it were better to meet it thus, and in this way end my life—not amid the horrors of the sacrifice and the *Mista Kosek*, but in a way which seemed natural to a seafaring man like myself, and with which I had long familiarized my thoughts. For I had fallen upon a world and among people which were all alien and unintelligible to me; and to live on would only open the way to new and worse calamities. There was peace also in the thought that my death would snatch the prospect of death from Almah. She would now be safe. It was only when we were together as lovers that death threatened her; but now since I was removed she could resume her former life, and she might remember me only as an episode in that life. That she would remember me I felt sure, and that she would weep for me and mourn after me was undeniable; but time as it passed would surely alleviate that grief, and Almah would live and be happy.

---

1 After the Greek inventor Daedalus created the labyrinth at Minos, he was imprisoned with his son Icarus to ensure that no one would discover its secrets. Daedalus made wings of wax and feathers so that they could fly away. Despite his father's warning, Icarus flew too close to the sun, which melted the wax, causing him to fall to his death in the sea. The story is told by Ovid in *Metamorphoses*.

Perhaps she might yet regain her native land and rejoin her loved kindred, whom she would tell of the stranger from an unknown shore who had loved her, and through whose death she had gained her life. Such were the thoughts that filled my mind as I floated over the black water with darkness all around, as I held Layelah in my arms, with my coat wrapped around her, and murmured in her ear tender words of consolation and sympathy.

A long, long time had passed—but how long I know not—when suddenly Layelah gave a cry, and started up on her knees, with her head bent forward listening intently. I too listened, and I could distinctly hear the sound of breakers.

It was evident that we were approaching some shore; and, from what I remembered of the shore of Magones, such a shore meant death, and death alone. We stood up and tried to peer through the gloom. At length we saw a whole line of breakers, and beyond all was black. We waited anxiously in that position, and drew steadily nearer. It was evident that the athaleb was desirous of reaching that shore, and we could do nothing but await the result.

But the athaleb had his wits about him, and swam along on a line with the breakers for some distance, until at length an opening appeared, into which he directed his course. Passing through this we reached still water, which seemed like a lagoon surrounded by a coral reef. The athaleb swam on farther, and at length we saw before us an island with a broad, sandy beach, beyond which was the shadowy outline of a forest. Here the monster landed, and dragged himself wearily upon the sand, where he spread his vast bulk out, and lay panting heavily. We dismounted—I first, so as to assist Layelah; and then it seemed as if death were postponed for a time, since we had reached this place where the rich and rank vegetation spoke of nothing but vigorous life.

Fortune had indeed dealt strangely with me. I had fled with Almah, and with her had reached one desolate shore, and now I found myself with Layelah upon another shore, desolate also, but not a savage wilderness. This lonely island, ringed with the black ocean waters, was the abode of a life of its own, and there was nothing here to crush the soul into a horror of despair like that which was caused by the tremendous scenes on Magones.

In an instant Layelah revived from her gloom. She looked around, clapped her little hands, laughed aloud, and danced for joy.

"Oh, Atam-or," she cried, "see—see the trees, see the grass, the bushes! This is a land of wonder. As for food, you can call it down from the sky with your *sepet-ram*, or we can find it on the rocks. Oh, Atam-or! life is better than death, and we can live here, and we can be happy. This shall be better to us than the lands of the Orin, for we shall be alone, and we shall be all in all to one another."

I could not help laughing, and I said:

"Layelah, this is not the language of the Kosekin. You should at once go to the other side of this island, and sit down and wait for death."

"Never," said Layelah; "you are mine, Atam-or, and I never will leave you. If you wish me to die for you, I will gladly lay down my life; but I will not leave you. I love you, Atam-or; and now, whether it be life or death, it is all the same so long as I have you."

Our submersion in the sea and our long exposure afterward had chilled both of us, but Layelah felt it most. She was shivering in her wet clothes in spite of my coat, which I insisted on her wearing, and I determined, if possible, to kindle a fire. Fortunately my powder was dry, for I had thrown off my flask with my coat before jumping into the sea, and thus I had the means of creating fire. I rubbed wet powder over my handkerchief, and then gathered some dried sticks and moss. After this I found some dead trees, the boughs of which were dry and brittle, and in the exercise I soon grew warm, and had the satisfaction of seeing a great heap of fagots accumulating. I fired my pistol into the handkerchief, which, being saturated with powder, caught the fire, and this I blew into a flame among the dried moss. A bright fire now sprang up and blazed high in the air; while I, in order to have an ample supply of fuel, continued to gather it for a long time. At length, as I came back, I saw Layelah lying on the sand in front of the fire, sound asleep. I was glad of this, for she was weary, and had seemed so weak and tremulous that I had felt anxious; so now I arranged my coat over her carefully, and then sat down for a time to think over this new turn which my fortune had taken.

This island was certainly very unlike Magones, yet I had no surety but that it might be equally destitute of food. This was the first question, and I could not think of sleep until I had found out more about the place. The aurora light, which constantly brightens and lessens in this strange world, was now shining gloriously, and I set forth to explore the island. The beach was of fine sand all the way. The water was smooth, and shut in on every side by an outer reef against which the sea-waves broke incessantly. As I walked I soon perceived what the island was; for I had often seen such places before in the South Pacific. It was, in fact, a coral islet, with a reef of rocks encircling it on every side. The vegetation, however, was unlike anything in the world beyond; for it consisted of many varieties of tree-ferns, that looked like palms, and giant grasses, and bamboo. The island was but small, and the entire circuit was not over a mile. I saw nothing that looked like food, nor did it seem likely that in so small a place there could be enough sustenance for us. Our only hope would be from the sea, yet even here I could see no signs of any sort of shell-fish. On the whole the prospect was discouraging, and I returned to the starting-point with a feeling of dejection; but this feeling did not trouble me much at that time: my chief thought was of rest, and I flung myself down on the sand and fell asleep.

I was awakened by a cry from Layelah. Starting up, I saw her standing and looking into the sky. She was intensely excited. As soon as she saw me she rushed toward me and burst into tears, while I, full of wonder, could only stare upward.

"Oh!" cried Layelah, "they've turned back—they've found us! We shall have to leave our dear, lovely island. Oh, Atam-or, I shall lose you now; for never, never, never again will you have one thought of love for your poor Layelah!"

With these words she clung sobbing to me. For my part I do not remember what I said to soothe her, for the sight above was so amazing that it took up all my attention. The aurora shone bright, and in the sky I saw two vast objects wheeling and circling, as if about to descend. I recognized them at once as athalebs; but as their backs were hid from view by their immense wings, I could not make out whether they were wanderers about to alight of their own accord, or guided here by riders—perhaps by the Kosekin from whom we had been parted.

This much at least I remember. I said to Layelah that these athalebs were wild ones, which had come here because they saw or scented our wounded one; but Layelah shook her head with mournful meaning.

"Oh no," said she; "Almah has come back for you. This fire-light has guided them. If you had not made the fire, they never, never, never could have found us; but now all is lost."

There was no time for conversation or discussion. The athalebs drew swiftly nearer and nearer, descending in long circuits, until at length they touched the ground not far away on the wide sandy beach. Then we saw people on their backs, and among them was Almah. We hurried toward them, and Almah rushed into my arms, to the great disgust of Layelah, for she was close beside me and saw it all. She gave an exclamation of grief and despair, and hurried away.

From Almah I learned that our disappearance had caused alarm; that two of the athalebs had come back in search of us; that they had been to Magones, and had searched over the seas, and were just about giving us up as lost, when the fire-light had attracted their attention and drawn them here.

I said nothing at that time about the cause of our disappearance, but merely remarked that the athaleb had fallen into the sea and swam here. This was sufficient. They had to remain here for some time longer to rest their athalebs. At length we prepared to depart. Our wounded athaleb was left behind to take care of himself. I was taken with Almah, and Layelah went on the other. We were thus separated; and so we set forth upon our return, and at length arrived at the *amir*.

[TO BE CONTINUED.]

Illustration 17: "The Atolls." Or coral islands.

PART 17 (28 APRIL, 1888)

CHAPTER XXVI.[1]
GRIMM'S LAW AGAIN.

DINNER was now announced, and Oxenden laid the manuscript aside; whereupon they adjourned to the cabin, where they proceeded to discuss both the repast and the manuscript.

"Well," said Featherstone, "More's story seems to be approaching a crisis. What do you think of it now, Melick? Do you still think it a sensational novel?"

"Partly so," said Melick; "but it would be nearer the mark to call it a satirical romance."

"Why not a scientific romance?"[2]

"Because there's precious little science in it, but a good deal of quiet satire."

"Satire on what?" asked Featherstone. "I'll be hanged if I can see it."

"Oh, well," said Melick, "on things in general. The satire is directed against the restlessness of humanity; its impulses, feelings, hopes, and fears—all that men do and feel and suffer. It mocks us by exhibiting a new race of men, animated by passions and impulses which are directly the opposite of ours, and yet no nearer happiness than we are. It shows us a world where our evil is made a good, and our good an evil; there all that we consider a blessing is had in abundance—prolonged and perpetual sunlight, riches, power, fame—and yet these things are despised, and the people, turning away from them, imagine that they can find happiness in poverty, darkness, death, and unrequited love. The writer thus mocks at all our dearest passions and strongest desires; and his general aim is to show that the mere search for happiness per se is a vulgar thing, and must always result in utter nothingness. The writer also teaches the great lesson that the happiness of man consists not in external surroundings, but in the internal feelings, and

1 The *Harper's Weekly* serial mistakenly numbers this chapter XXXVI.

2 Scientific Romance is used increasingly from the 1840s onward, at first to refer to popularized and erroneous science and then to speculative fiction. For example, on 24 March 1866, Charles Dickens refers to Henri de Parville's "Un Habitant de la Planète Mars" as a "scientific romance" in his weekly journal *All the Year Round* (251). In his introduction to the 1873 first American edition of Jules Verne's *A Tour of the World in Eighty Days*, Adrien Marx characterizes Verne's fiction as "scientific romance" (12).

that heaven itself is not a place, but a state. It is the old lesson which Milton extorted from Satan:

> 'What matter where, if I be still the same—'

Or again:

> 'The mind is its own place, and of itself
> Can make a heaven of hell, a hell of heaven.'"[1]

"That's good too," cried Oxenden. "That reminds me of the German commentators who find in the Agamemnon of Æschylus or the Œdipus of Sophocles or the Hamlet of Shakespeare[2] motives and purposes of which the authors could never have dreamed, and give us a metaphysical, beer-and-tobacco, High-Dutch[3] Clytemnestra or Antigone or Lady Macbeth.[4] No, my boy, More was a simple sailor, and had no idea of satirizing anything."

"How, then, do you account for the perpetual undercurrent of meaning and innuendo that may be found in every line?"

"I deny that there is anything of the sort," said Oxenden. "It is a plain narrative of facts; but the facts are themselves such that they give a new coloring to the facts of our own life. They are in such profound antithesis to European ways that we consider them as being written merely to indicate that difference. It is like the

---

1 See John Milton's *Paradise Lost*, Book I, lines 254-56. Melick reverses the order, quoting line 256 before lines 254-55. In Book I, Satan has just awoken in hell.

2 Ironically, all of the tragedies mentioned here are especially resonant with the Kosekin world view. *Agamemnon*, the first play of the Greek Tragedian Æschylus' *Oresteia*, first performed in 458 BCE, dramatizes the homecoming of Agamemnon, King of Argos, from the Trojan War, and his subsequent murder. Sophocles' *Oedipus the King* was first performed in Athens in 429 BCE. *The Tragedy of Hamlet, Prince of Denmark* was written between 1599 and 1601 by William Shakespeare.

3 High-Dutch is German. Notably, in the context of a discussion about satire, Gulliver likens the Houyhnhnm language to High Dutch in Part 4, Chapter 3 of *Gulliver's Travels*.

4 While accounts vary, in the *Oresteia* Clytemnestra, Queen of Argos and wife of Agamemnon, kills her husband and the Trojan Cassandra; she is later killed by her son Orestes. Antigone, in Sophocles' play of the same name, is the daughter of the incestuous marriage between Oedipus and Jocasta; she tries to gain a proper burial for her brother Polyneices, but her struggle ends in disaster. Lady Macbeth, in Shakespeare's tragedy *Macbeth* (1603-07), convinces her husband Macbeth to kill the king of Scotland, suffers intense guilt, and appears to commit suicide.

Germania of Tacitus, which many critics still hold to be a satire on Roman ways,[1] while as a matter of fact it is simply a narrative of German manners and customs."

"I hope," cried Melick, "that you do not mean to compare this awful rot and rubbish to the *Germania* of Tacitus?"

"By no means," said Oxenden; "I merely asserted that in one respect they were analogous. You forced on the allusion to the *Germania* by calling this 'rot and rubbish' a satirical romance."

"Oh, well," said Melick, "I only referred to the intention of the writer. His plan is one thing and his execution quite another. His plan is not bad, but he fails utterly in his execution. The style is detestable. If he had written in the style of a plain seaman, and told a simple unvarnished tale, it would have been all right. In order to carry out properly such a plan as this the writer should take Defoe as his model, or, still better, Dean Swift. *Gulliver's Travels* and *Robinson Crusoe*[2] show what can be done in this way, and form a standard by which all other attempts must be judged. But this writer is tawdry; he has the worst vices of the sensational school—he shows everywhere marks of haste, gross carelessness, and universal feebleness. When he gets hold of a good fancy, he lacks the patience that is necessary in order to work it up in an effective way. He is a gross plagiarist, and over and over again violates in the most glaring manner all the ordinary proprieties of style. What can be more absurd, for instance, than the language which he puts into the mouth of Layelah? Not content with making her talk like a sentimental boarding-school, bread-and-butter English miss, he actually forgets himself so far as to put in her mouth a threadbare joke, which everyone has heard since childhood."

"What is that?"

"Oh, that silly speech about the athaleb swallowing its victuals whole."

"What's the matter with that?" asked Oxenden. "It's merely a chance resemblance. In translating her words into English they

---

1 De Mille is one such commentator. In *The Elements of Rhetoric*, De Mille suggests that Tacitus' *Germania* can be read as "a satire on the Romans" (463).

2 The English writer Daniel Defoe (1659-1731) and the Irish satirist Jonathan Swift (1667-1775) are both significant influences for De Mille, if not for More, as Melick's highly reflexive intertextual reference suggests. Defoe's *Robinson Crusoe* (1719), which is a fictional autobiography about a castaway, is often considered to be the first English novel. Swift's satire *Travels into Several Remote Nations of the World, in Four Parts. By Lemuel Gulliver, First a Surgeon, and then a Captain of several Ships* was first published in 1726.

fell by accident into that shape. No one but you would find fault with them. Would it have been better if he had translated her words into the scientific phraseology which the doctor made use of with regard to the ichthyosaurus? He might have made it this way: 'Does it bite?' 'No; it swallows its food without mastication.'[1] Would that have been better? Besides, it's all very well to talk of imitating Defoe and Swift; but suppose he couldn't do it?"

"Then he shouldn't have written the book."

"In that case how could his father have heard about his adventures?"

"His father!" exclaimed Melick. "Do you mean to say that you still accept all this as *bona fide*?"

"Do you mean to say," retorted Oxenden, "that you still have any doubt about the authenticity of this remarkable manuscript?"

At this each looked at the other; Melick elevated his eyebrows, and Oxenden shrugged his shoulders; but each seemed unable to find words to express his amazement at the other's stupidity, and so they took refuge in silence.

"What do you understand by this athaleb, doctor?" asked Featherstone.

"The athaleb?" said the doctor. "Why, it is clearly the pterodactyl."[2]

"By-the-bye," interrupted Oxenden, "do please take notice of that name. It affords another exemplification of 'Grimm's Law.' The Hebrew word is 'ataleph,'[3] and means bat. The Kosekin word is 'athaleb.' Here you see the thin letter of Hebrew represented by the aspirated letter of the Kosekin language, while the aspirated Hebrew is represented by the Kosekin medial."

"Too true," exclaimed Melick, in a tone of deep conviction; "and now, Oxenden, won't you sing us a song?"

"Nonsense," said Featherstone; "let the doctor tell us about the athaleb."

---

1 That is, without chewing, biting, crushing or grinding the food.

2 Pterosaurs were flying reptiles that lived from the Triassic through the Cretaceous periods (225-65 million years ago). Their wingspans range from 50 cm to 13 m in length. See Appendix B1 for Richard Owen's description of the pterodactyl.

3 aTaleph (אֲטַלֵּף) has several mentions in the Bible, including Leviticus 11:19, Deuteronomy 14:18, and Isaiah 2:20. The King James translation of Isaiah directly associates bats with darkness and makes a comment on the renunciation of wealth: "In that day a man shall cast his idols of silver, and his idols of gold, which they made [each one] for himself to worship, to the moles and to the bats" (2:20).

"Well," resumed the doctor, "as I was saying, it must be undoubtedly the pterodactyl. It is a most extraordinary animal, and is a species of flying lizard, although differing from the lizard in many respects. It has the head and neck of a bird, the trunk and tail of an ordinary mammal, the jaws and teeth of a reptile, and the wings of a bat. Owen[1] describes one whose sweep of wings exceeded twenty feet, and many have been found of every gradation of size down to that of a bat. There is no reason why they should not be as large as More says; and I for my part do not suspect him of exaggeration. Some have supposed that a late, lingering individual may have suggested the idea of the fabulous dragon—an idea which seems to be in the minds of nearly all the human race, for in the early records of many nations we find the destruction of dragons assigned to their gods and heroes. The figure of the pterodactyl represents pretty closely that which is given to the dragons.[2] It is not impossible that they may have existed into the period which we call prehistoric, and that monsters far larger than any which we have yet discovered may have lingered until the time when man began to increase upon the earth, to spread over its surface, and to carve upon wood and stone representations of the most striking objects around him. When the living pterodactyls had disappeared the memory of them was preserved; some new features were added, and the imagination went so far as to endow them with the power of belching forth smoke and flames. Thus the dragon idea pervaded the minds of men, and instead of a natural animal it became a fabulous one.

"The fingers of the forelegs were of the ordinary dimensions, and terminated with crooked nails, and these were probably used to suspend themselves from trees. When in repose it rested on its hind legs like a bird, and held its neck curving behind, so that its enormous head should not disturb its equilibrium. The size and form of the feet, of the leg, and of the thigh prove that they could hold themselves erect with firmness, their wings folded, and move about in this way like birds, just as More describes them as doing. Like birds they could also perch on trees, and could crawl like bats and lizards along the rocks and cliffs.

"Some think that they were covered with scales, but I am of the opinion that they had a horny hide, with a ridge of hair running down their backs—in which opinion I am sustained by More's

---

1 Richard Owen. See Appendix B1.

2 In *The Testimony of Rocks,* Hugh Miller likens pterodactyls "to flying dragons,—real existences of the Oolitic period" (116).

account. The smaller kinds were undoubtedly insectivorous, but the larger ones must have been carnivorous, and probably fed largely on fish."

"Well, at any rate," said Melick, gravely, "this athaleb solves the difficult question as to how the Troglodytes emigrated to the South Pole."

"How?" asked the doctor.

"Why, they must have gone there on athalebs! Your friends the pterodactyls probably lingered longest among the Troglodytes, who, seeing that they were rapidly dying out, concluded to depart to another and a better world. One beauty of this theory is that it cannot possibly be disproved; another is that it satisfies all the requirements of the case; a third is that it accounts for the disappearance of the pterodactyls in our world, and their appearance at the South Pole; and there are forty or fifty other facts, all included in this theory, which I have not time just now to enumerate, but will try to do so after we have finished reading the manuscript. I will only add that the athaleb must be regarded as another link which binds the Kosekin to the Semitic race."

"Another link?" said Oxenden. "That I already have; and it is one that carries conviction with it."

"All your arguments invariably do, my dear fellow."

"What is it?" asked the doctor.

"The Kosekin alphabet," said Oxenden.

"I can't see how you can make anything out of that," said the doctor.

"Very well, I can easily explain," replied Oxenden. "In the first place we must take the old Hebrew alphabet. I will write down the letters in their order first."

Saying this he hastily jotted down some letters on a piece of paper, and showed to the doctor the following:

	Labials.	Palatals.	Linguals.[1]
A	B	C (or G)	D
E	F	Ch (or H)	Dh (or Th)
I	Liquids, L	M	N
O	P	K	T

1 The table refers to three different types of consonants, speech sounds created by closure of the vocal tract. Labials occur when one or both lips produce the consonant. Palatals are produced when the body of the tongue is raised against the roof of the mouth. Linguals are created by the tongue.

"That," said he, "is substantially the order of the old Hebrew alphabet."

"But," said the doctor, "the Kosekin alphabet differs in its order altogether from that."

"That very difference can be shown to be all the stronger proof of a connection between them," said Oxenden.

"I should like to know how."

"The fact is," said Oxenden, "these letters are represented differently in the two languages in exact accordance with Grimm's Law."

"By Jove!" cried Featherstone, "Grimm's Law again!"

"According to that law," continued Oxenden, "the letters of the alphabet ought to change their order. Now let us leave out the vowels and linguals, and deal only with the mutes. First, we have in the Hebrew alphabet the medials B, G, and D. Very well; in the Kosekin we have standing first the thin letters, or tenues, according to Grimm's Law, namely, P, K, T. Next we have in the Hebrew the aspirates F, Ch, Dh. In the Kosekin alphabet we have corresponding to them the medials B, G, D. Next we have in the Hebrew the tenues, or thin letters P, K, T. In the Kosekin we have the corresponding aspirates F, Ch, Th. The vowels, liquids, and sibilants need not be regarded just here, for the proof from the mutes is sufficient to satisfy any reasonable man."

"Well," said Melick, "I for one am thoroughly satisfied, and don't need another single word. The fact is, I never knew before the all-sufficient nature of Grimm's Law. Why, it can unlock any mystery! When I get home I must buy one—a tame one, if possible—and keep him with me always. It is more useful to a literary man than to any other. It is said that with a knowledge of Grimm's Law a man may wander through the world from Iceland to Ceylon, and converse pleasantly in all the Indo-European languages. More must have had Grimm's Law stowed away somewhere about him; and that's the reason why he escaped the icebergs, the volcanoes, the cannibals, the subterranean channel monster, and arrived at last safe and sound in the land of the Kosekin. What I want is Grimm's Law—a nice tidy one, well trained, in good working order, and kind in harness; and the moment I get one I intend to go to the land of the Kosekin myself."

CHAPTER XXVII.[1]
OXENDEN PREACHES A SERMON.

"MAGONES," said the doctor, "is clearly a volcanic island, and, taken in connection with the other volcanoes around, shows how active must be the subterranean fires at the South Pole. It seems probable to me that the numerous caves of the Kosekin were originally fissures in the mountains, formed by convulsions of nature; and also that the places excavated by man must consist of soft volcanic rock, such as pumice-stone, or rather tufa,[2] easily worked, and remaining permanently in any shape into which it may be fashioned. As to Magones, it seems another Iceland; for there are the same wild and hideous desolation, the same impassable wildernesses, and the same universal scenes of ruin, lighted up by the baleful and tremendous volcanic fires."

"But what of that little island on which they landed?" asked Featherstone. "That, surely, was not volcanic."

"No," said the doctor; "that must have been a coral island."[3]

"By-the-bye, is it really true," asked Featherstone, "that these coral islands are the work of little insects?"

"Well, they may be called insects," replied the doctor; "they are living zoophytes[4] of most minute dimensions, which, however, compensate for their smallness of size by their inconceivable numbers. Small as these are they have accomplished infinitely more than all that ever was done by the ichthyosaurus, the plesiosaurus, the pterodactyl, and the whole tribe of monsters that once filled the earth. Immense districts and whole mountains have been built up by these minute creatures. They have been at work for ages, and are still at work. It is principally in the South Seas that their

---

1 The *Harper's Weekly* serial mistakenly numbers this Chapter XXVIII.

2 The doctor means tuff, a rock made from volcanic ash. Tuff is sometimes called tufa, but tufa is properly the name for a type of limestone. Pumice-stone is rock formed when frothy lava is ejected and cools suddenly while rapidly depressurized. The depressurization creates bubbles that are then solidified in the rock.

3 Islands of live coral that grow on top of piles of dead coral only occur in subtropical and tropical seas and oceans. The formation of coral islands and the fact that coral are animals wasn't understood until the early 1800s. See Charles Darwin's *The Structure and Distribution of Coral Reefs* (1842).

4 An animal that appears to be a plant. In the class *Anthozoa*, phylum *Cnidaria*, coral are marine organisms that live in colonies.

labors are carried on. Near the Maldive Islands[1] they have formed a mass whose volume is equal to the Alps. Around New Caledonia[2] they have built a barrier of reefs four hundred miles in length, and another along the northeast[3] coast of Australia a thousand miles in length. In the Pacific Ocean, islands, reefs, and islets innumerable have been constructed by them, which extend for an immense distance.

"The coral islands are called 'atolls.' They are nearly always circular, with a depression in the centre. They are originally made ring-shaped, but the action of the ocean serves to throw fragments of rock into the inner depression, which thus fills up; firm land appears; the rock crumbles into soil; the winds and birds and currents bring seeds here, and soon the new island is covered with verdure. These little creatures have played a part in the past quite as important as in the present. All Germany rests upon a bank of coral; and they seem to have been most active during the Oolitic Period."[4]

"How do the creatures act?" asked Featherstone.

"Nobody knows," replied the doctor.

A silence now followed, which was at last broken by Oxenden.

"After all," said he, "these monsters and marvels of nature form the least interesting feature in the land of the Kosekin. To me the people themselves are the chief subject of interest. Where did they

---

1 Located southwest of Sri Lanka in the Indian Ocean, the Maldive Islands, now the Republic of Maldives, consist of 1,192 small coral islands.

2 Located in Melanesia in the south-west Pacific ocean (21° 30′ S 165° 30′ E), *Nouvelle-Calédonie* became a French possession in 1853. The New Caledonia Barrier Reef is about 1,500 kilometers long, making it the second largest coral reef in the world.

3 At more than 344,400 square kilometers in size, the Great Barrier Reef is the world's largest coral reef. Both the serial and the 1888 book have "northwest," but the reef is northeast of Australia (see Parks li).

4 That is, the Jurassic period (199.6-145.5 million years ago), the "Age of the Reptiles." The term Oolitic, from Oolite or egg-stone, names a type of limestone that formed in the Jurassic period. This Oolitic limestone was used to identify the period until the middle of the nineteenth century. The term is used by Louis Figuier, Charles Lyell, Hugh Miller, Joseph Jukes, and others that De Mille consulted. However, it is mistakenly transcribed as "Eolithic" (the early stone age when eoliths were used as tools) in the *Harper's Weekly* serial and "Colitic" (apparently pertaining to Colitis, the disease of the colon, or perhaps just a typo) in the 1888 Harper's Brothers' book edition.

get that strange, all-pervading love of death, which is as strong in them as love of life is in us?"

"Why, they got it from the imagination of the writer of the manuscript," interrupted Melick.

"Yes, it's easy to answer it from your point of view; yet from my point of view it is more difficult. I sometimes think that it may be the strong spirituality of the Semitic race, carried out under exceptionally favorable circumstances to the ultimate results; for the Semitic race more than all others thought little of this life, and turned their affections to the life that lives beyond this. The Kosekin may thus have had a spiritual development of their own, which ended in this.

"Yet there may be another reason for it, and I sometimes think that the Kosekin may be nearer to the truth than we are. We have by nature a strong love of life—it is our dominant feeling—but yet there is in the minds of all men a deep underlying conviction of the vanity of life, and the worthlessness. In all ages and among all races the best, the purest, and the wisest have taught this truth—that human life is not a blessing; that the evil predominates over the good; and that our best hope is to gain a spirit of acquiescence with its inevitable ills. All philosophy and all religions teach us this one solemn truth, that in this life the evil surpasses the good. It has always been so. Suffering has been the lot of all living things, from the giant of the primeval swamps down to the smallest zoophyte. It is far more so with man. Some favored classes in every age may furnish forth a few individuals who may perhaps lead lives of self-indulgence and luxury; but to the mass of mankind life has ever been, and must ever be, a prolonged scene of labor intermingled with suffering. The great Indian religions, whether Brahmanic[1] or Buddhistic,[2] teach as their cardinal doctrine that life is an evil. Buddhism is more pronounced in this, for it teaches more emphatically than even the Kosekin that the chief end of man is to get rid of the curse of life and gain the bliss of Nirvana,[3] or annihilation. True, it does not take so practical a form as among the Kosekin, yet it is believed by one-third of the human race

---

1 The religious teaching and practices of Hinduism are founded in the Vedas of ancient India.

2 The religious and philosophical teachings and practices that derive in large part from Siddartha Gautama or Buddha, originating in India after the sixth century BCE.

3 An important concept in Buddhism, Hinduism, and Jainism, Nirvana is a state free from suffering and delusion that involves moving beyond identity, appetite and craving, hatred and greed.

as the foundation of the religion in which they live and die. We need not go to the Kosekin, however, for such maxims as these. The intelligent Hindoos, the Chinese, the Japanese,[1] with many other nations, all cling firmly to this belief. Sakya-mouni Gautama Buddha,[2] the son and heir of a mighty monarch, penetrated with the conviction of the misery of life, left his throne, embraced a life of voluntary poverty, want, and misery, so that he might find his way to a better state—the end before him being this, that he might ultimately escape from the curse of existence. He lived till old age, gained innumerable followers, and left to them as a solemn legacy the maxim that not to exist is better than to exist; that death is better than life. Since his day millions of his followers have upheld his principles and lived his life. Even among the joyous Greeks we find this feeling at times bursting forth; it comes when we least expect it, and not even a Kosekin poet could express this view more forcibly than Sophocles in the *Œdipus at Colonus*:[3]

"'Not to be born surpasses every lot;
And the next best lot by far, when one is born,
Is to go back whence he came as soon as possible;
For while youth is present bringing vain follies,
What woes does it not have, what ills does it not bear—
Murders, factions, strife, war, envy!
But the extreme of misery is attained by loathsome old age—
Old age, strengthless, unsociable, friendless,
Where all evils upon evils dwell together.'"

"I'll give you the words of a later poet," said Melick, "who takes a different view of the case. I think I'll sing them, with your permission."

---

1 This list emphasizes how emphatically the Kosekin are constructed as Orientalist projections. (See the Introduction for a discussion of Orientalism.)

2 Siddhartha Gautama (sixth to fourth centuries BCE) became Buddha ("awakened one") at the age of thirty-five. He was born a prince of the Sakya people and is also known as "sage of the Sakyas," thus Sakya-mouni. "Sakyamoum," which occurs in both the serial and the book (every existing edition), seems to be a typographical error; "Sakya-mouni" is used commonly throughout the nineteenth century, and so I have used it here.

3 Written shortly before Sophocles' death in 406 BCE, the action of *Œdipus at Colonus* takes place between the Theban plays *Oedipus the King* and *Antigone*. At the end of his life, Oedipus considers his crimes of incest and murder, and he gains absolution.

Melick swallowed a glass of wine and then sang the following:

"'They may rail at this life: from the hour I began it
I found it a life full of kindness and bliss,
And until they can show me some happier planet,
More social and bright, I'll content me with this.
As long as the world has such lips and such eyes
As before me this moment enraptured I see,
They may say what they will of their orbs in the skies,
But this earth is the planet for you, love, and me.'[1]

"What a pity it is," continued Melick, "that the writer of this manuscript had not the philological, theological, sociological, geological, palæological, ontological, ornithological,[2] and all the other logical attainments of yourself and the doctor! He could then have given us a complete view of the nature of the Kosekin, morally and physically; he could have treated of the geology of the soil, the ethnology of the people, and could have unfolded before us a full and comprehensive view of their philosophy and religion, and could have crammed his manuscript with statistics. I wonder why he didn't do it even as it was. It must have been a strong temptation."

"More," said Oxenden, with deep impressiveness, "was a simple-minded though somewhat emotional sailor, and merely wrote in the hope that his story might one day meet the eyes of his father. I certainly should like to find some more accurate statements about the science, philosophy, and religion of the Kosekin; yet, after all, such things could not be expected."

"Why not?" said Melick; "it was easy enough for him."

"How?" asked Oxenden.

"Why, he had only to step into the British Museum, and in a couple of hours he could have crammed up on all those points in science, philosophy, ethnology, and theology, about which you are so anxious to know."

---

1 Melick is quoting the Irish poet Thomas Moore (1779-1852). "They May Rail at This Life" is a four-stanza lyric found in volume 7 of *Irish Melodies*.

2 Philology is the humanist study of language. Theology is the study of religion and/or the divine. Sociology is the study of human social behaviour. Geology is the study of the origin, history, and structure of the earth. Paleontology is the study of prehistoric antiquities. Ontology is the metaphysical investigation of the nature of being. Ornithology is the branch of zoology that studies birds.

"Well," said Featherstone, "suppose we continue our reading? I believe it is my turn now. I sha'n't be able to hold out so long as you did, Oxenden, but I'll do what I can."

Saying this, Featherstone took the manuscript and went on to read.

[TO BE CONTINUED.]

PART 18 (5 MAY, 1888)

CHAPTER XXVIII.
IN PRISON.

IT was with hearts full of the gloomiest forebodings that we returned to the *amir*, and these we soon found to be fully justified. The athalebs descended at that point from which they had risen—namely, on the terrace immediately in front of the cavern where they had been confined. We then dismounted, and Layelah with the Kosekin guards accompanied us to our former chambers. There she left us, saying that a communication would be sent to us.

We were now left to our own conjectures.

"I wonder what they will do to us?" said I.

"It is impossible to tell," said Almah.

"I suppose," said I, "they will punish us in some way; but then punishment among the Kosekin is what seems honor and reward to me. Perhaps they will spare our lives, for that in their eyes ought to be the severest punishment and the deepest disgrace imaginable."

Almah sighed.

"The Kosekin do not always act in this matter as one would suppose," said she. "It is quite likely that they may dread our escaping, and may conclude to sacrifice us at once."

On the next *jom* I had a visit from the Kohen Gadol. He informed me that the paupers had held a Council of State, in which they had made a special examination of our late flight. He and Layelah had both been examined, as well as the Kosekin who had gone after us; but Layelah's testimony was by far the most important.

The Council of State gathered from Layelah's report that we had fled to Magones for the especial purpose of gaining the most blessed of deaths; that she pursued us in the interest of the state; and that we on her arrival had generously surrendered our own selfish desires, and had at once returned.

We learned that much gratification was felt by the council, and also expressed, at Layelah's account and at our action.

First, at our eager love of death, which was so natural in their eyes; secondly, at the skill which we had shown in selecting Magones; and finally, at our generosity in giving up so readily the blessed prospect of exile and want and death, so as to come back to the *amir*. Had we been Kosekin our acts would have been natural enough; but, being foreigners, it was considered more admirable in us, and it seemed to show that we were equal to the Kosekin themselves. It was felt, however, that in our eager rush after death we had been somewhat selfish; but as this probably arose from our ignorance of the law, it might be overlooked. On the whole it was decided that we ought to be rewarded, and that, too, with the greatest benefits that the Kosekin could bestow. What these benefits were the Kohen Gadol could not say; and thus we were left, as before, in the greatest possible anxiety. We still dreaded the worst. The highest honors of these men might well awaken apprehension; for they thought that the chief blessings were poverty and darkness and death.

Layelah next came to see me. She was as amiable as ever, and showed no resentment at all. She gave me an account of what had happened at the Council of State, which was the same as what I had heard from the Kohen Gadol.

I asked her why she had made such a report of us.

"To conciliate their good-will," said Layelah. "For if they thought that you had really fled from death from a love of life, they would have felt such contempt for you that serious harm might have happened."

"Yes," said I; "but among the Kosekin what you call harm would probably have been just what I want. I should like to be viewed with contempt, and considered unworthy of death and the *Mista Kosek*, and other such honors."

"Oh yes," said Layelah; "but that doesn't follow; for you see the paupers love death so intensely that they long to bestow it on all; and if they knew that you were afraid of it, they would be tempted to bestow it upon you immediately, just to show you how delightful a thing it is. And that was the very thing that I was trying to guard against."

"Well," said I, "and what is the result? Do you know what their decision is?"

"Yes," said Layelah.

"What is it?" I asked, eagerly.

Layelah hesitated.

"What is it?" I cried again, full of impatience.

"I'm afraid it will not sound very pleasant to you," said Layelah, "but at any rate your life is spared for the present. They have decided to give you what they call the greatest possible honors and distinctions."

Layelah paused, and looked at me earnestly. For my part these words sounded ominous, and were full of the darkest meaning.

"Tell me all," I said; "don't keep me in suspense."

"Well," said Layelah, "I'm afraid you will think it hard; but I must tell you. I will tell it, therefore, as briefly and formally as possible.

"First, then, they have decreed the blessing of separation. You and Almah must now be parted, since this is regarded as the highest bliss of lovers.

"Secondly, they have decreed the blessing of poverty. All these luxuries will be taken away, and you will be raised to an equality in this respect with the great paupers.

"Thirdly, you are to have the blessing of darkness. You are to be removed from this troublesome and vexatious light, which here is regarded as a curse, and henceforth live without it.

"Fourthly, the next decree is the high reward of imprisonment. You are to be delivered from the evils of liberty, and shut up in a dark cavern, from which it will be impossible to escape or to communicate with anyone outside.

"Fifthly, you are to associate with the greatest of the paupers, the class that is the most honored and influential. You will be present at all their highest councils, and will have the privilege of perpetual intercourse with those reverend men. They will tell you of the joys of poverty, the happiness of darkness, and the bliss of death."

Layelah paused, and looked at me earnestly.

"Is there anything more?" I gasped.

"No," said she. "Is not that enough? Some were in favor of bestowing immediate death, but they were outvoted by the others. You surely cannot regret that."

Layelah's words sounded like the words of a mocking demon. Yet she did not wish to distress me; she had merely stated my sentence in formal language, without any attempt to soften its tremendous import. As for me, I was overwhelmed with despair. There was but one thought in my mind—it was not of myself, but of Almah.

"And Almah?" I cried.

"Almah," said Layelah—"she will have the same; you are both included in the same sentence."

At this a groan burst from me. Horror overwhelmed me. I threw myself down upon the floor and covered my face with my hands. All was lost! Our fate—Almah's fate—was darkness, imprisonment, and death. Could anything be imagined that might mitigate such woes as these? Could anything be conceived of as more horrible? Yes; there remained something more, and this was announced by Layelah.

"Finally," said she, "it has been decreed that you shall not only have the blessing of death, but that you shall have the rare honor of belonging to the chosen few who are reserved for the *Mista Kosek*. Thus far this had not been granted. It was esteemed too high an honor for strangers; but now, by an exercise of unparalleled liberality, the Grand Council of Paupers have added this, as the last and best, to the high honors and rewards which they have decreed for you and Almah."

To this I had nothing to say; I was stupefied with horror. To such words what answer could be made? At that moment I could think of nothing but this tremendous sentence—this infliction of appalling woes under the miserable name of blessings! I could not think of Layelah; nor did I try to conjecture what her motives might be in thus coming to me as the messenger of evil. I could not find space amid my despair for speculations as to her own part in this, or stop to consider whether she was acting the part of a mere messenger, or was influenced by resentment or revenge. All this was far away from my thoughts; for all my mind was filled with the dread sentence of the Council of Paupers and the baleful prospect of the woes that awaited us.

On the next *jom* I saw Almah. She had already learned the awful tidings. She met me with a face of despair; for there was no longer any hope, and all that remained for us was a last farewell. After this we parted, and each of us was taken to our respective prison.

I was taken along dark passages until I came to a cavern with a low, dark portal. Upon entering I found the darkness deeper than usual, and there was only one solitary lamp, which diffused but a feeble ray through the gloom. The size of the place could not be made out. I saw here a group of human beings, and by the feeble ray of the lamp I perceived that they were wan and thin and emaciated, with scant clothing, all in rags, squalor, misery, and dirt; with coarse hair matted together, and long nails and shaggy beards. They reminded me in their personal appearance of the cannibals of the outer shore.[1] These hideous beings all gathered around me, blinking at me with their bleary eyes and grinning with their abominable faces and then each one embraced me. The filth, squalor, and unutterable foulness of these wretches all combined to fill my soul with loathing, and the inconceivable horror of that embrace well-nigh overwhelmed me. Yet, after all, it was

1 This association on More's part suggests that his early encounter with the savages in Part 3, Chapter 4 may need to be re-evaluated.

surpassed by the horror of the thought that Almah might be at that very moment undergoing the same experience; and for her such a thing must be worse than for me.

I retreated as far as possible from them, deep into the thick darkness, and sat down. No convicted felon at the last hour of life, no prisoner in the dungeons of the Inquisition, ever could have suffered more mental agony than I did at that moment. The blessings, the awful blessings of the Kosekin were descending upon my miserable head—separation from Almah, squalor and dirt, imprisonment, the society of these filthy creatures, darkness, the shadow of death, and beyond all the tremendous horrors of the *Mista Kosek*!

I do not know how the time passed, for at first I was almost stupefied with despair; nor could I ever grow reconciled to the society of these wretches, scarce human, who were with me. Some food was offered me—filthy stuff, which I refused. My refusal excited warm commendation; but I was warned against starving myself, as that was against the law. In my despair I thought of my pistol and rifle, which I still kept with me—of using these against my jailors, and bursting forth; but this wild impulse soon passed away, for its utter hopelessness was manifest. My only hope, if hope it was, lay in waiting, and it was not impossible that I might see Almah again, if only once.

*Jom*s passed away, I know not how. The Chief Pauper, who is the greatest man in the land of the Kosekin, made several attempts to converse with me, and was evidently very condescending and magnanimous in his own eyes; but I did not meet his advances graciously—he was too abhorrent. He was a hideous wretch, with eyes nearly closed and bleary, thick, matted hair, and fiendish expression—in short, a devil incarnate in rags and squalor.

But as the *jom*s passed I found it difficult to repel my associates. They were always inflicting their society upon me, and thrusting on me nasty little acts of kindness. The Chief Pauper was more persistent than all, with his chatter and his disgusting civilities. He was evidently glad to get hold of a fresh subject for his talkative genius; he was a very garrulous cannibal, and perhaps my being a foreigner made me more interesting in his eyes.

The chief topic of his discourse was death. He hated life, loved death, longed for it in all its forms, whether arising from disease or from violence. He was an amateur in corpses, and had a larger experience in dead bodies than any other man in the nation.

I could not help asking him once why he did not kill himself, and be done with it.

"That," said he, "is not allowed. The temptation to kill one's self is one of the strongest that human nature can experience, but it is one that we must struggle against, of course, for it is against all law. The greatest blessing must not be seized. It must be given by nature or man. Those who violate the blessed mystery of death are infamous."

He assured me that he had all his life cultivated the loftiest feelings of love to others. His greatest happiness consisted in doing good to others, especially in killing them. The blessing of death, being the greatest of all blessings, was the one which he loved best to bestow upon others; and the more he loved his fellow-creatures the more he wished to give them this blessing. "You," said he, "are particularly dear to me, and I should rather give to you the blessing of death than to any other human being. I love you, Atam-or, and I long to kill you at this moment."

"You had better not try it," said I, grimly.

He shook his head despondingly.

"Oh no," said he; "it is against the law. I must not do it till the time comes."

"Do you kill many?" I asked.

"It is my pleasing and glorious office," he replied, "to kill more than any other; for, you must know, I am the *Sar Tabakin*" (chief of the executioners).

The Chief Pauper's love of death had grown to be an all-absorbing passion. He longed to give death to all. As with us there are certain philanthropists who have a mania for doing good, so here the pauper class had a mania for doing what they considered good in this way. The Chief Pauper was a sort of Kosekin Howard or Peabody,[1] and was regarded by all with boundless reverence. To me, however, he was an object of never-ending hate, abhorrence, and loathing; and, added to this, was the thought that there might be here some equally hideous female—someone like the nightmare hag of the outer sea—a torment and a horror to Almah.

---

1 John Howard (1726-90) was an English prison reformer and philanthropist; George Peabody (1795-1869) was an American entrepreneur who dramatically influenced modern philanthropy; in the 1860s, he founded the Peabody Trust to provide housing for the poor. While Peabody did move to London in 1837, he wasn't known for his philanthropic work until the 1850s.

CHAPTER XXIX.
THE CEREMONY OF SEPARATION.

SEPARATED from Almah, surrounded by foul fiends, in darkness and the shadow of death, with the baleful prospect of the *Mista Kosek*, it was mine to endure the bitterest anguish and despair; and in me these feelings were all the worse from the thought that Almah was in a similar state, and was enduring equal woes. All that I suffered in my present condition she too was suffering—and from this there was no possibility of escape. Perhaps her surroundings were even worse, and her sufferings keener; for who could tell what these people might inflict in their strange and perverted impulses?

Many *jom*s passed, and there was only one thing that sustained me—the hope of seeing Almah yet again, though it were but for a moment. That hope, however, was but faint. There was no escape. The gate was barred without and within. I was surrounded by miscreants, who formed the chief class in the state and the ruling order. The Chief Pauper was the highest magistrate in the land, from whose opinion there was no appeal, and the other paupers here formed the Kosekin senate. Here, in imprisonment and darkness, they formed a secret tribunal and controlled everything. They were objects of envy to all. All looked forward to this position as the highest object of human ambition, and the friends and relatives of those here rejoiced in their honor. Their powers were not executive, but deliberative.[1] To the Meleks and Athons was left the exercise of authority, but their acts were always in subordination to the will of the paupers.

"I have everything that heart can wish," said the Chief Pauper to me once. "Look at me, Atam-or, and see me as I stand here: I have poverty, squalor, cold, perpetual darkness, the privilege of killing others, the near prospect of death, and the certainty of the *Mista Kosek*—all these I have, and yet, Atam-or, after all, I am not happy."

To this strange speech I had nothing to say.

"Yes," continued the Chief Pauper, in a pensive tone, "for twenty seasons I have reigned as chief of the Kosekin in this place. My cavern is the coldest, squalidest, and darkest in the land. My raiment is the coarsest rags. I have separated from all my friends. I

1 That is, each member contributes a point of view, decisions are made through voting or consensus, and the group acts in the name of the entire group.

have had much sickness. I have the closest captivity. Death, darkness, poverty, want, all that men most live and long for, are mine to satiety; and yet, as I look back and count the *jom*s of my life to see in how many I have known happiness, I find that in all they amount to just seven! Oh, Atam-or, what a comment is this on the vanity of human life!"[1]

To this I had no answer ready; but by way of saying something, I offered to kill him on the spot.

"Nay, nay, Atam-or," said he, with a melancholy smile, "do not tempt me. Leave me to struggle with temptations by myself, and do not seek to make me falter in my duty. Yes, Atam-or, you behold in me a melancholy example of the folly of ambition; for I often think, as I look down from my lofty eminence, that after all it is as well to remain content in the humble sphere in which we are placed at birth; for perhaps, if the truth were known, there is quite as much real happiness among the rich and splendid—among the Athons and Meleks."

On this occasion I took advantage of the Chief Pauper's softer mood to pour forth an earnest entreaty for him to save Almah's life, or at least to mitigate her miseries. Alas! he was inexorable. It was like an appeal of some mad prisoner to some gentle-hearted governor in Christendom, entreating him to put some fellow-prisoner to death, or at least to make his confinement more severe.

The Chief Pauper stared at me in horror.

"You are a strange being, Atam-or," said he, gently. "Sometimes I think you mad. I can only say that such a request is horrible to me beyond all words. Such degradation and cruelty to the gentle and virtuous Almah is outrageous and forever impossible; no, we will not deprive her of a single one of those blessings which she now enjoys."

I turned away in despair.

At length one *jom* the Chief Pauper came to me with a smile and said,

"Atam-or, let me congratulate you on this joyous occasion."

"What do you mean?" I asked.

"You are to have your ceremony of separation."

"Separation!" I repeated.

"Yes," said he. "Almah has given notice to us. She has announced her intention of giving you up, and separating from you.

1 "Vanity of vanities, all is vanity": Ecclesiastes 1:2. In "Thoughts on Various Subjects," Alexander Pope writes, "The vanity of human life is, like a river, constantly passing away, and yet constantly coming on" (309-10).

With us the woman always gives the announcement in such cases. We have fixed the ceremony for the third *jom* from this, and I hope you will not think it too soon."

This strange intelligence moved me greatly. I did not like the idea of a ceremony of separation; but behind this there rose the prospect of seeing Almah, and I felt convinced that she had devised this as a mode of holding communication with me, or at least of seeing me again. The thought of Layelah was the only thing that interfered with this belief, for it might be her doings after all; yet the fact remained that I was to see Almah, and in this I rejoiced with exceeding great joy.

The appointed *jom* came. A procession was formed of the paupers. The chief did not go, as he never left the cavern except on the great sacrifices and *Mista Kosek*s. The door was opened, and I accompanied the procession. On our way all was dark, and after traversing many passages we came at length to the door of a cavern as gloomy as the one I had left. On entering this I found all dark and drear; and a little distance before me there was a light burning, around which was gathered a group of hags hideous beyond all expression. But these I scarcely noticed; for there amid them, all pale and wan, with her face now lighted up with joyous and eager expectation, I saw my darling—my Almah! I caught her in my arms, and for a few moments neither of us spoke a word. She sobbed upon my breast, but I knew that the tears which she shed were tears of joy. Nor was our joy checked by the thought that it was to be so short-lived. It was enough at that moment that we saw one another—enough that we were in one another's arms; and so we mingled our tears, and shared one common rapture. And sweet it was—sweet beyond all expression—the sweetest moment in all my life; for it had come in the midst of the drear desolation of my heart and the black despair. It was like a flash of lightning in the intense darkness, short and sudden indeed, yet still intense while it lasted, and in an instant filling all with its glow.

"I did this," murmured Almah, "to see you and to save you."

"Save me!" I repeated.

"Yes," said she. "I have seen Layelah. She told me that there is this chance and this one only to save you. I determined to try it. I cannot bear to think of you at the sacrifice—and for love of me meeting your death—for I would die to save you, Atam-or."

I pressed her closer in my arms.

"Oh, Almah," said I, "I would die to save you! and if this ceremony will save you I will go through with it, and accept my fate whatever it may be."

We were now interrupted.

The women—the hags of horror—the shriek-like ones, as I may call them, or the fiend-like, the female fiends, the foul ones—they were all around us; and one there was who looked so exactly like the nightmare hag of the outer sea that I felt sure she must be the same, who by some strange chance had come here. Such, indeed, is quite likely, for there may have been a pass over the mountains to the land of the Kosekin; and those savage cannibals may all have been honored Kosekin exiles, dwelling in poverty, want, woe, and darkness, all of which may have been allotted to them as a reward for eminent virtues. And so here she was, the nightmare hag, and I saw that she recognized me.

A circle was now formed around us, and the light stood in the middle. The nightmare hag also stood within the circle on the other side of the light opposite us. The beams of the lamp flickered through the darkness, faintly illuminating the faces of the horrible creatures around, who, foul and repulsive as harpies, seemed like unclean beasts, ready to make us their prey. Their glances seemed to menace death; their blear eyes rested upon us with a horrid eager hunger. My worst fears at that moment seemed realized; for I saw that Almah's associates were worse than mine, and her fate had been more bitter. And I wondered how it had been possible for her to live among such associates; or, even though she had lived thus far, whether it would be possible for her to endure it longer.

And now there arose a melancholy chant from the old hags around—a dreadful strain, that sounded like a funeral dirge, sung in shrill, discordant voices, led by the nightmare hag, who as she sang waved in her hand a kind of club. All the time I held Almah in my arms, regardless of those around us, thinking only of her from whom I must soon again be separated, and whom I must leave in this drear abode to meet her fearful fate alone. The chant continued for some time, and as long as it continued it was sweet to me; for it prolonged the meeting with Almah, and postponed by so much our separation.

At length the chant ceased. The nightmare hag looked fixedly at us, and spoke these words:

"You have embraced for the last time. Henceforth there is no more sorrow in your love. You may be happy now in being forever disunited, and in knowing the bliss of eternal separation. As darkness is better than light, as death is better than life, so may you find separation better than union."

She now gave a blow with her club at the lamp, which broke it to atoms and extinguished the flame. She continued:

Illustration 18: "The women—the hags of horror—the shriek-like ones, as I may call them, were all around us."

"As the baleful light is succeeded by the blessed darkness, so may you find the light of union followed by the blessed darkness of separation."

And now in the deep darkness we stood clasped in one another's arms; while around us, from the horrible circle of hags, there arose another chant as harsh and discordant as the previous one, but which, nevertheless, like that, served at least to keep us together a little longer. For this reason it sounded sweeter than the sweetest music; and therefore, when at last the hideous noise ended, I felt a pang of grief, for I knew that I must now give up Almah forever.

I was right. The ceremony was over. We had to part, and we parted with tears of despair. I was led away, and as I went I heard Almah's sobs. I broke away, and tried to return for one more embrace; but in the darkness I could not find her, and could only hear her sobs at a greater distance, which showed that she too was being led away. I called after her,

"Farewell, Almah!"

Her reply came back broken with sobs.

"Farewell forever, Atam-or!"

I was once more led away, and again traversed the dark passages, and again came back to my den, which now seemed dark with the blackness of despair.

On my return I was formally and solemnly congratulated by all the paupers. I should not have received their congratulations had I not expected that there would be something more. I expected that something would be said about the result of this act of separation; for Almah had believed that it would be the means of saving my life, and I believed that it would be the means of saving her life, and for this reason each of us had performed our part; although, of course, the joy of meeting with one another would of itself have been sufficient, and more than sufficient, to make that ceremony an object of desire. I thought, therefore, that some statement might now be made to the effect that by means of this ceremony my status among the Kosekin would be changed, and that both I and Almah, being no longer lovers, would be no longer fit for the sacrifice. To my intense disappointment, however, nothing whatever was said that had the remotest reference to this.

On the following *jom* I determined to ask the Chief Pauper himself directly; and accordingly, after a brief preamble, I put the question point-blank:

"Will our ceremony of separation make any difference as to our sacrifice?"

"What?" he asked, with a puzzled expression.

I repeated the question.

"I don't understand," said he, still looking puzzled.

Upon this I once more repeated it.

"How can that be?" said he at length; "how can the ceremony of separation have any effect upon your sacrifice? The ceremony of separation stands by itself as the sign and symbol of an additional blessing. This new happiness of separation is a great favor, and will make you the object of new envy and admiration; for few have been so fortunate as you in all the history of the Kosekin. But you are the favorite of the Kosekin now, and there is nothing that they will not do for you."

"But we were separate before," said I, indignantly.

"That is true," said he, "in point of fact; but this ceremony makes your separation a legal thing, and gives it the solemn sanction of law and of religion. Among the Kosekin one cannot be considered as a separate man until the ceremony of separation has been publicly performed."

"I understood," said I, "that we were chosen to suffer the sacrifice together because we were lovers; and now, since you do not any longer regard us as lovers, why do you sacrifice us?"

At this question the Chief Pauper looked at me with one of those hungry glances of his, which showed how he thirsted for my blood, and he smiled the smile of an evil fiend.

"Why do we sacrifice you, Atam-or?" he replied. "Why, because we honor you both, and love you both so dearly that we are eager to give you the greatest of all blessings, and to deny you nothing that is in our power to bestow."

"Do you mean to sacrifice both of us?" I gasped.

"Of course."

"What! Almah too?"

"Certainly. Why should we be so cruel to the dear child as to deprive her of so great a boon?"

At this I groaned aloud and turned away in despair.

Many *jom*s now passed away. I grew more and more melancholy and desperate. I thought sometimes of fighting my way out. My fire-arms were now my chief consolation; for I had fully made up my mind not to die quietly like a slaughtered calf, but to strike a blow for life, and meet my death amid slain enemies. In this prospect I found some satisfaction, and death was robbed of some of its terrors.

[TO BE CONTINUED.]

PART 19 (12 MAY, 1888)

CHAPTER XXX. THE DAY OF SACRIFICE.

AT last the time came.

It was the end of the dark season. Then, as the sun rises for its permanent course around the heavens, when the long day of six months begins, all in the land of the Kosekin is sorrow, and the last of the loved darkness is mourned over amid the most solemn ceremonies, and celebrated with the most imposing sacrifices. Then the most honored in all the land are publicly presented with the blessing of death, and allowed to depart this hated life, and go to the realms of that eternal darkness which they love so well. It is the greatest of sacrifices, and is followed by the greatest of feasts. Thus the busy season—the loved season of darkness—ends, and the long, hateful season of light begins, when the Kosekin lurk in caverns, and live in this way in the presence of what may be called artificial darkness.

It was for us—for me and for Almah—the day of doom. Since the ceremony of separation I had not seen her; but my heart had been always with her. I did not even know whether she was alive or not, but believed that she must be; for I thought that if she had died I should have heard of it, as the Kosekin would have rejoiced greatly over such an event. For every death is to them an occasion of joy, and the death of one so distinguished and so beloved as Almah would have given rise to nothing less than a national festival.

Of time I had but a poor reckoning; but, from the way in which the paupers kept account of their *jom*s, I judged that about three months had elapsed since the ceremony of separation.

The paupers were now all joyous with a hideous joy. The Chief Pauper was more abhorrent than ever. He had the blood-thirst strong upon him. He was on that *jom* to perform his horrible office of *Sar Tabakin*, and as he accosted me he smiled the smile of a demon, and congratulated me on my coming escape from life. To this I had no word of answer to make; but my hands held my rifle and pistol, and these I clutched with a firmer grasp as my last hour approached.

The time of departure at length arrived. Soldiers of the Kosekin came, following the paupers, who went first, while the guards came after me. Thus we all emerged into the open air. There the broad terrace already mentioned spread out before my eyes, filled with thousands upon thousands of human beings. It seemed as though the entire population of the city was there, and so densely packed was this great crowd that it was only with great difficulty that a way was laid open for our passage.

Above was the sky, where the stars were twinkling faintly. There was no longer the light of the aurora australis; the constellations glimmered but dimly, the moon was shining with but a feeble ray; for there far away over the icy crests of the lofty mountains I saw a long line of splendid effulgence, all golden and red—the light of the new dawn—the dawn of that long day which was now approaching. The sight of that dawning light gave me new life. It was like a sight of home—the blessed dawn, the sunlight of a bright day, the glorious daybreak lost for so long a time, but now at last returning. I feasted my eyes on the spectacle, I burst into tears of joy, and I felt as though I could gaze at it forever. But the sun as it travelled was rapidly coming into view; soon the dazzling glory of its rim would appear above the mountain crest, and the season of darkness would end. There was no time to wait, and the guards hurried me on.

There in the midst of the square rose the pyramid. It was fully a hundred feet in height, with a broad flat top. At the base I saw a great crowd of paupers. Through these we passed, and as we did so a horrible death-chant arose. We now went up the steps and reached the top. It was about sixty feet square, and upon it there was a quadrangle of stones set about three feet apart, about sixty in number, while in the midst was a larger stone. All of these were evidently intended for sacrificial purposes.

Scarcely had I reached the top when I saw a procession ascend from the other side. First came some paupers, then some hags, and then, followed by other hags, I saw Almah. I was transfixed at the sight. A thrill passed through every nerve, and a wild impulse came to me to burst through the crowd, join her, and battle with them all for her life. But the crowd was too dense. I could only stand and look at her, and mark the paleness of her face and her mute despair. She saw me, waved her hand sadly, and gave a mournful smile. There we stood separated by the crowd, with our eyes fastened on each other, and all our hearts filled with one deep, intense yearning to fly to one another's side.

And now there came up from below, louder and deeper, the awful death-chant. Time was pressing. The preparations were made. The Chief Pauper took his station by the central stone, and in his right hand he held a long, keen knife. Toward this stone I was led. The Chief Pauper then looked with his blear and blinking eyes to where the dawn was glowing over the mountain crest, and every moment increasing in brightness; and then, after a brief survey, he turned and whetted his knife on the sacrificial stone. After this he turned to me with his evil face, with the glare of a horrid death-hunger in his ravenous eyes, and pointed to the stone.

I stood without motion.

He repeated the gesture and said, "Lie down here."

"I will not," said I.

"But it is on this stone," said he, "that you are to get the blessing of death."

"I'll die first!" said I, fiercely, and I raised my rifle.

The Chief Pauper was puzzled at this. The others looked on quietly, thinking it probably a debate about some punctilio.[1] Suddenly he seemed struck with an idea.

"Yes, yes," said he. "The woman first. It is better so."

Saying this he walked toward Almah, and said something to the hags.

At this the chief of them—namely, the nightmare hag—led Almah to the nearest stone, and motioned to her to lie down. Almah prepared to obey, but paused a moment to throw at me one last glance and wave her hand as a last farewell. Then without a word she laid herself down upon the stone. At this a thrill of fury rushed through all my being, rousing me from my stupor, impelling me to action, filling my brain with madness. The nightmare hag had already raised her long keen knife in the air. Another moment and the blow would have fallen. But my rifle was at my shoulder; my aim was deadly. The report rang out like thunder. A wild, piercing yell followed, and when the smoke cleared away the nightmare hag lay dead at the foot of the altar. I was already there, having burst through the astonished crowd, and Almah was in my arms; and holding her thus for a moment, I put myself in front of her and stood at bay, with my only thought that of defending her to the last and selling my life as dearly as possible.

The result was amazing.

After the report there was for some moments a deep silence, which was followed by a wild, abrupt outcry from half a million people—the roar of indistinguishable words bursting forth from the lips of all that throng, whose accumulated volume arose in one vast thunder-clap of sound, pealing forth, echoing along the terraced streets, and rolling on far away in endless reverberations. It was like the roar of mighty cataracts, like the sound of many

1 A fine point of etiquette or strict observance of formalities.

waters; and at the voice of that vast multitude I shrank back for a moment. As I did so I looked down, and beheld a scene as appalling as the sound that had overawed me. In all that countless throng of human beings there was not one who was not in motion; and all were pressing forward toward the pyramid as to a common centre. On every side there was a multitudinous sea of upturned faces, extending as far as the eye could reach. All were in violent agitation, as though all were possessed by one common impulse which forced them toward me. At such a sight I thought of nothing else than that I was the object of their wrath, and that they were all with one common fury rushing toward me to wreak vengeance upon me and upon Almah for the slaughter of the nightmare hag.

All this was the work of but a few moments. And now as I stood there holding Almah—appalled, despairing, yet resolute and calm—I became aware of a more imminent danger. On the top of the pyramid, at the report of the rifle, all had fallen down flat on their faces, and it was over them that I had rushed to Almah's side. But these now began to rise, and the hags took up the corpse of the dead, and the paupers swarmed around with cries of "*Mut! mut!*" (dead! dead!) and exclamations of wonder. Then they all turned their foul and bleary eyes toward me, and stood as if transfixed with astonishment. At length there burst forth from the crowd one who sought to get at me. It was the Chief Pauper. He still held in his hand the long knife of sacrifice. He said not a word, but rushed straight at me, and as he came I saw murder in his look. I did not wait for him, but raising my rifle, discharged the second barrel full in his face. He fell down a shattered, blackened heap, dead.

As the second report thundered out it drowned all other sounds, and was again followed by an awful silence. I looked around. Those on the pyramid—paupers and hags—had again flung themselves on their faces. On the square below the whole multitude were on their knees, with their heads bowed down low. The silence was more oppressive than before; it was appalling—it was tremendous! It seemed like the dread silence that precedes the more awful outburst of the hurricane when the storm is gathering up all its strength to burst with accumulated fury upon its doomed victim.

But there was no time to be lost in staring, and that interval was occupied by me in hastily reloading my rifle. It was my last resource now; and if it availed not for defence it might at least serve to be used against ourselves. With this thought I handed the pistol to Almah, and hurriedly whispered to her that if I were killed, she could use it against herself. She took it in silence, but I read in her face her invincible resolve.

The storm at last burst. The immense multitude rose to their feet, and with one common impulse came pressing on from every side toward the pyramid, apparently filled with the one universal desire of reaching me—a desire which was now all the more intense and vehement from these interruptions which had taken place. Why they had fallen on their knees, why the paupers on the pyramid were still prostrate, I could not tell; but I saw now the swarming multitude, and I felt that they were rolling in on every side—merciless, blood-thirsty, implacable—to tear me to pieces. Yet time passed and they did not reach me, for an obstacle was interposed. The pyramid had smooth sides. The stairways that led up to the summit were narrow, and did not admit of more than two at a time; yet, had the Kosekin been like other people, the summit of the pyramid would soon have been swarming with them; but as they were Kosekin, none came up to the top; for at the base of the pyramid, at the bottom of the steps, I saw a strange and incredible struggle. It was not, as with us, who should go up first, but who should go up last; each tried to make his neighbor go before him. All were eager to go, but the Kosekin self-denial, self-sacrifice, and love for the good of others made each one intensely desirous to make others go up. This resulted in a furious struggle, in which, as fast as anyone would be pushed up the steps a little way, he would jump down again and turn his efforts toward putting up others; and thus all the energies of the people were worn out in useless and unavailing efforts—in a struggle to which, from the very nature of the case, there could be no end.

Now those on the pyramid began to rise, and soon all were on their feet. Cries burst forth from them. All were looking at us, but with nothing like hostility; it was rather like reverence and adoration, and these feelings were expressed unmistakably in their cries, among which I could plainly distinguish such words as these: "*Ap Ram!*" "*Mosel anan wacosek!*" "*Sopet Mut!*" (The Father of Thunder! Ruler of Cloud and Darkness! Judge of Death!) These cries passed to those below. The struggle ceased. All stood and joined in the cry, which was taken up by those nearest, and soon passed among all those myriads, to be repeated with thunder echoes far and wide.

At this it suddenly became plain to me that the danger of death had passed away; that these people no longer regarded me

Illustration 19: "I am Atam-or, the Man of Light."

as a victim, but rather as some mighty being—some superior, perhaps supernatural power, who was to be almost worshipped. Hence these prostrations, these words, these cries, these looks. All these told me that the bitterness of death had passed away. At this discovery there was, for a moment, a feeling of aversion and horror within me at filling such a position; that I, a weak mortal, should dare to receive adoration like this; and I recoiled at the thought: yet this feeling soon passed; for life was at stake—not my own merely, but that of Almah; and I was ready now to go through anything if only I might save her: so, instead of shrinking from this new part, I eagerly seized upon it, and at once determined to take advantage of the popular superstition to the utmost.

Far away over the crests of the mountains I saw the golden edge of the sun's disc, and the light flowed therefrom in broad effulgence, throwing out long rays of glory in a luminous flood over all the land. I pointed to the glorious orb, and cried to the paupers, and to all who were nearest, in a loud voice:

"I am Atam-or, the Man of Light! I come from the land of light! I am the Father of Thunder, of Cloud and Darkness; the Judge of Death!"

At this the paupers all fell prostrate, and cried out to me to give them the blessing of death.

I made no answer, but leading Almah to the edge of the pyramid, told her to fire the pistol. A million eyes were fixed on us. She held up the pistol and fired. Immediately after, I fired both barrels of the rifle; and as the reports rang out and the smoke cleared away, I heard a mighty murmur, and once more beheld all prostrate. Upon this I hurriedly loaded again, and waited for further revelations. All the time I could not help wondering at the effect produced by the rifle now, in comparison with the indifference with which it had been regarded at my first arrival in the country. I could not account for it, but supposed that the excitement of a great religious festival and the sudden death of the Chief Pauper and the Chief Hag had probably deeply impressed them. In the midst of these thoughts the whole multitude arose; and once more there came to my ears the universal uproar of innumerable cries, in the midst of which I could hear the words, "*Ap Ram!*" "*Mosel anan wacosek!*" "*Sopet Mut!*"

CHAPTER XXXI.
CONCLUSION.

IN the midst of this the paupers and the hags talked earnestly together. Some of those who had been nearest in rank to the late Chief Pauper and Chief Hag were conspicuous in the debate. All looked at me and at Almah, and pointed toward the sun, which was wheeling along behind the distant mountain crest, showing a golden disc. Then they pointed to the dead bodies; and the hags took the Chief Hag, and the paupers the Chief Pauper, and laid them side by side on the central altar. After this a hag and a pauper advanced toward us, each carrying the sacrificial knife which had belonged to the deceased.

The hag spoke first, addressing Almah, in accordance with the Kosekin custom, which requires women to take the precedence in many things.

"Take this," she said, "O Almah, consort of Atam-or, and Co-ruler of Clouds and Darkness. Henceforth you shall be Judge of Death to the women of the Kosekin."

She then handed Almah the sacrificial knife of the Chief Hag, which Almah took in silence.

Then the pauper presented me with the sacrificial knife of the Chief Pauper, with the following words:

"Take this, O Atam-or, Father of Thunder and Ruler of Clouds and Darkness. Henceforth you shall be Judge of Death to the men of the Kosekin, and *Sar Tabakin* over the whole nation."

I received the knife in silence, for I had nothing to say; but now Almah spoke, as was fitting for her to do, since with the Kosekin the women must take the precedence; and here it was expected that she should reply in behalf[1] of both of us.

So Almah, holding the sacrificial knife, stood looking at them, full of dignity, and spoke as follows:

"We will take this, O Kosekin, and we will reward you all. We will begin our reign over the Kosekin with memorable acts of mercy. These two great victims shall be enough for the *Mista Kosek* of this season. The victims designed for this sacrifice shall have to deny themselves the blessing of death, yet they shall be rewarded in other ways; and all the land from the highest to the lowest shall have reason to rejoice in our rule.

"To all you hags and paupers we grant the splendid and unparalleled boon of exile to Magones. There you can have all

1 The phrase "in behalf" rather than "on behalf" emphasizes that she speaks for their benefit.

the suffering which heart can wish, and inevitable death. To all classes and ranks in the whole nation we promise to grant a diminution in their wealth by one-quarter. In the abundance of our mercy we are willing ourselves to bear the burden of all the offerings that may be necessary in order to accomplish this. All in the land may at once give up one-quarter of their whole wealth to us."

At this the hags and paupers gave a horrible yell of applause.

"As rulers of Light and Darkness, we will henceforth govern the nation in the light as well as in the dark. We will sacrifice ourselves so far to the public good as to live in the light, and in open palaces. We will consent to undergo the pains of light and splendor, to endure all the evils of luxury, magnificence, and boundless wealth, for the good of the Kosekin nation. We will consent to forego the right of separation, and agree to live together, even though we love one another. Above all, we will refuse death and consent to live. Can any rulers do more than this for the good of their people?"

Another outburst of applause followed.

"In three *joms*," continued Almah, "all you hags and paupers shall be sent to exile and death on Magones. As for the rest of the Kosekin, hear our words. Tell them from us that the laborers shall all be elevated to the rank of paupers, the artisans shall be made laborers, the tradesmen artisans, the soldiers tradesmen, the Athons soldiers, the Kohens Athons, and the Meleks Kohens. There shall be no Meleks in all the land. We, in our love for the Kosekin, will henceforth be the only Meleks. Then all the misery of that low station will rest on us; and in our low estate as Meleks we shall govern this nation in love and self-denial. Tell them that we will forego the sacrifice and consent to live; that we will give up darkness and cavern gloom and live in light. Tell them to prepare for us the splendid palaces of the Meleks, for we will take the most sumptuous and magnificent of them all. Tell all the people to present their offerings. Tell them that we consent to have endless retinues of servants, soldiers, followers, and attendants. Tell them that with the advent of Almah and Atam-or a new era begins for the Kosekin, in which every man may be as poor as he likes, and riches shall be unknown in the land."

These extraordinary words seemed to fill the paupers with rapture. Exclamations of joy burst from them; they prostrated themselves in an irrepressible impulse of grateful admiration, as though such promises could only come from superior beings. Then most of them hurried down to communicate to the people below the glorious intelligence. Soon it spread from mouth to mouth, and all the people were filled with the wildest excitement.

For never before had such a thing been known, and never had such self-sacrifice been imagined or thought possible, as that the rulers of the Kosekin could consent to be rich when they might be paupers; to live together when they might be separate; to dwell in the light when they might lurk in the deepest cavern gloom; to remain in life when they might have the blessing of death. Selfishness, fear of death, love of riches, and love of luxury, these were all unintelligible to the Kosekin, as much as to us would be self-abnegation, contempt of death, voluntary poverty, and asceticism. But as with us self-denying rulers may make others rich and be popular for this, so here among the Kosekin a selfish ruler might be popular by making others poor. Hence the words of Almah, as they were made known, gave rise to the wildest excitement and enthusiasm, and the vast multitude poured forth their feelings in long shouts of rapturous applause.

Amid this the bodies of the dead were carried down from the pyramid, and were taken to the *Mista Kosek* in a long and solemn procession, accompanied by the singing of wild and dismal chants.

And now the sun, rolling along behind the icy mountain crest, rose higher and higher every moment, and the bright light of a long day began to illumine the world. There sparkled the sea, rising far away like a watery wall, with the horizon high up in the sky; there rose the circle of giant mountains, sweeping away till they were blended with the horizon; there rose the terraces of the *amir*, all glowing in the sunlight, with all its countless houses and cavern-openings and arching trees and pointing pyramids. Above was the canopy of heaven, no longer black, no longer studded with stars or glistening with the fitful shimmer of the aurora, but all radiant with the glorious sunlight, and disclosing all the splendors of the infinite blue. At that sight a thrill of joy passed through me. The long, long night at last was over; the darkness had passed away like some hideous dream; the day was here—the long day that was to know no shadow and no decline—when all this world should be illuminated by the ever-circling sun—a sun that would never set until his long course of many months should be fully run. My heart swelled with rapture, my eyes filled with tears. "O Light!" I cried; "O gleaming, golden Sunlight! O Light of Heaven!—light that brings life and hope to man!" And I could have fallen on my knees and worshipped that rising sun.

But the light which was so glorious to us was painful and distressing to the Kosekin. On the top of the pyramid the paupers crouched, shading their eyes. The crowd below began to disperse in all directions, so as to betake themselves to their coverts and to the caverns, where they might live in the dark. Soon nearly all were gone except the paupers at the foot of the pyramid, who were awaiting our commands, and a crowd of Meleks and Athons at a distance. At a gesture from me the few paupers near us descended and joined those below.

Almah and I were alone on the top of the pyramid.

I caught her in my arms in a rapture of joy. This revulsion from the lowest despair—from darkness and from death back to hope and light and life—was almost too much to endure. We both wept, but our tears were those of happiness.

"You will be all my own now," said I, "and we can fly from this hateful land. We can be united—we can be married—here before we start—and you will not be cruel enough to refuse. You will consent, will you not, to be my wife before we fly from the Kosekin?"

At this Almah's face became suffused with smiles and blushes. Her arms were about me, and she did not draw away, but looked up in sweet confusion and said,

"Why, as to that—I—I cannot be more your—your wife than I am."

"What do you mean?" I exclaimed, in wonder. "My wife!"

Her eyes dropped again, and she whispered:

"The ceremony of separation is with the Kosekin the most sacred form of marriage. It is the religious form; the other is merely the civil form."

This was unintelligible, nor did I try to understand it. It was enough to hear this from her own sweet lips; but it was a strange feeling, and I think I am the only man since Adam that ever was married without knowing it.

"As to flight," continued Almah, who had quite adopted the Kosekin fashion, which makes women take the lead—"as to flight, we need not hurry. We are all-powerful now, and there is no more danger. We must wait until we send embassies to my people, and when they are ready to receive us, we will go. But now let us leave this, for our servants are waiting for us, and the light is distressing to them. Let us go to the nearest of our palaces and obtain rest and food."

Here Featherstone stopped, yawned, and laid down the manuscript.[1]

"That's enough for to-day," said he; "I'm tired, and can't read any more. It's time for supper."

THE END

1 The manuscript evidently continues.

Appendix A: Antarctic Exploration

[*A Strange Manuscript* works closely with the history of Antarctic exploration. Beginning with James Cook's exploratory discoveries, De Mille references Charles Wilkes's US expedition (1839-40) and James Ross's British naval expedition (1841). Excerpts from Cook, Wilkes, and Ross are included below.]

Antarctica Exploration Timeline

150	Ptolemy draws maps of the hypothetical southern continent *Terra Incognita.*
1520	Ferdinand Magellan, sailing into the Pacific Ocean, reaches Tierra del Fuego.
1773	James Cook crosses the Antarctic Circle (66° 33′ 44″) and reaches latitude 66° 36′ 30″ S.
1774	Cook sees "mountains of ice" at latitude 71° 10′ S.
1790	Sealing industry begins on South Georgia Island.
1818	John Cleves Symmes publishes his theory that the Earth is hollow with solid concentric spheres accessible via openings at the poles.
1820	Russian Fabian Gottlieb von Bellingshausen on the *Vostok* circumnavigates Antarctica and is the first person to see the Antarctic continent.
1823	John Weddell on the *Jane* (sealing expedition) reaches 74° 15′ S and finds open water (the Weddell Sea).
1839	Charles Wilkes's US expedition makes first attempt to reach the South Pole.
1840	Wilkes claims to have evidence of an Antarctic continent.
1841	British expedition led by James Ross enters Ross Sea and discovers Mount Erebus and Mount Terror.
1898	Adrien de Gerlache and his crew on the *Belgica* survive an Antarctic winter.
1911	Roald Amundsen's team reaches the South Pole.

1. From James Cook and Tobias Furneaux, *A Voyage Towards the South Pole and Round the World*, Volume 1 (1777)

[In Chapter 2 of *A Strange Manuscript*, More compares the southward progress of the *Trevelyan* with that of James Cook. At latitude 65° S and longitude 60° E, the *Trevelyan* is said to be "far within that impenetrable icy barrier which in 1773 had arrested the progress of Captain

Cook." Cook made two attempts to reach the South Pole during his second voyage (1772-75) aboard the HMS *Resolution*. In January 1773, they were stopped by ice at latitude 66° 36′ 30″ S, longitude 39° 35′ E. In January 1774, they encounter "mountains of ice" at latitude 71° 10' S, longitude 106° 54′ W. In both cases, Cook was farther south than the *Trevelyan*.]

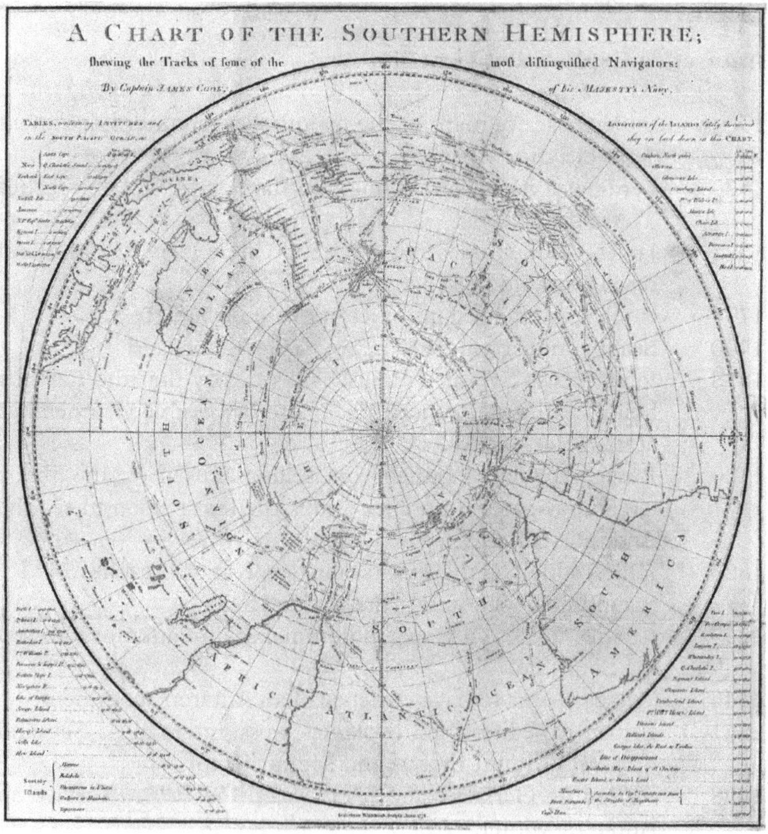

Figure 1: "A chart of the Southern Hemisphere; shewing the tracks of some of the most distinguished navigators," by Captain James Cook, engraved by William Whitchurch (Cook, Vol. 1, Plate number 1). The tracks show the routes of Mendana (1595), Quiros (1606), Le Maire and Schouten (1616), Tasman (1642), Halley (1700), Roggewein (1722), Bouvet (1738-39), Byron (1765), Wallis (1767), Bougainville (1768), Surville (1769), and Cook. Note that there is no Antarctic continent.

a. Book 1, Chapters 2-3, January 1773

As the wind remained invariably fixed at E. and E. by S., I continued to stand to the south; and on the 17th, between eleven and twelve o'clock, we crossed the Antarctic Circle in the longitude of 39° 35′ E., for at noon we were by observation in the latitude of 66° 36′ 30″ S. The weather was now become tolerably clear, so that we could see several leagues round us; and yet we had only seen one island of ice since the morning. But about four p.m. as we were steering to the south, we observed the whole sea in a manner covered with ice, from the direction of S.E., round by the S. to W.

In this space, thirty-eight ice islands, great and small, were seen, besides loose ice in abundance, so that we were obliged to luff[1] for one piece, and bear up[2] for another, and as we continued to advance to the south, it increased in such a manner, that at three quarters past six o'clock, being then in the latitude of 67° 15′ S., we could proceed no farther; the ice being entirely closed to the south, in the whole extent from E. to W.S.W., without the least appearance of any opening. This immense field was composed of different kinds of ice; such as high hills, loose or broken pieces packed close together, and what, I think, Greenlandmen call field-ice. A float of this kind of ice lay to the S.E. of us, of such extent, that I could see no end to it from the mast-head. It was sixteen or eighteen feet high at least; and appeared of a pretty equal height and surface. Here we saw many whales playing about the ice.

[...]

After meeting with this ice, I did not think it was at all prudent to persevere in getting farther to the south; especially as the summer was already half spent, and it would have taken up some time to have got round the ice, even supposing it to have been practicable; which, however, is doubtful. I therefore came to a resolution to proceed directly in search of the land lately discovered by the French. And, as the winds still continued at E. by S., I was obliged to return to the north, over some part of the sea I had already made myself acquainted with, and, for that reason, wished to have avoided. But this was not to be done, as our course made good, was little better than north. In the night the wind increased to a strong gale, attended with sleet and snow, and obliged us to double-reef our top-sails. About noon the next day the gale abated, so that we could bear all our reefs out; but the wind still remained in its old quarter.

---

1 Steer closer into the wind.

2 To put the helm to windward and keep the vessel more off the wind.

b. Book 2, Chapter 6, January 1774

On the 30th, at four o'clock in the morning, we perceived the clouds, over the horizon to the south, to be of an unusual snow-white brightness, which we knew denounced our approach to field-ice. Soon after, it was seen from the top-mast-head; and at eight o'clock, we were close to its edge. It extended east and west, far beyond the reach of our sight. In the situation we were in, just the southern half of our horizon was illuminated, by the rays of light reflected from the ice, to a considerable height. Ninety-seven ice hills were distinctly seen within the field, besides those on the outside; many of them very large, and looking like a ridge of mountains, rising one above another till they were lost in the clouds. The outer or northern edge of this immense field, was composed of loose or broken ice close packed together, so that it was not possible for any thing to enter it. This was about a mile broad, within which, was solid ice in one continued compact body. It was rather low and flat (except the hills), but seemed to increase in height, as you traced it to the south; in which direction it extended beyond our sight. Such mountains of ice as these, I believe, were never seen in the Greenland seas, at least, not that I ever heard or read of, so that we cannot draw a comparison between the ice here and there.

[...]

I will not say it was impossible any where to get farther to the south; but the attempting it would have been a dangerous and rash enterprise, and what, I believe, no man in my situation would have thought of. It was, indeed, *my* opinion, as well as the opinion of most on board, that this ice extended quite to the pole, or perhaps joined on some land, to which it had been fixed from the earliest time; and that it is here, that is to the south of this parallel, where all the ice we find scattered up and down to the north, is first formed, and afterwards broken off by gales of wind, or other causes, and brought to the north by the currents, which we always found to set in that direction in the high latitudes. As we drew near this ice some penguins were heard, but none seen; and but few other birds or any other thing that could induce us to think any land was near. And yet I think, there must be some to the south behind this ice; but if there is, it can afford no better retreat for birds, or any other animals, than the ice itself, with which it must be wholly covered. I, who had ambition not only to go farther than any one had been before, but as far as it was possible for man to go, was not sorry at meeting with this interruption, as it in some measure relieved us, at least shortened the dangers and hardships inseparable from the navigation of the southern polar regions. Since, therefore, we could not proceed one inch farther to the south, no other reason need be assigned for my tacking and standing back to the north; being at this time in the latitude of 71° 10′ S., longitude 106° 54′ W.

2. From Charles Wilkes, *Synopsis of the Cruise of the U.S. Exploring Expedition During the Years 1838-1842* (1842)

[The United States Exploring Expedition, which took place between 1838 and 1842, included two attempts (February-March 1839 and January-February 1840) to reach the South Pole. It was during the second attempt that Charles Wilkes believed he had discovered sufficient evidence of an Antarctic continent. In Chapter 7 (p. 103) of *A Strange Manuscript*, Dr. Congreve refers to Wilkes: "Wilkes pretends to have found a continent, but his account of it makes it quite evident to my mind that he saw nothing but ice. I believe that Wilkes's antarctic continent will some day be penetrated by ships, which will sail for hundreds of miles farther south." The following excerpt is taken from a synopsis of the expedition that Wilkes delivered to the National Institute on 20 June 1842.]

The Vincennes and Porpoise[1] continued along the icy barrier to the longitude of 97° east, seeing the land, and at times approaching it to within from three-quarters of a mile to ten miles, when the icy barrier would permit.

On the 29th of January we entered what I have called Piners Bay, the only place where we could have landed on the naked rocks. We were driven out of it by one of the sudden gales usual in those seas. We got soundings in thirty fathoms. The gale lasted thirty-six hours, and after many narrow escapes, I found myself some sixty miles to leeward of this bay. It now became probable that this land which we had discovered was of great extent, and I deemed it of more importance to follow its trend than to return to Piners Bay to land, not doubting I should have an opportunity of landing on some portion of it still more accessible; this, however, I was disappointed in, the icy barrier preventing our approach, and rendering it impossible to effect.

Great quantities of ice, covered with mud, rock, and stone, presented themselves at the edge of the barrier, in close proximity to the land; from these our specimens were obtained, and were quite as numerous as could have been gathered from the rocks themselves. The land, covered with snow, was distinctly seen in many places, and between them such appearances as to leave little or no doubt in my mind of its being a continuous line of coast, and deserving the name bestowed upon it, of the *Antarctic Continent*, lying as it does under that circle. Many

1 Four ships comprised the Wilkes expedition. During the second attempt on the South Pole, the *Peacock* and the *Flying Fish* were forced to return north before seeing land, but the *Vincennes* (the flagship) and *Porpoise* continued.

phenomena were observed here, and observations made, which will be found under their appropriate head in the sequel.

On reaching 97° east we found the ice trending to the northward and continuing to follow it close, we reached to within a few miles of the position where Cook was stopped by the barrier in 1773.

3. From Captain Sir James Clark Ross, *A Voyage of Discovery in the Southern and Antarctic Regions (During the Years 1839-43)*, Volume 1 (1847)

[The Antarctic expedition commanded by James Ross between 1839 and 1843 is referred to several times in *A Strange Manuscript*, by both Adam More and Agnew, in the manuscript proper (see Chapter 3), and by Dr. Congreve, who provides a detailed summary of Ross's discoveries (see Chapter 7). Melick entertains the possibility that the manuscript "may have been written by one of Ross's men and thrown overboard." These mentions focus on Mount Erebus and Mount Terror, which Ross discovered in January 1841, three years before More sights similar volcanoes in Chapter 3. Dr. Congreve places the volcanoes sighted by More and Agnew on the opposite side of Antarctica from Erebus and Terror. Note also the descriptions, especially of the seals.]

a. Volume 1, Chapter VII, 10 January 1841

We now shaped our course directly for the Magnetic Pole, steering as nearly south by compass as the wind, which soon afterwards veered to the south-east, admitted. Our hopes and expectations of attaining that interesting point were now raised to the highest pitch, too soon, however, to suffer as severe a disappointment. A strong "land-blink" made its appearance in the horizon as the ships advanced, and had attained an elevation of several degrees by midnight. All of us were disposed to doubt that which we so much apprehended, owing to its much paler colour than the land-blinks we had seen in the northern regions, but soon after 2 A.M. the officer of the watch, Lieutenant Wood, reported that the land itself was distinctly seen directly ahead of the ship.

It rose in lofty peaks, entirely covered with perennial snow; it could, be distinctly traced from S. S.W. to S. E. by S. (by compass), and must have been more than one hundred miles distant when first seen.

[...]

b. Volume 1, Chapter VII, 27 January 1841

Franklin Island is situated in lat. 76° 8′ S., long. 168° 12′ E. It is about twelve miles long and six broad, and is composed wholly of igneous rocks; the northern side presents a line of dark precipitous cliffs, between five and six hundred feet high, exposing several longitudinal

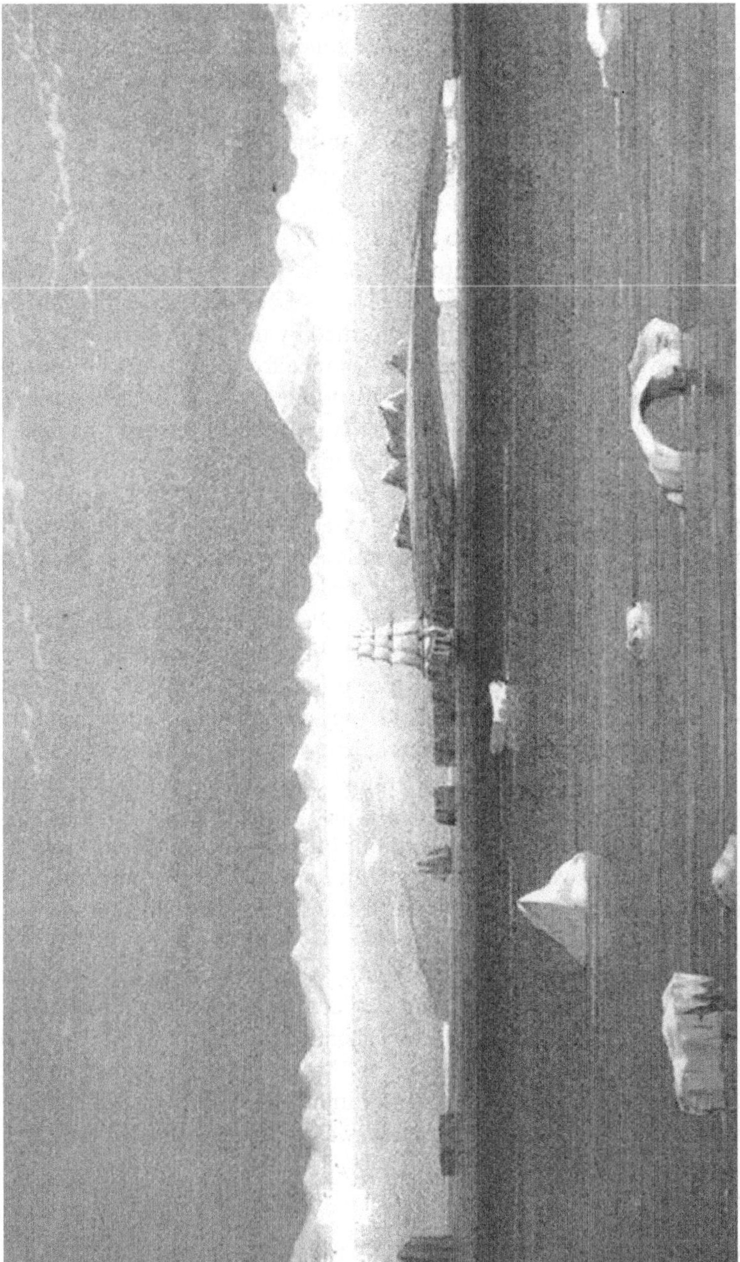

Figure 2: Mount Sabine and Possession Island Discovered 11th January 1841, by J.E. Davis.

broad white, probably aluminous, bands of several feet thickness; two or three of them were of a red ochre colour, and gave a most strange appearance to the cliffs. We could not perceive the smallest trace of vegetation, not even a lichen or piece of sea-weed growing on the rocks; and I have no doubt from the total absence of it at both the places we have landed, that the vegetable kingdom has no representative in antarctic lands. We observed that the white petrel had its nests on the ledges of the cliffs, as had also the rapacious skua gull; several seals were seen, and it is by no means improbable that the beach on which we in vain attempted to land may, at the proper season, be one of their places of resort, or "*rookeries*" as they are termed by the seal fishers.

At between two and three miles distance from the land, the soundings were regular, in thirty-eight to forty-one fathoms, on a bed of fine sand and black stones, and probably good anchorage might be found near the shore with southerly winds. A high cliff of ice projects into the sea from the south and south-west sides, rendering it there quite inaccessible, and a dangerous reef of rocks extends from its southern cape at least four or five miles, with apparently a deep water passage between them and the cape; several icebergs of moderate size were aground on the banks to the northward and westward of the island. At midnight the bearings of eight separate islands are given in the log of the Erebus; but as these afterwards proved to be the summits of mountains, at a great distance, belonging to the mainland, they do not appear upon the chart as islands. With a favourable breeze, and very clear weather, we stood to the southward, close to some land which had been in sight since the preceding noon, and which we then called the "High Island"; it proved to be a mountain twelve thousand four hundred feet of elevation above the level of the sea, emitting flame and smoke in great profusion; at first the smoke appeared like snow drift, but as we drew nearer, its true character became manifest.

The discovery of an active volcano in so high a southern latitude cannot but be esteemed a circumstance of high geological importance and interest, and contribute to throw some further light on the physical construction of our globe. I named it "Mount Erebus," and an extinct volcano to the eastward, little inferior in height, being by measurement ten thousand nine hundred feet high, was called "Mount Terror."

[...]

c. Volume 1, Chapter VIII, 28 January 1841

At 4 P.M. Mount Erebus was observed to emit smoke and flame in unusual quantities, producing a most grand spectacle. A volume of dense smoke was projected at each successive jet with great force, in a vertical

Figure 3: Beaufort Island and Mount Erebus, Discovered 25th January, 1841, by J.E. Davis.

column, to the height of between fifteen hundred and two thousand feet above the mouth of the crater, when condensing first at its upper part, it descended in mist or snow, and gradually dispersed, to be succeeded by another splendid exhibition of the same kind in about half an hour afterwards, although the intervals between the eruptions were by no means regular. The diameter of the columns of smoke was between two and three hundred feet, as near as we could measure it; whenever the smoke cleared away, the bright red flame that filled the mouth of the crater was clearly perceptible; and some of the officers believed they could see streams of lava pouring down its sides until lost beneath the snow which descended from a few hundred feet below the crater, and projected its perpendicular icy cliff several miles into the ocean. Mount Terror was much more free from snow, especially on its eastern side, where were numerous little conical crater-like hillocks, each of which had probably been, at some period, an active volcano; two very conspicuous hills of this kind were observed close to Cape Crozier. The land upon which Mount Erebus and Terror stand comprised between Cape Crozier and Cape Bird, had the appearance of an island from our present position; but the fixed ice, not admitting of our getting to the westward of Cape Bird, prevented our ascertaining whether it was so or not at this time.

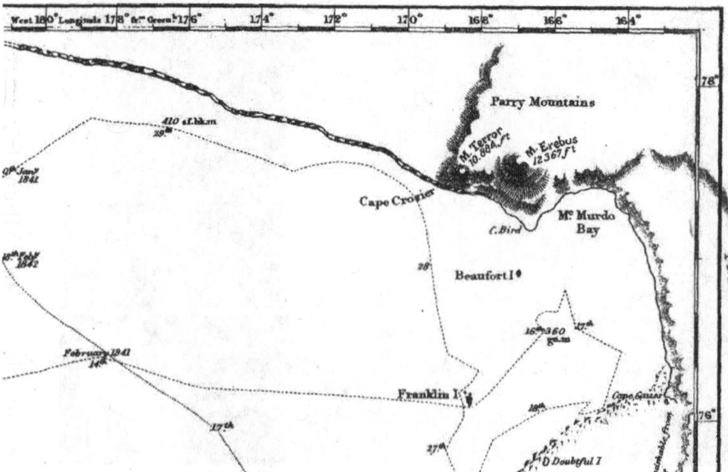

Figure 4: Inset from Ross's Chart of Victoria Land, January 1841: Mt. Terror and Mt. Erebus.

Appendix B: Nineteenth-Century Geology and Paleontology

[There are two levels identifying the various monstrous creatures encountered by Adam More as dinosaurs: 1) More's first-hand description and 2) the doctor's scientific naming and explanation, especially in Chapter 17. De Mille is drawing on recent geological and paleontological findings to imagine the fantastic monsters of myth and fiction (e.g., of the Sinbad voyages mentioned by Melick) in terms of an evolutionary environmental niche at the South Pole. He draws from different eras and periods of geological time: the dinosaurs belong to the Mesozoic Era, predominantly the Jurassic period, but also the Cretaceous period. The vegetation belongs to the Carboniferous period. Here is a simplified Geological Time Chart:

Era	**Period**	**Age (millions of years ago)**
Cenozoic	Quaternary	1.8 – 0 mya
	Neogene	23 – 1.8 mya
	Paleogene	65 – 23 mya
Mesozoic	Cretaceous	146 – 65 mya
	Jurassic	208 – 146 mya
	Triassic	245 – 208 mya
Paleozoic	Permian	286 – 245 mya
	Carboniferous	360 – 286 mya
	Devonian	410 – 360 mya
	Silurian	440 – 410 mya

This appendix provides excerpts from some of his main scientific sources to illustrate how De Mille is drawing directly from contemporary geological discourse to construct plausibility. And it features illustrations from these sources to help readers both visualize De Mille's descriptions and see how closely they are based on the paleontological literature.]

1. From Richard Owen, *Geology and the Inhabitants of the Ancient World* (1854)

[Richard Owen (1804-92) played a central role in nineteenth-century British comparative anatomy and paleontology. He first named dinosaurs, distinguishing them from lizards and introducing the term *Dinosauria*. For the 1851 Great Exhibition in Hyde Park, Owen worked with Benjamin Waterhouse Hawkins to make full-sized sculptures of dinosaurs based on fossils. Owen published several works, including his guide to the Crystal Palace sculptures, *Geology and the Inhabitants of the Ancient World*. De Mille probably visited the Great Exhibition, which opened in the same month that James and his brother returned to London from the continent. In any case, he was definitely influenced by Owen's guide to the Crystal Palace. As the following excerpts show, many of the creatures that More encounters at the South Pole are found at the Crystal Palace, and Dr. Congreve's descriptions of some of them are based on Owen's descriptions.]

Figure 5: Restored Extinct Animals on the Geological Islands in the great lake in the Gardens of the Crystal Palace.

a. Pterodactyle

Nos. 2 and 3[1] are restorations of a flying reptile or dragon, called Pterodactyle, from the Greek words *pteron*, a wing, and *dactylos*, a finger; because the wings are mainly supported by the outer finger, enormously lengthened and of proportionate strength, which, nevertheless, answers to the little finger of the human hand. The wings consisted of folds of skin, like the leather wings of the bat; and the Pterodactyles were

1 The numbers refer to exhibits of restorations of extinct animals located throughout the Crystal Palace and its gardens.

covered with scales, not with feathers: the head, though somewhat resembling in shape that of a bird, and supported on a long and slender neck, was provided with long jaws, armed with teeth; and altogether the structure of these extinct members of the reptilian class is such as to rank them amongst the most extraordinary of all the creatures yet discovered in the ruins of the ancient earth.

Remains of the Pterodactyle were first discovered, in 1784, by Prof. Collini, in the lithographic slate of Aichstadt, in Germany, which slate is a member of the oolitic formations: the species so discovered was at first mistaken for a bird, and afterwards supposed to be a large kind of bat, but had its true reptilian nature demonstrated by Baron Cuvier, by whom it was called the *Pterodactylus longirostris*, or Long-beaked Pterodactyle: it was about the size of a curlew.[1]

[...]

Remains of the largest known kinds of Pterodactyle have been discovered more recently in chalk-pits, at Burham, in Kent. The skull of one of these species—the *Pterodactylus Cuvieri*—was about twenty inches in length, and the animal was upborne on an expanse of wing of probably not less than eighteen feet from tip to tip. [...] The long, sharp, conical teeth in the jaws of the Pterodactyles indicate them to have preyed upon other living animals; their eyes were large, as if to enable them to fly by night. From their wings projected fingers, terminated by long curved claws, and forming a powerful paw, wherewith the animal was enabled to creep and climb, or suspend itself from trees. [...]

b. Iguanodon

Mr. W.H. Bensted, of Maidstone, the proprietor of a stone-quarry of the Shanklin-sand formation [...] had his attention one day, in May, 1834, called by his workmen to what they supposed to be petrified wood in some pieces of stone which they had been blasting. He perceived that what they supposed to be wood was fossil bone, and with a zeal and care which have always characterised his endeavours to secure for science any evidence of fossil remains in his quarry, he immediately resorted to the spot. [...] He succeeded after a month's labour in exposing them to view, and in fitting the fragments to their proper places. This specimen is now in the British Museum. Many other specimens of detached bones, including vertebrae or parts of the back-bone, especially that part resting on the hind limbs, and called the "pelvis," bones of the limbs, down to those that supported the claws, together with jaws

1 Large migratory birds of the sandpiper family.

and teeth, which have since been successively discovered, have enabled anatomists to reconstruct the extinct Iguanodon, and have proved it to have been a herbivorous reptile, of colossal dimensions, analogous to the diminutive Iguana in the form of its teeth, but belonging to a distinct and higher order of reptiles, more akin to the crocodiles. The same rich materials, selecting the largest of the bones as a standard, have served for the present restorations (Nos. 4 and 5) of the animal, as when alive: all the parts being kept in just proportion to the standard bones, and the whole being thus brought to the following dimensions:—

Total length, from the nose or muzzle to the end of the tail	34 feet, 9 inches
Greatest girth of the trunk	20 feet, 5 inches
Length of the-head	3 feet, 6 inches
Length of the tail	25 feet, 6 inches

[...]

c. Hylaeosaurus

The animal, so called by its discoverer, Dr. Mantell, belongs to the same highly organised order of the class of reptiles as the Iguanodon, that, viz.,[1] which was characterised by a longer and stronger sacrum and pelvis, and by larger limbs than the reptiles of the present day possess; they were accordingly better fitted for progression on dry land, and probably carried their body higher and more freely above the surface of the ground.

Visiting, in the summer of 1832, a quarry in Tilgate Forest, Dr. Mantell had his attention attracted to some fragments of a large mass of stone, which had recently been broken up, and which exhibited traces of numerous pieces of bone. The portions of the rock, which admitted of being restored together, were cemented, and then the rock was chiselled from the fossil bones, which consisted of part of the back-bone or vertebral column, some ribs, the shoulder bones called scapula and coracoid, and numerous long angular bones or spines which seemed to have supported a lofty serrated or jagged crest, extended along the middle of the back, as in some of the small existing lizards. [...] Many small dermal bones were also found, which indicate the Hylæosaurus to have been covered by hard tuberculate scales, like those of some of the Australian lizards, called *Cyclodus*. This character of the skin, and the serrated crest, are accurately given in the restoration, the major part

1 As follows.

of which, however, is necessarily at present conjectural, and carried out according to the general analogies of the saurian form.

[...]

d. Megalosaurus

The Megalosaurus, as its name implies (compounded by its discoverer, Dr. Buckland, from the Greek *megas*, great, and *sauros*, lizard), was a lizard-like reptile of great size. [...]

The restoration of the animal has been accordingly effected, agreeably with the proportions of the known parts of the skeleton, and in harmony with the general characters of the order of reptiles to which the Megalosaurus belonged. This order—the Dinosauria (Gr. *demos*, terribly great, *sauros*, a lizard)—is that to which the two foregoing huge reptiles of the Wealden series belong, viz., the Iguanodon and Hylaeosaurus, and is characterized by the modifications already mentioned, that fitted them for more efficient progression upon dry land. The Iguanodon represented the herbivorous section of the order, the Hylæosaurus appears, from its teeth, to have been a mixed feeder, but the Megalosaurus was decidedly carnivorous, and, probably, waged a deadly war against its less destructively endowed congeners and contemporaries.

Figure 6: Megalosaurus (restoration No. 7).

Baron Cuvier [see p. 177, note 1] estimated the Megalosaurus to have been about fifty feet in length; my own calculations, founded on more complete evidence than had been at the Baron's command, reduce its size to about thirty-five feet: but with the superior proportional height and capacity of trunk, as contrasted with the largest existing crocodiles, even that length gives a most formidable character to this extinct predatory reptile.

As the thigh-bone (*femur*) and leg-bone (*tibia*) measure each nearly three feet, the entire hind-leg, allowing for the cartilages of the joints, must have attained a length of two yards: a bone of the foot (metatarsal) thirteen inches long, indicates that part, with the toes and claws entire, to have been at least three feet in length. The form of the teeth shows the Megalosaurus to have been strictly carnivorous, and viewed as instruments for providing food for so enormous a reptile, the teeth were fearfully fitted to the destructive office for which they were designed. They have compressed conical sharp-pointed crowns, with cutting and finely serrated anterior and posterior edges; they appear straight, as seen when they had just protruded from the socket, but become bent slightly backwards in the progress of growth, and the fore part of the crown, below the summit, becomes thick and convex.

[...]

e. Teleosaurus

On the shore beneath the overhanging cliff of oolitic rock are two restorations, Nos. 10 and 11, of a large extinct kind of crocodile, to which the long and slender-jawed crocodile of the Ganges, called "Gaviàl" or "Gharriàl" by the Hindoos, offers the nearest resemblance at the present day. Remains of the ancient extinct British gavials have been found in most of the localities where the oolitic formations occur, and very abundantly in the lias cliffs near Whitby, in Yorkshire. The name Teleosaurus (*telos*, the end, *sauros*, a lizard), was compounded from the Greek by Professor Geoffroy St. Hilaire, for a species of these fossil gavials, found by him in the oolite stone at Caen, in Normandy, and has reference to his belief that they formed one—the earliest—extreme of the crocodilian series, as this series has been successively developed in the course of time on our planet.

The jaws are armed with numerous long, slender, sharp-pointed, slightly curved teeth, indicating that they preyed on fishes, and the young or weaker individuals of co-existing reptiles. The nostril is situated more at the end of the upper jaw than in the modern gavial: the fore-limbs are shorter, and the hind ones longer and stronger than in the gavial, which indicates that the Teleosaur was a better swimmer; the vertebrae or bones of the back are united by slightly concave surfaces, not interlocked by cup and ball joints as in the modern crocodiles, whence it would seem that the Teleosaur lived more habitually in the water, and less seldom moved on dry land; and, as its fossil remains have been hitherto found only in the sedimentary deposits from the sea, it may be inferred that it was more strictly marine than the crocodile of the Ganges.

[...]

f. Enaliosauria (Ichthyosaurus and Plesiosaurus)

The creatures called Enaliosauria or Sea-lizards (from the Greek *enalios*, of the sea, and *sauros*, lizard), were vertebrate animals, or had back bones, breathed the air like land quadrupeds, but were cold-blooded, or of a low temperature, like crocodiles and other reptiles. The proof that the Enaliosaurs respired atmospheric air immediately, and did not breathe water by means of gills like fishes, is afforded by the absence of the bony framework of the gill apparatus, and by the presence, position, and structure of the air passages leading from the nostrils, and also by the bony mechanism of the capacious chest or thoracic-abdominal cavity: all of which characters have been demonstrated by their fossil skeletons. With these characters the Sea-lizards combined the presence of two pairs of limbs shaped like fins, and adapted for swimming.

The Enaliosauria offer two principal modifications of their anatomical, and especially their bony, structure, of which the two kinds grouped together under the respective names of Ichthyosaurus and Plesiosaurus are the examples.

THE ICHTHYOSAURUS

The genus Ichthyosaurus includes many species: of which three of the best known and most remarkable have been selected for restoration to illustrate this most singular of the extinct forms of animal life.

The name (from the Greek *ichthys*, a fish, and *sauros*, a lizard) indicates the closer affinity of the Ichthyosaur, as compared with the Plesiosaur, to the class of fishes. The Ichthyosaurs are remarkable for the shortness of the neck and the equality of the width of the back of the head with the front of the chest, impressing the observer of the fossil skeleton with a conviction that the ancient animal must have resembled the whale tribe and the fishes in the absence of any intervening constriction or "neck."

[...]

In its great length and gradual diminution we perceive its saurian character; the tegumentary nature of the fin, unsustained by bony fin-rays, bespeaks its affinity to the same part in the mammalian whales and porpoises; whilst its vertical position makes it closely resemble the tail-fin of the fish.

[...]

The vertical fin was a more efficient organ in the rapid cleaving of the liquid element, when the Ichthyosaurs were in pursuit of their prey, or escaping from an enemy.

That the Ichthyosaurs occasionally sought the shores, crawled on the strand, and basked in the sunshine, may be inferred from the bony structure connected with their fore-fins, which does not exist in any porpoise, dolphin, grampus, or whale.

[...]

Of no extinct reptile are the materials for a complete and exact restoration more abundant and satisfactory than of the Ichthyosaurus they plainly show that its general external figure must have been that of a huge predatory abdominal fish, with a longer tail, and a smaller tail-fin: scale-less, moreover, and covered by a smooth, or finely wrinkled skin analogous to that of the whale tribe.

The mouth was wide, and the jaws long, and armed with numerous pointed teeth, indicative of a predatory and carnivorous nature in all the species; but these differed from one another in regard to the relative strength of the jaws, and the relative size and length of the teeth.

[...]

PLESIOSAURUS

The discovery of this genus forms one of the most important additions that geology has made to comparative anatomy. Baron Cuvier deemed "its structure to have been the most singular, and its characters the most monstrous, that had been yet discovered amid the ruins of a former world." To the head of a lizard it united the teeth of a crocodile, a neck of enormous length, resembling the body of a serpent, a trunk and tail having the proportions of an ordinary quadruped, the ribs of a chameleon, and the paddles of a whale. "Such," writes Dr. Buckland, "are the strange combinations of form and structure in the Plesiosaurus, a genus, the remains of which, after interment for thousands of years amidst the wreck of millions of extinct inhabitants of the ancient earth, are at length recalled to light by the researches of the geologist, and submitted to our examination, in nearly as perfect a state as the bones of species that are now existing upon the earth." (Op. cit., vol. v. p. 203).

The first remains of this animal were discovered in the lias of Lyme Regis, about the year 1823, and formed the subject of the paper by the Rev. Mr. Conybeare (now Dean of Llandaff), and Mr. (now Sir Henry) De la Beche, in which the genus was established and named Plesiosaurus (from the Greek words, *plesios* and *sauros*, signifying "near" or "allied to," and "lizard"), because the authors saw that it was more nearly allied to the lizard than was the Ichthyosaurus from the same formation.

[...]

No. 15.—PLESIOSAURUS MACROCEPHALUS

The first of these has been called, from the relatively larger size of the head, the *Plesiosaurus macrocephalus* (No. 15), (Gr. *macros*, long, *cephale*, head). The entire length of the animal, as indicated by the largest remains, and as given in the restoration, is eighteen feet, the length, of the head being two feet, that of the neck six feet; the greatest girth of the body yields seven feet.

[...]

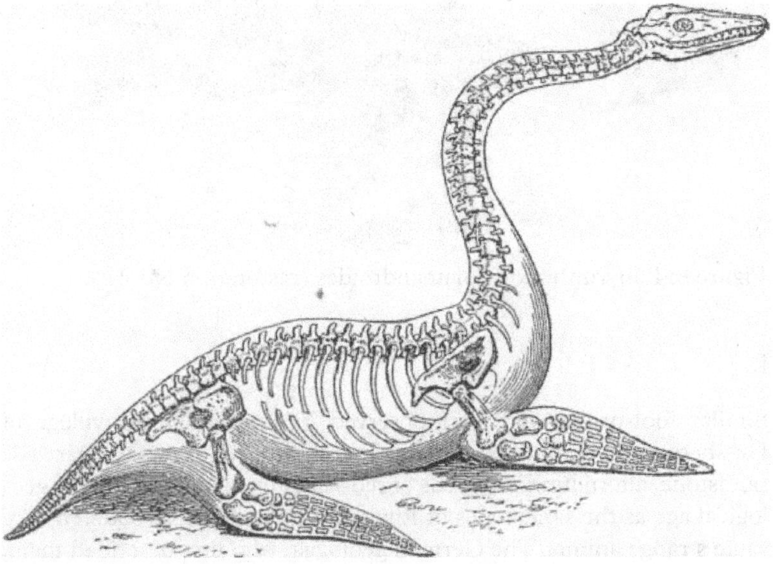

Figure 7: Plesiosaurua macrocephalus (restoration No. 15).

g. Labyrinthodon

The skull of the Labyrinthodon is attached to the neck-bones by two joints or condyles, and the teeth are situated both on the proper jaw-bones, and on the bone of the roof of the mouth called "vomer": both these characters are only found at the present day in the frogs and salamanders.

The hind-foot of the Labyrinthodon was also, as in the toad and frog, much larger than the fore-foot; and the innermost digit in both was short and turned in, like a thumb.

Consecutive impressions of the prints of these feet have been traced for many steps in succession (as is accurately represented in the new red sandstone part of the Secondary Island) in quarries of that formation in Warwickshire, Cheshire, and also in Lancashire, more especially at a quarry of a whitish quartzose sandstone at Storton Hill, a few miles from Liverpool.

Figure 8: Labyrinthodon Salamandroides (restoration No. 18).

[...]

Similar foot-prints were first observed in Saxony, at the village of Hessberg, near Hillburghausen, in several quarries of a gray quartzose sandstone, alternating with beds of red sandstone, and of the same geological age as the sandstones of England that had been trodden by the same strange animal. The German geologist, who first described them, proposed the name of *Cheirotherium* (Greek. *cheir*, the hand, *therion*, beast), for the great unknown animal that had left the foot-prints, in consequence of the resemblance, both of the fore and hind feet, to the impression of a human hand, and Dr. Kaup conjectured that the animal might be a large species of the opossum-kind. The discovery, however, of fossil skulls, jaws, teeth, and a few other bones in the sandstones exhibiting the footprints in question, has rendered it more probable that both the footprints and the fossils are evidences of the same kind of huge extinct Batrachian reptiles.

2. From Louis Figuier, *The World Before the Deluge* (1866)

[Louis Figuier's *La Terre avant le déluge* (1863) seems to be one of De Mille's sources. In Chapter 17, the doctor incorrectly notes that Emile Bayle calls the Ichthyosaurus the "whale of the saurians." Figuier also mistakenly attributes the analogy to Bayle. Included here are illustrations that Figuier calls "Ideal Landscapes of the Ancient World" by the famous Edouard Riou (1833-1900), who illustrated the novels of Jules Verne.]

a. "whale of the saurians"

The extraordinary creature which bears the name of *Ichthyosaurus*, from the Greek words Ιχθύς σαυρος, fish-lizard, presents certain dispositions and organic arrangements which are met with dispersed in certain classes of animals now living, but they never seem to be again reunited in any one. It possesses the muzzle of a porpoise, the head of a lizard, the jaws end teeth of a crocodile, the vertebræ of a fish, the sternum of the Ornithorhynchus, the paddles of a whale, and the trunk and tail of an ordinary quadruped.

Bayle appears to have given the best idea of the Ichthyosaurus by describing it as the whale of the Saurians—the Cetacea of the primitive seas. It was, in short, an animal exclusively marine: on shore it would be an immovable, inert mass: its paddles and fish-late vertebræ, the length of the tail and other parts of its structure, prove that its habits were aquatic, as the remains of fishes and reptile, and the form of its teeth, show that it was carnivorous. Like the whale, also, the Ichthyosaurus respired atmospheric air; so that it was under the necessity of coming frequently to the surface of the water, like that inhabitant of the deep. We can even believe with Bayle that, like the whale, it was provided with vents or blowers, through which it ejected the water it had swallowed in columns into the air.

The short thick neck of the Ichthyosaurus supported a voluminous head, which continued backwards from behind the eyes in vertebral column of more than a hundred vertebræ. The animal being created,

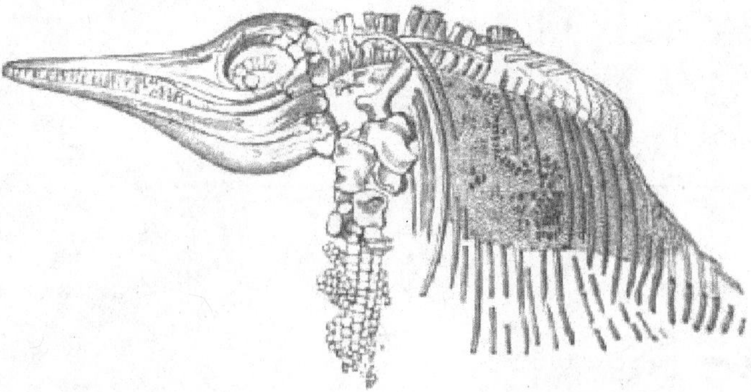

Figure 9: Skeleton of Ichthyosaurus. Containing teeth and bones of the fish in the coprolite form (Fig. 95).

like the whale, for rapid movement through the water, its vertebræ had none of the invariable solidity of the lizard or crocodile, but rather the structure and lightness of that of fishes. (193-194)

b. Ideal Landscapes

Figure 10: Icythyosaurus and Plesiosaurus, Edouard Riou (202-203).

Figure 11: Pteradactyle, by Riou (210-211).

Figure 12: Middle Oolitic Period with Teleosaurus and Hylaeosaurus, by Riou (222-223).

3. Coal Period Vegetation: From Louis Figuier, *The World Before the Deluge* (1866)

[In Chapter 17 (p. 177), the doctor notes, "I see that river, with its trees and shrubs, all unknown now except in museums—the vegetation of the Coal Period—the lepidodendron, the lepidostrobus, the pecopteris, the neuropteris, the lonchopteris, the odontopteris, the sphenopteris, the cyclopteris, the sigillaria reniformis, the sphenophyllum, the calamites—." Figuier's *La Terre avant le déluge* (1863) is one of De Mille's primary sources for the plants More observes growing at the South Pole. For information on the Carboniferous or "Coal" period, De Mille may have consulted Charles Lyell's *Elements of Geology* (1838), John William Dawson's *Air Breathers of the Coal Period* (1863), and Hugh Miller's *The Testimony of Rocks* (1865), but Figuier provided the most vivid illustrations recreating carboniferous vegetation, and he discusses all of the species mentioned by De Mille. Like Lyell and Dawson, Figuier uses the term "coal period" as synonymous with Carboniferous.]

To the Devonian succeeds, in the history of our globe, the carboniferous period, in whose bosom was concealed during many long ages the coal measures, which have done so much to enrich and civilize the world in our own age. [...] The monuments of this grand forest epoch discover themselves in the rich coal measures of England and Scotland. These give us some idea of the rich vestments which covered the nakedness of the earth newly risen from the bosom of the waves. It was the paradise of terrestrial vegetation. The grand *Sigillaria*, the *Stigmaria*, and the plant especially typical of this age—the arborescent fern—formed the woods, which were left to grow undisturbed, for as yet no living mammifera[1] violated the silent solitude: everything announces a uniformly warm, humid temperature, the only climate in which the gigantic ferns of the coal-measures could have attained their magnitude. In Fig. 34 the reader has a restoration of the arborescent and herbaceous ferns of the period. Conifers have been found of this period with concentric rings, whence it has been concluded that seasons existed; but these rings are more slightly marked than in existing trees of the same family, from which it is reasonable to think that the seasonal changes were less marked than they are with us.

Figure 13: Ferns restored (Fig. 34).

1 Mammals.

[...]

Coal, then, is the substance of the vegetation of the most remote ages of the world. Buried under an enormous thickness of rocks, they have been preserved to our days, after being modified in their inward nature and in their exterior. Having lost certain of their constituents, they have been transformed into a species of carbon, and impregnated with bituminous or tarry substances, the ordinary product of the slow decomposition of organic matter.

Thus coal, which feeds our manufactures and our furnaces, which is the fundamental agent of our productive industry and economy—the coal which warms our hearths and furnishes the gas which lights our streets and dwellings—is the substance of the plants which formed the forests, the grass, and the marshes of the ancient world at a period too distant for human chronology to assign a date to it.

[...]

What we can remark on with certainty as a striking characteristic in the vegetation of the globe during this phase of its history was the prodigious development its vegetation assumed. The ferns, which in our days and in our climate are only small herbaceous plants, in the carboniferous age presented themselves sometimes under a lofty form and port.

The marshy herbaceous plants with cylindrical stem, hollow, channeled, and articulated; whose articulations are furnished with a membranous, dentated[1] sheath, which bears the name of "mares-tail," their fructification forming a sort of catkin composed of many rings of scales, which bear on their lower surface sacs full of *spores* or seeds—these humble *Equisetii*, with fluted stem and whorled branches, represented during the coal period by herbaceous trees—immense asparagus—as it were, of forty to five-and-forty feet high, and four to six inches in diameter, their trunks hollowed and channeled longitudinally, and divided transversely by the lines of articulation, have been preserved: they bear the name of *Calamites*. The engraving (Fig. 35) represents one of these gigantic mares-tails, or calamites, of the coal period.

[...]

The *Lepidodendrons*, of which there are about forty species known, have a cylindrical stem or trunk bifurcated in the branches, that is, the branches were evolved in pairs, or *archotomous*. The extremities of the

1 Having tooth-like points.

branches were terminated by a fructification in the form of a cone, formed of linear scales, to which the name of *Lepidostrobus* has been given. In many of the coal-fields fossil cones have been found, to which this name has been given by earlier palaeontologists. They sometimes form a nucleus of concrete balls of clay ironstones, and are well preserved, having a conical axis, surrounded by scales compactly imbricated. The opinion of Brougniart is now generally adopted, that they are the fruit of the Lepidodendron.

[...]

Figure 14: Calamite restored, 30-40 feet high (Fig. 35).

M. Eugene Deslongchamps has successfully attempted the restoration of the tree discovered in the Bohemian colliery, which is here represented with its stem, its branches, fronds, and organs of fructification (Fig. 44). The ferns composed a great part of the vegetation of the carboniferous period, both in the herbaceous and arboraceous form.

The ferns differ chiefly in some of the details of the leaf. Pecopteris, for instance, have the leaves, once, twice, or thrice pinnated, with the

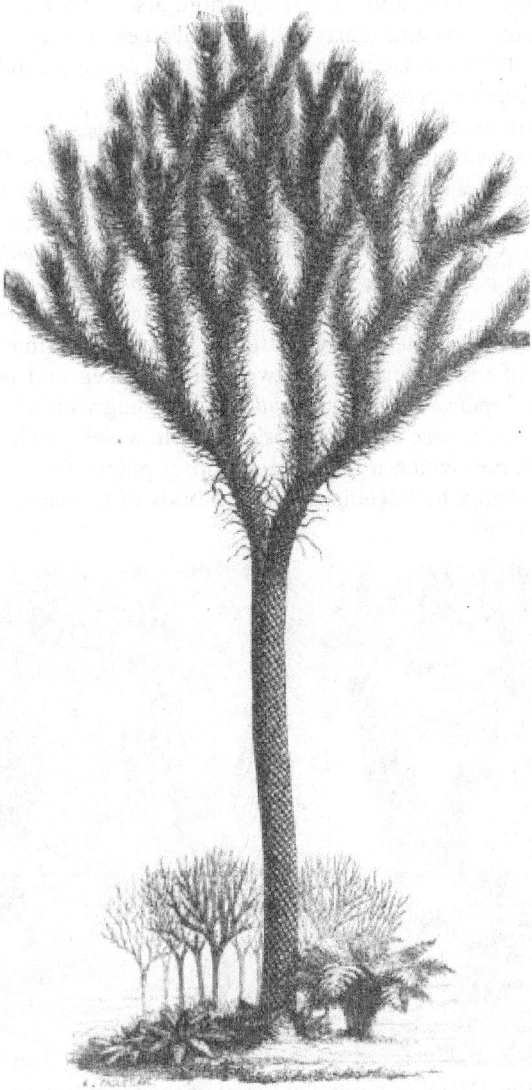

Figure 15: Lepidodendron Sternbergii restored, 40 feet high (Fig. 44).

leaflets adhering either by their whole base or by the centre leaves divided like Pecopteris, but the midrib does not reach the apex of the leaflets, but divides right and left into veins.

[...]

On the opposite page (Plate 11.), M. Riou has attempted, under the directions of M. Deslongchamps, to reproduce the aspect of nature during the period. A marsh and forest of the coal period are here represented with a short and thick vegetation, a sort of grass, composed of herbaceous ferns and mares-tail. Several trees of forest height raise their heads above this lacustrine vegetation. Here are the indications of the species represented:—

On the left are seen the naked trunk of a *Lepidodendron* and a *Sigillaria,* an arborescent fern rising between the two trunks. At the foot of these great trees an herbaceous fern and a *Stigmaria* appear, whose long ramification of roots, provided with reproductive spores, extend to the water. On the right the naked trunk of another *Sigillaria,* a tree whose foliage is altogether unknown, a *Sphenophyllum* and a *conifer.* It is difficult to describe with precision the species of this family, whose imprints are, nevertheless, very abundant in the coal formation.

In front of this group we see two trunks broken and overthrown. These are a *Lepidodendron* and *Sigillaria,* mingling with a heap of vegetable debris in course of decomposition, from which a rich humus will be formed, upon which a new generation of plants will soon develop themselves. Some herbaceous ferns and buds of *Calamites* rise out of the marshy water.

Figure 16: Ideal View of a marshy forest of the Coal Period (Plate 11), by Riou.

4. From Elijah H. Burritt, *Atlas Designed to Illustrate the Geography of the Heavens* (1845)

[More's description of the southern night sky in Chapter 18 is based on Plate 7, "Southern Circumpolar Map," found in the *Atlas Designed to Illustrate The Geography of the Heavens* by Elijah H. Burritt (Parks 299). The map is here reproduced with an expanded constellation Robur Caroli seen in the second figure.]

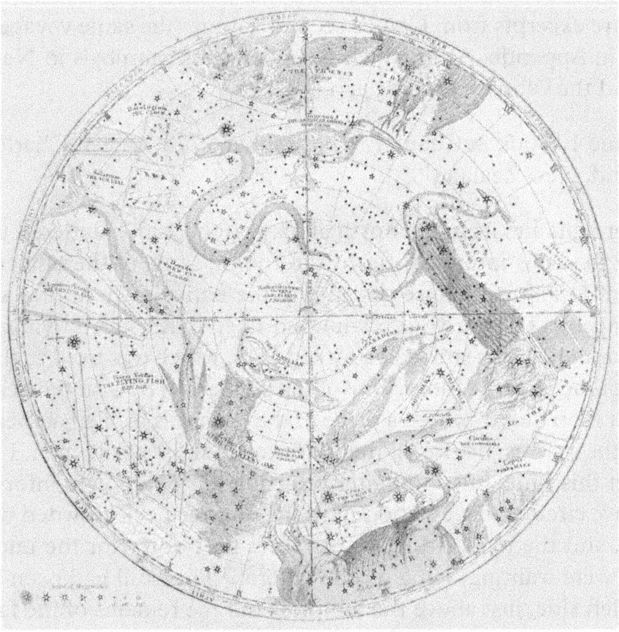

Figure 17: Burritt's Southern Circumpolar Map.

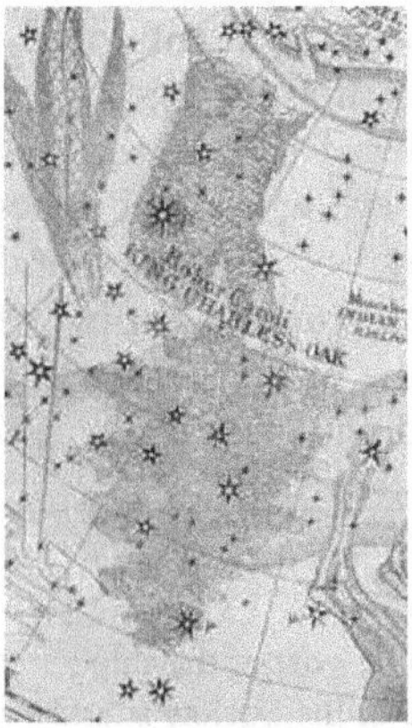

Figure 18: Constellation Robur Carolini (King Charles Oak).

Appendix C: Savages and Cannibals

[Cannibalism is a recurring issue in exploration narratives in the eighteenth and nineteenth centuries.]

1. From James Cook, *A Voyage Towards the South Pole and Round the World* (1777)

[Here are excerpts from Cook's second voyage (the same voyage represented in Appendix A) in which he encounters cannibals in New Zealand and the Vanuatu archipelago.]

a. Volume 1, Book 2, Chapter 5, November 1773, Queen Charlotte's Sound, New Zealand[1]

Calm or light airs from the north all day on the 23d,[2] hindered us from putting to sea as intended. In the afternoon, some of the officers went on shore to amuse themselves among the natives, where they saw the head and bowels of a youth, who had lately been killed, lying on the beach; and the heart stuck on a forked stick, which was fixed to the head of one of the largest canoes. One of the gentlemen bought the head, and brought it on board, where a piece of the flesh was broiled and eaten by one of the natives, before all the officers and most of the men. I was on shore at this time, but soon after returning on board, was informed of the above circumstances; and found the quarter-deck crowded with the natives, and the mangled head, or rather part of it, (for the under-jaw and lip were wanting) lying on the tafferal.[3] The skull had been broken on the left side, just above the temples; and the remains of the face had all the appearance of a youth under twenty.

The sight of the head, and the relation of the above circumstances, struck me with horror, and filled my mind with indignation against these cannibals. Curiosity, however, got the better of my indignation, especially when I considered that it would avail but little; and being desirous of becoming an eye-witness of a fact which many doubted, I ordered a piece of the flesh to be broiled and brought to the quarter-deck, where one of these cannibals eat it with surprising avidity. This had such an effect on some of our people as to make them sick. Oedidee[4] (who came on board with me) was so affected with the sight as to

1 On New Zealand's South Island.

2 23rd.

3 That is, the taffrail, the upper part of the ship's stern.

4 A native of Bora Bora, one of the Society Islands, whom Cook picked up in September of 1773. Cook later discovers that his proper name is Heete Heete.

become perfectly motionless, and seemed as if metamorphosed into the statue of horror. It is utterly impossible for art to describe that passion with half the force that it appeared in his countenance. When roused from this state by some of us, he burst into tears; continued to weep and scold by turns; told them they were vile men; and that he neither was, nor would be any longer their friend. He even would not suffer them to touch him; he used the same language to one of the gentlemen who cut off the flesh; and refused to accept, or even touch the knife with which it was done. Such was Oedidee's indignation against the vile custom; and worthy of imitation by every rational being.

I was not able to find out the reason for their undertaking this expedition; all I could understand for certain was, that they went from hence into Admiralty Bay (the next inlet to the west), and there fought with their enemies, many of whom they killed. They counted to me fifty; a number which exceeded probability, as they were not more, if so many, themselves. I think I understood them clearly, that this youth was killed there; and not brought away prisoner, and afterwards killed. Nor could I learn that they had brought away any more than this one; which increased the improbability of their having killed so many. We had also reason to think that they did not come off without loss; for a young woman was seen, more than once, to cut herself, as is the custom when they lose a friend or relation.

That the New Zealanders are cannibals, can now no longer be doubted. The account given of this in my former voyage, being partly founded on circumstances, was, as I afterwards understood, discredited by many persons. Few consider what a savage man is in his natural state, and even after he is, in some degree, civilized. The New Zealanders are certainly in some state of civilization; their behaviour to us was manly and mild, shewing,[1] on all occasions, a readiness to oblige. They have some arts among them which they execute with great judgment and unwearied patience; they are far less addicted to thieving than the other islanders of the South Sea; and I believe those in the same tribe, or such as are at peace one with another, are strictly honest among themselves. This custom of eating their enemies slain in battle (for I firmly believe they eat the flesh of no others) has undoubtedly been handed down to them from the earliest times; and we know it is not an easy matter to wean a nation from their ancient customs, let them be ever so inhuman and savage; especially if that nation has no manner of connexion or commerce with strangers. For it is by this that the greatest part of the human race has been civilized; an advantage which the New Zealanders, from their situation, never had. An intercourse with foreigners would reform their manners, and polish their savage minds.

1 Showing.

Or, were they more united under a settled form of government, they would have fewer enemies, consequently this custom would be less in use, and might in time be in a manner forgotten. At present, they have but little idea of treating others as themselves would wish to be treated, but treat them as they expect to be treated. If I remember right, one of the arguments they made use of to Tupia,[1] who frequently expostulated with them against this custom, was, that there could be no harm in killing and eating the man who would do the same by them if it was in his power. "For," said they, "can there be any harm in eating our enemies, whom we have killed in battle? Would not those very enemies have done the same to us?" I have often seen them listen to Tupia with great attention; but I never found his arguments have any weight with them, or that with all his rhetoric, he could persuade any one of them that this custom was wrong. And when Oedidee, and several of our people, shewed their abhorrence of it, they only laughed at them.

Among many reasons which I have heard assigned for the prevalence of this horrid custom, the want of animal food has been one; but how far this is deducible either from facts or circumstances, I shall leave those to find out who advanced it. In every part of New Zealand where I have been, fish was in such plenty, that the natives generally caught as much as served both themselves and us. They have also plenty of dogs; nor is there any want of wild fowl, which they know very well how to kill. So that neither this, nor the want of food of any kind, can, in my opinion, be the reason. But, whatever it may be, I think it was but too evident, that they have a great liking for this kind of food.

I must here observe, that Oedidee soon learnt to converse with these people, as I am persuaded, he would have done with the people of Amsterdam, had he been a little longer with them; for he did not understand the New Zealanders, at first, any more, or not so much, as he understood the people of Amsterdam.

b. Volume 2, Book 3, Chapter 5, August 1774, Vanuatu Archipelago

The preceding day, Mr. Forster[2] learnt from the people the proper name of the island, which they call Tanna;[3] and this day I learnt from them the names of those in the neighbourhood. The one we touched at last is called Erromango; the small isle, which we discovered the morning we landed here, Immer; the Table island to the east, discovered at

1 A Tahitian native who travelled with Cook.

2 The Polish Prussian Johann Reinhold Forster was the naturalist on this voyage.

3 Tanna is an island in the Vanuatu archipelago, a group of more than 80 islands approximately 1750 kilometers due east of northern Australia. The other islands mentioned by Cook here are near Tanna.

the same time, Erronan or Footoona; and an island which lies to the S.E. Annattom. All these islands are to be seen from Tanna.

They gave us to understand, in a manner which I thought admitted of no doubt, that they eat human flesh, and that circumcision was practised among them. They began the subject of eating human flesh, of their own accord, by asking us if we did; otherwise I should never have thought of asking them such a question. I have heard people argue, that no nation could be cannibals, if they had other flesh to eat, or did not want food; thus deriving the custom from necessity. The people of this island can be under no such necessity; they have fine pork and fowls, and plenty of roots and fruits. But since we have not actually seen them eat human flesh, it will admit of doubt with some, whether they are cannibals.

2. From Charles Darwin, *Journal of Researches into the Geology and Natural History of the Various Countries Visited by H.M.S. Beagle* (1846)

[In December 1832, Charles Darwin arrived in Tierra del Fuego, an archipelago off the southern tip of South America. Kenneth Hughes notes that, in Chapter 4 of *A Strange Manuscript*, More alludes to the following description Darwin provides of native Fuegians when he documents the second survey expedition of the H.M.S. Beagle from 1831-36 (Hughes 117). Almost immediately following this description, Darwin discusses the practice of cannibalism among the Fuegians.]

While going one day on shore near Wollaston Island, we pulled alongside a canoe with six Fuegians. These were the most abject and miserable creatures I anywhere beheld. On the east coast the natives, as we have seen, have guanaco cloaks, and on the west they possess seal-skins. Amongst these central tribes the men generally have an otter-skin, or some small scrap about as large as a pocket-handkerchief, which is barely sufficient to cover their backs as low down as their loins. It is laced across the breast by strings, and according as the wind blows, it is shifted from side to side. But these Fuegians in the canoe were quite naked, and even one full-grown woman was absolutely so. It was raining heavily, and the fresh water, together with the spray, trickled down her body. In another harbour not far distant, a woman, who was suckling a recently-born child, came one day alongside the vessel, and remained there out of mere curiosity, whilst the sleet fell and thawed on her naked bosom, and on the skin of her naked baby! These poor wretches were stunted in their growth, their hideous faces bedaubed with white paint, their skins filthy and greasy, their hair entangled, their voices discordant, and their gestures violent. Viewing such men, one can hardly make one's self believe that they are fellow-creatures, and inhabitants of the same world. It is a common subject of conjecture what pleasure in life some of the lower animals can enjoy: how much more reasonably the same question may be asked with respect to these barbarians! At night, five or six human beings, naked and scarcely protected from the wind and rain of this tempestuous climate, sleep on the wet ground coiled up like animals. Whenever it is low water, winter or summer, night or day, they must rise to pick shell-fish from the rocks; and the women either dive to collect sea-eggs, or sit patiently in their canoes, and with a baited hair-line without any hook, jerk out little fish. If a seal is killed, or the floating carcass of a putrid whale is discovered, it is a feast; and such miserable food is assisted by a few tasteless berries and fungi.

[...]

The different tribes when at war are cannibals. From the concurrent, but quite independent evidence of the boy taken by Mr. Low, and of Jemmy Button,[1] it is certainly true, that when pressed in winter by hunger, they kill and devour their old women before they kill their dogs: the boy, being asked by Mr. Low why they did this, answered, "Doggies catch otters, old women no." This boy described the manner in which they are killed by being held over smoke and thus choked; he imitated their screams as a joke, and described the parts of their bodies which are considered best to eat. Horrid as such a death by the hands of their friends and relatives must be, the fears of the old women, when hunger begins to press, are more painful to think of; we are told that they then often run away into the mountains, but that they are pursued by the men and brought back to the slaughter-house at their own firesides!

1 Jemmy Button is one of four Fuegians who returned to England with Robert Fitzroy during the 1830 voyage of H.M.S. *Beagle*. Button and two surviving companions returned to Tierra del Fuego with Darwin in 1832.

Appendix D: Historical Mythology: Caves and Troglodytes

1. From Plato, *The Republic of Plato* (c. 380 BCE): The Allegory of the Cave

[In Book 7 of Plato's *The Republic* (c. 380 BCE), Socrates introduces Glaucon to the allegory of the cave, using the cave as a metaphor for "the region which the eye reveals." Plato imagines prisoners in a cave, who mistake the shadows cast on the wall of the cave as reality; these prisoners stand up and go outside into daylight, a process akin to the philosophical recognition that eternal forms constitute the real. Key to De Mille's use of the Troglodyte Kosekin is Plato's ironic inversion of light and dark, blindness and seeing: that is, sight comes to be understood as a type of blindness. De Mille would have read *The Republic* in Greek, but here is a translation by John Llewelyn Davies and David James Vaughan (London: Macmillan and Co., 1912).]

Imagine a number of men living in an underground cavernous chamber, with an entrance open to the light, extending along the entire length of the cavern, in which they have been confined, from their childhood, with their legs and necks so shackled, that they are obliged to sit still and look straight forwards, because their chains render it impossible for them to turn their heads round: and imagine a bright fire burning some way off, above and behind them, and an elevated roadway passing between the fire and the prisoners, with a low wall built along it, like the screens which conjurors put up in front of their audience, and above which they exhibit their wonders.

I have it, he replied.

Also figure to yourself a number of persons walking behind this wall, and carrying with them statues of men, and images of other animals, wrought in wood and stone and all kinds of materials, together with various other articles, which overtop the wall; and, as you might expect, let some of the passers-by be talking, and others silent.

You are describing a strange scene, and strange prisoners.

They resemble us, I replied. For let me ask you, in the first place, whether persons so confined could have seen anything of themselves or of each other, beyond the shadows thrown by the fire upon the part of the cavern facing them?

Certainly not, if you suppose them to have been compelled all their lifetime to keep their heads unmoved.

And is not their knowledge of the things carried past them equally limited?

Unquestionably it is.

And if they were able to converse with one another, do you not think that they would be in the habit of giving names to the objects which they saw before them?

Doubtless they would.

Again: if their prison-house returned an echo from that part facing them, whenever one of the passers-by opened his lips, to what, let me ask you, could they refer the voice, if not to the shadow which was passing?

Unquestionably they would refer it to that.

Then surely such persons would hold the shadows of those manufactured articles to be the only realities.

Without a doubt they would.

Now consider what would happen if the course of nature brought them a release from their fetters, and a remedy for their foolishness, in the following manner. Let us suppose that one of them has been released, and compelled suddenly to stand up, and turn his neck round and walk with open eyes towards the light; and let us suppose that he goes through all these actions with pain, and that the dazzling splendour renders him incapable of discerning those objects of which he used formerly to see the shadows. What answer should you expect him to make, if some one were to tell him that in those days he was watching foolish phantoms, but that now he is somewhat nearer to reality, and is turned towards things more real, and sees more correctly; above all, if he were to point out to him the several objects that are passing by, and question him, and compel him to answer what they are? Should you not expect him to be puzzled, and to regard his old visions as truer than the objects now forced upon his notice?

Yes, much truer.

And if he were further compelled to gaze at the light itself, would not his eyes, think you, be distressed, and would he not shrink and turn away to the things which he could see distinctly, and consider them to be really clearer than the things pointed out to him?

Just so.

And if some one were to drag him violently up the rough and steep ascent from the cavern, and refuse to let him go till he had drawn him out into the light of the sun, would he not, think you, be vexed and indignant at such treatment, and on reaching the light, would he not find his eyes so dazzled by the glare as to be incapable of making out so much as one of the objects that are now called true?

Yes, he would find it so at first.

Hence, I suppose, habit will be necessary to enable him to perceive objects in that upper world. At first he will be most successful in distinguishing shadows; then he will discern the reflections of men and other things in water, and afterwards the realities; and after this he will raise his eyes to encounter the light of the moon and stars, finding it less difficult to study the heavenly bodies and the heaven itself by night, than the sun and the sun's light by-day.

Doubtless.

Last of all, I imagine, he will be able to observe and contemplate the nature of the sun, not as it appears in water or on alien ground, but as it is in itself in its own territory.

Of course.

His next step will be to draw the conclusion, that the sun is the author of the seasons and the years, and the guardian of all things in the visible world, and in a manner the cause of all those things which he and his companions used to see.

Obviously, this will be his next step.

What then? When he recalls to mind his first habitation, and the wisdom of the place, and his old fellow-prisoners, do you not think he will congratulate himself on the change, and pity them?

Assuredly he will.

And if it was their practice in those days to receive honour and commendations one from another, and to give prizes to him who had the keenest eye for a passing object, and who remembered best all that used to precede and follow and accompany it, and from these data divined most ably what was going to come next, do you fancy that he will covet these prizes, and envy those who receive honour and exercise authority among them? Do you not rather imagine that he will feel what Homer describes, and wish extremely "To drudge on the lands of a master, / Under a portionless wight," and be ready to go through anything, rather than entertain those opinions, and live in that fashion?

For my own part, he replied, I am quite of that opinion. I believe he would consent to go through anything rather than live in that way.

And now consider what would happen if such a man were to descend again and seat himself on his old seat? Coming so suddenly out of the sun, would he not find his eyes blinded with the gloom of the place?

Certainly, he would.

And if he were forced to deliver his opinion again, touching the shadows aforesaid, and to enter the lists against those who had always been prisoners, while his sight continued dim, and his eyes unsteady,—and if this process of initiation lasted a considerable time,—would he not be made a laughingstock, and would it not be said of him, that he had gone up only to come back again with his eyesight destroyed, and that it was not worth while even to attempt the ascent? And if any one endeavoured to set them free and carry them to the light, would they not go so far as to put him to death, if they could only manage to get him into their power?

Yes, that they would.

2. From *Penny Cyclopaedia of the Society for the Diffusion of Useful Knowledge*, Volume 25 (1843): Troglodytae

[Derived from the Greek Τρωγλοδύτης, to get into or dwell in a hole or cave, the word Troglodyte has a long history of representing a specific type of culture, whether it be African cultures in the age of Herodotus or, as this Victorian era encyclopedia article suggests, "people of the lowest stage of civilization." This entry in the 1843 *Penny Cyclopaedia* is representative, similar to other entries found in the likes of John Kitto's *Pictorial Bible* (1855) and *The Encyclopaedia Dictionary* edited by Robert Hunter (1888).]

TROGLODYTÆ

Under the term *Troglodytæ* the antients[1] appear to have comprised more than one race of men. The principal race, that referred to by Pliny (*Nat. Hist.*, v.8)[2] as excavating caves for habitations, feeding on serpents, and expressing their ideas by inarticulate sounds, 'stridor, non vox,'[3] is placed among the Æthiopians.[4] Again, in the twenty-ninth chapter of the sixth book, treating of the nations near the Red Sea, we find *Troglodytici* and the *Æthiopici.* The annotator, in the variorum Pliny (Lugd. Batav., Rotterdami, 1669, 8vo.) states in a note to the chapter last quoted, that a nation of Abyssinians near the Red Sea then went by the name *Troglodytæ*, and that the kingdom was called *Barnagas* by the natives.

These African Troglodytæ, according to Aristotle[5] and other antient writers who have treated on the subject, lived in caves, and buried their dead in a rather singular manner. They tied the corpse's neck and heels together, hung it up, pelted it with stones amid shouts of laughter, and, finally, after having covered it with a heap of stones and placed a horn upon the heap, departed. They made wars for food, and strangled weak

1 Ancients.

2 The Roman natural philosopher Gaius Plinius Secundus (23-79 CE), or Pliny the Elder, wrote the encyclopedic work *Naturalis Historia* ("Natural History").

3 *Stridor* is Latin for "hissing, buzzing, rattling, whistling, making a shrill sound." *Non vox* is Latin for "no voice."

4 People of Ethiopia, located in northeast Africa, in the Horn of Africa.

5 Greek philosopher who lived from 384-22 BCE.

and worn out individuals of their own nation with an ox's tail. This mode of disposing of such members of the community was considered a benefit, and the sick were treated in the same manner; for they held it to be the greatest evils that he who could no longer do anything worthy of life should continue to love it. They hissed rather than spoke, and lived on the flesh of serpents, some of which were found in their country twenty cubits[1] in length, but were so swift that they were able to run down the wild beasts which they hunted. In their territory some placed the Fountain of the Sun,[2] which was tepid in the morning, cold at noon, became warm in the evening, and at midnight poured forth streams of the hottest water.

A general description of the mode of living and of the habitations of the Troglodytæ on the Arabian Gulf (the Red Sea) is given in Strabo[3] (xvi., p.775, &c.). Their principal occupation was the breeding of cattle, and the highest power was in the hands of a number of chiefs. The men had wives and children in common, with the exception of the chiefs, who had wives belonging to them exclusively. They lived principally upon animal food and no part of an animal, not even the bones and skin, were despised as food. They were either naked or were only covered with the skins of animals, and the women tattooed their bodies, and wore necklaces of shells. These general features, and still more the detailed account of their life in Strabo, show that the Troglodytæ were people of the lowest stage of civilization.[4]

Aristotle makes the *Troglodytæ* pygmies,[5] and places them in the marshes whence the Nile flowed, in which locality they with their little horses made war against the cranes.

Cluverius[6] states that the Arabian Troglodytæ possessed the whole left side of the Arabian Gulf, whence the region itself was called *Troglo-*

---

6 An ancient unit of length measurement, originally equal to the length of the forearm from the tip of the middle finger to the elbow.

7 In Book 4 of *The Histories* (c. 430 BCE), the Greek Herodotus locates the Fountain of the Sun in Libya. He describes a spring that rises from the salt, warm in the morning, cold at noon, warmer through the afternoon, and "at midnight it boils furiously."

3 Greek philosopher, geographer, and historian who lived from 63 BCE to 24 CE.

4 Compare this with More's comment in Chapter 4: "These people were like human beings. The vilest and lowest savages that I had ever seen were not so odious as these."

5 A term for an ethnic group of short average height. See Appendix D3 in this regard.

6 The German geographer and historian Philipp Clüver (1580-1622) first published his *Introduction to Universal Geography* (*Introductio in Universam Geographiam*) in 1624.

dytica. In the fourth section of the fifth chapter of the sixth book, in which he treats of the 'Deserts of Libya, the Troglodytæ and Garamantes,'[1] he places the *Troglodytæ* beyond the Libyan Deserts, in the locality called, when he wrote, the Desert Berdoa; and he says that the Black Mountain (*Mons Ater*, so called from its sun-burnt appearance)[2] protected the *Troglodytæ* from the south wind; and that beyond them lay the Garamantes, called, when he wrote, the kingdom of 'Borno.' [BORNOU?][3]

The accounts of the almost mere animal life of the 'Boshiesmen,'[4] in South Africa, by Thunberg[5] and others, correspond in some particulars with those related of the *Troglodytæ*.

But there was also in Mœsia[6] a nation called *Troglodytæ*. Cluverius describes the *Peucestæ* and the *Troglodytæ* as inhabiting the lower part of Mœsia. (*Introd. Geog.*, iv. 16 and 17.) *Troglodytæ* are mentioned in Mauritania (Strab., xvii., p. 828); and on the northern side of the Caucasus. This tribe was well acquainted with the cultivation of corn. (Strab., xi., p. 506.)

The earliest extant account of *Troglodytæ* is by Agatharchides of Cnidos.[7] (Photius, *Biblietheca*, c. 250.)

3. From Thomas Hodgkin, "On the Ancient Inhabitants of the Canary Islands" (1848)

[These excerpts are taken from a paper read before the Ethnological Society of London on 21 May 1845 and published as an article in the *Journal of the Ethnological Society of London* (vol. 1, 1848): 167-81. Hodgkin argues that his inspection of the Guanchee mummies found on the Canary Islands indicates that the ancient inhabitants were "a diminutive people," and he associates them with the legendary Troglodytes of northeast Africa. Hodgkin's paper may help explain why De Mille's novel begins in sight of Mount Tenerife on the Canary Islands.]

It is many years since the inspection of Guanchee mummies induced me to believe that the ancient inhabitants of the Canary Islands were a

---

1 A Saharan people who founded a kingdom in Libya.

2 The Gebel as-Soda (Black Mountain or Mons Ater in antiquity) is a chain of mountains between the oases of Djofra and Sebha in the Libyan Desert.

3 Bornu, a Kanuri kingdom south and west of Lake Chad, was a dominant power in the central Sudan from the fourteenth to the nineteenth centuries CE. Variant spellings include Borno and Bornou.

4 The Bushmen are an indigenous people of southern Africa.

5 The Swedish naturalist, Carl Peter Thunberg (1743-1828).

6 An ancient region located in the Balkans, Moesia was the name of a Roman province.

7 See the Introduction (pp. 33-34) for information on Agatharcides of Cnidos.

diminutive people. It was, however, only a passing observation, which led to no particular inquiry at the time. It happened, however, that at the same period I was examining many of the animal productions of Northern and Southern Africa, in conjunction with my friend Dr. Knox of Edinburgh; and we were both of us impressed with the many points of resemblance between these productions in the remote parts of the Continent. The notorious fact of the existence of a once numerous, though now greatly reduced, race of diminutive human beings in the south of Africa—the Hottentots and the Bushmen—seemed to find their counterpart in the obscure, and, undoubtedly, in part fabulous, relations of Troglodytes, formerly supposed to exist towards the north-east of the Continent. I could not avoid associating these two points with the former existence of a small race in the islands of the western coast of the same Continent. I merely noticed the coincidence, without attempting to pursue any inquiry into the subject, or even supposing that materials could be collected subservient to the investigation.

[...]

The difficulty of the inquiry into the origin of the ancient inhabitants of the Canary Islands, is increased by the circumstance, that the African relations with the Canary Islands, in remote ages, would, in all probability, have been with the Northern tribes, of which, unhappily, too little is known. From the statues and drawings made by the ancient Egyptians, and which have been preserved to the present time, it would appear that there existed in the north of Africa a large proportion of individuals possessing the intermediate character between the Caucasian variety and that of the Negroes. The colour, which is not to be strictly relied upon, is a sort of swarthy red; the lips are thick; the eyes are full, and the nose somewhat flattened; yet these features, as contrasted with those of the Negro, are far more delicate and regular: the hair is not frizzled; and, in males, the chin is furnished with a beard of some length. Major Denham has described a people, still to be found in the northern parts of Africa, distinguished alike from the Caucasian Arabs who live near them, and from the numerous Negro tribes with which they are brought into contact by the slave-dealers, who collect their captives from various parts of the Continent. Their complexion is described by the Major as reddish, and his pen and his pencil alike suggest the resemblance between this people and the ancient race before alluded to.

[...]

It is well known, that the race which formerly inhabited the Island of Teneriffe resembled the ancient Egyptians in this particular, that they carefully preserved the bodies of their dead, having recourse to processes by which decomposition was retarded. There was also some resemblance in the destination of the bodies so prepared, as they were placed in regular order, in the erect posture, in dark and secluded chambers expressly devoted to this purpose, although the Egyptians reared those gigantic structures, to which Martial has applied the term of *barbara miracula*, and thus obtained sepulchral chambers which were altogether artificial; whereas the Guanchees took advantage of the natural caverns which their volcanic region offered them in ample numbers. The cave-temples and tombs of Upper Egypt sufficiently evince that even in this particular a resemblance existed.

The inspection of Guanchee mummies brought from the caves of Teneriffe to enrich anatomical collections, contrasting, by their small dimensions, with those of Egypt, had strongly impressed me with the idea that the extinct inhabitants of the Canaries must have been a people of rather diminutive stature, resembling, in this respect, the Hottentots of Southern Africa, and some of the past, if not of the present, inhabitants of the eastern part of the same continent.

Appendix E: Scientific Romance and Lost Worlds

[Readers of *A Strange Manuscript* have often traced a lineage of influence that includes Edgar Allan Poe's *The Narrative of Arthur Gordon Pym* (1838) and Samuel Taylor Coleridge's "The Rime of the Ancient Mariner" (1798). In the novel's frame narrative, Melick suggests that More should have taken Jonathan Swift's *Gulliver's Travels* (1726) and Daniel Defoe's *Robinson Crusoe* (1719) as his models, and he goes on to call More "a gross plagiarist." Moreover, as the reviews in Appendix F illustrate, when *A Strange Manuscript* was first published in 1888, readers immediately compared it to Samuel Butler's *Erewhon* (1872) and Rider Haggard's *King Solomon's Mines* (1885) and *She* (1886-87). This appendix selects from some of these antecedents and contemporaries.]

1. From John Cleves Symmes Jr., *Symzonia; Voyage of Discovery* (1820)

[Published in 1820 under the pseudonym Captain Adam Seaborn, *Symzonia* is a fictional narrative based on John Cleves Symmes Jr.'s theory, published as a pamphlet in 1818, that the Earth is hollow with solid concentric spheres accessible via openings at the poles. *Symzonia* documents the discovery of the utopian Symzonians, a subterranean race. The novel was part of Poe's inspiration for *The Narrative of Arthur Gordon Pym* and is directly mentioned by More, along with similar theories and works of fiction, in Chapters 3 and 5. The following excerpt is taken from Chapter 5 when Seaborn sails into the opening at the South Pole. The opening encompasses the pole and thus it is too large to see directly except by way of where the sun sets. Inversion is marked geographically both in terms of inside-outside and north-south.]

I kept near Cape Worldsend,[1] taking its bearings in a variety of positions, for the ostensible purpose of ascertaining its exact position, until four o'clock, when the larboard watch went below, I saw that both Albicore and Slim turned in to get some sleep, and immediately ordered Mackerel to keep the vessel on a course corresponding to south, and to press with both steam and canvass to the utmost. The wind was about N.W., fresh and very steady, which served as a guide, the helmsman being directed to keep the wind four points on the quarter. We ran at the rate of 16 knots. I gave strict orders that Albicore and Slim should not

1 A fictional land mass discovered by Seaborn.

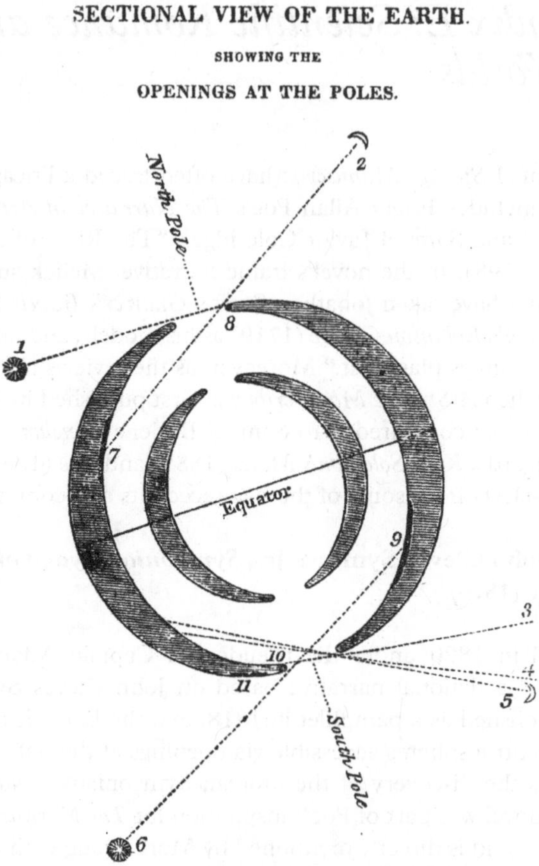

Figure 19: Frontispiece from Symzonia: Sectional View of a Hollow Earth (Symmes iv-v).

1. Rays of the sun when in the equator, refracted 3 degrees.
2. Moon's rays in 28° north declination.
3. Sun's rays in 9° south declination.
4. Sun's rays in 23° south declination.
5. Moon's rays in 28° south declination.
6. Sun's rays in 23° 27′ south declination, refracted 3°.
7. Supposed place of Belzubia.[1]
8. Place of exile.
9. Symzonia.[2]
10. Token Island.
11. Seaborn's Land.

---

1 Another continent inside the earth inhabited by people who historically oppressed the egalitarian Symzonians.

2 Utopian civilization inside the earth.

be disturbed at the usual hour of calling the dog watch; and when they came on deck at 10 P.M. there was no land in sight. The sun to their astonishment was just setting in the bosom of the ocean: they stared at one another, and looked at me, but said nothing. They were perfectly bewildered; they knew not which way was north, south, east or west. Had they now undertaken to direct the course of the vessel, they would have been more likely to run from the land than towards it. Mackerel was delighted to see the sun set once more; it seemed like old times; and the weather had been for some days so hot that a little night was very desirable.

[...]

The re-appearance of the stars, and the refreshing coolness of the night air delighted my people. At daylight we made sail, and set the paddles in motion. At noon we had the sun nearly overhead, and the declination being 20° 5′ S. Slim was positive that we were in latitude 28° S. and wondered why the compass would not traverse.[1] The next day we had a vertical sun, as I had predicted, and the weather as warm as I had ever known it at sea, with a fine breeze. No one knew which way we were steering but myself; and Slim's opinion confidently expressed that we were near the equator, and must soon make the continent of Asia, Africa, America, or the Asiatic islands, served to quiet the apprehensions of the men for their own safety, and at the same time to awaken their solicitude for the situation of Mr. Boneto's party, whom they said I had barbarously left to perish by the frosts of a polar winter, on Seaborn's Land.

The next day we observed the sun to the south of us, and nearly over head, and the compass began to traverse imperfectly. We had a regular recurrence of day and night, though the latter was very short, which I knew was occasioned by the rays of the sun being obstructed by the rim of the earth,[2] when the external side of the part we were on turned towards the sun. The nights were not dark, when no clouds intervened to obstruct the rays of the sun, reflected from the opposite rim, and from a large luminous body northward, in the internal heavens, which reflected the sun as our moon does, and which I judged to be the second concentric sphere, according to Capt. Symmes.[3] This gave us very pleasant nights, but not quite clear enough to render sailing through untried seas entirely safe.

1 That is, it is an optical illusion produced by their location inside the Earth.

2 They can see the hole they came through to gain access to the interior of the Earth.

3 See the Sectional View of the Earth above.

We continued running due north, *internal* three days, when the compass became pretty regular; but instead of the N. and S. points corresponding to the N. and S. points on the external world, as Capt. Symmes supposed it would do, the needle turned fairly end for end; the south end pointing directly into the globe towards the north pole, with some variation from the true north.

2. From Edgar Allan Poe, "The Narrative of Arthur Gordon Pym" in *The Works of the Late Edgar Allan Poe* (1859)

[If "MS. Found in a Bottle" (1833) has the most obvious resemblance to *A Strange Manuscript, The Narrative of Arthur Gordon Pym* (1838) has the most profound influence. As Wayne Kime observes in his study of the American antecedents of the novel, "De Mille has modeled his account (the early part of the novel) rather openly upon Pym" (283).]

a. Preface

[Like De Mille, Poe deliberately provokes a reader to question the believability of the narrative.]

Upon my[1] return to the United States a few months ago, after the extraordinary series of adventure in the South Seas and elsewhere, of which an account is given in the following pages, accident threw me into the society of several gentlemen in Richmond, Va., who felt deep interest in all matters relating to the regions I had visited, and who were constantly urging it upon me, as a duty, to give my narrative to the public. I had several reasons, however, for declining to do so, some of which were of a nature altogether private, and concern no person but myself, others not so much so. One consideration which deterred me was, that, having kept no journal during a greater portion of the time in which I was absent, I feared I should not be able to write, from mere memory, a statement so minute and connected as to have the *appearance* of that truth it would really possess, barring only the natural and unavoidable exaggeration to which all of us are prone when detailing events which have had powerful influence in exciting the imaginative faculties. Another reason was, that the incidents to be narrated were of a nature so positively marvellous, that, unsupported as my assertions must necessarily be (except by the evidence of a single individual, and he a half-breed Indian), I could only hope for belief among my family, and those of my friends who have had reason, through life, to put faith in my veracity—the probability being that the public at large would

1 Arthur Gordon Pym.

regard what I should put forth as merely an impudent and ingenious fiction. A distrust in my own abilities as a writer was, nevertheless, one of the principal causes which prevented me from complying with the suggestion of my advisers.

b. A History of Antarctic Exploration: Pym, Chapter 16

[As they prepare to sail south in an attempt to reach the pole, Pym reviews the history of exploratory attempts in the Antarctic, from James Cook (1728-79) to James Weddell (1787-1834). Poe is writing in the late 1830s, before the Wilkes and Ross expeditions that dominate De Mille's version of this exploration history in Chapters 3 and 7. His account of Weddell and Morrell below emphasizes the basis for a warm southern ocean found in both Poe and De Mille.]

In 1822, Captain James Weddell, of the British navy, with two very small vessels, penetrated farther to the south than any previous navigator, and this, too, without encountering extraordinary difficulties. He states that although he was frequently hemmed in by ice before reaching the seventy-second parallel, yet, upon attaining it, not a particle was to be discovered, and that, upon arriving at the latitude of 74 degrees 15′, no fields, and only three islands of ice were visible. It is somewhat remarkable that, although vast flocks of birds were seen, and other usual indications of land, and although, south of the Shetlands, unknown coasts were observed from the masthead tending southwardly, Weddell discourages the idea of land existing in the polar regions of the south.

On the 11th of January, 1823, Captain Benjamin Morrell, of the American schooner Wasp, sailed from Kerguelen's Land with a view of penetrating as far south as possible. On the first of February he found himself in latitude 64 degrees 52′ S., longitude 118 degrees 27′ E. The following passage is extracted from his journal of that date. "The wind soon freshened to an eleven-knot breeze, and we embraced this opportunity of making to the west; being however convinced that the farther we went south beyond latitude sixty-four degrees, the less ice was to be apprehended, we steered a little to the southward, until we crossed the Antarctic circle, and were in latitude 69 degrees 15′ E. In this latitude there was no field ice, and very few ice islands in sight.

3. From Edward Bulwer Lytton, *The Coming Race: or The New Utopia* (1871)

[Edward Bulwer Lytton's novel *The Coming Race*, published anonymously in 1871, tells the story of the discovery of a lost subterranean race called the Vril-ya. The Vril-ya, who are physically large and perfect, have evolved a nerve in their hands that allows them to manipulate vril, a powerful energy that they use to manipulate fantastic technologies, to destroy their enemies, and to heal themselves. There are a number of similarities between *A Strange Manuscript* and *The Coming Race*: the Vril-ya, who live underground and are a lost race associated with an Indo-European tribe, are based on European notions of the Orient; there is considerable attention to their language and its resemblance to Aryan or Indo-European languages; and there are several inversions of European norms, especially gender.]

a. Orientalism: The Coming Race, Chapter 4

[The Kosekin and Vril-ya are both subterranean races associated with Egypt. In this first excerpt, taken from Chapter 4, the explicit Orientalist construction of the Vril-ya is notable because it projects a super-human or post-human race (perhaps species), thus reflecting considerable anxiety with the prospect of non-European cultures making technological advances.]

I now came in full sight of the building. Yes, it had been made by hands, and hollowed partly out of a great rock. I should have supposed it at the first glance to have been of the earliest form of Egyptian architecture. It was fronted by huge columns, tapering upward from massive plinths, and with capitals that, as I came nearer, I perceived to be more ornamental and more fantastically graceful than Egyptian architecture allows. As the Corinthian capital mimics the leaf of the acanthus, so the capitals of these columns imitated the foliage of the vegetation neighbouring them, some aloe-like, some fern-like. And now there came out of this building a form—human—was it human? It stood on the broad way and looked around, beheld me and approached. It came within a few yards of me, and at the sight and presence of it an indescribable awe and tremor seized me, rooting my feet to the ground. It reminded me of symbolical images of Genius or Demon that are seen on Etruscan vases or limned on the walls of Eastern sepulchres—images that borrow the outlines of man, and are yet of another race. It was tall, not gigantic, but tall as the tallest man below the height of giants.

Its chief covering seemed to me to be composed of large wings folded over its breast and reaching to its knees; the rest of its attire was composed of an under tunic and leggings of some thin fibrous material. It wore on its head a kind of tiara that shone with jewels, and carried in its right hand a slender staff of bright metal like polished steel. But the face! it was that which inspired my awe and my terror. It was the face of man, but yet of a type of man distinct from our known extant races. The nearest approach to it in outline and expression is the face of the sculptured sphinx—so regular in its calm, intellectual, mysterious beauty. Its colour was peculiar, more like that of the red man than any other variety of our species, and yet different from it—a richer and a softer hue, with large black eyes, deep and brilliant, and brows arched as a semicircle. The face was beardless; but a nameless something in the aspect, tranquil though the expression, and beauteous though the features, roused that instinct of danger which the sight of a tiger or serpent arouses. I felt that this manlike image was endowed with forces inimical to man. As it drew near, a cold shudder came over me. I fell on my knees and covered my face with my hands.

b. Gender: The Coming Race, Chapter 26

[In this second excerpt, from Chapter 26 of *The Coming Race*, the issue of gender is considered. Like the Kosekin women, the Gy, women of the Vril-ya, are the dominant gender, notable especially because they take the initiative in courting. Unlike De Mille, the women have effaced their power historically by choosing to give up their wings once married. Gender in De Mille is striking because the inversions produced by the comparison of Kosekin and European values suggest that Kosekin women are closer to Europeans.]

I proceed to that very delicate question, urged of late as essential to the perfect happiness of our human species by the two most disturbing and potential influences on upper-ground society,—Womankind and Philosophy. I mean, the Rights of Women.

Now, it is allowed by jurisprudists that it is idle to talk of rights where there are not corresponding powers to enforce them; and above ground, for some reason or other, man, in his physical force, in the use of weapons offensive and defensive, when it come to positive personal contest, can, as a rule of general application, master women. But among this people there can be no doubt about the rights of women, because, as I have before said, the Gy, physically speaking, is bigger and stronger than the An; and her will being also more resolute than his, and will being essential to the direction of the vril force, she can bring to bear upon him, more potently than he on herself, the mystical agency which art can extract from the occult properties of nature. Therefore all that our female philosophers above ground contend for as to rights of women, is conceded as a matter of course in this happy commonwealth. Besides such physical powers, the Gy-ei have (at least in youth) a keen desire for accomplishments and learning which exceeds that of the male; and thus they are the scholars, the professors—the learned portion, in short, of the community.

Of course, in this state of society the female establishes, as I have shown, her most valued privilege, that of choosing and courting her wedding partner. Without that privilege she would despise all the others. Now, above ground, we should not unreasonably apprehend that a female, thus potent and thus privileged, when she had fairly hunted us down and married us, would be very imperious and tyrannical. Not so with the Gy-ei:[1] once married, the wings once suspended, and more amiable, complacent, docile mates, more sympathetic, more sinking their loftier capacities into the study of their husbands' comparatively frivolous tastes and whims, no poet could conceive in his visions of conjugal bliss. Lastly, among the more important characteristics of the Vril-ya, as distinguished from our mankind—lastly, and most important on the bearings of their life and the peace of their commonwealths, is their universal agreement in the existence of a merciful beneficent Deity, and of a future world to the duration of which a century or two are moments too brief to waste upon thoughts of fame and power and avarice; while with that agreement is combined another—viz., since they can know nothing as to the nature of that Deity beyond the fact of His supreme goodness, nor of that future world beyond the fact of its felicitous existence, so their reason forbids all angry disputes on insoluble questions. Thus they secure for that state in the bowels of the earth what no community ever secured under the light of the stars—all the blessings and consolations of a religion without any of the evils and calamities which are engendered by strife between one religion and another.

4. From Jules Verne, *A Journey into the Interior of the Earth* (1877)

[Influenced in part by the geological findings of Charles Lyell and others, Jules Verne's *Voyage au Centre de la Terre* (1864) is usually translated *Journey to the Centre of the Earth*. The novel follows a company of explorers who descend via an Icelandic volcano into the centre of the Earth, a journey that is also a trip back in geological time. Verne is one of the first novelists to recast the monstrous in terms of evolutionary plausibility—dinosaurs that have somehow survived because of their evolutionary niche. In this excerpt from the early English translation, *A Journey into the Interior of the Earth*, the narrator Axel, his uncle, professor Liedenbrock, and their guide Hans encounter a number of dinosaurs, including Ichthyosaurus and the Plesiosaurus.]

---

1 Plural.

TUESDAY, AUGUST 18. Evening came, or rather the time came when sleep weighs down the weary eyelids, for there is no night here, and the ceaseless light wearies the eyes with its persistency just as if we were sailing under an arctic sun. Hans was at the helm. During his watch I slept.

Two hours afterwards a terrible shock awoke me. The raft was heaved up on a watery mountain and pitched down again, at a distance of twenty fathoms.

"What is the matter?" shouted my uncle. "Have we struck land?"

Hans pointed with his finger at a dark mass six hundred yards away, rising and falling alternately with heavy plunges. I looked and cried:

"It is an enormous porpoise."

"Yes," replied my uncle, "and there is a sea lizard of vast size."

"And farther on a monstrous crocodile. Look at its vast jaws and its rows of teeth! It is diving down!"

"There's a whale, a whale!" cried the Professor. "I can see its great fins. See how he is throwing out air and water through his blowers."

And in fact two liquid columns were rising to a considerable height above the sea. We stood amazed, thunderstruck, at the presence of such a herd of marine monsters. They were of supernatural dimensions; the smallest of them would have crunched our raft, crew and all, at one snap of its huge jaws.

Hans wants to tack to get away from this dangerous neighbourhood; but he sees on the other hand enemies not less terrible; a tortoise forty feet long, and a serpent of thirty, lifting its fearful head and gleaming eyes above the flood.

Flight was out of the question now. The reptiles rose; they wheeled around our little raft with a rapidity greater than that of express trains. They described around us gradually narrowing circles. I took up my rifle. But what could a ball do against the scaly armour with which these enormous beasts were clad?

We stood dumb with fear. They approach us close: on one side the crocodile, on the other the serpent. The remainder of the sea monsters have disappeared. I prepare to fire. Hans stops me by a gesture. The two monsters pass within a hundred and fifty yards of the raft, and hurl themselves the one upon the other, with a fury which prevents them from seeing us.

At three hundred yards from us the battle was fought. We could distinctly observe the two monsters engaged in deadly conflict. But it now seems to me as if the other animals were taking part in the fray—the porpoise, the whale, the lizard, the tortoise. Every moment I seem to see one or other of them. I point them to the Icelander. He shakes his head negatively.

"Tva," says he.

"What two? Does he mean that there are only two animals?"

"He is right," said my uncle, whose glass has never left his eye.

"Surely you must be mistaken," I cried.

"No: the first of those monsters has a porpoise's snout, a lizard's head, a crocodile's teeth; and hence our mistake. It is the ichthyosaurus (the fish lizard), the most terrible of the ancient monsters of the deep."

"And the other?"

"The other is a plesiosaurus (almost lizard), a serpent, armoured with the carapace and the paddles of a turtle; he is the dreadful enemy of the other."

Hans had spoken truly. Two monsters only were creating all this commotion; and before my eyes are two reptiles of the primitive world. I can distinguish the eye of the ichthyosaurus glowing like a red-hot coal, and as large as a man's head. Nature has endowed it with an optical apparatus of extreme power, and capable of resisting the pressure of the great volume of water in the depths it inhabits. It has been appropriately called the saurian whale, for it has both the swiftness and the rapid movements of this monster of our own day. This one is not less than a hundred feet long, and I can judge of its size when it sweeps over the waters the vertical coils of its tail. Its jaw is enormous, and according to naturalists it is armed with no less than one hundred and eighty-two teeth.

The plesiosaurus, a serpent with a cylindrical body and a short tail, has four flappers or paddles to act like oars. Its body is entirely covered with thick armour of scales, and its neck, as flexible as a swan's, rises thirty feet above the waves.

Those huge creatures attacked each other with the greatest animosity. They heaved around them liquid mountains, which rolled even to our raft and rocked it perilously. Twenty times we were near capsizing. Hissings of prodigious force are heard. The two beasts are fast locked together; I cannot distinguish the one from the other. The probable rage of the conqueror inspires us with intense fear.

One hour, two hours, pass away. The struggle continues with unabated ferocity. The combatants alternately approach and recede from our raft. We remain motionless, ready to fire. Suddenly the ichthyosaurus and the plesiosaurus disappear below, leaving a whirlpool eddying in the water. Several minutes pass by while the fight goes on under water.

All at once an enormous head is darted up, the head of the plesiosaurus. The monster is wounded to death. I no longer see his scaly armour. Only his long neck shoots up, drops again, coils and uncoils, droops, lashes the waters like a gigantic whip, and writhes like a worm that you tread on. The water is splashed for a long way around. The spray almost blinds us. But soon the reptile's agony draws to an end; its movements become fainter, its contortions cease to be so violent, and the long serpentine form lies a lifeless log on the labouring deep.

As for the ichthyosaurus—has he returned to his submarine cavern? Or will he reappear on the surface of the sea?

5. From Samuel Butler, *Erewhon or Over the Range* (1880)

[Published anonymously in 1872, the satirical utopia *Erewhon* by Samuel Butler (1835-1902) tells the story of the discovery of a lost civilization that sees the world in strikingly different ways than Europeans. In the following excerpt, Higgs explains the Erewhonians' radically different notions of health and crime.]

This is what I gathered. That in that country if a man falls into ill health, or catches any disorder, or fails bodily in any way before he is seventy years old, he is tried before a jury of his countrymen, and if convicted is held up to public scorn and sentenced more or less severely as the case may be. There are subdivisions of illnesses into crimes and misdemeanours as with offences amongst ourselves—a man being punished very heavily for serious illness, while failure of eyes or hearing in one over sixty-five who has had good health hitherto is dealt with by fine only, or imprisonment in default of payment. But if a man forges a cheque, or sets his house on fire, or robs with violence from the person, or does any other such things as are criminal in our own country, he is either taken to a hospital and most carefully tended at the public expense, or if he is in good circumstances, he lets it be known to all his friends that he is suffering from a severe fit of immorality, just as we do when we are ill, and they come and visit him with great solicitude, and inquire with interest how it all came about, what symptoms first showed themselves, and so forth,—questions which he will answer with perfect unreserve; for bad conduct, though considered no less deplorable than illness with ourselves, and as unquestionably indicating something seriously wrong with the individual who misbehaves, is nevertheless held to be the result of either pre-natal or post-natal misfortune. I should add that under certain circumstances poverty and ill luck are also considered criminal.

6. From Jonathan Swift, *Travels into Several Remote Nations of the World, in Four Parts. By Lemuel Gulliver, First a Surgeon, and then a Captain of Several Ships*, Part II: A Voyage to Brobdingnag, Chapter 6 (1774)

[The Irish satirist Jonathan Swift (1667-1775) first published *Gulliver's Travels* in 1726. In each of Gulliver's adventures, he encounters a different imaginary society. Swift's satire works in part by subverting established social and political norms and practices. As Gulliver compares his experiences in Lilliput and Brobdingnag, for example, the opposed scales of diminutive and gigantic produce radical shifts in perspective and insight. In the following scene, the king of Brobdingnag draws conclusions that question an ideal assessment of European norms in a way that is similar to conversations Adam More has with the Kohen in *A Strange Manuscript*.]

He was perfectly astonished with the historical account I gave him of our affairs during the last century; protesting "it was only a heap of conspiracies, rebellions, murders, massacres, revolutions, banishments, the very worst effects that avarice, faction, hypocrisy, perfidiousness, cruelty, rage, madness, hatred, envy, lust, malice, and ambition, could produce."

His majesty, in another audience, was at the pains to recapitulate the sum of all I had spoken; compared the questions he made with the answers I had given; then taking me into his hands, and stroking me gently, delivered himself in these words, which I shall never forget, nor the manner he spoke them in: "My little friend Grildrig, you have made a most admirable panegyric upon your country; you have clearly proved, that ignorance, idleness, and vice, are the proper ingredients for qualifying a legislator; that laws are best explained, interpreted, and applied, by those whose interest and abilities lie in perverting, confounding, and eluding them. I observe among you some lines of an institution, which, in its original, might have been tolerable, but these half erased, and the rest wholly blurred and blotted by corruptions. It does not appear, from all you have said, how any one perfection is required toward the procurement of any one station among you; much less, that men are ennobled on account of their virtue; that priests are advanced for their piety or learning; soldiers, for their conduct or valour; judges, for their integrity; senators, for the love of their country; or counsellors for their wisdom. As for yourself," continued the king, "who have spent the greatest part of your life in travelling, I am well disposed to hope you may hitherto have escaped many vices of your country. But by what I have gathered from your own relation, and the answers I have with much pains wrung and extorted from you, I cannot but conclude the bulk of your natives to be the most pernicious race of little odious vermin that nature ever suffered to crawl upon the surface of the earth."

Appendix F: Reviews

[I have arranged these four reviews, all written in 1888, in chronological order. The novel was published anonymously because De Mille was not a US citizen and therefore the novel was more susceptible to piracy. But this secret was poorly kept: two of the reviews here identify De Mille or his earlier titles. Despite this, the two Canadian reviews, written later in the year, don't identify the author. The reviewers compare *A Strange Manuscript* to *King Solomon's Mines* (1885) and *She: A History of Adventure* (serialized in *The Graphic* in 1886-87) by Henry Rider Haggard (1856-1925) or to *Erewhon* (1872) by Samuel Butler (1835-1902). Such comparisons were a factor in the early assessment of the novel's merits.]

1. *New York Times*, 21 May 1888

It is now an open secret that this story, which has found its way to a handsome volume after its serial publication in *Harper's Weekly*, is the work of the late Prof. De Mille. The information is really needed to vindicate, not the literary honesty, but the literary originality, of the author. For if the author of "A Strange Manuscript" were living he would find it a quite hopeless task to persuade people that he had not read and imitated "She" and "King Solomon's Mines." No copyright can be made to cover the idea of appealing to a particular kind of interest, the interest of the purely marvellous. In fact it is as old as "The Arabian Nights," and older, and it is to his unquestioning confidence in it that Rider Haggard owes his enormous success. "She" is one of the luckiest books ever written, and its success shows what can be done by assuming that novel readers, instead of being students of scientific or aesthetic or psychological problems, are simply grown-up children. The assumption is completely justified, for every "thoughtful" reader also comprises a grown-up child, who delights in the "The Arabian Nights" and Defoe and Dumas and Jules Verne and Rider Haggard, and if a writer can attract all the grown-up children he is sure of the entire reading public. Though this is well known theoretically, few writers have the courage to act upon it practically in the thoroughgoing way that Rider Haggard pursues. He has written books which he doubtless thinks more of than he thinks of "King Solomon's Mines" or "She" or "Allan Quartermain," upon which he has spent more labor, and upon which he would rest his literary reputation with much more confidence. The public, however, declines to buy these works, except as it is lured by a hope of finding more outrageous wonders in them, and resents the absence from them of the incredible.

In his most successful books Haggard exceeds other producers of the same article, as we have said, by his implicit trust in the marvellous. No other modern writer of wonders has this in the same degree. All of them feel bound to make a pretense, at some information to convey. Even Jules Verne commonly has a scientific or pseudo-scientific thesis, of which the story is the illustration. The author of "A Strange Manuscript" is not quite free from the suspicion of allegorizing and of social satire. Where this is pervading and obtrusive, as in "Gulliver's Travels," the interest of the "story book" is correspondingly diminished. But in the present case this intention is not likely to be detected by the reader in quest of marvels, while the interest of the detecting it adds to the pleasure of the other kind of reader.

The first requirement of a wonder book is that the scene should be laid in some undiscovered country from whose bourne[1] no traveler has returned or is likely to return to contradict the story teller. The author of "A Strange Manuscript" has judiciously established his hero within the Antarctic circle, to which Poe referred in one of the most grisly of his tales. This is more eligible than the heart of Africa, which Mr Haggard prefers, and which is very rapidly losing the mystery that makes it suitable for his purpose, though on the other hand the author's own African knowledge enables him to give the air of reality to the doings of his explorers until they disappear from the confines of civilization and begin their astonishing experiences. One of the difficulties of wonder stories is to connect their heroes with ordinary life so as to make the incredibilities more plausible. Prof. De Mille manages this very cleverly by inventing a party of yachtsmen, who in the first place find the copper cylinder a derelict in mid-ocean, and who afterward act as an expository chorus to smooth away the reader's difficulties. To get the hero into his environment is another test of ingenuity, for unlike Haggard and Jules Verne, whose heroes go in parties, the subject of these adventures is a solitary castaway. The story of the journey from a boat "adrift in the Antarctic Ocean" to the country of the Kosekin has a weirdness that is much more suggestive of Poe or of "the Ancient Mariner" than of the prosaic Haggard.

The country of the Kosekin, into which the adventurer is shot through a tunnel under the mountains, is a country in which he lives fully up to the privileges of the only explorer. Prof. De Mille invents a circumpolar climate, in which the six months of Antarctic twilight become a blaze of sunlight, under which flourish a tropical fauna and flora, though by no means the fauna and flora known to our tropics. He revives in this land strange antediluvian[2] monsters—gorgons, hydras,

1 A boundary; a goal or destination.

2 Before the deluge or flood.

and chimeras dire—mainly habitants of the sea and sky. The common animal of draught is a bird, the opkuk, which trots as fast as a horse and is tireless, while for the saddle the Kosekin employ another bird, or rather bat, an interesting beast, that carries as many people as his back will hold, that measures 50 feet from tip to tip of his wings, and that makes his way through the air at an inconceivable speed. This attractive creature, as the chorus explains, is the pterodactyl, though the Kosekin call him the athaleb. With a reckless prodigality of invention, the author introduces a third bird of burden, the opmahara, which, according to the chorus,[1] is our respected fossil friend, Dinornis gigantean. One of the noblest lies in the volume is the account of a ride on a runaway opmahara, that had been scared by the discharge of the adventurer's rifle, which, with a sufficient quantity of ammunition, he continued to retain throughout his wanderings. The marine monsters are on an equally liberal scale, and the annual hunt of the Kosekin after beasts identified as the plesiosaurus and the megalosaurus and the iguanodon will give even the most hardened English pursuers of big game a new notion of the capabilities of "sport."

The Antarctic human being is quite as queer as his environment. Living six months in the blaze of day and six in darkness has a very marked effect upon his mind and morals, and circumpolar society is turned quite topsy-turvy. Light is painful and distressing to the Kosekin, and they rejoice in darkness. By an easy metaphor they rejoice also in death rather than life, and seek for poverty and wretchedness of all kinds. The rich are held in contempt, and the Chief Pauper, who is also the public executioner, is the most honoured man in the country, attaining the summit of human happiness and crowning his career by going to a barren island to die of starvation. It is in his description of the manners and customs induced by these ideals that the reader suspects the author of a satirical intention. He depicts a race of gentle, unselfish, and courteous murderers, and cannibals, who indeed can scarcely be called unselfish, since their selfishness is our unselfishness. Unrequited love is a great object of desire among the Kosekin and accordingly, in order to carry on the love story which is indispensable to the wonder book as understood by Haggard and De Mille, it is necessary to introduce a female foreigner also who takes the view of the tender passion that is entertained in extra-polar regions. There are some agnostics[2] among the Kosekin who have philosophic doubts whether darkness and death and misery are the unmixed blessings they are held to be, and one of these falls in love with the stranger, and brings on a complication which increases the resemblance of the story to "She." The readers for whom

1 That is, the four men on the yacht *The Falcon*.

2 Namely Layelah and her father, the Kohen Gadol.

the book is mainly meant will take little interest in tracing the satire or the philosophy; but nothing but a recent surfeit of Haggard can dull their interest in the marvels. Mr. Gaul's illustrations are admirably appropriate and admirably adapted to stimulate the curiosity which the text assuages.

2. *Brooklyn Daily Eagle*, 3 June 1888

The authorship of this somewhat belated story is ascribed here to the writer of the "Cryptogram," the "Dodge Club Papers," etc, its general and confident assertion not having been denied. The fact, if it is a fact, must have a somewhat curious interest for Mr. Rider Haggard and his fellow thaumaturgical[1] writers, who, had the story been published when written, might have found themselves with less of a vocation in the same line. And yet the public taste created by these writers has also curiously encouraged the publication of a posthumous work which does not seem to have had the courage of conviction to bring it to the birth of publicity during its author's life. It seems to have been, either carefully or carelessly, tucked away in a pigeon hole of the Messrs. Harpers' manuscript room for years, and now that novel readers still demand wonder tales it is brought forth, the dust is blown from its leaves and it is printed. Whether the fame of the author has been enhanced thereby may be questioned. At any rate it is fortunate for the book and the author's fame that "priority of invention" can be claimed, that the work was written before Haggard blossomed out in the field of literature with "She" and "Allan Quartermain," and so cannot be charged with plagiarism, in idea, if not in plot and incident. And yet what the French call the motive of the book is entirely different from anything that Haggard, at least, ever wrote. Haggard claims simply to construct a wonder story, with stirring adventure, narrated, it is true, with a sort of Crusoe good faith and verisimilitude, but in which the incidents and whole environment are unique. In Dr. De Mille's present book there is plenty of thrilling adventure, but it is not apparently its main purpose. A vein of speculative philosophy runs through it, scarcely satirical, and yet presenting a sharp contrast to all our conceptions of life. The story opens in the year 1850, with the becalming of an English yachting party off the Canary Islands. They see a queer object floating near them. It is taken aboard and proves to be a copper can encrusted with barnacles, evidently the sport of the waves for years. When opened it is found to contain a manuscript written upon a substance resembling the ancient papyrus. It purports to be the narrative of Adam More, an English sailor, who has committed his story to the sea in the hope of its

---

1 Relating to supernatural powers or magic.

reaching some civilized land with intelligence for his friends in England of his whereabouts and adventures. He tells how his ship visited the Antarctic ocean, and how a shipmate and himself went ashore to kill seals, were caught in an ocean current and carried southward for many days. Although More's companion is killed by cannibals, he himself escapes and is swept by the current into a mysterious opening which leads to subterranean passage beneath lofty mountains. He encounters the requisite monster on the way, but comes out whole at last in a strange land among a strange people. Although at the South Pole, these people enjoy a pleasant climate. In fact they belong to another geological era than the one More has been accustomed to, as he finds on looking at the fauna and flora about him. The Kosekin, the people themselves, are not only the antipodes of some of the world's people, but the antithesis of most of them in their ideas and conditions. They have the six months day and night which prevail at the poles, but they are fairly civilized, and yet they are strangely gentle, kind and considerate. Unselfishness is the rule of their life. Poverty is considered by them the most exalted condition. Darkness they prefer to light, and death to life. The rich are lowest in the social scale, paupers the highest. Crime results from the efforts of the rich to force their wealth, upon others and punishment consists in the imposition of more wealth. Though death is the greatest good it must not be accepted from the neighbor. Self denial is the rule in that as in other things. The beginning and the end of the dark season are marked by human sacrifices, and there is a holy cannibal feast. During the six months of sunshine the people live in caves as a protection from the light. The necessary love story is not wanting to the book, but it is brought to rather an abrupt ending, in harmony with its general somber tone. There is a lack of the breezy complacency in danger and healthful adventurous spirit of Haggard's narratives. The tale is rather one of the lamp than the mountains and forests, though strange enough for the most exacting sensation monger. It is illustrated by Gilbert Gaul's well known skillful pencil.

3. *The Week* [Toronto], July 1888

This anonymous novel will gratify lovers of the marvellous to their hearts' content. A party of English gentlemen, on board the yacht *Falcon*, which lay becalmed between the Canaries and Madeira Islands, while amusing themselves sailing paper boats—and betting on them, of course—discovered a slime-and-barnacle-covered copper cylinder floating in the ocean. On opening it they found two packages, one containing a letter in English, French and German, addressed to the finder, and the other the strange manuscript which is the story in this book. Both the letter and narrative were written on a vegetable substance, which the learned man of the party pronounced to be papyrus. The manuscript relates that Adam More, mate of the ship *Trevelyan*, while the vessel was becalmed off an ice-bound coast in the southern seas, went ashore with the second mate to hunt seals. They succeeded in killing a couple of seals, when it began to snow. They hastened to their boat, but in the storm and darkness they were unable to regain the ship. Powerful currents carried them among volcanic islands to one which was inhabited, where they landed, and where More's too trustful companion fell a victim to the cannibal savages. More escaped to his boat, which was caught by the current and borne through a long, awesome, subterranean channel to an open sea at the pole. Now our hero's adventures began: land was in sight, cities and cultivated fields could be seen, and on the sea floating craft of various kinds. He made for one of the largest galleys, was taken on board and kindly treated. He found himself among a strange people, who could not endure the light, and who dwelt in caverns during the long day of half a year, and pursued their business and festivities during the long night. Their aims and ambitions and customs were exactly the reverse of those of civilized nations. The Kosekin, as they called themselves, preferred darkness to light, poverty to riches, death to life. Poverty was happiness, darkness was delight, unrequited love was bliss, and death was the supreme blessing. Every one strove not to get but to give. Merchants traded, not to make money, but, if possible, to lose it. The wealthy embarked in business in the hope of getting rid of their fortunes, but, they seldom succeeded, for every one wanted to pay the utmost for what they got. The pauper class was of the highest, the chief or ruler, of the lowest rank in the State; the private soldier was superior to the commander, and the man who toiled at the oar, ranked higher than the admiral of the fleet.

Our readers must go to the book itself for an account of the wonderful adventures of Adam More—or Atam-or, as he was called by the Kosekin. The story seems to be a sensational satire. It has some of the characteristics of the *Arabian Nights*, and the works of Jules Verne and Rider Haggard. It ends abruptly, and without disposing of some of the principal characters. The illustrations are numerous and striking. The last one represents More standing on the summit of a pyramid, rifle in hand, after he has been hailed, "Father of Thunder and Ruler of Clouds and Darkness." By the way, he must have gone on his sealhunt with a magazine of ammunition. The supply seems to have been inexhaustible.

4. *The Athenaeum*, 15 December 1888

[*The Athenaeum* has been the official student newspaper at Acadia University, in Nova Scotia, Canada, since 1874. This review is of the British Chatto & Windus edition of the novel.]

An ingenious device has relieved the author of "A Strange Manuscript found in a Copper Cylinder" from the necessity of making his story bear any resemblance to what might be reality. The cylinder is picked up by a yacht, and the manuscript is supposed to have been written a long time ago. Nobody is responsible for its contents, and the author is able to give the comments of the yachtsmen upon it, and to display a considerable amount of varied information. It would have been a graceful act on the part of the author if he had acknowledged his debt to Mr. Samuel Butler's "Erewhon"; but authors of thrilling romances of impossible adventure do not brook charges of plagiarism, and humble critics must content themselves with wondering at the strange law which has led the human intellect in the year 1888 to light upon the same ideas of topsy-turvydom which occurred to Mr. Butler in 1872. The people who inhabit the shores of the summer seas around the South Pole invert our ideas upon life and death and upon wealth and poverty; their aim in life, so to speak, is to be killed, and the wealthy class among them is the class of paupers. The wit and satire with which Mr. Butler worked out his ideas of the race who treated crime as a disease and disease as a crime are wanting in the author of "A Strange Manuscript," &c.,[1] who has also to learn that a string of impossible adventures does not make a work of imagination.

1 Et cetera.

Works Cited and Recommended Reading

Works Cited

"Account of the Ruined Cities of Yucatan." *The Saturday Magazine* (Supplement) 24.743 (January 1844). London: John William Parker.

Agatharchides of Cnidus. *On the Erythraean Sea.* Trans. Stanley M. Burstein. London: Hakluyt Society, 1989.

Arnold, Angela. "'To Seize, to Slay, to Conquer': Satirising the Imperial Mission in James De Mille's *A Strange Manuscript Found in a Copper Cylinder.*" *Foundation: The International Review of Science Fiction* 30.81 (Spring 2001): 83-89.

Bailey, James Osler. *Pilgrims through Space and Time: Trends and Patterns in Scientific and Utopian Fiction.* New York: Argus, 1947.

Bakhtin, Mikhail. *Problems of Dostoevsky's Poetics.* Trans. Caryl Emerson. Minneapolis, MN: Minnesota UP, 1984.

Becker, Allienne. R. *The Lost Worlds Romance: From Dawn Till Dusk.* Westport, CT: Greenwood P, 1992.

Beddoes, Julie. "Inside Out: Finding the Author in James De Mille's *A Strange Manuscript Found in a Copper Cylinder.*" *Signature* 3 (1990): 1-12.

Bleiler, Everett F., ed. *The Checklist of Fantastic Literature: A Bibliography of Fantasy, Weird and Science Fiction Books.* Chicago: Shasta, 1948.

Bruce, James. *Travels to Discover the Source of the Nile, In the Years 1768, 1769, 1770, 1771, 1772, and 1773.* 6 volumes. Volume 3. Dublin: William Porter, 1791.

Burpee, Lawrence J. "Novels of James De Mille." *Nation* (16 Aug 1906): 138.

Burritt, Elijah H. *Atlas Designed to Illustrate the Geography of the Heavens.* New York: Huntington & Savage, 1845.

Burstein, Stanley M., ed. and trans. *Agatharchides of Cnidus on the Erythraean Sea.* London: The Hakluyt Society, 1981.

Butler, Samuel. *Erewhon or Over the Range.* 6th ed. London: David Bogue, 1880.

Cavell, Richard. "Bakhtin Reads De Mille: Canadian Literature, Postmodernism, and the Theory of Dialogism." *Future Indicative: Literary Theory and Canadian Literature.* Ed. John Moss. Ottawa: Ottawa UP, 1987. 205-10.

Clareson, Thomas D. "Lost Lands, Lost Races: A Pagan Princess of Their Very Own." *Journal of Popular Culture* 8.4 (Spring 1975): 714-23.

Coleridge, Samuel Taylor. *Bibliographia Literaria.* Ed. James Engell and W. Jackson Bate. Bollingen Series. Princeton: Princeton UP, 1983.

Colombo, John Robert. "Four Hundred Years of Fantastic Literature in Canada." *Out of This World: Canadian Science Fiction and Fantasy Literature*. Ed. Andrea Paradis. Kingston, ON: Quarry P, 1995.

Cook, James, and Tobias Furneaux. *A Voyage Towards the South Pole and Round the World*. 2 volumes. London: W. Strahan and T. Cadell, 1777.

Cuvier, Georges. *Essay on the Theory of the Earth*. 5th ed. Trans. London and Edinburgh: William Blackwood and T. Cadell, 1827.

Darwin, Charles. *Journal of Researches Into the Natural History and Geology of the Countries Visited During the Voyage of H.M.S. Beagle*. Volume 1. New York: Harper & Brothers, 1846.

——. "Observations of the Parallel Roads of Glen Roy, and of Other Parts of Lochaber in Scotland, with an Attempt to Prove that They Are of Marine Origin." *Philosophical Transactions of the Royal Society of London* 129 (1839).

Dawson, J.W. "The Air-Breathers of the Coal Period in Nova Scotia." *Canadian Naturalist and Quarterly Journal of Science* 8.1 (1863): 1-12.

——. "The Air-Breathers of the Coal Period in Nova Scotia." *Canadian Naturalist and Quarterly Journal of Science* 8.2 (1863): 81-92.

Defoe, Daniel. *Robinson Crusoe*. Ed. Evan Davis. Peterborough, ON: Broadview P, 2010.

De Mille, James. *A Strange Manuscript Found in a Copper Cylinder*. New York: Harper Brothers, 1888.

——. *A Strange Manuscript Found in a Copper Cylinder*. London: Chatto & Windus, 1888.

——. *A Strange Manuscript Found in a Copper Cylinder*. Ed. Malcolm Parks. Centre for Editing Early Canadian Texts. Ottawa: Carleton UP, 1986.

——. *The Elements of Rhetoric*. New York: Harper Brothers, 1878.

Dickens, Charles. *All the Year Round: A Weekly Journal*. Volume XV. London: Chapman & Hall, 1866.

——. *Dickens's Dictionary of London*. London: Charles Dickens, 1879.

Edwards, Justin D. *Gothic Canada: Reading the Spectre of a National Literature*. Edmonton: U of Alberta P, 2005.

"Egypt." *Penny Cyclopedia of the Society for the Diffusion of Useful Knowledge*. Volume 9. London: Charles Knight & Co., 1837.

Ellsworth, R.C. "Utopian Literature of Canada." *Canadian Notes and Queries* 12 (1973): 4.

Figuier, Louis. *The World Before the Deluge*. New York: D. Appleton & Co., 1866.

Frye, Northrop. *Anatomy of Criticism*. New Jersey: Princeton UP, 1957.

Gerson, Carole. "A Contrapuntal Reading of A Strange Manuscript Found in a Copper Cylinder." *Essays on Canadian Writing* 56 (Fall 1995): 224-35.

——. "De Mille, James (1833-80)." *Biographical Guide to Canadian Novelists*. Ed. Robert Lecker, Jack David, Ellen Quigley. Toronto: ECW, 1993.

——. "Three Writers of Victorian Canada: Rosanna Leprohon/James De Mille/Agnes Maule Machar." *Canadian Writers and Their Works*. Fiction Series. Volume 1. Ed. Robert Lecker, Jack David, Ellen Quigley. Toronto: ECW, 1983.

Gnarowski, Michael. *A Concise Bibliography of English-Canadian Literature*. Toronto: McClelland and Stewart, 1978.

Guth, Gwendolyn. "Reading Frames of Reference: The Satire of Exegesis in James De Mille's *A Strange Manuscript Found in a Copper Cylinder*." *Canadian Literature* 145 (Summer 1995): 39-59.

Guthrie, William and James Ferguson. *A New Geographical, Historical, and Commercial Grammar*. Edition 19. London: G. G. & J. Robinson & J. Mawman, 1801.

Haggard, H. Rider. *She: A History of Adventure*. Ed. Andrew Stauffer. Peterborough, ON: Broadview P, 2006.

——. *King Solomon's Mines*. Ed. Gerald Monsman. Peterborough, ON: Broadview P, 2002.

Henkin, Leo J. *Darwinism in the English Novel 1860-1910: The Impact of Evolution on Victorian Fiction*. New York: Russell & Russell, 1963.

Hodgkin, Thomas. "On the Ancient Inhabitants of the Canary Islands." *Journal of the Ethnological Society of London* 1 (1848): 167-81.

Huenemann, Karyn. "Dystopias in a New Land." *The Influence of Imagination: Essays on Science Fiction and Fantasy as Agents of Social Change*. Ed. Lee Easton and Randy Schroeder. Jefferson, NC and London: McFarland & Co., 2008.

Hughes, Kenneth J. "*A Strange Manuscript Found in a Copper Cylinder*: Sources, Satire, A Positive Utopia." *The Canadian Novel*. Volume 2, rev. ed. Ed. John Moss. Toronto: NC Press, 1984. 111-25.

"Ignoramus." *Hartford Courant* 21.27 (29 November 1856): 209.

Irvine, Dean. "Editing Archives/Archiving Editions." *Journal of Canadian Studies* 40.2 (Spring 2006): 183-211.

Ivison, Douglas. "James De Mille." *Canadian Fantasy and Science-Fiction Writers*. Ed. Douglas Ivison. Detriot, MI: Gale, 2002.

Kālidāsa. *The Megha Dūta, or Cloud Messenger*. Trans. H.A. Ouvry. London: Williams & Norgate, 1868.

Keefer, Janice Kulyk. *Under Eastern Eyes: A Critical Reading of Maritime Fiction*. Toronto: U of Toronto P, 1987.

Ketterer, David. *Canadian Science Fiction and Fantasy*. Bloomington and Indianapolis: Indiana UP, 1992.

Kilgour, Maggie. "Cannibals and Critics: An Exploration of James De Mille's Strange Manuscript." *Mosaic: A Journal for the Interdisciplinary Study of Literature* 30.1 (March 1997): 19-37.

Kilian, Crawford. "The Cheerful Inferno of James De Mille." *Journal of Canadian Fiction* 1.3 (1972): 61-67.

Kime, Wayne R. "The American Antecedents of James De Mille's *A Strange Manuscript Found in a Copper Cylinder.*" *Dalhousie Review* 55 (1975): 280-306.

La Bossière, Camille R. "The Mysterious End of James De Mille's Unfinished Strange Manuscript." *Essays on Canadian Writing* 27 (1983-84): 41-54.

Lamont-Stewart, Linda. "Misreading De Mille's *Strange Ms.*: Irony and Misdirection." *Essays in Canadian Irony*. Ed. Linda Hutcheon. Volume 3. Working Paper Series 89-W02. Toronto: Robarts Centre for Canadian Studies, 1989. 1-17.

——. "Rescued by Postmodernism: The Escalating Value of James De Mille's *A Strange Manuscript Found in a Copper Cylinder.*" *Canadian Literature* 145 (Summer 1995): 21-36.

Leane, Elizabeth. "Antarctica as a Scientific Utopia." *Foundation: The International Review of Science Fiction* 32 (89) (September 2003): 27-35.

——. "Romancing the Pole: A Survey of Nineteenth-Century Antarctic Utopias." *Australian Cultural History* 23 (2004): 147-71.

Lemaire, Gérard-Georges. *The Orient in Western Art*. English edition. Paris: Könemann, 2005.

Logan, J.D. and Donald G. French. *Highways of Canadian Literature*. Toronto: McClelland, 1924.

Lyell, Charles. *Principles of Geology*. 3 volumes. London: John Murray, 1830.

Lytton, Baron Edward Bulwer Lytton, *The Coming Race: or The New Utopia*. New York: Francis B. Felt & Co., 1871.

MacLeod, Douglas E. "A Critical Biography of James De Mille." Diss. Dalhousie U, 1968.

MacMechan, Archibald. "Concerning James De Mille." *Canadian Bookman* (4 April 1922): 125-26.

——. *The Headwaters of Canadian Literature*. 1924. Toronto: McClelland and Stewart, 1974.

——. Introduction. "A Voyage of Long Ago." *Canadian Geographical Journal* (11 September 1935): 148-60.

——. "James De Mille, the Man and the Writer." *Canadian Magazine* (27 September 1906): 404-16.

Mann, Robert James. *Lessons in General Knowledge*. London: Longman, Brown, Green, and Longmans, 1856.

McGaw, Danna. "A Re-Vision of the Reception of Three Nineteenth Century Canadian Texts." *University of Calgary Theses* 144 (1991): 132-44.

Matthews, Richard. *Fantasy: The Liberation of Imagination*. London: Routledge, 2002.

Miller, Hugh. *The Testimony of Rocks; or Geology in its Bearing on the Two Theologies, Natural and Revealed.* Boston: Gould & Lincoln, 1865.

Milnes, Stephen. "Colonialist Discourse, Lord Featherstone's Yawn and the Significance of the Denouement in *A Strange Manuscript Found in a Copper Cylinder.*" *Canadian Literature* 145 (Summer 1995): 86-104.

Milton, John. "Paradise Lost." *The Complete Poems*. Ed. John Leonard. London and New York: Penguin Classics, 1998. 120-405.

Monk, Patricia. *The Gilded Beaver: An Introduction to the Life and Work of James De Mille.* Toronto: ECW, 1991.

Moore, Thomas. *Irish Melodies*. Volume 7. London: Longmans, Green, & Co., 1866.

Multineddu, Flavio. "A Tendentious Game with an Uncanny Riddle: *A Strange Manuscript Found in a Copper Cylinder.*" *Canadian Literature* 145 (Summer 1995): 62-81.

New, William. *A History of Canadian Literature*. 2nd ed. Montreal: McGill-Queen's UP, 2003. Web.

Obeyesekere, Nananath. "'British Cannibals': Contemplation of an Event in the Death and Resurrection of James Cook, Explorer." *Critical Inquiry* 15 (Summer 1992): 630-54.

Owen, Richard. *Geology and the Inhabitants of the Ancient World.* London: Crystal Palace Library and Bradbury & Evans, 1854.

——. *Paleontology: A Systematic Summary of Extinct Animals and Their Geological Relations.* 2nd ed. Edinburgh: Adam & Charles Black, 1861.

Parker, George L. "De Mille, James." *The Oxford Companion to Canadian Literature.* Ed. William Toye. Toronto: Oxford UP, 1983. 183-84.

Parks, Malcolm G. "Introduction." *A Strange Manuscript Found in a Copper Cylinder.* By James De Mille. Ottawa: CEECT-Carleton UP, 1986. xvii-lix.

——. "Some Animadversions upon a Review of the CEECT Edition of De Mille's A Strange Manuscript." *Papers of the Bibliographical Society of Canada* 28 (1989): 70-73.

——. "Strange to Strangers Only." *Canadian Literature* 70 (1976): 61-78.

Parry, William Edward. *Journal of a Third Voyage for the Discovery of a Northwest Passage.* London: John Murray, 1826.

Pitcher, E.W.R. *Recalling Fiction's Cultural Context—Early Gothic and Utopian Romance: Cooper, Poe, Crane, Cather, Lawrence, Fitzgerald and West.* Lewiston, NY: Edwin Mellen, 2002.

Plato, *The Republic of Plato*. Trans. John Llewelyn Davies and David James Vaughan. London: Macmillan and Co., 1912.

Poe, Edgar Allan. "MS Found in a Bottle." *The Narrative of Arthur Gordon Pym of Nantucket and Related Tales.* Ed. J. Gerald Kennedy. Oxford: Oxford UP, 1994. 179-89.

——. "A Descent into the Maelström," *The Works of Edgar Allan Poe*. Volume 1. New York: W.J. Widdleton, 1865. 161-77.
——. "Narrative of A. Gordon Pym." *The Works of the Late Edgar Allan Poe*. Volume 4. New York: Blakeman & Mason, 1859. 13-188.
Pope, Alexander. *The Works of Alexander Pope*. Volume 7. London: J.M. McCreery, 1824.
Pordzik, R. *The Quest for Postcolonial Utopia: A Comparative Introduction to the Utopian Novel in the New English Literatures*. New York: Peter Lang, 2001.
Ptolemy. *Ptolemy's Geography: An Annotated Translation of the Theoretical Chapters*. Trans. J. Lennart Berggren and Alexander Jones. Princeton: Princeton UP, 2000.
"Recreations in Natural History—the Dodo." *Bentley's Miscellany*. Volume 15. London: Richard Bentley, 1844.
Rev. of *A Strange Manuscript Found in a Copper Cylinder*, by James De Mille. "The Novel of Adventure." *New York Times* 21 (May 1888): 3.
Rev. of *A Strange Manuscript Found in a Copper Cylinder*, by James De Mille. *Brooklyn Daily Eagle* 3 June 1888: 7.
Rev. of *A Strange Manuscript Found in a Copper Cylinder*, by James De Mille. *Week* 26 July 1888: 561.
Rev. of *A Strange Manuscript Found in a Copper Cylinder*, by James De Mille. *Athenaeum* 15 December 1888: 811.
Rieder, John. *Colonialism and the Emergence of Science Fiction*. Middletown CN: Wesleyan UP, 2008.
R.S. "Are Sensational Novels Superior to Novels Written With a Purpose?" *The British Controversialist and Literary Magazine*. London: Houlston & Wright, 1868.
Ross, Captain Sir James Clark. *A Voyage of Discovery in the Southern and Antarctic Regions (During the years 1839-43)*. 2 volumes. London: John Murray, 1847.
Ross, John. *A Voyage of Discovery, made under the orders of the admiralty, in his majesty's ships Isabella and Alexander, for the purpose of Exploring Baffin's Bay, and enquiring into the probability of a North-West Passage*. 2 volumes. London: John Murray, 1819.
Said, Edward W. *Orientalism*. New York: Vintage, 1979.
——. *Culture and Imperialism*. New York: Knopf, 1993.
Stevens, Peter. "Canada" (Chapter 2). *Literatures of the World in English*. Ed. Bruce Alvin King. London: Routledge, 1974. 42-60.
"A Strange Manuscript Found in a Copper Cylinder." *Harper's Weekly; A Journal of Civilization*. 32. 1620-38 (7 January-12 May 1888).
Swift, Jonathan. *Travels into Several Remote Nations of the World, in Four Parts. By Lemuel Gulliver, First a Surgeon, and then a Captain of Several Ships*. London: John Bell, 1774.
Symmes, John Cleaves (pseudonym: Captain Adam Seaborn). *Symzonia: Voyage of Discovery*. New York: J. Seymour, 1820.

"Troglodytæ." *Penny Cyclopaedia of the Society for the Diffusion of Useful Knowledge.* Volume 25. ed. Charles Knight. London: Charles Knight & Co., 1843.
Turcotte, Gerry. "'Generous, Refined, and Most Self-Denying Fiends': Naming the Abomination in James De Mille's Strange Manuscript." *Seriously Weird: Papers on the Grotesque.* Ed. Alice Mills. New York: Peter Lang, 1999. 77-88.
Vandervaart, Leonard. "Ideas in the Fiction of Victorian Canada: James De Mille, Agnes Maule Machar, and Robert Barr." *Dissertation Abstracts International* 50.7 (January 1990).
Verne, Jules. *A Journey into the Interior of the Earth.* London: Ward, Lock, & Co., 1877.
——. *A Tour of the World in Eighty Days.* Trans. George M. Towle. Boston: James R. Osgood & Co., 1873.
Watters, R.E. Introduction. *A Strange Manuscript Found in a Copper Cylinder.* By James De Mille. Toronto: McClelland & Stewart (NCL), 1969. vii-xviii.
Wilkes, Charles. *Synopsis of the Cruise of the U.S. Exploring Expedition during the years 1838, '39, '40, '41, & '42.* Washington: Peter Force, 1842.
Wilkinson, Sir J. Gardner. *A Popular Account of the Ancient Egyptians.* New York: Harper & Brothers, 1854.
Willmott, Glenn. "Canadian Ressentiment." *New Literary History: A Journal of Theory and Interpretation* 32.1 (Winter 2001): 133-56.
Wilson, Kenneth C. "The Nutty Professor: Or, James De Mille in the Fun House." *Essays on Canadian Writing* 48 (Winter 1992-93): 128-49.
Woodcock, George. "An Absence of Utopias." *Canadian Literature* 42 (1969): 3-5.
——. "De Mille and the Utopian Vision." *Journal of Canadian Fiction* 2.2 (1973): 174-79.

Recommended Reading

Brantlinger, Patrick. *Rule of Darkness: British Literature and Imperialism, 1830-1914.* Ithaca and London: Cornell UP, 1988.
Burgoyne, Daniel. "Coleridge's 'Poetic Faith' and Poe's Scientific Hoax." *Romanticism on the Net* 21 (2001).
Clarke, I.F. *The Pattern of Expectation 1644-2001.* London: Cape, 1979.
Coleman, Daniel. *White Civility: The Literary Project of English Canada.* Toronto and Buffalo: U of Toronto P, 2006.
D'Angelo, Frank. "Nineteenth-Century Forms/Modes of Discourse: A Critical Inquiry." *College Composition and Communication* 35.1 (February 1984): 31-42.

Davies, Gwendolyn. "An Introduction to James De Mille's 'Inaugural Discourse' of 1861." *University of Toronto Quarterly*, 64.3 (1995): 431-36.

Hofkosh, Sonia and Alan Richardson, eds. *Romanticism, Race and Imperial Culture, 1780-1834*. Bloomington: Indiana UP, 1996.

Hulme, Peter. *Colonial Encounters: Europe and the Native Caribbean, 1492-1797*. London and New York: Routledge, 1986.

Janes, Daniela. "Economies of Justice: Workers and Labour Reformers in Late-Victorian Canadian Industrial Fiction." Diss. U of Toronto, 2004.

Litch, Margaret Ann. *James DeMille: His Place and Significance in the History of Canadian Children's Literature*. Ottawa, ON: National Library of Canada, 1984.

Malmgren, Carl. *Worlds Apart: Narratology of Science Fiction*. Bloomington and Indianapolis: Indiana UP, 1991.

Moore-Gilbert, Bart. *Postcolonial Theory: Contexts, Practices, Politics*. London and New York: Verso, 1997.

Northey, Margot. *The Haunted Wilderness: The Gothic and Grotesque in Canadian Fiction*. Toronto: U of Toronto P, 1976.

Paradis, Andrea. *Out of This World: Canadian Science Fiction and Fantasy Literature*. Kingston, ON: Quarry P, 1995.

Rev. of *A Strange Manuscript Found in a Copper Cylinder*, by James De Mille. *Times* [Philadelphia] (31 May 1888): 5.

Rev. of *A Strange Manuscript Found in a Copper Cylinder*, by James De Mille. *Morning Journal* [Boston] (5 June 1888): 4.

Rev. of *A Strange Manuscript Found in a Copper Cylinder*, by James De Mille. *Critic* (15 September 1888): 125.

Rev. of *A Strange Manuscript Found in a Copper Cylinder*, by James De Mille. *Leeds Mercury* (1 October 1888): 8.

Rev. of *A Strange Manuscript Found in a Copper Cylinder*, by James De Mille. *Perthshire Advertiser and Strathmore Journal* [Perth] (1 October 1888): 4.

Rodinson, Maxime. *Europe and the Mystique of Islam*. Trans. Roger Veinus. London: I.B. Taurus, 1988.

Standish, David. *Hollow Earth: The Long and Curious History of Imagining Strange Lands, Fantastical Creatures, Advanced Civilizations, and Marvelous Machines Below the Earth's Surface*. Cambridge, MA: Da Capo Books, 2007.

Turcotte, Gerry. *Peripheral Fear: Transformations of the Gothic in Canadian and Australian Fiction*. New York: Peter Lang, 2009.